# The Taste of Love. . .

Lord Randal's strong arms slid about her tiny waist, and he pulled her snugly into his arms. Breathlessly, Cassie surrendered.

With deliberate slowness, Randal lowered his head. Gently, tentative lips touched hers, exploring, deepening the kiss. Her eyes closed as she felt for the first time what it was like to be kissed by a man; the strength of him, the touch of skin against skin, the first flush of passion.

Without a thought, her arms hugged his neck and she pressed closer to his lean, hard, frame. His tongue delicately probed, demanded entrance. Her mouth opened willingly to grant it.

All the heavenly sweetness of his kiss hit her. She was lost in delicious, overpowering sensation. Yet Cassie needed more, and she innocently urged him on, inflaming him until Randal had to pull back.

"The servants, my darling," he whispered.

"Oh, heavens!" Cassie pulled back from his arms. "We shouldn't have. Not here."

"Yes, we should. We couldn't help ourselves." Randal stroked her flushed cheek with one finger. "Trust me . . ."

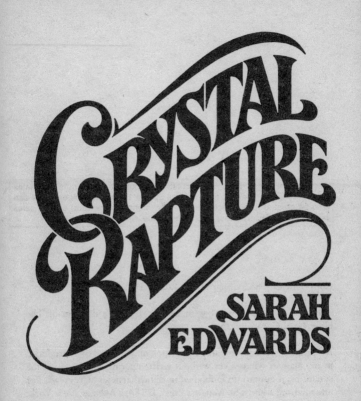

# CRYSTAL RAPTURE

## SARAH EDWARDS

ST. MARTIN'S PRESS/NEW YORK

# Prologue

"Yes, my lord," the real estate agent said expansively, "this is one of the finest neighborhoods in London. For the money, of course, for the money. Lord Griswold lived in the house at one time. This entire neighborhood is associated with the aristocracy, not like some places you might—" His voice died away as he realized that might not be a selling point.

His lordship sent a glance down his high-bridged nose and tightened the muffler about his neck. He hunched his shoulder against the sleet stinging their backs. "The charms of this street are lost upon me as night has fallen. If I might see inside?" He had seen the street in daylight. Pickering hadn't lied about its past. Its present wasn't so glorious.

Pickering's profuse apologies tumbled out as he unlocked the door and lit the lantern he'd placed inside. In the harsh light, the agent extolled the virtues of dilapidated reception rooms, principal bedrooms, and nurseries until only a single flight of stairs remained.

"Where do those go?" his lordship interrupted.

"Those, my lord? Well, let me tell you, the room at the top of those stairs is an extra feature of this particular house. It's a strong room for keeping valuables and the like."

The estate agent couldn't keep a hint of anxiety out of his voice. His lordship noticed and motioned the agent up the stairs. He followed silently, ignoring the steady flow describing the room's possible uses. Here the walls were solid, unmarked.

Once inside the room, he silenced Pickering with a gesture. No sound of the rising storm reached them. Good. No one would hear the child, then. But it was cold. Bitterly cold. He hugged his heavy black coat tightly to his slender body. The nights would be cool even in May. The child would need plenty of blankets. Or was there a fireplace?

"Why, no, my lord. What use would a fireplace be in a strong room?"

"This wasn't a strong room." This rotund little man with his excessive muttonchop whiskers and loud checked coat irritated him. "What was it?"

Pickering sighed. "Well, now, my lord. It's like this. Lord Griswold's wife was what you might call not quite right in the head. He had this room reinforced rather than turn her over to an asylum, poor lady. People don't like the house's history. That's why it's so cheap. Only a hundred pounds the year, and for such a good neighborhood."

"Could the neighbors hear her when she screamed?"

"No, my lord."

"Seventy-five pounds. In advance. I have a young relative who unfortunately displays symptoms of instability. I have just been named guardian. I shall be bringing him to London in the spring for medical aid. In the meantime, I shall need to furnish the house suitably."

"If I might suggest a dealer, my lord?"

His lordship's gray-blue eyes swept impatiently over Pickering. "If you wish."

He barely listened while Pickering gave him exact information on a furniture dealer in the neighborhood. Things couldn't be better. Reviewing the house as he followed the estate agent back down the four flights of stairs, he said a curt good night and strode off down the street, his mind full of plans.

Once the darkness had swallowed him, he glanced back at the house, darker against the dark sky. Pickering had fallen on the offer as expected. Now he had only to find the proper puppets to carry out his orders. And furnish the house, naturally. He would use Pickering's dealer. His lordship's teeth showed in a humorless smile. That should make it easy for Pickering and his dealer to identify him when he kidnapped the child.

# Chapter I

Mr. Marshall paused at the bottom of the steps leading up to the late Andrew Cardwell's large Georgian house near Grosvenor Square. The task before him was distasteful. He hoped to convince Miss Cassandra Cardwell to return to her home in Charleston, South Carolina. He considered telling her he'd found enough money to pay for her passage home. He hurried up the steps, anxious to get it over with, and rang the bell.

"Miss Cardwell," he said in surprise when the door swung open.

She stood before him, tiny, delicate, well-formed, looking more like a young girl than a woman just turned twenty-one a few days ago. The heavy golden brown hair which curled against her temples set off her youthful appearance. She met his gaze with clear, green-flecked hazel eyes. Only the assertive thrust of her strong, firm chin made him wonder whether most gentlemen would be quite content with the strength of her character. In any case, she'd never marry well in England as the penniless daughter of a suicide.

"The servants have already gone to other situations," she explained. "But won't you come in? The brokers left a few chairs uncovered in here."

Leading the way down the echoing hall to a spacious room bare of hangings and pictures, Cassie took one of the three chairs not shrouded in holland covers. A single candlestick stood on the mantel. Despite the March chill, no fire burned in the grate.

"My poor child, surely you haven't stayed here with—with—" He waved his hand about, indicating the desolation. "Without even a servant," he concluded.

"My maid went this morning," Cassie said quietly. "Won't you have a chair?"

Sitting down, Mr. Marshall began to discuss her present position. He watched carefully for her reactions; they were not what he'd expected. Didn't she understand? She was penniless, her father dead, with no place to turn. She listened intently, not interrupting until he suggested she return to Charleston.

"Thank you for the kind offer," Cassie said, tucking her shawl more tightly about her. Charleston beckoned enticingly for a moment. . . . To be warm again.

If she left London, though, she'd live with her aunt, who despised her for being prettier than her cousins. Three weeks of living with Aunt Dorothea from the time of her grandmother's death until the first ship left Charleston harbor for London had convinced her that anything was preferable. She doubted Mr. Marshall would understand. Men never did. He might understand her other, more important reason. "But I have to stay here, Mr. Marshall."

"But why, Miss Cardwell?" With his head cocked, a querulous look on his ascetic face, and the rumpled fringe of white hair, her father's kind solicitor reminded her of a sparrow.

"I can't go home until I discover who killed my father."

Mr. Marshall leaned forward as though to pat her hand. He was too far away. "Your complaint to Scotland Yard was relayed to me. I'm sorry, but there's no doubt your father's death was suicide."

Cassie shook her head stubbornly. "He was murdered." The words sounded harsh in the shrouded silence of the drawing room.

"It was suicide," he corrected her again as though she were a child rejecting an unpalatable truth.

Settling back into the chair more comfortably, Cassie shook her head. "It was meant to appear so." Without looking at it, she touched a letter on the table beside her. "I intend to prove as much."

"How? There was ample evidence." He was humoring her. But she'd caught his attention.

"How can the police be sure?" She leaned forward, her small, slender body tense. "They didn't bother to investigate. There wasn't an inquest."

"There was a suicide note," he reminded her. He frowned, though her criticism wasn't personal.

"I'm sorry, Mr. Marshall." Cassie forced herself to settle back in her chair. Forced herself to calm her voice. "I feel so frustrated trying to work within an unknown legal system." She smoothed the heavy skirt of her black wool dress.

"Not that you had much to do with the legal system in the United States, I'm sure."

Cassie smiled automatically at the gallantry. "Not much," she conceded. "But that's not important. The discrepancies are important. They would have been brought out at a coroner's inquest. But the doctor said the coroner wouldn't be paid for an inquest since there wasn't any sign of external violence."

"The doctor was quite correct. The coroner is paid for inquests which are 'duly held.' Without open violence, their Lordships would have ruled, very properly, that an inquest was not duly held. And, umnh, the note . . ." The solicitor shrugged. "Naturally the doctor gave a certificate of 'death by misadventure' to avoid disagreeable publicity. It's frequently done in these cases. Anything else would have been unpleasant for you. Especially with Lord Lytham's testimony."

Cassie's lips firmed and the cleft in her chin deepened. "Yes, Lord Lytham's testimony was most interesting. Perhaps that explains the errors in my father's suicide note."

"Errors in it?" He sat up very straight.

"Ignore the language." Cassie chopped the air sharply with one hand, then dropped it into her lap. "Papa may have picked up a lot of English phrases in the last two years. But the handwriting wasn't much like his. Nor does it explain why he said he was reduced to penury. Papa wasn't."

"Oh, but—"

"I know. His money was gone. But when my grandmother died two months ago, she left me a fortune in jewelry. More than fifty thousand pounds. I don't like it. It's old-fashioned and not very pretty, just valuable." Her hands gleamed palely against her skirts. "My father kept his financial problems secret, too. So whoever murdered him had to have that information."

"That's true only if your father was actually murdered. Why would anyone want to kill him?" Mr. Marshall's voice was gentle, apologetic.

"I don't know," Cassie agreed tiredly, then

straightened to tell Mr. Marshall earnestly, "I offered him my inheritance only the day before. So he
knew he wasn't penniless."

"I see." He paused. "Yes, I see. That might make
a difference. Do you have any other evidence?"

"Several things." Cassie ticked off points on the
fingers of one hand. "First of all, when I left the
house, Papa wasn't depressed—despite Lord
Lytham's testimony. Nor did Papa ever drink
heavily. I'll admit he'd been acting strangely since I
arrived, but it wasn't his impending bankruptcy. Or
he would have asked me to sell the jewels. And
there's the agony columns in the *Times*."

"The agony columns?"

"Yes. There are ciphers in it people use for personal messages. Papa and I used to write letters in
ciphers to each other when he had to travel. Or he'd
leave enciphered messages telling me where my
birthday or Christmas presents were hidden."

Her throat tightened at the memory. She had to
pause to regain control. Mr. Marshall stared at the
empty fireplace until she resumed.

"There was no one else who shared his love of
puzzles and ciphers." For a moment it seemed she
would stop again. But to Mr. Marshall's surprise,
she continued in a stronger voice. "When I arrived a
few weeks ago and found out about the agony column, I suggested to Papa we break the ciphers together." Cassie's tone grew puzzled. "Instead of
agreeing, Papa was furious and ordered me not to
fool around with them. Later he apologized, but he
was adamant." Her hands lifted from her lap, then
drifted back. "That wasn't like Papa. One of the
ciphers could have something to do with his death.
So you see, Papa knew there might be danger."

Frowning, Mr. Marshall thought for a moment
before he spoke. "Have you told anyone else?"

"Yes. Scotland Yard said his drunken state distorted his handwriting. And his prohibition against reading the *Times* was evidence of a proper feeling for me. Young ladies might be corrupted by crime and violence reported in the newspapers. They want something written, some concrete evidence, and I don't have it. Yet."

The solicitor looked faintly disapproving at her unladylike intentions.

"That's why"—Cassie took the letter from the table beside her and opened it—"I'm going to accept Lord Lytham's offer to be a companion to his wife at two hundred pounds a year." Cassie nodded as Mr. Marshall's brows rose. She handed him the letter. "Yes, two hundred. Have you ever heard of a companion earning that much? It's because Papa was his friend." Expression disbelieving, she nodded toward the letter. "Lord Lytham was the last one to see Papa alive that night. And he was the one who suggested the firm of McCrory and Chambers as Papa's investment advisors."

The solicitor cleared his throat. "Spying on Lord Lytham may be dangerous if what you suspect is true."

Cassie continued as if he hadn't spoken. "I believe Lord Lytham's involved somehow. At luncheon, Papa told me he intended to see him. I had hoped to learn something from Papa's papers, but there wasn't anything."

"This is an imprudent course for an unprotected young lady," the solicitor warned.

"Lord Lytham's not likely to suspect a female for precisely that reason." Determination firmed her soft lips. "Do you know of a trustworthy investigator? I need someone to check on McCrory and Chambers. Lord Lytham's home will be simple for me to investigate once I'm living there, but not McCrory and Chambers."

"I see," Mr. Marshall said thoughtfully. "You won't do anything foolish?"

"Of course not."

The solicitor leaned back in his chair and looked at her for several seconds over steepled fingers. Abruptly he straightened. "I've used a private enquiry agent a number of times. He's trustworthy and has always given satisfaction. I'll send you a note once I've arranged things," he said brusquely. "At Lord Lytham's."

The butler, Minton, placed a cup of coffee beside Lord Lytham's plate, then withdrew. Shepherding the footmen before him, he cast an experienced eye over the chafing dishes on the long sideboard against the wall. All were full despite his lordship's heaped plate and Lady Elaine's second helping. Lord Lytham insisted on surplus. Minton closed the door to his pantry behind him.

Lady Elaine barely waited for the latch to click before she burst into speech. "Did I tell you that Cassie Cardwell's coming today?"

Lytham glanced up from the newspaper. "I believe you mentioned it."

"It will be so delightful to have someone here each day." Her plump cheeks dimpling, Elaine batted her lashes at her husband. "If only you didn't spend so much time at the Home Office."

"It's merely my career," he answered mildly. "Speaking of the Home Office, I need to get there early today. Another flap concerning the Great Exhibition." His gaze drifted away from Elaine's face to the dining room windows. Trees, their leaves budding, dipped in the March wind. "Only a few more weeks until it opens," he said softly as though speaking to himself. "I'll be glad when it's over."

"So will I. Being in London is delightful at this season. But the summer! I do wish we didn't have to stay in town all summer."

Tossing his napkin beside his plate, Lytham rose from his chair and came around the table. "You'll have Miss Cardwell to keep you company," he reminded her. He started toward the door into the hall, then turned back. "Oh, Elaine, I found young Mary with my newspaper yesterday. If she does it again, you'll have to dismiss her."

Elaine's fair brows drew together over china-blue eyes. "Oh, dear. I shall speak to her. She's simply reading the Personals column for messages from her young man. They're so much in love." She swung around in her chair, knocking a litter of mail onto the floor. "I don't know why you're so against her reading the newspaper."

"Women's minds aren't suited for the sort of thing editors see fit to put in them, even the *Times*. I will not have any female in my household sully her mind with reports of crimes and politics." Elaine's unhappy nod satisfied him. Returning to her chair, he bent down to brush a kiss on her small nose. "Thank you, my dear. I'll see you tonight."

Cassie hesitated in the doorway of the empty morning room. It was just like Lady Lytham. Cushiony. Comfortable. Friendly. Not in the least fashionable like the Gothic chairs and shining suits of armor in the hallway. It was also cluttered. Portraits and knickknacks, small stuffed cushions, and lacy antimacassars covered walls, tables, sofas, and chairs. A flowery carpet covered the floor, and a dozen tables were scattered over it. An ormolu-mounted table contained both planter and bird cage. Inside, a small yellow canary chirped cheerfully. Lady Elaine whiled away her time here, isolated from the problems of the household.

A voice close behind brought Cassie around: "Oh, dear. And I meant to be here ahead of you. So awful for you to be shown into an empty room, too. The time just slipped away from me. It always does, and I simply never get anything done. Sit down, my dear. Minton is bringing us tea. I'm sure you haven't been eating properly since your bereavement."

The voice was breathless and childlike, but the body wasn't. Lady Lytham swayed down the hall, her yellow skirts minimizing the full roundness above her waist. A flush colored her round cheeks, and she was breathless from hurrying. Altogether an amiable absurdity, Cassie thought, then chastised herself for thinking it. She stepped from the doorway to allow Lady Elaine to pass.

"My dear, do sit down. That chair is most comfortable and perfectly placed so that we may chat while I regain my strength. I've been so busy all morning. No time to rest for a wee bit, as they say in Scotland. The dear Queen and Prince Albert have made all things Scottish so fashionable."

Lady Elaine sank onto the green sofa, a fat cushion at her back. She swung her feet up on the flowered hassock and cast a brown shawl over them, so that she resembled a gigantic sunflower.

"I've noticed—" Cassie began but was cut off.

"Here's our tea. Do you mind pouring? Put it down beside Miss Cardwell, Minton." The thin, stately butler placed the tea tray on an inlaid table beside Cassie. "Thank you so much. Now, my dear Miss Cardwell, or may I call you 'Cassie' as your dear father did? We were so sorry when we heard the news, and my dearest Lytham feels absolutely responsible." Lady Elaine's large eyes filled with tears. "So I insisted I simply must have you for my companion."

Cassie stared at her, shocked for a moment, wondering what Lady Elaine could possibly know about Lytham's involvement and her own suspicions. No, she didn't know anything, Cassie surmised, though if she did, she couldn't be so guileless.

"That's very kind of you, Lady Elaine," Cassie countered, "but I'm sure Lord Lytham did everything possible."

Lady Elaine chattered on, and Cassie filled a small flowered china plate with a slice of dundee cake, a scone filled with clotted cream and raspberry jam, a muffin, and a strawberry tart to accompany the cup of tea. She remembered her father's description of Lady Elaine's appetite and thought to please her with this show.

"Exactly as I like my tea," Elaine admired, then continued: "I'm so sorry I couldn't be with you during this awful time. But my physician, Sir James, insisted I keep to my bed. Just a small indisposition that could have been made much worse if I hadn't stayed out of the March wind." Her double chin wobbled with emotion.

"Thank you, Lady Elaine." The golden-haired girl was not sure how to respond.

"Do call me Elaine. We shall be such friends." She smiled as she popped a bit of scone oozing cream into her mouth. Licking her long fingers, Elaine giggled. "Do try the scones. They're delicious. Our Emil has such a light touch. There, there, I know you haven't been eating properly; you're too thin."

Cassie delicately nibbled the corner of her scone, suddenly not hungry. The older woman noticed, sighed, and patting her hand maternally asked Cassie's forgiveness for "going on so about something you'd much rather forget."

Quick color rose in Cassie's cheeks; she seemed on the verge of tears. If only this woman knew what I came into her house to do, she thought, trembling to control her emotions.

"Oh, but you needn't worry so. The worst is over, and you'll soon be out of your blacks." Elaine stopped talking and looked hard at Cassie. The lovely curve of her cheeks, her small, straight nose, and bright, tear-filled green-flecked hazel eyes satisfied Elaine. But had that lady been a more astute judge of character, she would have noticed a hint of defiance burning in those appealing features. Instead, she studied how well the curly, golden brown hair combined with the slender figure and stated, "We shall find it easy to make an excellent match for you."

A startled Cassie said, "I hardly think it appropriate."

"Oh, but it is. Matchmaking's my only hobby, and I think I can arrange a brilliant match for you. A most perfect husband. But I shall be quite selfish and keep you with me for a while. First, you may help me pair Miss Madeline Edgar and the Honorable Welton Sinclair. They'll make such a lovely couple. If only her parents weren't so foolish."

"I shall be glad to help any way I can." Cassie giggled. "But isn't it wicked to encourage them against her parents' wishes?"

"Her parents are much too ambitious. They want a wealthy marquess. Lady Albinia does, actually. Madeline wants love. And she and Welton love each other. It's so affecting. And you too, my dear, will find love and happiness, if I have anything to say about it."

As she said that, Cassie refilled the lady's plate and took a second scone which Elaine forced on her.

Standing alone in the middle of the dark and spotless yet incredibly large library at Lytham House several days later, Cassie wondered where to start her search. The week had been filled with surprises. Lady Elaine's plans for her made her think more about love and marriage than she ever had. She hoped to find someone whose magic would change her life, but unfortunately, her purpose in this house was to find out if foul play had ended her beloved Papa's life.

A portrait of the previous Lord Lytham peered at her almost disapprovingly from above the huge fireplace. Heavy crimson plush drapes were drawn against the chill gray rain outside, and a fire kept the damp out. A desk stood in the middle of an elegant oriental carpet. Chairs were scattered invitingly about.

Listening for footsteps, Cassie found herself standing before Lytham's desk—the most obvious place to look for any papers, though it wasn't likely that the lord had kept a record of his plans to murder her father! But there should be something, she hoped. Some reference to the investments, some inconsistency, something.

She discovered, much to her surprise, only the desk's top was neat. Each of the desk drawers was stuffed with papers. Scanning them hastily, she noted that they all pertained to the forthcoming Great Exhibition. Not one referred to her father or his investments. And why would they, she chided herself.

Carefully trying to return each paper to where she found it, Cassie looked forlornly at all the books that were stacked on the heavily carved shelves that stretched to the ceiling. Could something be hidden behind or in them? For that matter, there must be a safe. A household this size required large sums of cash to pay servants and tradesmen.

She stiffened. There was a noise in the hall. Steadying herself, she was sure it was only the old house creaking. The servants were all down in the servants' hall taking a rest. Elaine was napping, and Lord Lytham was at his government office.

Resolutely, Cassie took the library steps over to the shelves nearest the desk. Methodically, she searched behind the books lining the shelves. The panel was so cunningly hidden that she almost didn't see the handle set into the wall.

When she realized what it was, Cassie paused. The panel rim, like the edge of a door, ran beyond the shelf above. How did it open with the shelf in front of it? It did open; she could see the smudge where someone's hand had brushed countless times.

Cassie carefully put the load of books on the library stool and straightened up. She tugged at the shelf. And nearly fell backward when both shelf and panel swung smoothly, effortlessly open.

Her stomach fluttering, Cassie paused. No gruesome sight, however often promised by novels, lay behind the panel. Her heart pounding, she saw the strongbox, the sort she'd hoped to find, which occupied the small niche behind the panel.

She lifted the box out and looked behind it. Only dust and bare plaster walls remained within. Placing it on the desk, she tugged on the handle to see if Lytham had forgotten to lock it. He hadn't, and there wasn't a key in the desk. She searched the room for a key. There wasn't one.

How did you pick a lock? she wondered, but she had no idea. And this was no time to experiment. Cassie placed the box back carefully into its niche and closed the panel. Balzac and Dumas had been nearest the side which swung open. When she found the key, if she found it, she wouldn't need to remove the books, just grasp the shelf and tug gently . . .

Sounds from the hallway startled her. She listened tensely. Suppose Lytham was returning. A flutter of panic tightened her stomach. He couldn't find her with the books that hid the strongbox's niche. Furiously, she thrust them into their proper places, then leaned back to see if it looked right.

"Excuse me, miss—"

His voice startled her as only the guilty can be startled, and her foot slipped on the narrow step. She grabbed for something, anything, but missed. Cassie fell backward awkwardly, gasping when a strong pair of arms caught and held her close to a masculine body. They cradled her gently for a moment too long before swinging her free of the library stool. Safely. Cassie savored the sensation.

The fine wool of his jacket which brushed her cheek carried the misty chill of outdoors. Beneath it, through the hard muscles, she could feel his heart race. A tingle she'd never felt before shot through her, leaving behind a peculiar ache.

Cassie stiffened. Who was he? And what was she doing letting him cradle her like this? She pushed against his chest. His arms only tightened in response, supporting her slight weight easily. His warm breath stirred the tangle of loose curls on her forehead. She'd never been held in a man's arms before. That explained the way he affected her, the way her breath caught in her throat each time she inhaled his clean male scent.

For a moment she thought he didn't intend to put her down. For a moment she hoped he wouldn't. Then slowly the taut muscles binding her relaxed,

and he set her on her feet. Cassie breathlessly shook
out her skirts, reluctant to look at him. Face flaming, she took a quick step back and tilted her head.
She knew, without knowing why, that she needed
the distance.

"Thank you, I'm—" she began. Her voice died as
she looked at him. A sunburst of pleasure warmed
her.

"Are you all right?" he asked at the same instant.

From blue-gray eyes surrounded by feathery dark
lashes to tawny brown hair glinting with gold lights
and waving across his forehead, strong jaw, high-
bridged nose, and full lips lifted in a questioning
half-smile, he was classically handsome. And he reminded her of someone.

"Yes, thank you," Cassie said after a long pause.
"Who are you?"

Perplexity and something else darkened her eyes.
This was a man she could love. She dismissed the
notion. She didn't even know his name. Love
at first sight belonged in novels, not in the real
world.

"Randal," he answered. His deep voice sent an
uncomfortable thrill through her. "Randal Wakefield. Who are you?" His voice was as quiet as hers.

"I'm Cassandra Cardwell." She sounded soft,
breathless.

"How very pleasant to meet you, Miss Cardwell.
Are you sure you're all right?"

Did she sound that shaken? "Yes, quite all right,
Mr. Wakefield. Thank you."

"It's Lord Randal Wakefield, Marquess of Rydal,
actually. But won't you call me Randal? If I may
call you Cassandra?" His smile was devastating.

"My friends call me Cassie," she responded
breathlessly.

Her voice finally sounded normal. Good. She

must be getting over the shock of her near accident. Could he be Elaine's wealthy marquess? The one Madeline Edgar's parents wanted instead of Mr. Sinclair? But how was it possible that Madeline could prefer another man?

"May I call you Cassie?"

"If you like." The impact of his smile nearly made her gasp. She must not be as recovered as she thought. She controlled her reaction, asking firmly, "Is there any way I can help you? Lord Lytham isn't at home today."

"He will be shortly. We have several things to discuss about some of the exhibits."

"Oh, you're involved with the Great International Exhibition of Arts and Industry?" Cassie asked eagerly. Interest gilded her hazel eyes with green and gold flecks.

Startled by her enthusiasm, Randal nodded, his face suddenly taut. "You could say that." There was a strange note in his voice. "A great deal rides on the opening of it." Slowly his intent face relaxed. He looked carefully at her, and his expression warmed. He gestured toward one of the chairs near the fire. "Why don't we sit down? I'm sure you're still feeling a bit wobbly after your fall."

A slow flush climbed Cassie's cheeks. It wasn't the fall, it was him. The amazing effect he'd had on her when he held her so effortlessly in his arms. Her flush deepened. She skirted him and took the chair nearest the door.

"Do you help Lord Lytham in his work on the Great Exhibition?"

She deliberately chose a safe topic. The mention of it invariably brought a burst of enthusiasm. It was to be the first international exhibition dedicated not only to arts and industry, but encompassing all the wonders of the age, and housed in a fairy-tale

building of glass which towered above the trees in
Hyde Park. Ever since her arrival in London, she'd
been fascinated with the Exhibition, but the men
she'd met thought a woman couldn't be interested—although a few suggested she might want to
see the food-storage machinery, the furniture, the
paintings, and the porcelain dolls. And, of course,
she'd want to taste the jellies and ice cream to be
sold at the Exhibition. But not the machinery or the
great engines.

"You could say Lytham helps me. I'm coordinating the Exhibition," Randal said, taking the chair
opposite. His long legs extended across the hearth
almost to the edge of her black wool skirt.

"Then perhaps you can tell me," Cassie began,
realizing there could be no overcoming her intense
reactions to him, "whether Babbage's calculating
engine will be displayed? I've been wanting to see it
ever since I arrived, but no one seems to know anything about it."

Randal's dark brows rose. "Babbage's calculating
engine?" he said, chuckling. "I don't recall. Why do
you ask? Surely—"

"I love mathematics." Cassie cut him off de-
fiantly. "And ciphers."

She thought of her father and their games with
ciphers, and shivered. What if he had arrived a moment sooner when she had had Lytham's strongbox
in her hands? She shivered again.

"Are you warm enough? Should I ring for a maid
to fetch a shawl?" Randal asked with quick concern.
He leaned forward in the chair, his gaze searching
her now pale face.

How easily he'd noticed her tiny shiver. His gaze
paused at her small waist, at the swell of her breasts
tautening the somber, close-fitting wool of her
high-necked gown. It brought back the sensation of

being caught and held in his arms. She shivered again, and color flared in her cheeks. What would it be like to curl down beside him in the safe haven of his arms?

Unconsciously, she shifted to rise before she caught herself. Had he noticed? How could she weave fantasies about a handsome face? Yet nothing destroyed the small, irrational core of warmth inside her. It had blossomed when he held her, and she couldn't banish it.

"No, I'm quite all right." The returning hint of breathlessness made Cassie clasp her hands firmly in her lap. She would be sensible, and waited for him to continue.

Certainty that she was politely evading him flickered in his eyes before he smiled blandly. "Why mathematics?"

"I enjoy mathematics, just like Caroline Herschel and Ada, Countess of Lovelace. I was looking for books on the subject when . . ."

At his quizzical look, she started to explain. "Ada Byron, who married the Earl of Lovelace, Lord Byron's daughter—" The clock on the mantelpiece chimed. "Oh, Elaine will be wondering what's become of me." Cassie jumped to her feet and hurried to the door.

Randal rose to his lean height. "Elaine's never thought that hard in her life." There was indulgent affection in his voice. "Unless . . . are you Elaine's new companion?"

"I'll be her former new companion unless I start doing my job." She opened the door and paused. "I'd like to thank you for saving me from a nasty fall. When I have the time, I'll find a book about lady mathematicians to show you they really do exist."

Cassie slipped out of the library, the sound of his deep laughter following her. A close call, but she couldn't help wondering why Madeline Edgar chose to give her love to another man.

# Chapter II

Jim Barnthorpe flicked his handkerchief fastidi-
ously over the crusted bench and sighed. Alfie chose
such disgusting places for their rendezvous. Jim
spread the linen handkerchief over the bench before
lowering himself onto it. With only the small table
between them, Alfie's beer-laden breath struck him
in the face. Jim pulled a scented silk handkerchief
from his pocket and held it up to his nose. The class
of criminal his lordship wanted was not the sort he
was accustomed to dealing with.

"You wanted to see me?" Jim asked. Careful, he
warned himself. Don't let the man see what you
think of him. Jim buried his nose in the handkerchief.

Alfie drained his mug and slammed it down. Jim
winced and glanced around warily. No one paid attention to their small side table. Men who frequented this inn were used to ignoring louder
noises.

"O' course I wanted to see yer. You tell 'is lordship we needs more than the couter or two 'e give us."

"His lordship's given you twenty pounds," Jim protested automatically.

"That was two weeks ago. And we still don't know what we're supposed ter be doin'. W'en's 'e going ter show 'is face and tell us wot 'e's plannin'? We don't 'old wi' waitin' around."

"Now, Alfie," Jim said soothingly, "you know his lordship said we could expect more money shortly. He said so in his last cipher."

"We don't 'old wi' no ciphers neither. 'is lordship's got to show 'isself. Wot's 'e afraid of? That we'll run ter the ruddy bobbies?" Alfie spat on the floor and demanded, "Wot's more, we got to know wot 'e's got planned."

Alfie swiveled around without waiting for Jim's answer. He patted a barmaid on the rump as she passed and gestured at his mug. Wearily she pushed his hand away and clapped the empty mug onto her tray. Expertly threading her way through the ragged crowd to the dirt-crusted bar, she loaded her tray with filled mugs and plopped them before customers, collecting their money as she went.

"'at's better," Alfie sighed when he received his mug. He wiped the foam from his lip. "We got a right ter meet 'is lordship and take 'is instructions personal."

Alfie's glare emphasized the underlying threat. Jim swallowed hard behind the scented handkerchief and nodded. "I'll tell his lordship what you said. But I'm sure he wants to put off any meeting until a little nearer the time."

"Wot's 'e doing 'iring us so soon? Tain't reasonable, 'at's what it is. And you tell 'is lordship so. We needs some action, ter keep our 'ands in, like."

"I . . . I'll tell his lordship." Jim pulled out his wallet. "Will another pound help?"

"A quid for three of us? Garn. You know better nor 'at." Alfie rose from his bench to tower over Barnthorpe, his powerful frame blocking the light from the central lamp.

"Then . . ." Jim paused, wishing he'd refused to meet Alfie in Bluegate Fields. "How about a fiver?" He extended it. Alfie scooped it up, stuffing it into his shirt, and sat back down. "That should hold you and your friends until I can arrange things with his lordship." A scuffle broke out across the room, forcing Jim to raise his voice. "Meet me at the Alderman's Inn a week from today."

At the Alderman's Inn, he wouldn't be at Alfie's mercy as he was here. Did Alfie realize that? No. That was one of the advantages he had in dealing with the lower classes. They never planned ahead the way the educated did.

"Awright. Alderman's Inn. But don' you go tryin' to cross us. We'll find you wherever yer are." Alfie shoved the bench back. "Don't yer ferget it, neither."

Mouth dry, Jim watched Alfie push his way through the boisterous crowd. Why did he put up with this? At times like these, he wasn't sure. He strode through the crowd once Alfie was beyond the door; still, there was money in it. Far more money than the two hundred pounds his lordship had already paid down.

Barnthorpe paused outside the door, darting glances into the shadows, before striding on down the street with his silk handkerchief pressed to his nose. The street smelled even worse than the tavern. He brushed at his new pale gray suit, the one his lordship's advance had paid for. Once he learned precisely why his lordship had hired these ruffians, he'd have a good many more new suits at his lordship's expense. Jim smiled slyly. Although his high-and-mighty lordship didn't know it yet.


"How lovely to see you smiling." Elaine looked up from her needlework as Cassie entered the morning room. "Has something happened?"

"Not really. Just—" Cassie paused. "Just I met the most interesting gentleman. The Marquess of Rydal. I had to tell him I was your companion. You'd think he would've guessed with my American accent."

"But it's charming, my dear. Just the slightest hint of a southern drawl, as you call it. It falls softly on the ear. Tell me, what did you think of him?" Elaine waited expectantly, her hand poised over the altar cloth she was embroidering, mischievous light dancing in her eyes.

"Lord Randal?" Cassie asked cautiously.

"No, the man in the moon." Elaine giggled.

Randal was tantalizing. And totally impractical. Cassie brought herself up sharply. Memories of his smiling eyes and handsome face couldn't distract from the fact that as Elaine's companion, she was hardly a suitable match.

Elaine watched her with bright interest. "He's charming, attractive. Terribly so, in fact. He's also funny. That's very nice in a man," Cassie said demurely.

Elaine's embroidery dropped onto her voluminous garnet silk lap. The altar cloth's green and gold embroidery clashed garishly. "He's one of the biggest catches I know, and already he's past thirty." Elaine paused, shaking her head solemnly. "You'd think by now he'd be married, especially since he's the last of his name. But no. I've introduced him to I don't know how many lovely young girls. Even he agrees they're charming and will make excellent wives. But does he marry? Of course not. Men. They're so difficult." Her pale fingers picked up her sewing carelessly.

Cassie fixed her attention back on her petit point. If she hinted any more that Randal interested her, Elaine's matchmaking attempts would be relentless. Yet she was curious to learn more about him. If what she felt in his arms was given a chance to grow, Cassie knew that she wouldn't need the help of a matchmaker. But it was all too impractical.

"Is Lord Randal the wealthy marquess that Miss Edgar's parents are trying to snare for her?" Cassie asked. Behind her, rain stung windowpanes cloaked with heavy velvet drapes.

"Yes." Elaine paused to take a strand of embroidery silk from the small inlaid sewing table placed beside her. "At least he seems wealthy. Margaret Tilson would have it Randal's almost broke and in dire need of money. But that's just because he showed no interest in marrying her daughter. Oh, dear. Now where was I before I got distracted?" She frowned in deep concentration. "Of course. Madeline. Well, Madeline is a dear sweet girl. But she has no intellectual interests at all."

Cassie looked up from her petit point. "And Lord Randal does?"

"Yes, he took a First at Oxford in history or some such thing. I don't really remember what the subject was, but it makes him invaluable at the Home Office. Why, the Prince actually listens to his ideas. They're designing housing for the poor together. It's to be displayed at the Prince's Great Exhibition. Or I think it is. I wasn't attending closely, I'm afraid. You'll have to ask him when he comes to dinner. Oh, dear!" Elaine sat abruptly erect. "Is it Wednesday today?"

"Yes, why?"

"Did I remember to tell Emil that we were dining thirty tonight?" Elaine struggled to lift herself off the sofa.

"I told Emil on Monday that you were expecting guests. Everything's been taken care of," Cassie assured her soothingly.

"Even the seating arrangements?" Elaine gratefully sank back down.

Cassie returned to her needlepoint. "Even the seating arrangements. I made up the seating chart yesterday." Pausing, Cassie looked up from her canvas. "Unfortunately, Lady Carruthers has sent her regrets. That makes your table uneven."

"Really? Why, how wonderful. I only invited Lady Carruthers because she's dear Lytham's godmother. But this gives me the grandest notion. You'll be my junior hostess. That will allow me to conserve my strength," Elaine said triumphantly.


Randal bounded up the front steps of his house off Belgrave Square. "Find Glanville for me, please, Pryor," Randal told his butler. "I'll be in the library."

Randal scanned the shelves. Not a thing on mathematics beyond a few texts that had survived his schooldays. They wouldn't have the sort of information he was looking for.

"My lord, you're to have dinner at Lytham House tonight," his secretary said, closing the door. Glanville was a small man with a worried, overly precise air. His lordship's easy habits upset him.

Randal waved an impatient hand. "I'll start dressing in a bit. I've got an important task for you."

"Yes, my lord?" Glanville brightened.

"Find all the information you can during the next couple of hours on Caroline Herschel and Ada, Countess of Lovelace. She's Lord Byron's daughter."

"Caro—" Frowning, Glanville cut himself short. "Yes, my lord. Are you to meet the ladies in question tonight?"

Randal fought a smile at Glanville's suppressed curiosity. "I sincerely hope not. I seem to remember hearing that at least one of the ladies has been dead for several years. Both ladies are or were renowned for their mathematical abilities. See if you can find something on lady mathematicians in general as well, Glanville, before I leave for Lytham's. You might try one of the scientific bookstores. Failing that, Lord Wheatstone or Lord Playfair may be able to help you. Or try Babbage."

"Yes, my lord." Glanville hesitated, then continued in a rush, "My lord, your man of business requested another interview. He says it's urgent." Glanville fidgeted at Randal's prolonged silence.

"Did he specify the reason for this urgent interview?" Randal asked.

"Between your gamble in backing the Great Exhibition, milord, and your heavy expenditures in . . . in Bluegate Fields, he feels you're seriously overextended," Glanville finished guiltily. "I know he shouldn't have mentioned it to me, milord, but—" Glanville stopped short when Randal held up his hand.

"Nonsense. I'm glad he's worried. I am a trifle short." Randal's lips twisted in an ironic smile. "But I'll make a complete recovery at the Exhibition opening."

Glanville, fearful he'd gone too far, said nothing.

"But my first priority, Glanville, is to learn about

these learned females. I intend to be an expert on Caroline Herschel and Ada Byron by tonight."

Glanville relaxed. The twinkle had reappeared in his lordship's eyes.

Randal strode out of the library. That would give Glanville something useful to do. A chuckle escaped him as he ran up the stairs to dress. What sort of speculation would occupy them in the upper servants' sitting room tonight?

Several hours later, Cassie rushed into the drawing room to check the arrangements. Despite the two huge Gothic armchairs which stood either side of the fireplace, everything was ready.

That morning the room had been filled with a profusion of small inlaid tables and occasional chairs with no space for the ladies' voluminous crinstiffened skirts. Cassie had instructed Minton to remove all but two of the tables and arrange the chairs in small groups. Those tables now stood near one wall, crystal punch bowls on their inlaid tops. Beside them, footmen stood ready to serve the guests.

"Miss." Minton stood beside her, preventing her from going to check the refreshment tables.

"Yes, Minton?"

"I wished to ascertain whether the placement of Lady Elaine's new chairs is satisfactory."

Cassie looked at the Gothic monsters near the fireplace and nodded. "They're excellently arranged, Minton."

"Thank you, miss."

He retreated to the door, and Cassie looked for either Elaine or Lord Lytham to introduce her to the few guests who had already arrived. Elaine wasn't here. Where was she? When Cassie left Elaine's room three-quarters of an hour ago, Elaine had been ready to come down. Getting her to that point had taken Cassie's and her maid's combined efforts. While the maid coped with Elaine's hair and the various fastenings to her gown, Cassie searched for mislaid jewelry and fans.

Once she'd finished, Cassie had less than thirty minutes to change into a suitable gown and dress her hair before the first guest arrived. It had taken her forty-five instead. Twice, Elaine had tapped on Cassie's door to inspect her choice of clothes. Twice, she'd requested Cassie change into something more festive. Cassie had finally chosen an elegant black silk dress, one of her best. When Elaine tapped on the door again, Cassie hadn't answered. Everything from the deep flounces to the heavy lace and ribbon knots trimming the bodice were as festive as she could make them and still remain in mourning.

"Miss Cardwell." Randal's deep, resonant voice sounded behind her.

Cassie spun around, her silk and lace flounces brushing his legs. With one hand she clutched her black lace fan. He'd been attractive in ordinary clothes. But in the stark black and white of evening clothes he was superb. The very lack of color emphasized the hint of gold in his tawny brown hair and deepened the blue of his eyes. Madeline Edgar must be an idiot.

"Lord Randal! At least I wasn't on a stool this time." She instinctively hid behind teasing.

"Unfortunately for me."

Dropping her eyes for an instant, she smiled, then met his gaze fearlessly again. "I'm—" She paused delicately, deliberately." . . . surprised a gentleman would mention such a thing." With hands clasped demurely before her, she let her fan swing on a cord about one wrist.

His eyes darkened while his smile indented the

corners of his mouth. "Gentlemen remain silent," he answered softly, "only if the memory was less than complimentary to the lady in question."

"Less—" Cassie barely stopped herself from repeating his words. Devil. She controlled the laughter bubbling inside. "However complimentary," she continued gravely, "it was highly improper."

"Why?" Randal asked with an air of bright interest. It didn't fool her in the least.

"Any young lady could tell you that."

"But no young lady ever has. Won't you enlighten my ignorance?"

Cassie opened her eyes wide. "We hadn't been introduced," she explained innocently, "when you saved me from a fall. It was a shock to my sensibilities to be held by a strange man."

"Ah," Randal said, nodding in enlightenment. "I see. Once we've been introduced, your sensibilities won't be shocked when I hold you in my arms?"

"Not in the least," she assured him. She paused, smiling. "On the dance floor. Once we've been properly introduced."

"Then let's find Lytham. I'm sure he'll do the honors." Randal's hand took her arm while he searched for his host.

Before he could move, they were interrupted. "Ah, Lord Randal. We're delighted to find you among the guests."

A middle-aged woman of overpowering aspect planted herself beside him. Her beaky nose and imposing bosom made a mockery of the ingratiating condescension of her smile. She dismissed Cassie with a single glance.

Randal hesitated briefly before he bowed over her hand in acknowledgment. "Lady Albinia. May I present Miss Cassandra Cardwell? Lady Albinia Edgar," he said formally, no pleasure in his voice.

Dipping a curtsy, Cassie realized that this was Madeline Edgar's mother. Did Madeline take after her?

"Miss Cardwell," Lady Albinia acknowledged flatly. She looked at Cassie's mourning and added, "The governess. No. You're companion to Lady Elaine, aren't you? American, too, I believe."

"Correct on both counts, Lady Albinia." Reluctantly, she pulled away from Randal's restraining hand. "I'm Lady Elaine's co-hostess, so I must ask you to excuse me. If I can perform any service for you, Lady Albinia, please tell me. Lord Randal."

She swept curtsies to both of them, and turned away in a rustle of silk skirts. Lady Albinia's remarks forced her back to reality.

"The cheek of the girl," clucked the older woman, searching for someone to support her views. "So common, too. And that dress—far too rich for the daughter of a bankrupt suicide."

Cassie had moved away quickly. She didn't want to hear the low rumble of Randal's reply. In case, she thought, he might agree with the hateful woman. Lady Albinia's remarks recalled her to her real mission. She hoped that this dinner party would provide the perfect opportunity to learn more about Lytham and his habits.

Cassie glanced around the room, looking for someone she recognized. Strangers, black-and-white-clad men with brandy glasses, their wives and daughters with milder claret cup, surrounded her. The women wore the latest fashion. She felt like a raven in a forest of exotic birds.

She drifted hesitantly toward a group of ladies. Where was Elaine? It was too forward to introduce herself. She looked for a familiar face. With relief, she saw Lord Lytham signaling.

She dipped a slight curtsy when she stopped before him. His black and white evening dress accented the purity of his face with its gray-blue eyes and high-bridged nose. He seemed too civilized to have committed murder. Yet he must have.

"Yes, my lord?"

"Cassie." A smile lit his fair, handsome face. "Do you know what's happened to Elaine? She said she'd be ready on time for this party, and the Prime Minister's already arrived."

"I thought Elaine was here. We had her ready nearly"—Cassie glanced at the clock on the mantel—"an hour ago. Surely nothing's happened in the kitchens. I'll look for her."

"Don't bother." Lytham rubbed his aristocratically high-bridged nose and took her arm. "She'll turn up. If you're to assist Elaine, I'd best make you known to people."

Cassie shifted uneasily. Why did he have to stand so close? "Shouldn't I go up to see if Elaine's all right?"

"No, my dear. Elaine is invariably late no matter how she tries or what she promises. It's one of her many endearing characteristics. No one seems to mind. Although I can't think of anyone else who could get away with it." Warm affection lit his face for a moment. "She'll be down before we go in to dinner."

During the next quarter hour, Lytham introduced her to more than a dozen people. Somehow, she always seemed to see Randal. Even when she didn't look for him, she knew where he was. She'd only met him this afternoon, but she was sensitive to his presence. A lady should have better self-control, she chided herself. If she'd just escaped from the schoolroom, it might be different, although she doubted it. She wondered whether they'd ever be alone together again. Would she dare?

Like Randal and Lytham, most of those present were in some way connected with the Great Exhibition. While she received some sharp looks when Lytham said her name, no one mentioned her father. Until she met Mr. Edgar, Lady Albinia's husband.

"Miss Cardwell." He bowed ceremoniously over her hand when Lytham presented her. "I'm most pleased to meet you. I was truly sorry to hear of your father's death. Will you permit me to extend my condolences. I didn't have the opportunity at the funeral."

"Of course, Mr. Edgar. It's most kind of you." Cassie looked more closely at him. She vaguely remembered seeing him. But he faded into the background wherever he stood. Understandably. He was a good three inches shorter than his wife. Only his beautiful green eyes were memorable. "Are you connected with the Great Exhibition in some way?"

He beamed with enthusiasm. "Just the question answerer. Somebody has to do it to let the others work."

"The question answerer?"

"Quite simple, Miss Cardwell. Reporters always ask such tomfool questions. How can the building be moved after the Exhibition? Will the vibrations of all those people walking about shatter the Crystal Palace? Since it's made of glass, how will it withstand wind and hailstorms? By making the Exhibition international, aren't we risking inviting too many foreigners to our shores? Won't that make the Queen more vulnerable to further assassination attempts? Why finance something sure to lose money? I could go on, but you follow me."

"I do indeed. But are they worried about assassination?"

Just then she heard Randal's voice. Cassie knew if

she turned around, she'd find him within a few feet. Color tinted her cheeks, setting off the golden brown of her hair.

"There's fear something's up," Edgar's voice continued. "Especially after last year. Two attempts on her life the month after Prince Arthur was born. Security's bad, too. Thank the Lord that's not my department. Randal's the man in charge of that. Coordination, that is. Doesn't have to plan it himself."

"That's quite a large responsibility for Lord Randal," Cassie murmured.

"There'll be no repeat of last year," Lytham interrupted.

Eager to hear Lytham discuss the subject further, Cassie was disappointed as Lytham's attention wandered from the conversation to Elaine, who, glittering with diamonds, flitted toward them. In a magnificent green velvet dress spread over whalebone- and crin-stiffened petticoats, Elaine exchanged greetings with a number of people, moving lightly for a woman of her size. Becomingly flushed, she stopped neatly before Lytham.

"My dear, my apologies. I'm so late. But Emil had a crisis when the squabs didn't arrive. Now, I'm afraid everyone must hurry into the dining room. Emil has something spectacular planned for us."

Elaine claimed the Prime Minister, Lord John Russell, while Lord Lytham escorted Lady Russell into the dining room. Cassie stood to one side, trying to remember her escort's name. To her surprise, Randal, who had been watching her with admiration, claimed her.

"You're supposed to take—" Cassie stopped. On the arm of another gentleman, Lady Albinia passed them with a disapproving glance. The place card be-

side Randal's read "Lady Albinia Edgar." Cassie
was certain of it. She'd written and placed the china
cards herself.

"You, Miss Cardwell. Elaine told me so."

His eyes dared her to protest again. Heart racing,
Cassie lowered her lashes and refused the challenge.
Quietly she took his arm.

When they entered the dining room, Cassie
glanced at the cards along the gleaming length of
the table. The small china card to the right of Randal's carried her name. Elaine was exercising her
matchmaking skills. Was Randal as surprised as she?

Randal's hand brushed her bare shoulder when he
seated her. It was shockingly cool and smooth
against her flushed skin. She tried to smile politely
at an unknown lady across the table, grateful at least
that it wasn't Lady Albinia seated there. She would
have spent the next two hours glaring at Cassie for
being partnered by the most eligible man in the
room.

In fact, Lady Albinia was seated near Lord
Lytham. And staring nastily, as expected. She was
aiming her looks at the couple across from Randal
and Cassie. They must be Elaine's latest matchmaking subjects. Welton Sinclair—the man Madeline
preferred to Lord Randal.

Madeline was a softly pretty brunette girl with
green eyes, flirting happily with the man beside her
and ignoring her mother. Cassie looked curiously at
Welton, a bluff soldierly type.

"You aren't supposed to ignore me, you know,"
Randal said, reproachfully innocent. His breath
stirred a tendril beginning to work its way loose
from her neat coiffure. "Not as Elaine's co-hostess."

"I'm not supposed to be your dinner partner, either." The realization of his nearness struck her with renewed force.

"Of course you are. As the Marquess of Rydal, I'm the highest-ranking man here except for the Prime Minister. Therefore I rate the co-hostess as my dinner partner while Elaine has the PM. I'm part of your duties."

"But instead of Elaine's companion, you should have one of the ladies. Lady Albinia, for example."

"Lady Albinia? Spare me, please. She'd spend the time extolling Madeline's virtues."

Cassie stole a glance at Randal's confident expression. Confident of her, she realized. Confident that she wouldn't be able to resist his attentions for long. She knew he was right.

"I'm sure Miss Edgar has many virtues. Aren't you in the least bit interested?" When Randal denied it strongly, she shook her head, overemphasizing regretfulness. "Then perhaps you're right. Lady Albinia would make an uncomfortable dinner companion." Sighing, she looked the length of the table again and nodded toward a massive matron with too many diamonds and a shelflike bosom. "What about that lady? She'd be the perfect dinner partner for you."

Cassie stole a glance at Randal in time to catch his appalled expression. To hide her amusement, she sipped the clear court bouillon in her red and gold porcelain bowl.

"My dear girl, do you know who that is?"

Cassie shook her head. She made her smile innocent but politely questioning.

"That is Lady Helen Mowbray. A lady of no conversation and less tact. She uses these occasions to pound into the head of her hapless partner the importance of her latest cause. She is *not* a desirable dinner partner."

"If she's such a bore, why is she invited?"

"Such an innocent." Randal shook his head and took a spoonful of soup. "She happens to be excessively wealthy and well connected. Besides, she means well. It's hard not to sympathize. She tries to help people." He smiled at Cassie. "Unfortunately, they usually don't want to be helped."

Cassie choked. Her eyes dancing, she looked up at Randal and told him sternly, "Finish your soup, Lord Randal. The footmen wish to clear for the next course."

"Yes, Miss Cardwell. Whatever you say, Miss Cardwell." His deadpan response left her choking with amusement.

He applied himself earnestly to the bowl of bouillon, finishing it in time for the footman to replace it with a plate of fish napped in lemon sauce. With a sense of reprieve, Cassie turned dutifully to the man seated at her right. Randal politely turned to the lady at his left. As he did, his sleeve brushed against her bare arm. Shivering, Cassie smiled tentatively at the small bespectacled man. His place card read: Lord Playfair.

"Miss Cardwell," he acknowledged her, "I understand you're interested in mathematics."

"Why, yes, how did you know?"

"The young man on your right told me. Ladies tell me he's absolutely fascinating. We'll have to hope this course passes quickly so you can return to a more interesting conversation than an old dodderer like me can provide." He surveyed the flush deepening on Cassie's cheeks with approval. "Mathematics, hmnh? It's a good occupation for a girl. D'you intend to follow up on it?"

"I must earn my living," Cassie said regretfully, relieved to return to mathematics.

"I don't think mathematics is your future." Lord

Playfair smiled and glanced past her to Randal. "Do you like ciphers? Please, try your fish, it's excellent. Elaine always sets a good table." He took a bite himself, watching her with bright interest.

"Ciphers? I've loved them since I was a little girl." Cassie obediently took a small forkful of fish.

"The *Times* prints whole columns every day," Lord Playfair continued, not recognizing her interest, "the agony column. Fools think they're hiding their love affairs by putting them in cipher. Simplest sort, too. They shift every letter over so that *y* becomes *z* and *z* becomes *a*. But the business ciphers are much more interesting.

"Wheatstone and I used to solve them. We've been so busy recently we haven't had the time. Why don't you take up where we left off? That is, if Lytham will let the women in his household read the *Times*. I understand he's persuaded that women need protection from the sordid realities of life."

Afraid her frustration would show, Cassie lowered her eyes to her barely touched fish. "I've been trying to get the *Times*, but the butler thinks Lord Lytham wouldn't approve."

"Shortsighted of Lytham." Lord Playfair finished his last bite of fish and leaned back for the footman to take the plate. "Still, it's easy enough to circumvent. Tell Elaine about the enciphered love notes. She'll get the papers for you. She's a delightfully foolish woman; everyone adores her. And she loves a romance. I assure you, what isn't available to the companion is easily accessible to the mistress. With Lytham never the wiser. Now, you've been a good girl and politely talked to me without once looking to your left. Here's the entrée. Back to young Rydal with you."

Elated with his suggestion of how to get the newspapers, Cassie spent the rest of dinner alternating between Randal and Lord Playfair. Taken one course at a time, Randal's laughing flirtation was much easier to handle. She turned to Lord Playfair with each change of plate for more mathematical information. And the chance to catch her breath after Randal.

She'd forgotten Lady Albinia. Until she got to the door as Elaine led the ladies out. Then her haughty voice rang out clearly.

". . . disgraceful the way the girl's setting her cap for Rydal."

# Chapter III

When they entered the drawing room, Lady Albinia began dissecting Cassie's appearance with the other ladies. Cassie flushed. She looked beautiful and vulnerable in her black gown. Soon, she knew she would have to talk with the other women as part of her responsibilities. She knew she could defend herself against Lady Albinia, but that would embarrass Elaine.

"Cassie dear," Elaine interrupted her thoughts, "what did you think of Emil's surprise? Everyone said I was foolish to hire an Austrian chef, even one trained in France. Have you ever seen such a superlative finish to a meal? But, of course, you ate nothing. She's as slender as a bird, isn't she, Lady Albinia?" said Elaine as if to provoke her guest.

Before she could reply, Cassie answered, "It was delicious, all of it." She glanced over her shoulder at the ladies hovering nearby.

"So original to have those lovely Austrian desserts. What were they called?" Elaine paused and

frowned. "Oh, I can't remember the German, but
Emil translated for me. Moor in a Shirt and Rich
Man. Quite amusing, isn't it? And so different from
the usual Gateau Ste. Honore or Charlotte Russe, or
an ordinary apple pie?"

Since those desserts, plus fresh fruit served on a
silver epergne that sprouted plates and candles in all
directions, had also been served, Cassie wasn't sure
what to say. Dinner had been lavish. Dish had followed dish on matched red-and-gold-banded china.
Ranks of footmen had paraded interminably between pantry, sideboard, and table.

Her mistress continued as happily as if Cassie had
answered. "Just a tidy little dinner. Now, Cassie
dear, would you be so kind, I feel the chill on these
spring evenings. Would you run up to my room for
the paisley shawl? It has a green background exactly
this color."

Cassie stifled a groan. Search Elaine's room? It
would take forever. Shawls, dresses, lingerie, shoes,
and nightdresses overflowed cupboards and dressers. Yes, it *would* take forever. Or at least long
enough for the men to finish their port and join the
ladies. Cassie smiled. Lady Albinia's efforts at confrontation would have to wait for another day.

"It should be in the dresser nearest the windows
beside the bed. Or did I leave it in the morning
room? I'm not sure, so try there as well." As
though she knew it was an impossible task, Elaine
shrugged apologetically.

Shortly, Cassie was up the stairs and entering the
heated luxury of Elaine's bedroom. The bed stood
in solid splendor near the front of the room. Beneath a gathered canopy of red silk, it perched on an
inverted seashell of mahogany and gilt. The seven
ornately carved cupboards and three dressers lining

the walls of the bedroom and dressing room repeated the shell motif.

But no dresser stood near the window by the head of the bed. A cupboard occupied that space. Cassie approached it with a sigh. She'd have to search all of them.

Stiffened petticoats and day dresses bulged out as soon as she released the catch. Pushing through mounds of fabric, Cassie fought her way to the back where several shawls hung. When she brought them out to inspect in flickering candlelight, none of them proved to be paisley with a deep green background.

She checked the rest of the cupboards, then the dressers. When she finished the last cupboard, she was flushed and disheveled. She'd found every variety of shawl from a heavy knit in ugly brown to the lightest of lacy summer wraps. But not a paisley with a deep green background.

That left the morning room. Sighing, Cassie turned to go, but as she did, she noticed that the door connecting to Lord Lytham's room was partly opened. She knew she had to seize the opportunity to search it. Taking one tentative step forward, then another, she listened intently. Only the crackling sound of a low-burning fire came through the door as she opened it slowly. Cautiously, Cassie stepped into the room. Lytham's valet, like Elaine's maid, was comfortably below stairs. Holding a single flaring candle, Cassie crept quietly about the silent room.

At Lytham's elaborate dressing table, she paused and delicately lifted a discarded collar and tie. She shook her head disapprovingly. Papa's valet would never have left a room in such disarray, she thought. There'd been plenty of time after Lytham went downstairs for the man to clear up. Perhaps he intended to straighten up after he had his own dinner. He could reappear momentarily.

Hurrying now, Cassie glanced quickly in the dresser and secretary drawers. She found no keys. Frowning, Cassie turned to the night table next to Lytham's bed. Bed and table matched those in Elaine's room, but Lytham's wasn't cluttered with half-empty boxes of comfits and jars of complexion cream. A single unlit candle waited on top. And inside the single drawer lay a ring of keys.

Breath catching in her throat, Cassie reached for them, then stopped. She couldn't take them. They'd be missed. But now she knew where they were.

Footsteps coming down the hall startled her. She couldn't be found searching Lytham's bedroom. Sliding the drawer closed, Cassie turned toward Elaine's dressing room. The candle flame flickered and died with her movement.

A few steps across the room brought her to the deeper shadows before the hall door opened. Lytham walked in, a distracted scowl on his face. Cassie froze. As a thin plume of smoke wavered up from the candle, she watched him and waited.

Lurid visions of what he'd do to her if he saw her raced through her head. If only this wasn't his bedroom. Frantically, she searched for an excuse and discarded them all. They were too feeble. There was no reason, no decent reason, for her to be in his bedroom. Especially with him in it.

She waited for him to speak. And kept on waiting while he walked to his dressing room and entered it. She remained frozen for several seconds, expecting him to return. He hadn't seen her. Then she realized that, in the dim light, her mourning clothes had blended into the shadows.

Moving quietly, she started toward Elaine's dressing room again. The silk of her skirts swished dangerously in the dead stillness. At last she reached the safety of Elaine's dressing room; her heart pounded alarmingly in her throat. Cassie took several deep breaths. She was safe.

Her fingers trembling, she finally relit the candle. Going to the dressing room mirror, she checked her appearance. Plunging into Elaine's cupboards had destroyed whatever style her hair had. Pins stuck out, and golden brown tendrils curled wildly about her face and neck. Rapidly she pulled the pins from her hair until it tumbled, curling and silken, past her waist.

"What are you doing in here?" Lytham demanded, his deep voice echoing in Elaine's small dressing room.

Hair swirling in a glittering cape about her shoulders and breasts, she swung to face him. He must have seen the candlelight through the partially open door. "Lord Lytham, you startled me."

"That doesn't answer my question." Lytham took an impulsive step toward her, then halted.

"Lady Elaine wanted her green paisley shawl and asked me to find it for her." There was a suspicious glitter in his gray-blue eyes. Assuming a soothing calmness she didn't feel: "She thought it was up here in one of the cupboards, but I can't find it." She gave him a dazzling smile and returned to the mirror, comb in hand. "I mussed my hair searching for it."

She hoped Lytham couldn't see the way her hands shook. Still smiling at him in the mirror, Cassie put the comb down and twisted the thick, curly mass into a soft chignon at the nape of her neck.

"Why were you looking for it in my room?" He watched her intently. But his voice no longer rang with certainty.

Cassie straightened in righteous indignation. "I am not in the habit of visiting a gentleman's bedroom, my lord. Whether the gentleman is absent or not." She paused deliberately and let the silence stretch. Then she relaxed and smiled forgivingly. "You probably heard me through the door. I believe it was ajar." Cassie increased the warmth of her smile. "I can certainly understand why Elaine keeps it that way."

Lytham's intentness vanished and he returned her smile. He offered no apology, but Cassie couldn't imagine him ever apologizing to an employee.

"You might try the morning room, Cassie. That seems to be the graveyard for most of Elaine's lost treasures." He relaxed further. "And you shouldn't let Elaine use you as a drudge. We have maids for that sort of thing. I have to get back to my guests. Can I escort you down?"

When he smiled like that, Cassie didn't even want to be in the same house. "No, thank you, Lord Lytham. I want to look over the bedroom one more time to be certain I didn't miss it."

"With the amount of clothing she has, I don't understand how you hope to find anything. Be sure to hurry down. You're the co-hostess for this evening's entertainment." He shook his head firmly when her lips parted. "No, I'm not upset. I've been married to Elaine too long for that."

Laughing, he returned to his room. Cassie let the breath she'd kept trapped inside her escape in a long sigh and shuddered with relief. He believed her! What might have happened, she didn't dare consider. A burst of elation filled her. She'd outsmarted Lytham, found the strongbox and probably the key to open it.

She turned back to the mirror. Beneath the golden brown mass of her hair, riotous despite her efforts to subdue it, her face glowed with excitement in stark contrast to the black silk and lace of her dress. She'd gotten away with it. But anyone seeing her now would know something had happened. Taking several deep breaths, she went to the door. Sedately closing it behind her, she went down the corridor, a spring in her step.

Her hand on the bannister, she cautioned herself again. She had to be more careful. Trying to calm herself, she descended the final staircase. By the time she entered the morning room, Cassie had managed to hide most of her elation. Lady Albinia, no doubt, would blame Lord Randal for her ebullience. Let her. That was a safe reason.

In the dim light of her single candle and the banked fire, shadows shrouded the morning room furniture. Cassie moved among the scattered low chairs and occasional tables, candle held high. Every chair seemed to have a shawl or throw of some sort draped over it. Had Elaine really left the room in such disorder? The parlor maid certainly had her task cut out for her each day.

Finally, she spotted the shawl tucked down in one corner of the daybed. Elaine must have used it as a foot cover during her afternoon nap.

"Hello again."

Cassie froze, her heart racing. Almost being caught in Lytham's room had her more on edge than she realized. Unconsciously, she pressed one hand to her throat and turned around slowly to face Randal.

"Are you all right?" he asked, a worried note in his deep voice.

"Yes." She smiled at him. "You seem to make a habit of startling me."

Then it hit her. He must have followed her, and now they were alone together. Tension crackled, sending nervous shivers through her. Why had he come after her?

He stood in shadow just inside the closed door. The flickering light from her candle caught the buttons marching down his vest and the single diamond pinning his cravat. He took a slow, measured step toward her, then another, mischief filling his eyes. Her smile faded. A curious intentness shadowed his gaze.

"I do, don't I? I saw you flitting in here when I left the dining room," he said, his voice a deep purr. "Looking for something?"

Cassie held up the shawl. "Elaine was chilly."

In the half-light, he was a large cat, stalking. And she his prey.

"Umnh, it is chilly for the time of year." His gaze fastened on her. He took step after slow step, skirting the furniture without looking at it.

"Quite chilly," Cassie agreed. Chills ran up her spine as he stopped before her and looked down into her eyes. "London always seems chilly to me."

"May I take that for you?" Randal extended his hand for the shawl.

"It isn't heavy."

"I didn't think it was."

The candle flame glittered in his eyes. They beckoned her. She stared up at him, mesmerized.

And nearly jumped when he courteously offered her his arm. A turmoil of relief and disappointment filled her as she placed her hand on his arm.

Eyes still dancing with mischief, he looked down at her. "I wasn't certain we'd have the chance to be alone."

Mouth dry, Cassie watched him.

"So we could talk about Ada Byron," he continued smoothly. "You did know she's working on the calculating engine with Babbage? When her duties

as the Countess of Lovelace don't take precedence."
He smiled when Cassie nodded. "There was something else I wanted you to explain. What was it?
Ah, yes. How does one calculate the orbit of a
comet? Caroline Herschel discovered eight of
them."

Cassie turned toward the desk. Paper and pen
were available, and the prospect of staying here
alone with him was enticing. Too enticing. Turning
back, she caught a glimpse of his face. It was full of
sensuous deviltry. He waited expectantly. Instead of
fulfilling his expectations, she smiled serenely up at
him.

"Perhaps another day. The math is too complex
for an exhibition coordinator to master quickly."
She took his arm.

Smiling, he pressed her hand into his side. "Another day, then. Shall we join your guests in the
drawing room?"

The stairs led interminably up from the street
door, a thin film of dust in the corners. Gathering
her plain muslin skirt with one kid-gloved hand,
Cassie firmly grasped the handrail with the other.
This was the address off Chancery Lane. At the top
of the stairs was the office of the private enquiry
agent that Mr. Marshall had recommended.

Excitement and tension welled up in her. She'd
made progress, but she needed help. Mr. Neville
could search McCrory and Chambers' offices. Once
she learned what part the firm had played in her father's death and opened that strongbox, she'd be
that much closer to her goal. Breath coming
quickly, she started up the stairs.

Pausing on the landing, she released her skirt and
rapped on the door. Black lettering on the opaque
glass's upper half gave Mr. Neville's name. The rest

was the same dark, dull wood as the stairs and aged wainscoting lining them. She knocked more firmly.

The door opened. "Miss Cardwell?" a middle-aged gentleman asked. He stepped aside to let her enter. "Mr. Marshall told me you'd be visiting. How can I help you?" The smile and tone were paternal, intended to set her at ease.

Flicking a handkerchief over a clean Windsor chair, he invited her to take a seat. Neville was medium height, neither portly nor slender. From his graying muttonchop whiskers to his unobtrusive checked trousers and sober frock coat, nothing about him stood out. Except, she noted, for his eyes, which were a penetrating deep brown. He examined her with equal attention. Here was a man who was used to observing others without being observed.

Cassie tossed her head and began her tale. Neville made no notes as she spoke. At each pause, he asked a question that started her talking again. Eventually she'd told him everything, even about her discovery of the strongbox and the keys. And her father's warning against following the *Times* ciphers.

"So you see," she finished breathlessly, "it was good I didn't take the keys. If Lytham had seen me with them, I don't know what he would've done. I didn't want to run any more risks until I talked to you."

"Wise decision on your part, Miss Cardwell. Very wise." Neville studied his hands for a moment before looking up at her. "You realize, if your suspicions are correct, you are in grave danger?"

"I'm determined to learn the truth behind my father's death."

"If Lord Lytham killed your father, he won't stick at killing you."

Her hands tightening on her reticule, Cassie nodded calmly despite the turmoil inside her. "Then I shall have to be very careful he doesn't discover me again, shan't I?"

"Good girl." Neville nodded approvingly. "I'll concentrate my efforts on McCrory and Chambers. In the meantime, don't take the keys from Lord Lytham's drawer to try on the strongbox. Make impressions of them, and I'll have a set of keys made for you. They may do no good, though. There may not be any evidence in the strongbox," he pointed out.

"Impressions?" Cassie echoed. "How can I do that?"

Smiling at the intelligent young woman who sat before him, he rose from his chair and went to a narrow door. Opening it, he stepped into a small room and began searching through the shelves. A strange collection of things lined them. Wire, rope, and a litter of unidentifiable objects covered one side. At the back, there were stacks of books, ledgers, and bottles of ink.

"Here it is." He emerged from the closet, faintly flushed from stooping. "This is wax for making impressions. Press each side of a key straight into it for a complete impression. Return it to me, and I'll get keys made. Lord Lytham will never know you've had your hands on them." Anxiety flickered across his face. "You will be careful, won't you; it could be dangerous. I can't emphasize that too much."

Cassie accepted the wax with trembling hands and tucked it in her reticule. He was right. She'd been careful to appear an innocent, but resolved to take extra care. Especially since Lytham had caught her. She'd allayed his suspicions. Next time wouldn't be so easy.

Cassie started to rise when she remembered. "About your fee. Mr. Marshall didn't tell me how these things are usually arranged. I don't have much cash, but I brought this." She handed him an ornate garnet pin. "The jewelers valued this at thirty pounds. Is that enough to start with?"

"Certainly, Miss Cardwell. Although I'm afraid I won't be able to get more than ten or perhaps twelve pounds for it. You do understand?"

Cassie nodded and smiled to soothe the anxiety she saw in his kindly face. "The jeweler told me. In fact, he only offered me eight. I hoped you might be able to get a better price for it. If you need more, I have a number of similar pieces."

"No, this should be sufficient to start. I'll let you know if I need more. . . . Or"—he smiled warmly—"when I have information for you. How do I contact you?"

"I thought through Mr. Marshall. Neither Lord nor Lady Lytham will think it odd if I receive messages from Papa's solicitor."

"Perfectly sound reasoning. Now, don't you worry," he said, coming around his table to hold her chair, "and do be careful. This could be dangerous business."

Cassie rose and extended her hand. "Thank you, sir. I'll be careful."

Randal sipped his brandy while he waited for Welton Sinclair to join him. The grand opening plagued him. Even here, his thoughts refused to stray far from it. Except when he thought of Cassie, the enchanting creature in black he'd met at Lytham's. Between thoughts of her—her hazel eyes and bewitching smile—and the grand opening, he needed the peace the Merton Club provided.

If his carefully laid plans were successful, the Rydal family fortune would be restored to a sound footing. If not . . . Randal slowly took another sip of the excellent brandy. If only he could have forced those incompetent idiots on the committee to complete the Crystal Palace earlier. Completion one month before the opening left too little time, too many chances for his plans to go awry.

"Rydal," Tollaston's voice broke into his thoughts. "If I might have a word with you?"

The club secretary stood beside Randal's chair, tall, thin, pasty, self-important, yet nervous at bothering one of the club's prominent members. "Yes, Tollaston?" Randal deliberately didn't invite him to take a chair.

Mouth tightening, the secretary seated himself in the chair next to Randal's. "There have been reports," he began primly, "that certain members of this club have been frequenting, uh, an insalubrious locale."

"Insalubrious," Randal repeated. A muscle twitched at the corner of his firm mouth. "I'm not on the standards and admissions committee. Why bring it to my attention?"

"I wish to solicit your advice. Forays into Bluegate Fields could pose a health hazard to our members. While no epidemic is currently scourging that pestilential area, smallpox is always a danger." Tollaston placed his hands on his knees and looked down his nose. "The Merton Club has always been the club of choice for society during the half century we've been in existence. The members would not care to see that record blemished."

Randal took another sip of his brandy to hide both amusement and annoyance. "You've identified this culprit?" he asked, brows raised in polite interest.

Tollaston nodded, waiting.

"Then"—Randal put his brandy snifter down on the mahogany table beside him with a click—"you

have a greater problem. If one member has seen another in that, uh, 'insalubrious locale' "—he imitated
Tollaston's tone—"he must have been there himself.
And if more than one member has seen another, the
entire club may have already been contaminated.
Perhaps you should warn the club members. Oh,
are you going already? Well, I hope my advice
helped."

Randal watched Tollaston, his frock coat flapping
behind him, stride across the room. Who had seen
him? It didn't matter. His efforts in Bluegate Fields
couldn't be terminated. Even after his task there was
complete, it had to lie in obscurity. Would he have
to change his plans now? Publicity was the last
thing he could tolerate for his efforts in that "insalubrious locale."

"What did you do to Tollaston?" Looking weary,
Welton Sinclair slumped into the chair the secretary
had occupied. "He bolted out of here like a scalded
cat."

"I offended his sense of propriety."

"Is that all?"

Randal nodded. "Tollaston felt it necessary to
warn me to avoid visiting 'insalubrious locales.'
Our secretary feels I'm likely to contract bubonic
plague and might imperil the health of members."

Welton sat up sharply, anger washing the weariness out of his fair skin. "How dare he concern
himself with your movements? I've half a mind to
call a board meeting and have the man replaced."

"Sit back and relax." Picking up the snifter to
take the last sip from it, Randal smiled with wry
irony. "Besides, I've set him back a bit." He
chuckled at Welton's questioning look. "Several
members must be visiting these infamous haunts or
they couldn't have seen me there. He didn't like the
implication."

Welton's chuckle echoed Randal's, but he soon subsided into weary gloom again. After signaling the waiter for two brandies, Randal waited for his friend to finish brooding. It took half a glass before Welton met Randal's gaze and smiled apologetically.

"If you're really enjoying this slumming our secretary disapproves of, I may ask to come with you next time."

Taking another sip, Randal identified the source of Sinclair's problem. "Madeline?" he asked sympathetically.

Welton checked to make sure no one else could hear. They were nearly alone in the smoking room. Only an elderly man, a survivor of Waterloo, occupied a comfortable chair before the fire, and he was too deaf to hear.

"Her mother's becoming more insistent."

"Relax, I'm not going to marry her. It'd be like marrying my sister. If I had one."

Looking gloomy, Sinclair took another sip of brandy and leaned forward, bracing his elbows on his knees. "Lady Albinia's pushing Madeline at Carsbrooke."

"Carsbrooke! She can't be serious."

"I think he's just a threat," Sinclair said slowly. "For the moment. But eventually she might try to force Madeline into marriage with the man."

"You won't be able to wait, then?" Randal asked.

"No. It's two years before Madeline comes of age. Lady Albinia's patience won't last that long."

"Come along, old man. Dinner will help you face it." He rose to his feet and touched Welton's shoulder. Pausing, Randal looked at his friend. "If you decide to do something drastic, and I don't recommend it, I'll help any way I can."

When Cassie entered the morning room, Elaine was settled on the rose velvet daybed. After the ex-

ertions of the dinner party, it was necessary to re-
coup her strength. She had turned all the
housekeeping over to Cassie and had spent yesterday reading novels and munching on fruit and
boxes of sweets. But this morning she was restless.
Her embroidery didn't interest her, while the
thought of planning her next entertainment tired
her.

"You got them?" Elaine demanded. Once Cassie
explained about the ciphers, Elaine had arranged to
have the *Times* set aside for them.

In answer, Cassie held up the papers. "I'll find the
agony column."

"Oh, let me help."

Elaine rose from the daybed, her pale pink morning gown flowing limply with less than her usual
number of petticoats. They weren't comfortable
when she'd intended to spend the day lying down.
She picked up a newspaper and glanced through it.

Mouth pursed and nose wrinkled, Elaine read one
of the articles reporting a debate in Parliament.
"How can men read such things every day?"

"They find them interesting," Cassie said absently. She turned page after page, looking for the
ciphers. Finally she found them.

"Here they are," Cassie said happily. She showed
the paper to Elaine. "Look in this section."

Elaine obediently turned the pages and found a
similar column in her paper. "N.Z. M.P.W.F.,
D.P.N.F. U.P. N.F? What sort of language is that?
There's only one recognizable word in the whole
thing."

Taking Elaine's paper, Cassie looked at the long
paragraphs that started with those peculiar letter
groups. "Lord Playfair said most of the ciphers
were simple alphabetic shifts. We shouldn't have too
much trouble figuring it out." She carefully avoided
mention of her father and his interest in ciphers.

Bewilderment filled Elaine's pale blue eyes. "I don't understand."

Cassie pointed at several coded groups. "D'you see how each of these words ends in the same letter? What do you want to bet that *f* is the same as *e*?"

"How did you figure that out so fast?" Elaine asked.

"Simple statistics." Cassie wrote out the code on a piece of paper and wrote the letters she thought corresponded below them. "*E* is the most common letter in the English language. It frequently ends words or appears somewhere in the middle. These people have moved each letter over one, just as Lord Playfair said. At least, this makes sense."

"What does it say?" Elaine drew up a chair and sat down so that she could read over Cassie's shoulder.

"'My love, come to me. All is discovered. We must flee to Scotland before your parents force you into this obnoxious marriage. Not for worlds . . .'" Cassie paused and scribbled down some more code groups and their translation. "'Not for worlds would I sully your pure name.'" Cassie paused and frowned, then, "Oh, the typesetter made a mistake. 'Meet me at the station at half past two before they tear you from my arms. Elopement is all that is left to us. I shall never abandon you.'"

Giggling, Cassie turned to Elaine. "There's more in the same vein. Isn't it silly?"

"Silly? I think it's perfectly wonderful." Elaine sighed. "To think of giving up everything for your love. I'm sure it's quite wonderful."

"But—" Elaine's expression stopped her. "Would you like me to try solving another one? Or better still, you might try some of these." Cassie gave Elaine another page with ciphers.

"Oh, but I'm not smart enough to do these," Elaine protested.

"Of course you are. Just copy down the word groups of this one and this one. They look like normal words. Try the letter on either side of the one in the code group. See, if the code letter is *t*, try *u* or *s* to see which make up intelligible words. Or reverse the alphabet. Papa used to write me letters in a cipher like this when I was very little."

"You've done these before?"

"Lots of times. If you have a problem, let me know and I'll help."

Cassie bent over another cipher. This one looked far more interesting. Was this the one her papa had warned her against? It was more complex than the others in the paper. Carefully she analyzed it for frequencies and patterns, but could find none. She needed a longer message. Frowning, she put it aside. Once Minton provided them with back issues, she would search for more messages in that cipher. In the meantime, Elaine would be entertained with the personal messages.

"No, my lord. There'll be no difficulty at the opening on the first of May," Randal said. "But it's important to the Exhibition's success that the Queen attend. Some of the newspapers have speculated—"

"Newspapers, pah!" The Prime Minister gestured sharply as though he pushed all the newspapers in England away. "They're worse than a bunch of elderly gossips hanging over the back fence. Of course Frau Albert will open the exhibition. Not only is it her beloved Prince's creation, but the papers have put her in an absolutely untenable position. She looks cowardly if she doesn't." Anger flared in Lord John Russell's deeply set eyes.

"We're taking precautions against another assassination attempt," Randal offered mildly.

"What about the threats against Her Majesty?"

Lord Russell pushed back the fine dark hair drooping over his high forehead.

"Despite Irish agitation and the assassination attempts against the Queen, the threats seem to be just hot air." Randal's normally twinkling eyes narrowed. "Scotland Yard maintains that assassins don't publicize their attempts in advance. They plot in secret. They've investigated, naturally, but nothing's come of it. They don't expect any problem."

Lord Russell tensed. "But they're not certain."

Randal didn't answer the implied question. "I just wish it hadn't been necessary to involve the military at all. This division of security between the military and Scotland Yard is inviting trouble."

"There's no help for it. We can't afford any more dissension at this time." Lord Russell toyed with the papers littering his desk. He looked into Randal's eyes. "The present government could fall if the Exhibition fails. Keep me informed, Rydal. And keep any assassins away from the Queen."

"I shall do my best, my lord."

Randal left the office. No assassins would get near the Queen at the grand opening. He was confident of that. He'd carefully planned everything. But if his gamble failed . . . His strong shoulders tensed as he hurried down the stairs. Thoughts about the Great Exhibition gave way to the person invading his mind ever since he met her. Cassie.

Would Cassie be home if he visited Lytham's? He needed to see her desperately, and he had the excuse of thanking Elaine for her hospitality.

The other night, she'd acted skittish after rejoining the others in the drawing room. Had he been too forward? He didn't want to frighten her off. What did he want from her? What he wanted was becoming clearer to him with each passing hour. He was bewitched. Cassie Cardwell. An American.

It was unnerving. But exhilarating. He hailed a cab and directed it to Lytham House.

# Chapter IV

Elaine held up a blue damask ball dress from another age. For nearly seventy-five years, it had lain packed in a trunk in the Lytham House attics. "Look at this, Cassie. It's beautiful. What sort of charade could we use it for?"

That morning, Elaine had decreed, should be devoted to her forthcoming evening of tableaux. Consequently, they were in the attics exploring trunks and furniture that were stored there.

Skirting a closed trunk, Cassie took the dress and held it up. Cobweb-shrouded windows grayed the light, but the blue damask retained its glow. Even with its antique styling, it was lovely. Its wide sleeves dripped with heavy lace that matched the lace-trimmed underskirt. The damask overskirt was split and caught up at the sides. It required an elbow hoop to keep from dragging on the floor. Did Elaine know where one was?

"The hoop. Oh, dear. Where did I see— Oh, yes. Over there. Timpkins," Elaine instructed a foot-

man, "take those hoops down to the sun room,
please." She turned to Cassie while Timpkins ma-
neuvered the awkward hoop down the narrow
stairs. "What sort of tableau could we use it for?"

Finger on one cheek, Cassie cocked her head.
"I'm not sure. It has a rather 'let them eat cake' air
to it, doesn't it? We could do places instead of
quotations. Perhaps Versailles."

"That would make my tableaux different," Elaine
said, pleased. She looked at the forest of trunks and
boxes they hadn't opened yet. "Let's see what else
we can find for people to act out places. I shall have
to ask my dearest Lytham what he thinks. He actually offered to make up the list of topics. It's so
sweet of him." Elaine hesitated. "He doesn't usually
take quite so much interest in my little entertain-
ments."

A troubled expression settled on Elaine's round
face when she spoke of her husband. Cassie eyed
Elaine narrowly as she laid down the damask dress
on the pile of clothes they'd chosen. Something was
bothering Elaine, something she'd nearly mentioned
a number of times. But she always stopped, not
ready to confide in her companion yet.

Tactfully, Cassie plunged into the nearest trunk.
It held gloves, fans, trinkets, and other discards.
From the sounds, Elaine followed her example.
After a few seconds of rummaging, she gasped with
delight. Troubles forgotten, Elaine held up an elaborate man's gold brocade coat with oyster satin
smalls.

"How would Randal look in these?" she asked casually, watching Cassie closely.

Expression determinedly composed, Cassie rose
slowly from her knees. "Lord Randal? I wasn't
aware he was on the guest list."

"I expanded it. He was so sweet when he came to

thank me for my hospitality after my little dinner party. I couldn't help myself. Besides"—Elaine laid the suit of clothes down across a trunk—"I want Madeline to come. Lady Albinia won't let her if Randal's not here."

"I'm not sure Lord Randal would appreciate being dangled as bait for an eligible young lady."

She quickly bent back to her task. If only Elaine wouldn't talk about him. She must sense how he crept into Cassie's mind a dozen times a day. Despite Elaine's promises, all her matchmaking instincts were in full play.

"He doesn't mind," Elaine said airily. Her pale blue eyes sharpened. "He knows my plans—for Madeline and Sinclair. Aren't they the sweetest, dearest couple?"

"Lady Albinia will be among the invited guests?" Her mouth firmed, and the cleft in her chin deepened before Cassie bent over another trunk. It muffled her voice, fortunately, masking the feelings she couldn't suppress.

"It's the only way Madeline will be allowed to come."

Cassie recognized what would follow. First Elaine would discuss Welton Sinclair's chance of marrying Madeline. Then, somehow, she would steer the conversation over to Randal and her desire to see him married. Cassie decided to deflect Elaine.

"Look at what I've found." She held up a number of scarves in silk and lace, natural blonde, and in colors, some spangled. "I'm not sure what these could be used for, but it's a shame to leave them up here."

Elaine stood up with difficulty. "You're quite right. Such lovely laces. Are there more of them? We could use them for a bride or someone in a harem."

"It would help if we knew what Lord Lytham's chosen." Several more lace scarves went on the growing pile.

"Not knowing makes it more fun. Besides, people will use any props we can find. Like that table over there. It will do to set a scene."

Cassie looked dubiously at the rickety old table. "Fine, but it still would be easier if we knew."

"As host and hostess, dearest Lytham and I can't form one of the teams. Of course, you'll be in the tableaux. Without you we won't have an even number." Elaine paused guiltily. "I wanted to surprise you. Anyway, I can't tell you the subjects, since Lytham hasn't told me. He knows I'll forget and chatter about it. And he has such clever ideas."

"Yes, he does."

Cassie plunged into another trunk. Discussing Lytham with Elaine always made her uncomfortable. Elaine had become her friend. And she was spying on her friend's husband. She was glad the trunk hid her face.

"I shall assign teams for the tableaux. Three teams, I think. Madeline and Sinclair on one. And Lady Albinia shall have to be on another. So difficult to do these things without being obvious." Elaine sighed. "I can't have Lady Albinia on the same team with either Sinclair or Lord Randal. It would make the evening too interesting."

It made sense. Then she saw Elaine's delightful trap. Madeline and Sinclair would be in one group, Lady Albinia and Mr. Edgar in a second, while she'd be in the third. With Randal. Warmth filled her. Cooling only when she realized that she still hadn't been able to make wax impressions of the keys she'd found. Lord Lytham had remained stubbornly, erratically at home. She hoped he'd go back to his office soon before thoughts of the Marquess of Rydal distracted her even more.

His lordship glanced up at the knock on the library door. He covered the message before him with a blank sheet of paper, and called, "Enter." Tensely alert, he sat erect behind his desk in the tall, narrow black leather chair.

"Your sherry, milord." The butler closed the door behind him and advanced across the long room in the stately fashion that suited his dignity. He set the tray down on his master's desk precisely within reach but not in danger of being knocked over.

"I hope all is going well with your work, milord," the butler said with just the touch he wished. To express believable concern in a voice devoid of emotion was a rare talent.

"The Exhibition's grand opening should be truly spectacular." His lordship looked down his high-bridged nose at the desk. "People will talk about it for years."

"Thank you, that's all. If anyone calls, I'm not at home." He fingered the page covering the message.

"Very good, m'lord."

His lordship glanced up again when the door latched firmly behind the butler. Pouring a glass, he sipped the excellent sherry, a cheerless smile lifting his lips. So the pawns wanted more money. Greedy fools. The money was important. But Barnthorpe's identification of his patron was even more so. His testimony would be useful at the trial.

Decisively, his lordship returned the glass to the silver tray. He took the message from beneath the clean sheet of paper. Best to let Barnthorpe believe he was frightened.

He scratched out a few words, then added others, his gray-blue eyes narrowed consideringly. Yes, that should do it. Just the right touch of nerves. Now to encipher it and get it to the *Times*.

He took his small cipher engine and put it on the blotter. Rapidly, he enciphered the message, then copied it out in block letters for the newspaper.

What would have happened, he wondered as he folded the letter, if he hadn't thought to have the cipher engine's wooden strips carved and hadn't given a set to Barnthorpe? It had been difficult enough to teach the lout a simple cipher. Barnthorpe thought he was so smart. And he was. Just enough to be useful. His lordship's lips stretched in another mirthless smile.

Lytham would never spend the day at his government office again, Cassie thought as she closed the morning room door. Elaine had lain down for her nap, and the rest of the afternoon was free. The perfect time to continue her search, if it hadn't been for Lytham's presence in the house. Until he went to the Home Office, she couldn't safely make impressions of the keys in his bedroom. Neville's warning still chilled her. If Lytham decided to return to his room while she was there . . . She shivered.

Cassie turned toward the library for a book to read until time for her appointment with Mr. Marshall. A burst of rain spat against the windowpanes, making her draw the warm woolen shawl more closely about her shoulders. It was a chill, blustery day. One she wouldn't willingly go out in unless she had an errand. Or an impression of the keys.

"Don't go in, miss," Minton called as she reached the library door. "They're still cleaning the chimneys in his lordship's office. He's using the library and doesn't wish to be disturbed."

"Will he be long, Minton?" Hope flared as she waited for the answer.

"All afternoon, miss. Would you like me to fetch a book for you?" Although he liked her otherwise, he couldn't approve of her unladylike predilection for books. Unless they were novels.

"I have a book in my room." Cassie grimaced up at Minton, deliberately inviting a smile. "And some mending to do that I'd much rather put off."

He'd believe she was quietly occupied in her room and warn the other servants. No one would disturb her. Nor would the maids come upstairs, since the bedrooms were finished for the day. Lytham's room would be empty.

Excited at the opportunity, Cassie excused herself as calmly as she could and went up the steps. She took the last flight of stairs at a run, unable to stop herself. It felt as though every eye in Lytham House watched her and knew what she planned. She scuttled into her room as if someone chased her, and banged the door closed behind her.

Cassie leaned against the closed door, breathing deeply. Had anyone heard her? Of course not. No one was upstairs at this time of day. She took another deep breath to control her excitement. If she went down the hall to Lytham's room and anyone saw her like this, he'd be suspicious. Or she'd carelessly leave some trace behind.

Hands on her flushed cheeks, Cassie calmed herself. Finally, under control, she walked sedately across to her small bedside table and bumped into the bed. So much for her efforts. A flicker of humor lit her eyes and tugged at the corners of her generous mouth. Cassie took the keys from her pocket.

The impression wax was hidden inside the locked drawer where the maid wouldn't find it.

With the wax tucked safely in her petticoat pocket, Cassie went to the door. After several deep breaths, she opened it slowly. The hall was as silent and empty as it had been when she flew into her room. Now she listened so closely that she could hear the steady ticking of the clock in the hall below.

Keeping her movements natural, she walked quietly down the hall. No one would consider it unusual if he saw her going into Elaine's room. She even had an explanation ready for Elaine's maid or Lytham's valet, if they were still above stairs.

The stillness and the faint scent of her mistress's favorite perfume enfolded her. Gray light seeped through the windows of Elaine's room, dulling the vibrant red and gilt of the furniture. The room was as neat as it ever was. A platoon of maids couldn't keep up with the trail of belongings Elaine left behind.

What if Lytham's valet was still around? She'd simply tell him she was searching for one of Elaine's lost scarves or gloves. The entire household had been sent on wild-goose chases often enough to accept that explanation. But there would be no chance to make impressions of the keys.

The dressing room was empty, and the door into Lytham's was ajar. Cassie went to the cupboard nearest his room and opened it. Other than the fire's crackle, there was no sound. Then a coal popped loudly.

An even better excuse for being in Lytham's room . . . *I feared a spark had fallen onto the hearth rug,* she rehearsed to herself. She went boldly through the door and strode toward the fireplace. A burning fragment lay on the tile hearth perilously close to the lush, floral-patterned rug. Cassie picked up the brass-handled fire shovel and brush, and swept up the spark to toss back into the fire.

As on the night of the dinner party, the room was shadowed but empty. The valet had cleared away his master's nightclothes and shaving gear. Lytham's dressing table stood bare except for a pair of nail scissors, a brush, and a candlestick. None of the drapes had been drawn in preparation for the evening, and there was light enough from the windows to complete her task.

Pulse beating hard in her throat, Cassie approached the huge, red-shrouded bed resting on its inverted seashell. Were the keys still there? Or did Lytham have them? She pulled the nightstand drawer open slowly. They were there, the same ring she'd seen before.

Fingers trembling, she took the impression wax from her petticoat pocket. How had Neville said to do it? A clear impression of both sides of the key pressed straight into the wax. There were five keys on the ring. She had just enough wax.

Despite her shaking hands, Cassie made the impressions with careful precision. Each clink of a key, every pop of the fire made her start. Someone was bound to hear. The hall was a mere fifteen feet from where she stood. And she was in Lord Lytham's bedroom.

Finally the three pieces of wax held ten clear impressions. Cassie sighed soundlessly and thrust the wax back in her pocket. She dropped the keys into the drawer and closed it. Had she left a trace of her presence? Yes.

Her breath hissed through her teeth. A smear of wax marked the front of the drawer. Hastily taking her handkerchief, she rubbed at it. The candlestick rattled atop the nightstand from the fury of her attack. It nearly clattered off the edge before she caught it. Almost sick with relief that it hadn't fallen, Cassie looked at the smear again. Most of it was gone. What remained looked like a careless maid's polishing job, and there were plenty of careless maids in Lytham House.

With the treasured impressions bumping against the whalebone stiffening her bottom petticoat, Cassie hurried toward the dressing room. Once beyond it to the safety of Elaine's room, she stopped to breathe. How could people actually do such nerve-racking things for a living? Perhaps it got easier with practice, but Cassie doubted it.

When she entered the hall, the clock chimed the hour. Only three. She had plenty of time to stop at Neville's office before her appointment with Mr. Marshall. With her heaviest cloak over her arm, Cassie hurried downstairs. Minton would call a hansom for her. Once on her way, she'd ask the driver to stop at Neville's office first.

Pleased with how well everything was going, Cassie hummed softly as she reached the ground floor. Pausing before the mirror, she settled the cloak over her wool marocain dress and pulled the hood over her hair. It was already riotous from the damp weather. Cassie tucked a stray curl firmly beneath the hood and fastened her gloves at the wrist. At the doorbell's chime, her eyes went to the door. No one should be visiting this afternoon.

Minton appeared from the drawing room to answer the bell. "Is Lytham in?" Randal asked the butler. He stepped into the hall, his fawn carrick misted with rain, and removed his top hat.

"He is here, my lord," Minton began, "but he's not in."

"Don't disturb him," Randal said absently. No longer caring whether he saw Lytham, his eyes warmed to a deeper blue with only a hint of gray. He had seen Cassie. "On your way out, Miss Cardwell?" He thrust a packet of papers at Minton and stepped around him.

"I have an errand to run."

Randal looked quickly about the hall. The clock ticked ponderously in the quiet. Minton was the only servant in sight. Beneath Minton's dignified mask, a smile of satisfaction lurked.

"Without a maid or footman to accompany you? Elaine wouldn't approve." Randal took an impetuous step toward Cassie.

"Oh, but—" Cassie retreated a step. Randal's unexpected appearance flustered her. "But I'm just going to Mr. Marshall's office in a cab and then straight back home."

"Mr. Marshall?" Randal questioned, closing the gap again.

Randal looked down into her flushed face. How lovely she looked with her green-flecked hazel eyes and golden brown hair peeping from beneath her hood. Her creamy skin accented the soft perfection of her face.

"My father's solicitor. There are some papers I have to sign," she explained softly.

Cassie lowered her eyes to cut off some of his impact. He could so easily distract her from her purpose. She would get to Neville. And Randal wouldn't stop her. No matter how much she wanted to let him. She stepped around him.

"If you'll excuse me, I must go or I'll be late." Her voice was pleasant, she realized gladly, pleasant but firmly dismissive.

Only, he refused to be dismissed. One tawny brown brow arched. "I couldn't allow you to go unescorted. Highly improper for a young lady. Whatever would Elaine think of my manners?"

Randal smiled and held the door. "If you'll wait
here for a moment?" he commanded firmly, ignoring her half-formed protest. Not sure what to do
next, Cassie stood in the shelter of the portico. He
lifted his walking stick to signal a passing hansom.
"Here we are."

As though her broken protest hadn't been spoken, Randal took her arm in one strong hand and
helped her into the carriage. The strength of his
grasp gave Cassie a warm feeling of safety, the first
she'd had in days. Yet she couldn't relax and let
Randal rule her life this way.

She looked into his face to protest, then dropped
her gaze to her clasped hands. Something more than
warm interest lit his blue-gray eyes. Something that
made them more blue than gray. Something that
was more than friendly.

In the next instant, Randal was seated in the
hansom close beside Cassie. He got her solicitor's
address and passed it to the driver. As he settled
back into the seat, their shoulders brushed. Waves of
pleasure coursed through her.

Maybe he could accompany her to Mr.
Marshall's. Then she could claim an errand for
Elaine. Or that Mr. Marshall would escort her
home. A dozen plans for ridding herself of his company while enjoying it for the maximum time flitted
through her head. But she had to deliver the wax
impressions and couldn't go to a private enquiry
agent with Randal. She frowned and peered around
the fold of her hood as the horse jerked the hansom
into motion. Why did her duty and her desires have
to be in such conflict?

"It's not necessary," she tried again.

He smiled down at her, oblivious to the rain spit-
ting into the cab. "What isn't?" Randal asked innocently.

"Escorting me to my solicitor's," Cassie said repressively.

"I never shirk any task no matter how dark, dangerous, or unpleasant." The look he gave her clearly said she was neither dark nor unpleasant, but he considered her dangerous. And he found that danger enticing.

"That's absurd. I'm old enough to take care of myself." Cassie looked as stern as she could. But his absurdity had brought laughter to the surface. The cleft in her firm chin deepened when she primmed her mouth to restrain her amusement. "I'm quite old enough," she repeated.

"Possibly. But I couldn't allow someone as ancient and infirm as you to brave the perils of this trip alone."

Randal opened his eyes wide, the picture of innocence. Although he couldn't suppress his appreciation of the situation entirely. Placing one gloved hand on his chest, he lifted his head proudly.

"I'm only doing what any gentleman would." He glanced down at her, a smile warming his eyes. "My mother would be proud."

"She wouldn't be proud of you for ignoring your duty. You're supposed to speak to Lord Lytham about the Great Exhibition."

"I haven't ignored my duty," Randal protested. "I delivered a copy of the report I promised Lytham. There's nothing pressing for the rest of the day. I have plenty of time to escort you to your solicitor's."

No matter how she tried to escape, he came up with new reasons to accompany her, teasing unmercifully. Shortly, they became so absurd that she had tears in her eyes from laughing and almost forgot her mission.

"And"—he finished his last absurdity and looked

out at the buildings surrounding them—"we're here. I'll escort you into his office and wait." He took her chin in his hand and tipped her face up. "I'm not as easy to get rid of as you seem to think." He paused and the smile became less teasing, somehow warmer. "Then if you have the time, perhaps I could persuade you to take tea with my aunt? Aunt Maude's an invalid who enjoys cheerful young people about her. With her children all married and living in the country, she never sees enough young faces."

Paying the driver, Randal swung down from the hansom and supported her onto the wet cobblestone pavement. Cassie promptly forgot all her wild schemes to send him away. She couldn't simply refuse his escort again. Any more protests, and he would begin to suspect something. At least it was a comforting excuse.

As the cab drew away, the horse's hooves clopping and splashing, they stood looking at each other. Then what he'd suggested dawned on her. He was taking her to see his aunt. Why? She couldn't ask, and Randal wasn't volunteering reasons. He smiled down at her, silent.

Cassie was content to stand, her head tilted back. The hood of her cloak belled about her curly hair in the wind as she gazed up into his face. She found nothing strange in it. The noise of cabs rattling over the cobblestones and the sharp click of footsteps hurrying to reach shelter faded. Then a particularly sharp blast of wind stung her face with rain. Cassie freed her hand from his.

"I must go in," she said, her voice soft, breathless. "I'll be late."

"You will come?"

"To visit with your Aunt Maude? But I haven't a maid or footman to act as chaperone." Cassie peeped up beyond the edge of her dark hood, her lips quivering with demure laughter. How could she be angry with him?

"True. But Aunt Maude is most unconventional. However, I could persuade her to lend you a maid to chaperone us when I return you to Lytham House."

"Well—"

"Do say you'll come."

There was something like entreaty in his voice. Why did Randal want her to meet his Aunt Maude in such a casual way? She couldn't resist him as he stood over her. As she nodded, another gust of sharp wind drove into them.

It brought her back to reality. "I must go," she exclaimed.

She swung about and hurried toward the door leading to Mr. Marshall's office. As she did, the wax impressions bumped against her. Could she pass them to Mr. Marshall? He would send them to Neville. But Mr. Marshall's office was one large room filled with clerks; she couldn't hand them over in Randal's presence.

When could she get them to the enquiry agent? Not for the next few days at least. Elaine had too many plans to keep her busy. If only Randal hadn't come to Lytham House at just that moment. Even with his impromptu invitation to meet his Aunt Maude.

As she chastised herself, she smiled up at Randal. Tea at his aunt's house. Vaguely she recalled Elaine telling her that Randal's mother and father were both dead. His Aunt Maude was his favorite relation. Tea with his favorite aunt.

The thought remained with her while she discussed with Mr. Marshall a minor matter concerning her father's estate. Throughout the discussion, Cassie was unnervingly aware of Randal's discreet presence at the other end of the large room. Tea with his Aunt Maude.

She didn't fully believe it until the cab stopped before a small, charming house in Belgravia. In seconds, they were in the drawing room and Randal was leading her forward for an introduction.

If Aunt Maude had been able to stand, she would have been of medium height. Her silvered blond hair was styled in the fashion of twenty-five years ago with curls framing her face and piled on the back of her head. A network of fine wrinkles marked her eyes and the corners of her generous mouth. A slender woman dressed in current fashion in a heavy sapphire velvet gown. She didn't rise, although her dark blue eyes lit with pleasure when she saw Randal.

"This is Miss Cassandra Cardwell, Aunt," Randal said when he rose from kissing her cheek. "My aunt, the Dowager Countess of Enniscorthy."

"Milady." Cassie curtsied briefly, startled by the intent look on Lady Maude's face. It faded, and the old lady nodded and gestured to the other end of the sofa beside her.

"I've been wondering if you'd ever remember your aunt," Lady Maude said, directing a tart glance at Randal. "Sit down." She gestured imperiously at a chair across from her. "I'll get a crick in my neck if you insist on towering over me like that."

Controlling a smile, Randal settled easily in the small lady's chair indicated. As its size was more suited to Cassie, he seemed ludicrous in it. Cassie had to work hard to control her amusement.

And missed Lady Maude's first scathing comments.

". . . Bluegate Fields, and don't pretend you haven't been seen there," Lady Maude concluded.

"I'd never pretend with you, Aunt. I wouldn't dare." Randal shifted uneasily in the miniature chair. Did everyone know his business?

"Well, what were you doing there? No—" Lady Maude raised a hand to stop the explanation he clearly didn't intend to give. "You were up to no good. If we were alone, I'd give my opinion of such goings-on, but we aren't. I won't have you sully young, innocent ears with your misdeeds."

"Whatever you say, Aunt Maude." His frown clearing, he smiled with tender amusement. "Isn't it reprehensible what single men find to amuse themselves when their female relations ignore them? You haven't rung a peal over me for at least four days. How can any man stay on the path of righteousness for that long?"

"That's as may be. But you take after your father, young man. Not that my sister didn't choose well when she accepted his offer."

"The Rydals are glad you approve, Aunt."

"Tush. You go find my fan while I soothe this young girl's sensibilities. Your antics have undoubtedly shocked her to the core."

Outside, gusts of chill rain hit the windowpanes. Inside, it was comfortable but cool. Lady Maude no more needed a fan than Cassie needed a light summer dress. Her hostess wanted the opportunity to interrogate her alone. Ignoring the concerned question in Randal's face, Cassie turned to his aunt.

After Randal's exit, the interrogation materialized rapidly. Using an older woman's prerogative, Lady Maude subjected Cassie to a catechism about her antecedents, fortune, and prospects. Cassie told the story everyone believed.

"Well, I won't say you're not a good girl, because you are. But you're holding something back. It's not a little thing, either." Lady Maude's gaze narrowed. "I won't have my nephew hurt."

Cassie met the deep blue eyes and replied seriously, "It's nothing that would harm Randal."

Lady Maude stiffened. "You call him Randal?"

Always before, Cassie'd been careful to call him "Lord Randal" or "Rydal" in public. Talking so much with Elaine about him had allowed it to slip out. "What is Bluegate Fields?" She changed the subject quickly as if she had to ask the question before Lord Randal's return.

"Bluegate Fields? Where'd you hear about that place? It isn't a decent place for a lady of quality to know about."

"You warned Lord Randal about going there." Cassie's lips twisted.

"I did no such thing. I've never heard of Bluegate Fields." Lady Maude frowned. "It's not a decent place," she repeated, adding to herself, "and I don't like Randal going there." Cassie's puzzlement finally registered. "Only the lowest sort of people live in Bluegate Fields," Lady Maude explained. "Thieves, murderers, and . . . and worse. Fortunately, or unfortunately if you look at it from Randal's viewpoint, I have the best intelligence system in London. I hear all the gossip." Lady Maude looked hard at Cassie. "I don't believe all I hear. But I hear it all. Remember that. And don't tell Randal about all this. He might not visit as often if he knew I'm not left lonely."

"I won't tell him," Cassie said slowly. Why did Randal go to that sort of place?

"I wouldn't go to Bluegate Fields," Lady Maude said, chuckling. "No young lady would." She emphasized the word *lady* faintly. "But young gentlemen have the lowest tastes at times, as I'm sure your mother told you."

Still frowning, Cassie nodded. Her mother had died while she was a child. But she recalled some of Grandmother's comments on Papa's starts. Apparently men found amusement in the strangest places and in even stranger ways.

"Don't worry about it, my dear. Men are a separate species. Love them but don't try to understand them. You'll go crazy if you do. Ah, here's Randal. Have you brought my fan, dear boy?" She held out her hand for it.

"I didn't realize you wanted it, Aunt." Randal perched on the small chair he'd occupied before and grinned at his aunt. "Did I leave you alone long enough?"

"Quite long enough. And did you tell them to bring in tea?"

Nodding, Randal started to lean back in the chair and barely stopped himself in time. "Are you planning on going somewhere? During my banishment, I noticed a number of trunks."

"I'm about to become grandmother to the future Earl of Enniscorthy. Maybe. The procedure requires supervision, or that girl will do something foolish. I never understood what he saw in her, but at least she's been prompt in fulfilling her matrimonial duties."

Randal's grin widened. "I know exactly what Cousin Alfred saw in Frances."

"Don't be vulgar. Her obvious attributes are not compensation for inadequate lineage. But as long as she ensures the succession, I'll accept her as a daughter-in-law."

"That's good, Aunt. I doubt Cousin Alfred intends to divorce her. Even to please you. Frances may have the brains of a rabbit, but she's still a corker."

Sitting quietly in her corner of the couch, Cassie

listened to the pair spar cheerfully with each other. The only disturbance came after Randal offered to see his aunt off.

"Nonsense! I will *not* have you making a nuisance of yourself at the railway station. You fuss so much that it takes three times as long as it should to get anything accomplished. It's one of his more endearing male foibles, Miss Cardwell. Still, it gets on my nerves."

"Endearing or not, Aunt, I'm going to exercise another of my endearing foibles and wish you good-bye. You look tired, and you need your strength for the journey." Randal rose gracefully and stood waiting for Cassie. "I wish you'd reconsider going." He stopped when the fire flared in Lady Maude's eyes. "I know, you want to see your first Enniscorthy grandchild born. I wish you joy of it. Just be sure you rest, or your arthritis will be worse than ever in Ireland."

"Undoubtedly. But summer, such as it is, will be here soon, and I shan't tire myself." An impish smile lit her face. "I shall tire others instead. Now"—she turned to Cassie who stood beside Randal—"be sure you come to visit me when I return in June. And don't wait for this rapscallion to bring you."

"By the way, favorite of all my aunts, may we borrow a maid to chaperone us as I escort Miss Cardwell back to Lord Lytham's? Miss Cardwell is a stickler for propriety." Randal's firmly cut mouth twitched as he felt Cassie's indignation.

Lady Maude looked hard at him. "As your only aunt, I believe Miss Cardwell could use a chaperone to help keep you in hand. Take Perkins. She'll report to me if you give this young lady any trouble." She pulled the throw covering her legs higher on her lap, then looked over at Cassie. "I don't believe all the gossip I hear. I like you."

# Chapter V

Gliding through the small, chattering groups gathered in the drawing room, Cassie searched for Lord Lytham. Already, Madeline Edgar, Welton Sinclair, and the other four members of their team were prepared to stage the first charade of their tableau. From behind a red plush drapery over the arch at the far end of the room came muffled giggles and the scuffle of furniture being moved. The curtain would go up on their first tableau shortly, and Elaine wasn't down yet. Lytham wouldn't be pleased.

Despite there being only thirteen people in the room, Lytham wasn't easy to find. Cassie's gaze meshed with Randal's for an instant before she tore free. Not him. Not now. Finally, she caught sight of Lytham stepping around one of Elaine's newest acquisitions, a tall, ornately carved wooden screen. He was talking with Madeline Edgar's father, laughing lightly.

Cassie hurried over and bobbed a curtsy to both

men. She exchanged a few polite words with Mr. Edgar, then Lytham excused himself and led her away.

"Did you find her?" he asked. "Has she decided what to wear yet? You should have helped her there, child. You always show such excellent taste."

Startled at the fulsome compliment, Cassie recited her message quickly. "Lady Elaine is on her way down, my lord. There was a minor problem with one of the maids." Cassie finished breathlessly, unable to concentrate on anything but his smile.

Lytham always made her uncomfortable. Was it because of her suspicions or something to do with him personally? She didn't know. She simply knew she least wanted to be near him when he smiled at her like this.

"Poor little Cassie." Lytham took one of her hands and stroked it. "We work you too hard. A gently reared female shouldn't have to cope with such responsibility. When I asked you to find out what was keeping my wife, I expected you to ring for one of the servants. I never expected you to run up and down all those stairs."

"It was nothing, my lord."

A shiver of distaste coursed through her. Why was he stroking her hand like that? She tried to tug free.

"Such things are part of my duties," she countered.

A harder tug, then she searched the small chattering groups near them for a familiar face. A message for someone, anyone, would give her a polite reason to escape. The only face near her that she recognized was Lady Albinia's. Not even escaping Lord Lytham could induce Cassie to use her as a refuge.

At that moment Lady Albinia looked at Cassie, then turned back intent on her gossip. Had Lady

Albinia seen that moment when Cassie's glance meshed with Randal's? Undoubtedly. And she'd make capital of it. Cassie returned her attention to her mistress's husband and tried to free her hand again.

"Nonsense. You let us impose on your good nature far too much. Forgive us. I want your stay to be as happy as possible." The sweep of his free hand indicated her simple black taffeta dress.

"There's nothing to forgive. It's part of my duties." At last she freed her hand. "If you'll excuse me, I must—"

"My dearest Lytham, I'm sorry to be late." Elaine stopped beside them. She waved her silver, lace, and ivory fan briskly to cool her flushed face.

Simmons had convinced Elaine to wear a new nacre velvet gown with mameluke sleeves puffed with lace and satin ribbons. The silver ground gave the deep blue of the velvet pile the shimmer of moonlit clouds in the candlelight Elaine had decreed for tonight.

"For," she had told Cassie that morning, "however modern gas lighting is, it gives a harsh light, and it hisses so. Not at all the sort of thing for the tableaux tonight."

"You always are, my dear," Lytham answered her. A smile reached his somber gray-blue eyes for a fraction of a second. "But I really must take you to task this time."

"Task? Whatever for, dearest sir?" Elaine cocked her head coquettishly.

"You've been working this child too hard. All day long she's been running up and down stairs organizing this evening's entertainment. Now you've had her soothing your newest maid. That duty shouldn't have been Cassie's."

Elaine's rich chuckle floated out to attract the attention of those guests who weren't already listening. She wasn't taking his light scolding seriously.

But Lytham was serious. Why? His behavior was definitely odd. Was he trying to show his guests what a kind and generous employer he was to the poor, penniless orphan?

Something Papa had said about Lytham floated into her mind. About how important others' opinions were to him. Apparently the dozen guests present tonight in the drawing room were to be impressed. At least he didn't behave this way when they were alone.

Elaine's happy chatter caught Cassie's attention again. "But, dear, I told you," Elaine was saying, quite firmly for her, "Cassie makes up one of the teams. If she doesn't, my numbers are uneven. With Cassie, there'll be just enough for three teams."

"There's no need for three teams. This poor child has worked enough for today. I've watched her, and she hasn't even had time to sit down for tea. Have her join us as part of the audience. She deserves the rest."

"Nonsense. I must have three teams. And Cassie doesn't know what the tableau subjects are any more than I do, so it's proper for her to participate. Come along, dear. I believe Mr. Sinclair and Lord Harwell are ready to start their set of charades. You must hurry to join your team before the curtain rises."

"Which team is Cassie on?" Lytham asked sharply.

"Why, Randal's, of course." Elaine widened her eyes innocently, but she couldn't hide the mischief shining there. "It's by far the best place for Cassie." She fluttered her fan flirtatiously.

Color rose in his cheeks, and he darted an emotion-filled glance at Cassie. It was almost compassionate, as if she was to be pitied, Cassie realized, puzzled. Her mouth tightened. She didn't want Lytham's pity any more than she wanted Lady Albinia's dislike. But she had both.

"Nonsense, dear husband." Elaine responded to Lytham's protest with a playful rap of her fan and took Cassie by the hand. "You'll see how wrong you are. Come, Cassie. It's time for you to join your team."

As Elaine towed her resistlessly away, Cassie caught a fleeting glimpse of Lytham's anger-filled face. Why was he angry at his wife's wanting three teams? She glanced back over her shoulder at Lytham again.

The fury was gone. He turned to say something light to Mr. Edgar, who must have heard most of the argument. It was puzzling. Edgar's opinion must mean a great deal to him. Then both Edgar and Lytham faded from her mind.

In seconds, Randal would be . . . her partner? escort? whatever, for the second set of charades. How could Elaine be so blatant? Cassie shrugged inwardly. It was part of Elaine's charm.

Thoughts of her mistress faded as they approached Randal. His magnetism surrounded her even this far away. The murmur of the other guests drained away until, for an instant, she and Randal might have been alone. A shout of laughter broke her trance. Cassie turned to her mistress.

"The curtain is about to go up, Elaine. Shouldn't we take our seats?"

Several people had already drifted to the far end of the room. There the servants had arranged more than a dozen small chairs facing the stage. No sound came from behind the red plush curtain hiding the players from the audience. Clearly, the first tableau was about to begin.

"What? Oh, thank you, Cassie. You're so kind. You've been such a good companion, I shall be sorry to see you mar—" She broke off, blushing.

Cassie stood in shocked silence. Elaine had done that deliberately, and Randal knew it. He shook with suppressed mirth. What could she say? He didn't give her the chance.

"You may be sorry to see Cassie, but I never shall." He took Cassie's hand and gazed down at her. "I find looking at her quite pleasant." A thread of laughter tinged his voice.

Cassie stared hard at her mistress. "Isn't Lord Lytham waiting for you, Elaine?"

Elaine left, a gleam of satisfaction in her eyes. Cassie waited until her mistress couldn't hear, then promised Randal under her breath, "I'll get even with you for that."

"I look forward to it."

Maintaining a dignified silence, Cassie followed him to where three people waited. Fortunately, no one seemed to have heard Elaine's faux pas. As Cassie sat down, she spotted Lord Lytham.

Lytham stood alternately watching his wife and the rest of the audience. He seemed over his temper, although Cassie dreaded the party's aftermath. What a strange thought that was. Lytham might get annoyed, but he never raged at the household.

"I hope I haven't done something to annoy you," Randal said after a moment's silence.

"What?" His fleeting touch burned through her sleeve. "Not in the least. I should be accustomed to your reprehensible sense of humor. Someday I may be. I'm just—" Cassie quickly changed the subject. "Have you ever played at charades before, Lord Randal? I'm afraid I'm quite a novice at it. In America, tableaux are seldom played."

Cheeks burning, Cassie shifted in the small, gilt-

and–blue plush chair. When his hand brushed against her again, she shot a quick glance at him. That wasn't accidental. How to retaliate? For a well-bred young lady, ignoring him was the only option now available.

Nodding a greeting to the other members of the team, Cassie concentrated on the stage being slowly revealed as the curtain inched up in jerks. Were the small tremors shaking her fingers on her fan visible? She stole a look in Randal's direction.

His long, strong fingers stroked and curled a slip of paper. Her eyes fastened on the slow, sensuous strokes. Her palms tingled as though he stroked them instead of the paper. The fine tremor in her increased. He shifted in his chair. Deliberately?

Yes. Doubts faded once she realized his satisfaction. The way he'd entangled his leg in the rustling black taffeta of her plain skirt proved it. The muted sheen of her dress blended indissolubly with the fine black broadcloth of his breeches.

Cassie paled. His every move was deliberate, aimed at affecting her. She shot Randal a defiant look and shifted so that his trousers no longer melded with her skirt. The effort of solving the charade should help her ignore him.

The stage was draped in white, and all the actors wore vaguely medieval costumes in the same color. Madeline and Sinclair stood side by side, hands clasped, while a man wearing white vestments mimed a marriage ceremony. The other members of their team played the role of attendants.

A hum rose from the small audience as discussion broke out, anger from Lady Albinia's group, interest from Cassie's. "The word must be *bride,*" Lady Constance, a plump young woman, told Randal firmly.

"That's what we're meant to think, but have you

ever seen a wedding party where everyone was
dressed in white?" Randal asked.

"You mean the word is *white?*" Cassie asked, glad
her voice sounded clear and normal.

"Yes, but—"

The sounds of a muted altercation interrupted
him. The other team was arguing fiercely. Lady Albinia's sharp-edged voice rode over the others' protests. While she decreed her team's guess, she
divided venomous glances among Elaine, Sinclair,
and Cassie. The more her team argued, the louder
her voice became. Eventually, the other members of
her team gave in for the sake of peace, and Edgar
rose.

"My wife . . . that is, we all believe the answer is
*bride,*" he said.

The priest, Lord Harwell, shook his head and resumed his pose. As Edgar sat down, Randal looked
at the faces gathered around him. They nodded, and
he rose.

*"White?"* he asked, and Lord Harwell bowed.
The curtain fell, closing the white-draped stage to
their view.

"I hope Lady Albinia manages to restrain herself," Randal said softly to Cassie as a babble of discussion rose from the audience.

Somehow he had shifted closer to her in the pro-
cess of regaining his chair. Cassie retained her mask
of social politeness despite his nearness. Once again,
his shoe disappeared beneath the hem of her skirt.

"She isn't particularly happy." Amusement
threaded through Randal's voice. But his gaze on
Cassie's face was warmly caressing.

Cassie kept her tone cool. "Unfortunately, she's
got a lot of cause. And Elaine's machinations
haven't helped the poor woman."

His startled gaze flew up to tangle with hers.

Sparks of silver lit their blue depths. "I cannot like her," Cassie continued, "but it's never comfortable to be the butt of gossip."

Randal glanced down at the dull sheen of her black evening dress. It was made high to her throat and fastened with a mourning brooch. It made her waist seem tiny below the swell of her breasts. He longed to see her in colors—what would she look like in white? he wondered.

"No, it's not. But I side with Sinclair. He loves Madeline, and he's a very eligible match." He smiled down at her. "Besides, he's my friend."

"Hush. The curtain's going up." Cassie softened the admonition with an understanding smile and a daring touch to his tense hand.

Again, all six members of the team were onstage. But this time they wore their ordinary clothes. Their charade was to be taken from their actions, not from their surroundings. One after the other, Lord Harwell and Sinclair towed a protesting female across the makeshift stage. While the others acted their parts well, Cassie noticed Madeline struggled very little when Sinclair took her hand.

After brief conferences, both Randal and Edgar rose to ask for a tableau of the whole. In a few short minutes, the curtain rose again. A green carpet had been laid down, and a backdrop meant to suggest a stone wall covered the back of the stage. A plain wooden chest occupied the center and a black-hooded man stood grimly to one side with what appeared to be a tall battle-ax in his hand. Sinclair, in a costume with Elizabethan overtones, escorted Madeline, who was again dressed in white. She knelt and extended her neck over the chest while the women behind her wept.

Immediately both teams buzzed with suggestions. Each member of Randal's team presented a guess to him. He considered them, yet was dissatisfied with their solutions. But he didn't have an alternative.

Her drawl a little more pronounced than usual, Cassie asked, "Didn't they execute members of the nobility at the Tower of London?"

"Yes, but no one's been imprisoned there recently, have they, Lord Randal?" Lady Constance asked.

"They haven't," he agreed absently, "but they did execute people on Tower Green. Miss Cardwell's right." He shook his head and glanced keenly at the stage again. "That green rug could be taken as grass. But the first tableau was white. So it can't be the Tower of London."

"When I visited all the sights after I arrived," Cassie offered, "I saw several buildings inside the Tower of London walls."

"Of course." Randal leaned forward eagerly. "It's been years since I visited it as a schoolboy. But there's a White Tower inside the walls."

Two of the others nodded doubtfully. "I believe that's right," a slight matron with graying hair agreed. "Unfortunately, I'm not certain. The governess always takes the children on expeditions like that."

"Well, let's try *White Tower* as our guess. Edgar's team doesn't seem to be any more aware of our national buildings than we are. Except for Miss Cardwell."

His approving gaze brushed Cassie's face like a kiss. Instinctively she lowered her lashes as a tremor shook her. Not looking at him, she waited for Randal to present their solution.

"We believe," Randal said, rising to his feet, "your tableau is the White Tower." Lord Harwell bowed and the curtain came down.

"Now," Randal continued, "shall we present our

own tableau?'' He waited until they were outside in the hall to tell them what it was to be. "Lord Lytham has given us the word *Newgate* to portray. Newgate prison," he said slowly. Randal tapped a small slip of paper he'd held all evening against his thumb. "Interesting. The White Tower's a prison. Now Newgate. I wonder if Lytham gave Edgar's group another prison?"

"Oh, how exciting!" Lady Constance exclaimed. "It's so different. How will we do Newgate prison, Lord Randal?" She fluttered her lashes at him rapidly. To no noticeable effect.

Briefly he sketched his ideas, and listened to their suggestions for improvements. Finally, when they agreed, he nodded. "Then let's find the props and change into our costumes. Harwell and Sinclair should have nearly cleared the stage by now."

"But we've got to do it, Welton," Madeline whispered.

The door into the hall had shut firmly an instant earlier. Boldly, she cradled his hand in hers and pressed it to her soft breasts. Green eyes glowing softly, she gazed pleadingly up into his bluff, square face.

"It's not right," he protested, but his hand moved softly, compulsively in her grasp, his fingers brushing the soft mounds.

"Mama warned me. Either I give up all idea of marrying you, or it's back to Carroll Hall and she'll bring my sister out. I shan't see you again until I become twenty-one, and that's nearly two years away."

Neither mentioned Lady Albinia's other threat: Carsbrooke. The idea of her forced to wed that disreputable lecher tore at Welton's resolution. And Madeline knew it.

After a quick check that the door was still firmly shut, he pulled her into his arms. "Why won't your father consider my suit?"

Madeline shook her head slowly. The soft, smooth knot of her chignon brushed her rounded shoulders. "He won't cross Mama in this. She has this bee in her bonnet that the granddaughter of a duke should marry at least a marquess, and preferably a wealthy marquess. But I'd rather be the Honorable Mrs. Welton Sinclair than a marchioness."

"Can't understand why you prefer me to Randal."

Madeline grinned and twined her arms about Sinclair's neck. "Because you're you. Besides, marrying Randal would be like marrying my own brother. We grew up together."

"Well, that's lucky."

As his hands gently searched, Sinclair's lips found hers. He molded her supple body tautly to his muscular length. Moments stretched into minutes as they savored each other. Eventually he lifted his head and looked down into her flushed face.

"The next team will be here soon. We can't be found."

Sighing, Madeline moved fractionally away from him, her lashes drooping disconsolately before she remembered her goal. She looked urgently up at him, and her fingers tightened painfully on his arms.

"You will meet me, won't you?"

"How can I, darling? Your reputation—" He stroked her cheek soothingly.

"My parents would have to consent. And you'd be mine. What could be more important than that?" Pouting softly, she drew the tip of one finger over the full curve of his lips. "Don't you want me?"

"Of course I do." He sounded strangled. "Madeline, don't—"

The words were a low groan of protest. But Sinclair didn't fight when Madeline insistently tugged his head down again. With deliberation, she scattered nibbling kisses along the firm line of his jaw.

Leaning her pliant body against his powerful frame until he supported most of her weight, she stretched to reach the bristles of his mustache. With intentional sensuality she took one end into her mouth and tugged on it. With a low groan, he captured her lips, his tongue plunging deeply into her mouth.

A sound of furniture moving out in the hall brought them back to their surroundings and to awareness of the flimsiness of the curtain separating them from Lady Albinia. Madeline, eyes flaring with the deep glow of desire, gazed pleadingly up at him. Slowly sinking back from her toes, she took a tiny step away.

"You will, won't you?" she asked.

"You're absolutely sure you want to go through with this?"

Madeline nodded mutely.

"All right," Sinclair agreed slowly. "When I send word, meet me at Miss Norworth's, New Bond Street."

"Miss Norworth's? Really?" Madeline's brows rose in astonishment. "I'd never have thought—"

"Most people wouldn't," Sinclair agreed dryly. "That's why it's so useful. Hush, now. Here are the servants." He escorted her out into the hall under the amused gaze of a pair of footmen carrying a birdbath.

★     ★     ★

"But I can't," Cassie protested in a low voice. She stood on the improvised stage beside Randal. The other members of their team flitted in and out, checking the final bits of their costumes and props.

She had to appear to the world as a proper lady's companion. Ordinarily, she could protest appearing onstage while in mourning. But Elaine's request of her companion made it proper. Yet Elaine and Randal were contriving to break every other convention regarding her position. If they persisted, she might lose it as a result of gossip.

That specter heightened the butterflies from stage fright. She'd never appeared on the stage. Not even an amateur stage like this one. Living quietly with her father and grandmother in Charleston, South Carolina, hadn't given her much scope, despite a debut when she turned eighteen three years earlier.

His lips twitching, Randal thrust the doll swathed in a long baptismal gown into her arms. "But you must. Lady Constance would be embarrassed." Devil. He was enjoying this. "And you can't have your guests embarrassed, can you?"

Cassie suppressed a strong urge to throw the doll at his head. He knew who would be embarrassed standing before a priest, a child—their child—in her arms, while the infant was baptized. It would have been easier if he'd decided on a wedding scene as Lady Constance suggested. Plainly Lady Constance had seen herself as the bride. Well, Lady Constance could see herself as his wife if she liked. Cassie didn't want the job. Or the gossip this role would cause. Neither Elaine nor Lady Albinia would be able to resist voicing her view.

"Randal, I can't," she whispered pleadingly.

"You must. Lady Constance's mother has decided I'm the perfect husband for her daughter."

The doll in her arms, Cassie stepped back, disturbed at the sudden realization that she didn't want him as Lady Constance's husband. "Wouldn't you be?"

"We're holding up the tableau."

He matched her cool tone, but his hand beneath her elbow stroked the silken skin into tingling warmth. She'd changed into a costume more suitable for a christening, which left too much of her vulnerable to his probing eyes and gentle touch.

Cassie neither heard nor cared how the two teams in the audience did in guessing the first syllable of their word. Only Randal's presence mattered in the haze surrounding her. While she stood onstage, the doll in her arms, he touched her lightly, warily. He made the gentle stroke of his hand on her arm or brushing against her as he took the doll look perfectly normal to the onlookers. For Cassie it was seductive torture. Each touch sent shock waves through her. She nearly gasped aloud when his knuckles brushed against her breast.

Even worse was to come. The next scene of the charade was of a girl swinging on a gate while she chatted with her beau. As Cassie was the smallest of the young ladies on their team, she starred again. Her cheeks becomingly flushed, Cassie stepped up to the gate the men had somehow contrived from the props in the sun room. Randal's hands closing about her waist and lifting her onto the step behind the gate made her gasp audibly. Grasping the palings, she glared at Randal when he came around to the other side just before the curtain went up.

"You should smile at your beau," he commanded in a whisper. Mischief sparkled in his eyes.

"The curtain," Cassie warned him. Silence was her best defense. Anything else he would find a way to deliberately misunderstand.

After what seemed hours, Randal helped her down from the gate. No one had guessed the charade yet. They had requested the tableau of the whole. Fortunately, only Randal would appear in that. Taking the bonnet dangling by its ribbons from around her neck, Cassie started past Randal. The others had already filed out into the hall.

"Don't go yet," Randal said softly, catching her hand.

"But . . . I must. The ladies— They'll expect help with their costumes. It's part of my duties." Involuntarily, she looked up into his face.

"What you're doing here bothers me."

The intimate look on Randal's handsome face spelled danger to her plans. "Ignore Lord Lytham's nonsense. I do nothing more than the daughter of the household would." She paused to gain control. He was too near, and his constant playful touches had had their effect. "And you can't accuse Elaine of being a harsh taskmistress."

Randal smiled roguishly and shook his head. "No, not at all. Still, I'd be happier if you weren't here."

The slow, steady brush of his fingertips—from her palm to the delicate skin of her wrist—sent tingles coursing along her nerves. She couldn't think straight.

"Randal?" she said, softly questioning.

"Oh, it's no use."

His strong arms slid about her tiny waist, and he pulled her snugly into his arms. Breathlessly, Cassie surrendered. Once again she'd found a safe haven. Then all safety gave way to abandon that became delicious.

With deliberate slowness, Randal lowered his head, a lock of his brown, waving hair falling over his brow. Gently, tentative lips touched hers, exploring, deepening the kiss. Her eyes closed as she felt for the first time what it was like to be kissed by a man: the strength of him, the touch of skin against skin, the first flush of passion.

Without a thought, her arms hugged his neck and she pressed closer to his lean, hard frame. His tongue delicately probed, demanded entrance. Her mouth opened willingly to grant it.

All the heavenly sweetness of his kiss hit her, and he swooped to take advantage of her passion. Her tentative fingers touched the crisp waves of silken hair at his neck, went on to explore the enticing smoothness of his temple. She was lost in delicious, overpowering sensation. Yet Cassie needed more, and she innocently urged him on, inflaming him until Randal had to pull back.

His eyes a magnificent bright blue sparked with silver, he whispered, "The servants, my darling." He stole one more kiss from her moist, swollen lips. "I hear them coming. We'll have to go."

"Go?" Cassie's voice was husky with newly awakened passion. She could hardly believe what was happening. "Go?" she repeated. "Oh, heavens." She pulled back from his arms. "We shouldn't have. Not here."

"Yes, we should. We couldn't help ourselves." Randal stroked her worried cheek with one finger. "Trust me."

# Chapter VI

Since returning to the drawing room, she hadn't done anything right, to Randal's glee. Everyone must know what had happened behind the stage curtain. It must be written on her face. Cassie had volunteered to find a book on skin care Elaine had recommended for Lady Constance. She needed the time to regain control of her own complexion. If only Elaine had remembered the title!

Now she couldn't find the book. Or go back without it. Elaine said it was on the étagère in this drawing room. But which étagère?

There were three, all crammed with books and porcelain figurines. Candles in two of the sconces shed dim light, but not enough to read the titles easily. Cassie went to the third étagère in the dimmest part of the room. There among a clutter of books and pamphlets, she found it: *On the Improvement and Protection of a Gentlewoman's Complexion by a Doctor of the Medical Arts.*

Holding it against her waist, she reluctantly

turned; she didn't want to go back to the dining room. Even with Randal there. And especially with Randal there.

"My dear Cassie." Lytham's quiet, compassionate voice stopped her short.

"Yes, my lord?"

Cassie held her head erect and faced him. She wished he hadn't come upon her in the drawing room. Somehow she felt vulnerable alone with him and only the tick of the clock to break the silence. He was becoming more and more distasteful to her.

"I'm not quite sure how to tell you this," he began uncomfortably. Lytham darted a glance at her face, then fixed his eyes over her head.

"Yes, sir?"

Cassie braced herself. Did he intend to dismiss her for loose behavior? She had to be in Lytham House! Her throat was dry.

"I know how attractive Rydal is to women." He shifted uneasily. The flickering candles in the sconces at either end of the room no longer shone on his face. "I've seen it happen many times. His father was a notorious womanizer, and Rydal's following in his footsteps. I'd hate to see you made unhappy through his games."

"I'm not the first young lady he's approached?" How steady her voice sounded, as though she didn't care. Relief strengthened her.

Lytham's expression lightened. With greater certainty, he continued, "Precisely. You're under my protection in Lytham House, and I must warn you. Although he may make you an offer"—he cleared his throat—"Rydal's not the marrying kind. It's a terrible change for you, being reduced to a paid companion. But don't be seduced by Rydal's entreaties."

Randal's voice asking her to trust him echoed in

her ears. She wanted to, desperately, but suppose Lytham was right. Cassie smiled tightly. It might be foolish, but she trusted Randal—although disagreeing with Lytham might arouse his anger.

"Even if Lord Randal believed I was an heiress with no scandal in my background, he wouldn't harbor serious intentions. That's what you mean, isn't it?"

Lytham nodded, his smile strained. "Naturally, he'll marry for the succession. But, forgive me, not for a girl in your circumstances. Rydal's finances are such that he requires an heiress. I know this is difficult. Rydal must be most attractive to you."

"Yes," Cassie murmured. Her arms crossed instinctively, pressing the book comfortingly into her stomach.

"I realize," Lytham continued more smoothly, "that eventually you'll wish to marry. If I might—"

"Yes?" Cassie prompted, her head coming up alertly. Was Lytham's conscience bothering him? She watched him closely.

"When your mourning is over, I'll introduce you to several families in the City. Quite good families, though not, of course, members of Society. Several have sons of marriageable age; others are widowers. But you Americans don't consider being in trade a hindrance. Your father's sui— problems and your lack of wealth will be no bar to contracting a suitable marriage." He smiled charmingly at her.

Cassie hoped her smile remained in place. It wasn't his conscience. He wanted to present himself as Lord Bountiful, even to her. He actually believed he could sell her to a merchant's family? As if her father's death had stained her character? As if Lytham didn't know better. Her lack of guilt over acting as a spy no longer bothered her. Besides, she couldn't love anyone else—love on command, she corrected herself hastily.

"Now, don't you believe a word my dear Lytham says."

Starting, Cassie and Lytham turned toward Elaine. Neither had heard the drawing room door open. Elaine chattered blithely while taking her husband confidingly by the arm.

"It's nonsense. I have the perfect marriage in mind for you once you put off your blacks." Elaine winked conspiratorially at Cassie. "A marriage in our own class. Now, come along. Our guests are ready to leave. Did you find that book for me?"

On a wave of exclamations over how well the tableaux had gone, Elaine bore her husband and Cassie back to the dining room where refreshments had been laid out as a buffet. Little was left on the tables, and already several of the guests had sent for their wraps. Her stance frigid, Lady Albinia had positioned herself near one of the doors, her husband and daughter standing chastened beside her. Clearly she was offended that both her host and hostess had left their guests for even a short time.

When Elaine and Lytham hurried up to her, abandoning Cassie, Lady Albinia's stare was icy and her handshake reserved. Was it really Elaine's absence, Cassie wondered, or the charade which had married Madeline to Welton Sinclair? Her eyes caught and held Randal's for an instant. Did he have the same suspicion? There was no chance to ask. Shortly after Lady Albinia's party left, all the guests were gone, and Randal with them.

Lytham started to speak, then shook his head. Mouth tight, he glanced from his wife to her companion. Something had upset him further. But what? Elaine's calling his warning nonsense? He turned on his heel and strode out of the dining room.

"Now wasn't that an absolutely delightful evening," Elaine said, putting her arm about Cassie's waist. "I declare, I'm simply exhausted. Not even a chance to touch my supper. And you haven't eaten a bit. Let's have a small snack before we go to bed."

Unable to avoid Elaine's inquisition, Cassie followed her obediently to the refreshment table. The appetites of twenty people had left little food and only a few clean plates. Elaine pounced on one and loaded it high with a selection of lobster patties, cakes, pastries, and jellies. She waited while Cassie helped herself to a slice of asparagus roulade and one of the small cakes.

"How you survive on so little, I'll never know," Elaine exclaimed. She poured a cup of tea laced with cream and sugar. "Now, come along. There's a fire in the morning room. We can be comfortable while the servants clear away. The aftermath of a party is so dismal."

Silently, Cassie poured a cup of tea and followed Elaine. Better let Elaine quiz her now. If she put it off until tomorrow, it would be worse. She wanted neither Randal's intentions nor her own behavior discussed and analyzed. As the only one concerned with his intentions, she wouldn't misread his flirtatiousness.

Mouth set, Cassie took a chair near the fire in the morning room, the canary silent in its covered cage behind her. Over soothing sips of tea, she watched Elaine settle on her favorite sofa. The silvered dark blue of her deeply flounced gown flowed over the entire cushion. Could she distract Elaine? The party, perhaps? But that would bring them back to Randal. All paths led back to Randal. But there must be some way. . . . Cassie considered her mistress.

Elaine nibbled at one of the lobster patties and took a sip of tea before directing a beaming smile at Cassie.

"It's so exhausting, hostessing parties during the Season. If you're not giving one, you're going to another. I wouldn't do it if it weren't for Lytham's position in the government. You'll understand when you're married." Elaine tore off a bit of cake and sighed.

A flush mounted Cassie's cheeks. She replaced her cup in its saucer with a distinct clink. "I don't think, Elaine, that I—"

"I was delighted to see Randal so attentive tonight. His expression while you stood before the font! I've never seen anyone so devoted."

"I thought Mr. Sinclair looked quite devoted to Miss Edgar."

"My dear, of course he's devoted. I do believe"—Elaine's smile widened until the dimples in her plump cheeks looked like small thumbprints—"we can expect an interesting announcement in that quarter soon."

"Lady Albinia won't like it," Cassie observed quietly, willing to discuss anything but Randal.

"Oh, Lady Albinia." Elaine shrugged and licked some cream from the tip of her finger. She looked speculatively at Cassie. "She'll be quite upset when you marry Randal, you know. But since I expect dear Madeline to— My dear, are you all right?" she asked as Cassie choked.

Elaine put her plate and cup down on the table and struggled to her feet. Moving lightly to Cassie's side, she rescued the teacup and plate before Cassie spilled anything. Elaine's hard pats on the back stopped Cassie's choking. Pulling out a hand-kerchief to cover her mouth while she coughed,

Cassie mopped her streaming eyes after she caught her breath.

"I'm sorry, my dear. I shouldn't have sprung it on you like that. Especially not after Lytham so sweetly tried to save you from heartbreak. He's doing what he thinks best, but we know better, don't we? Men. They never give these affairs of the heart the attention they deserve until they fall in love themselves. Then they can't seem to apply the lessons they learn to anyone else's interests. Are you better, dear? Have a sip of tea and blow your nose."

Throat raw, Cassie nodded feebly. Elaine had caught her off guard. "I'm all right, thank you, Elaine," she finally managed. Cautiously she took a sip of tea. It soothed her throat.

"I apologize for being so tactless. But we both know Randal's taken with you."

Cassie blotted the last tear from her eyes and looked sternly across at Elaine. "*We* know nothing of the kind. He's been courteous to me. Nothing more. And Randal needs an heiress."

Forget the way he kissed her. That meant nothing. Randal had asked her to trust him, and she did. He wouldn't try to ruin her reputation, as Lytham warned. But Elaine's certainty that Randal would marry her was nonsense. He enjoyed flirting with a pretty girl. Yet the look in his eyes haunted her.

"Don't be absurd," Elaine said roundly. "Randal's still wealthy. That's just gossip. There's not an ounce of truth in it. He just bought a new carriage," Elaine said. "And I saw him when he came back to the drawing room. Don't tell me he didn't kiss you in the alcove. I know perfectly well he did. Some lucky girl always receives a kiss when we play charades," Elaine added at Cassie's raised brows. "Some of the sweetest romances have started that

way. That's why young people love playing charades so. And I do want you to be happy."

Elaine did know what happened. How many others did? Cassie took a bite of cake to hide her frown.

"Elaine . . ." Cassie began cautiously. The cake
formed a lump in the pit of her stomach. "You
shouldn't assume the Marquess of Rydal intends to
marry me because he forgot himself for an instant."

"My dear, don't take Lytham's warning seriously. He means well, but he doesn't understand.
He doesn't pay attention to people the way he used
to. Why, from the moment I saw the two of you
together I knew you were meant for each other.
Randal couldn't keep his eyes off you at that dinner.
And he did entertain you. I've never seen you laugh
so much. Then the way he looked at you when he
called to thank me for my hospitality. And tonight.
Minton told me how he insisted on escorting you to
your solicitor. That can't be anything but love."

"Or courtesy."

Cassie sighed tiredly. If Elaine knew Randal had
taken her to meet his aunt, she'd be ready to send an
announcement to the newspaper. Cassie's head
ached from tension. Living behind a mask while she
searched for her father's murderer was one thing.
She could live with her guilt over betraying Elaine
by spying on her husband, but Randal . . . She had
to fight both herself and him. Now it seemed half
the people at the party tonight must have guessed
her indiscretion. If only she'd had time to compose
herself before anyone saw her. She jerked her attention back to Elaine.

". . . flirtation. I've seen men who had no serious
intentions, and Randal isn't one of them. I think the
wedding should wait at least six months, though,
don't you? By then you will have put off your

blacks, this tiresome Exhibition will be over, and Madeline and Welton will have been married long enough."

Cassie watched her with exhausted interest. From out in the hall came the sound of the servants returning props to the conservatory and sun room. Elaine was relishing her final jelly and licking her fingers as a coal popped in the fire.

"Long enough for what?" Cassie asked.

She was too tired to protest more tonight. Let Elaine build castles in the air if it made her happy. Soon Elaine would learn how wrong she was. Or how right?

"For Lady Albinia to become accustomed, of course. She's so intent on poor Madeline marrying for a high title that I've heard rumors she's even considering the Marquess of Carsbrooke's offer. Frightful. The man's a toad. He practically bought the title by forcing his distant cousin into a duel with a dead shot. Not that I believe a word of it."

"I thought dueling was illegal."

"It is." Elaine chased the last crumbs on her plate and looked hungrily at Cassie's asparagus roulade.

Cassie gave it to her. "What did he do?"

"He bribed the other man. I forget the details, but it was a great scandal. Carsbrooke has never been accepted since. One might forget that, but one can't forget that his mother was a member of the demimonde and was married a bare month before Carsbrooke's birth." Elaine gasped guiltily. "Oh, dear, I shouldn't have mentioned such a thing to you."

"Never mind, Elaine. Being raised by a widower christened my delicate ears long ago. Though he would never explain."

Elaine leaned forward confidentially. "Well, you can see how Lady Albinia could use the threat of marriage to Carsbrooke quite easily."

"Are you certain she is?" Cassie asked, mildly interested. How gossip flew about in Society.

"No. But it's the most delicious speculation. And it may convince Madeline to elope," Elaine said, withdrawing a bit. "It's not at all to the point, anyway. I think the fall would be the perfect time for your wedding, don't you?"

"Elaine," Cassie said, "if Randal asks me to marry him, I'll listen. But I don't think he will. He's simply amusing himself with a flirtation, as Lord Lytham said." Randal's voice echoed warmly in her mind again, asking for her trust. But she couldn't bring herself to admit that to her mistress. "Now I'm going to bed. Good night, Elaine."

Feeling uncomfortable at Elaine's crushed look, Cassie rose from her chair and marched to the door. Hand on the doorknob, she paused. Elaine had become her friend. She couldn't leave her so downcast. Sighing, she returned and bent to hug Elaine affectionately.

"I'm sorry, Elaine. I can't allow myself to believe anything will come of Lord Randal's attentions. If it didn't happen, I couldn't bear the disappointment."

The clop of the horses' hooves over the rain-shimmered streets formed a steadying counterpoint to Randal's restless thoughts. He shouldn't have done it, and he wouldn't have if his game of touching and teasing hadn't made him lose control. The effect he had on her was heady. And the effect she had on him . . .

He moved restlessly against the squabs. How soft her lips were. So pure, as if she'd never been kissed before. Yet she learned quickly. He twisted in his Macfarlane cloak, trying to find a comfortable spot. Outside the carriage windows, the sputtering street lamps reflected on the wet cobblestones.

The thought of taking Cassie into his arms again made him ache. Second by second, Randal relived Cassie's tender lips beneath his own, her soft body pressed trustingly to his, her horrified expression when she realized what she'd done. What might have happened if they'd been safe from interruption made him groan softly with hunger.

The first time he'd met her in the library, he'd learned how soft and slender she was: small, yet fully formed beneath the bulwark of her corset and stiffened petticoats. Those few seconds had acted powerfully on him. So powerfully, he'd made excuses to call at Lytham House in the hope of seeing her. And his Aunt Maude liked her. That counted for something.

Should he marry Cassie? He'd have to marry someday. He couldn't die without an heir: the title would die as well. But he'd hoped to postpone it for a few more years. When he considered marrying, he'd envisioned a wife who wouldn't interfere with his pleasures, just produce a child every other year or so.

With Cassie . . . Yet her background wasn't the sort he'd wanted in a wife. She was an American, even ignoring her father's suicide. And with no dowry.

Still, he wanted her. He wanted her so much that the thought of going to bed alone was torture, while the thought of seeking the companionship of his current mistress held no appeal. Was he actually in love?

"My lord?" A footman held the door open and looked in inquiringly.

Drawing his cloak tightly about his body, he stepped down from the carriage with brief thanks. Nodding to his butler in the hall, he dismissed everyone. He wasn't ready for bed. Not the way he felt.

Free of his cloak and hat, Randal loosened the single-ended tie at his throat. Why did that female have to disturb his well-ordered existence now? Randal poured a large brandy from the decanter concealed in the cabinet beneath the spiral staircase leading to the second floor of books.

He dropped into a maroon leather wing chair with matching hassock placed comfortably near the warmth of the fire. Its crackle offered solace, but no answers. Knowing he needed to forget Cassie didn't change anything. He wanted her. Not just in his bed, but beside him on nights like this. And when he wanted a companion after a long day's work.

Barnthorpe shivered and glanced resentfully at the small fire burning fitfully in the grate. Why did his lordship have to send such long messages? After an evening of gambling with young Alston, he wanted his bed. Dawn had begun to break through the thin layer of clouds outside the dirty windows when he arrived home. But the message in the *Times* demanded immediate attention.

Barnthorpe pulled out the ridiculous pair of wooden sticks his lordship had given him. Letters were incised in them: three complete alphabets. As if he couldn't decipher the messages without them. Let's see, the stick with the two alphabets stayed still, didn't it?

With bloodshot eyes, he peered at the pair. First you put the *a* of the single alphabet beneath the— What was the key? Barnthorpe jerked open the desk drawer and fumbled about for the cipher key he kept there. Ah, yes. *Die*. What a ghastly key. Just likc the gentry to choose that. With more certainty, he deciphered the message.

More than an hour later, Barnthorpe slumped back in his chair. Running fingers through his thinning hair, he reread the message. Still slack-jawed, he read the message for the third time. A kidnapping. Good God, he'd never been involved in anything that big before.

A thin smile stretched his lips. It wouldn't matter to Alfie, although it might cost a little more. After the kidnapping was done and the ransom collected, Alfie would disappear back into Bluegate Fields with his gang. But Jim Barnthorpe wouldn't fade from his lordship's life so easily.

Triumph tinged his smile. Already his lordship had agreed to meet later this week. That would give him the chance to be sure. Once he had proof of his lordship's identity, he was set for life. Not just the paltry two hundred pounds his lordship had promised in the cipher, but a regular income, a gentleman's income.

But he had to be cautious for the time being. It wasn't wise to ask for more so early in the game. The two hundred pounds . . . well, part of it would hold Alfie and his gang. In the meantime, he needed more information. He had to have time to plan. His lordship had hinted that the kidnapping would take place by the beginning of May. That was too little time. It would hurt his pride if it didn't go well.

Once it was done, his lordship would be just where Barnthorpe wanted him. Then Jim Barnthorpe would live the kind of life he was meant to. No more lodgings with inadequate fires. No more worthless servants who didn't understand the importance of hot bathwater and clean linens. Yes, his lordship would pay. And pay.

*    *    *

Cassie shivered in the quiet of her room. Even though it wouldn't help, she added more coal to the low-burning fire. Despite blood accustomed to southern winters and warm springs, the temperature of her room had little to do with her chill.

Exhaustion. Exhaustion and Lytham's warning were the cause. Along with Elaine's airy certainty that Randal would marry her. Cassie wished she could be so certain. Proving Lytham was her father's killer had seemed so simple. She shivered and rubbed her arms.

While the coals caught, she slowly unhooked her dress. As always, the last hook in the middle of her back nearly defeated her. Pushing energetically, Cassie brought it around to the front and unfastened it. Cool air struck at her bare shoulders. She stepped quickly out of her dress and stripped off petticoats, corset cover, corset, pantalets, and chemise.

What if Randal were here now? Hot color burned from her small rounded breasts to her forehead and faded as quickly. She shouldn't think such things.

Avoiding the small mirror above her dressing table, Cassie dove into her warm linen nightgown. Only when she had the buttons fastened firmly up to her throat did she approach the dressing table to unpin her hair. He would never see her like this.

But after she'd proven her father wasn't a suicide? And revealed herself as an heiress? After all, he'd taken her to meet his aunt. No, she told herself sternly, marquesses don't marry companions. Even when he found out about her dowry, she would still have been just a lady's companion.

Cassie pulled the last pin out of her hair. It tumbled down, a golden brown, curly torrent flowing past her waist to pool on the dressing table bench. With each stroke of her brush, she reminded herself of how to behave. Cool. Polite. Don't take anything that devastating man said seriously. He wasn't trifling. She knew he wasn't trifling. But he wasn't serious, either.

# Chapter VII

The sound of someone clearing his throat jerked Randal around. Contemplation of the carved wooden paneling climbing the wall beside his desk had brought him no closer to solving the puzzle.

Welton Sinclair, his bluff face flushed, occupied most of the door frame leading into Randal's office. Welton looked defensive, uncertain. Randal had never seen him like that. Welton needed to talk.

"Come in and shut the door. They get noisier out there every day."

"You're not too busy?" Welton didn't wait for an answer. He came through the doorway and closed off the hall's racket.

"Nothing urgent." Randal pushed a folder of papers marked "urgent" aside. "I'm feeling lazy with the warm weather." He gestured toward the cold marble-manteled fireplace behind him. "Besides, I'd rather not work. Would you care for some Madeira? Or a cup of tea?"

"No . . . No, nothing, thanks."

Welton hesitated before sinking into the heavily stuffed armchair across from Randal. Thin early morning sunlight streaming through the tall window disclosed the strain in his shadowed eyes and glistened on his fair hair. Randal wondered if he'd slept last night.

"Your men having a problem fitting in an exhibit?" Randal asked after the silence had stretched for several minutes.

"What?" Welton's soft blond brows drew together in a frown, which didn't break his contemplation of the toe of one shiny black boot. "No. That's not it. It's, well, I need some advice. It's rather personal." He looked quickly up at Randal, then as quickly back at the toe of his boot. "Quite personal, in fact."

"It won't go beyond these walls."

Randal recognized the signs. Woman problems. A pang of sympathy went out to a fellow sufferer.

The toe of Welton's boot rotated in a tiny circle. He kept his eyes fixed on it as he began to speak slowly. "What would you do if someone you cared about wanted you to do something somewhat unusual?"

"Depends . . ." Randal shrugged and fingered the fountain pen lying on his desk. It had dripped on the blotter. Putting it in the stand, he looked at Sinclair again. "Would it harm anyone?"

"No. It wouldn't harm anyone," Welton said, even more slowly. The name *Madeline* hung in the air unspoken between them. "But it's not proper." The toe of his boot froze in midair, then resumed rotating in the opposite direction.

What was Madeline up to? She had been determinedly attached to Welton the night before. Who could have missed it? Or her mother's disapproval? Welton was a good match; Madeline would be Viscountess Linlithgow when Welton's father died. But a mere viscount wasn't good enough for the grand-daughter of a duke, according to Lady Albinia.

"It won't harm anyone?" Randal repeated carefully. Having known Madeline since schooldays, he feared the worst.

Welton lifted clear blue eyes to meet his friend's. "I wouldn't let it," he said simply.

"Then . . . if it'll make her happy, I'd do it."

The late morning sunshine felt welcome on her shoulders. Cassie looked nervously around, aware of attention from the few people present in Hyde Park. Perhaps it'd been wrong to suggest a meeting here. But she felt nervous at the thought of going to Neville's office again. If someone saw her enter the office of a private enquiry agent . . . It was foolish, but she couldn't shake the feeling. The wax key impressions in her petticoat pocket thumped against her leg with each step to underline her tension.

A light breeze ruffled the surface of the Serpentine. Pacing slowly alongside it, Cassie drew her cloak more closely around her. Where was Neville? All around, the trees and bushes filled out under the April sun. Daffodils and tulips bowed to the breeze. The serene spring day failed to calm her. She needed to see Neville. The breeze strengthened, making the daffodils bend to kiss the dark, wet soil around them.

On the path curving around the Serpentine, Cassie spotted a dapper figure strolling and enjoying the fresh greenery. Neville? It could be any habitué of Hyde Park sauntering down one of the paths leading up to the long, artificial lake. Neville had the faculty of blending with his surroundings, and something about the relaxed figure seemed familiar. Cassie quickened her pace. At the sound of hurrying footsteps on the gravel path, the man turned to face her. It was Neville. He smiled and waited.

"Miss Cardwell," he said when she stood beside him.

Cassie glanced quickly around. No one was near enough to hear them. They stood in an open area where the breeze off the Serpentine blew cool and unimpeded.

"Have you learned anything?" Cassie asked. There was something reassuring about Neville. She knew he had good news for her.

"All in good time. You shouldn't have hurried, you're out of breath. I'd have waited for you, especially on such a lovely day. Would you care to stroll in the park before we discuss the results of my investigations?"

"Oh, no, thank you. I have to get back." Darting a glance around, she reached into her petticoat pocket. "I have the impressions for you."

"Don't give them to me here," Neville ordered. His hard grasp on her arm prevented her from taking the impressions from beneath her cloak.

Skin prickling, Cassie started to look over her shoulder again before she caught herself. Had he seen someone? She raised tense eyes to his.

"It's all right," he reassured her. "It's just too public to pass anything. Call me overly cautious, but you learn caution in my business. Now, take my arm and we'll stroll down to the lake."

Cassie nodded and placed her hand beneath his elbow. They walked quietly down to the Serpentine while her heartbeat subsided to normal.

Some distance along the lake, she looked up at him. "Do you have any news?"

"Not as much as I'd like, but some." He directed their steps to one of the small teahouses. "Tea, Miss Cardwell?"

The concern in his face stopped Cassie, who was about to refuse. "Thank you." She took the chair he held before speaking again. "Is it all right for me to give you the impressions here?"

He nodded, and she slipped her hand into her petticoat pocket again. The table masked the movement from the few people in the restaurant. Keeping her hand beneath the table, she handed her prize to him and waited for the verdict. Had she done them properly? A qualm shook her.

After ordering tea, he inspected the impressions closely without raising them above the table's edge. Then slipped them in one pocket before shifting his chair closer to the table.

"Very good indeed. We'll have no trouble making keys from these. They're paired quite nicely." Humor lit his opaque brown eyes. "You have considerable talent for this business. Perhaps I should hire you to help me with my Society investigations."

"I couldn't possibly." She shook her head, smiling ruefully. "I was terrified the entire time. What if someone found me in Lord Lytham's bedroom?" She paused. "Don't such things ever bother you?"

"You get used to it. Ah, here's our tea. Would you pour, please?"

Cassie filled their cups and extended a plate of small cakes the waiter had brought. She felt trapped in a fairyland. If anyone had ever suggested she would sit in a teahouse with a private enquiry agent calmly discussing illegal entry, she wouldn't have believed him. Taking a bite of one of the cakes, she swallowed her first sip of tea.

He chatted about other cases for a bit, laughing at his own youthful nerves, before giving her his news. "Since you came to my office," he began quietly, cradling his second cup of tea in one pudgy hand and leaning confidentially forward, "I've had McCrory and Chambers' offices under surveillance. Only a few clerks work there along with a manager. Someone else is the firm's principal."

"Do you have any idea who?"

"Not yet. But I must warn you I may not be successful. Silent partners are sometimes quite well hidden."

"You'll find out. Have you learned anything else?" Cassie took a burning gulp of tea and clutched the cup, waiting.

"One of the clerks seems open to bribery. I hope to have news for you soon." His tone was patient.

"I'm sorry," she apologized. "It's wrong of me to press you, but Papa was killed more than a month ago. It's April already."

"We should have an answer by the end of May. Now, drink your tea and eat your cake. You must keep up your strength."

Cassie smiled wanly. "Especially with all the errands Lady Elaine can think of for me to run. Today I have to find her favorite sweets, the novel everyone is talking about, and pick up a hat for her in New Bond Street."

"That should keep you busy. You'll accept my escort until you find a cab?"

Cassie bade Neville good-bye and climbed into the cab he'd summoned. She stared sightlessly at the tangled traffic along the road while the driver took her to Miss Norworth's, New Bond Street.

She found herself thinking about Randal again. Well, she might not be able to control her mind, she told herself, but she'd try to control her actions next time they met.

Cassie hopped down from the cab and looked about. The milliner's shop was located in a large building in an older section of New Bond Street. Carriages and horse-drawn drays clopped down the streets or turned into the alleys.

While paying the driver, Cassie caught a glimpse of Madeline entering Miss Norworth's. Chatting with Madeline would take her mind off her problems. Smiling absently, Cassie crossed the street and entered the shop.

Inside, in a large showroom, stands displayed bonnets and hats. Reels of ribbon hung on one wall, adding brilliant color to the discreet pearl gray and white walls. Another wall held a honeycomb of small shelves filled with perfectly formed artificial fruits and flowers. Along one side, feathers in every imaginable shade and size beckoned. Small dressing tables offered ornate mirrors for ladies to view Miss Norworth's creations. A woman in a circumspect dove-gray dress with white lace collar and cuffs stood behind the counter. Otherwise the shop was empty.

"May I help you, miss?" The woman's voice was hoarse.

Cassie turned sharply; she hadn't heard her approach. Surveying the shop again, Cassie frowned, puzzled. Except for a curtained arch leading to the back premises, there were no alcoves where Madeline could be.

"I beg your pardon," Cassie said. The plain-faced woman raised her brows questioningly. "I thought I saw a young lady of my acquaintance enter here. Have you seen her? Miss Madeline Edgar?"

"You're the only customer to enter the shop in the past quarter hour, miss. Is there something I could show you?" The woman's eyes swept over Cassie's black merino dress and the mourning brooch at her throat. "Perhaps a new hat. We have some lovely things for ladies who are going into

half-mourning." She picked up a small silky straw
hat in white with lilac ribbons and a bunch of vio-
lets peeping over the brim. "This would suit your
lovely complexion and enhance the shade of your
hair."

"No, thank you. I shan't be out of my blacks for
several more months." Cassie looked covetously at
it. It was lovely. But it wasn't proper. Yet.

"Then perhaps you'd care for this lovely bonnet."
The woman held up one in black grosgrain with a
fluffy black feather pointing down to brush shoulder
and cheek. A jet pin, brilliant against the dull
grosgrain, held the feather in place. It gave the impression of color without being colorful. "It's quite
dashing without being the least bit improper," the
salesclerk assured Cassie.

Touching the silken fluff of the feather with a
longing finger, Cassie shook her head firmly. "Are
you quite sure Miss Edgar didn't come in here? I
was sure I saw her."

"I'm quite sure, miss. She must have stepped into
another shop along the street." The salesclerk
seemed offended that Cassie questioned her about
Madeline again.

"I'm sure it was Miss Norworth's she entered."
Frowning, Cassie shook her head. "Well, no matter.
If she isn't here, she isn't here. I've come to pick up
Lady Elaine Lytham's new hat."

"Certainly, miss." Interest died from the
woman's face. If Cassie ran errands for Lady Elaine,
she wasn't a prospective customer, despite her
clothing. "If you'll just wait here, I'll fetch it for
you from the back."

The woman marched briskly to the curtained
archway. While she was gone, Cassie picked up the
white straw and looked at it longingly. How pretty
it was. For an instant, she imagined wearing it while

walking with Randal in Hyde Park. He was lost in admiration of her and of the new lilac walking dress she wore with the hat. Cassie sighed and smiled at the fantasy. Perhaps this fall.

Behind her, the shop's doorbell jingled, and she thrust the hat back on its stand. Welton Sinclair stood uncomfortably just inside the door. It wasn't only his stance that seemed out of place. The delicate femininity of the hat shop emphasized his size and bluffly masculine appearance.

"Mr. Sinclair," she exclaimed with pleasure. Cassie went toward him, holding out her hand.

A fiery blush climbed his cheeks. "M-Miss Cardwell. I-I didn't expect— Uh, I'm here to pick out a bonnet for my mother." He looked about the shop quickly. "May I escort you back to Lytham House?"

Lips twitching at his embarrassment, Cassie let her eyes travel the long distance up to his flushed face. "That's not necessary. I'm just here to pick up a hat for Lady Elaine. Then I must stop for a book, and some of her special scented soap. There are other things on my list, as well. However, I'll be happy to help in choosing a hat for your mother."

What imp had prompted her to make that offer? Sinclair looked even more uncomfortable. Cassie smiled with as much innocent eagerness as she could muster.

"Th-that's very kind of you," he stuttered, swallowed, then recovered. "But as you haven't a maid, I'll postpone my gift-buying and see you home. A gentleman is always pleased to be seen escorting such a lovely lady." The gallantry seemed forced. Then Welton brightened and said, as if it clinched the matter, "And Randal wouldn't care to hear you'd been out alone."

Stiffening, Cassie felt her eyebrows rise in annoyance. Had everyone noticed last night? Sinclair, at least, had decided it gave Randal the right to dictate her actions. Well, she hadn't given that right, and the sooner Randal realized it, the better.

"Lord Randal is not the arbiter of my actions, and you may tell him so. I'm here on an errand for Lady Elaine. My reputation couldn't possibly be sullied by going alone to a respectable shop in a respectable neighborhood."

"I didn't mean that. It's just— Well, will you allow me to escort you? I'm afraid I haven't a carriage, but let me find a cab for you."

The poor man grew more flustered with each word. His reaction softened her sharp annoyance, and she smiled at him. It wasn't his fault. The thought of him tagging along behind like a huge, friendly puppy was appealing. But no, she didn't need an escort. And certainly not to please Lord Randal.

"No, thank you. Besides, I wouldn't want you to disappoint your mother. There are perfectly lovely bonnets here." Cassie couldn't resist stroking the plume on the black grosgrain bonnet. "Here's Lady Elaine's hat." She took the hatbox from the saleswoman's hand. "I must be going, or I won't be finished before Lady Elaine's at-home today. Goodbye, Mr. Sinclair."

He opened the door for her with some reluctance, but Cassie was intent on going alone. She wouldn't let Randal govern her actions. She went to the curb and signaled a passing cab before Sinclair could protest again.

Late that afternoon, Randal rang the doorbell at Lytham House. Once again, Lytham hadn't arrived at the Home Office. His attendance was becoming highly erratic, and his duties were suffering. Who would actually exhibit their products was now in question. Several exhibits had withdrawn because their planned displays couldn't be ready on time.

"Good afternoon, Minton." Randal handed him gloves, cane, and hat. "Is Lord Lytham at home?"

"Not at present, my lord," Minton said. "We expect him within the hour if you would care to wait."

Randal brightened. "Is Lady Elaine at home today?" Minton admitted that she was. "Until Lord Lytham returns, I'll pay my respects."

"Certainly, my lord. This way, if you please."

Minton passed Randal's things to a waiting footman and led the way to the west drawing room. Fragments of sunshine filtered through the fanlight above the door to reflect off two sparkling suits of armor guarding the staircase.

Minton announced him, then withdrew. Randal's eyes narrowed thoughtfully. A group of ladies were gathered around Elaine. She sat behind an elaborate tea tray and a cake stand with tiers for tea cake, muffins, tarts, and thinly sliced bread and butter. Warmed by the sun streaming through tall windows, the air bore the welcome scents of food and tea, mixed with the ladies' perfumes and a bouquet of spring flowers as charmingly haphazard as Elaine.

Where was Cassie? Randal surveyed the drawing room quickly while he crossed the ornate Aubusson carpet. There she was, behind one of the massive, carved wooden screens Elaine had found recently. She occupied a chair set back from the group, needlepoint frame before her. As though aware of his gaze, her eyes rose from her needlework. Then she busied herself with selecting a new color for her tapestry. While he greeted Elaine, who had risen from her chair, Cassie concentrated on her petit point. She refused to gratify him by showing anything.

"Yes, Lady Constance," Randal's voice floated clearly over to Cassie in her retired position, "my plans for the grand opening are proceeding famously. There's just one minor point I need to discuss with Lord Lytham. But I don't wish to interrupt you. I only stopped to thank Elaine for last night's wonderful hospitality. The tableaux subjects she and Lord Lytham chose were quite original."

Gratified by his praise for her husband, Elaine smiled up at him. "Thank you, Randal, but Lytham chose the tableaux subjects. He should be home shortly. Won't you have a cup of tea while you wait? And may I prevail upon your good nature to take Cassie a cup?"

"Thank you. Would Miss Cardwell care for some cake?"

Cassie felt him looking at her. She kept her head down, ignoring him.

"I doubt it," Elaine answered. "She never does when working on her needlepoint. The dear child is creating a medieval tapestry to go with my latest furniture finds." Elaine pointed at the massive Gothic chair near Cassie. "You might wish to try that chair. Lytham assures me it's uncommonly comfortable." She poured tea into two delicate red-and-gold-banded cups and handed them to him.

He took them and bowed, excusing himself. Withdrawing from the ladies gathered around Elaine, he joined Cassie behind her screen. Randal placed the cups on a small drum table, then drew around the armchair Elaine had indicated and seated himself close to Cassie. She watched as he strategically placed the chair to block the avid gaze of the other ladies in the room.

"Good afternoon, Miss Cardwell." The gentle caress in his tone transcended the stock greeting.

"Good afternoon, Lord Randal."

"You agreed to call me Randal." Cassie glanced past the high back of the chair. He read the concern in her eyes. "They can't hear us, Cassie."

"Maybe not," Cassie admitted. "But they can imagine."

"I know they can." He smiled ruefully. "You should have heard the inquisition I faced from Lady Albinia last night after the tableaux."

"She didn't?" Cassie wasn't sure whether she was shocked or amused. "That's not the way to induce you to become a member of her family."

Randal shrugged easily and stirred his tea. "Lady Albinia is doomed to disappointment, I'm afraid."

Cassie looked quickly up into his eyes. Even more quickly, she looked back at her petit point and changed to a bit of background. That required a simple tent stitch only. She couldn't make a mistake with that.

"I don't want to lose one of my best friends," Randal continued easily. "For once, Elaine's right. Madeline and Welton are ideally suited to each other."

"Yes, I know. That was one of the first thoughts that crossed my mind when I saw Mr. Sinclair today."

Cassie took a scalding sip of tea and nearly choked when it burned her tongue. It covered the sudden memory of her anger. She couldn't tell him. To mention Sinclair's assumption that Randal had the right to approve of her behavior could only cause embarrassment. Cassie set the cup down in its saucer with a distinct click.

"You saw Sinclair today? Where?"

The sharpness of Randal's question startled her. Without moving, his entire body tensed. Cassie saw it clearly through her lowered lashes. Why should he care where she'd met Welton Sinclair? Surely he didn't suspect—? The cleft in her chin deepened at the thought. She wasn't Randal's private possession.

"When I picked up Lady Elaine's hat at Miss Norworth's," she said coolly. Her hands oddly steady, her needle drew the grass-green wool in and out steadily. The field grew rapidly larger beneath the dog's feet.

Eyes narrowed to blue-gray slits, Randal nodded. "At Miss Norworth's? Well, well. The little vixen. Tell me, what sort of needlepoint is that?" he asked, abstraction masking his deep voice.

Why had he so obviously changed the subject? What was going on with Madeline and Sinclair? Then she remembered her decision to keep this difficult male at arm's length.

And she did throughout what remained of a difficult hour. When she finished telling him about the medieval tapestry she was working on, she ruthlessly kept the conversation on neutral topics. Topics they could have discussed with anyone listening. When he excused himself to find Lytham, pain lurked in his eyes. Cassie nearly called him back, but couldn't.

# Chapter VIII

While Elaine saw her guests out, Cassie slumped in her medallion-backed armchair with a weary sigh. She sipped lukewarm tea and stared sightlessly at the door. This was going to be harder than she'd dreamed. Randal's hurt gaze haunted her. But finding her father's murderer came first.

For now, her position was companion to Lady Elaine Lytham. And daughter of a suicide. It would harm Randal's career to be connected with her. How long could she act cold toward him? Could she relinquish her control and still hold him at arm's length? She doubted it, especially when the memory of his warm kiss was so vivid and so disturbing.

While she considered the possibility, Elaine bustled through the door, exhilarated at the past two hours' gossip. "My dear, you'll never guess. Miss Pearce has eloped."

"Miss Pearce?" Cassie asked, trying to sound interested. "I'm afraid—"

"Oh, of course, you've never met. Well, it seems

she's eloped to Scotland with a half-pay officer. He stands to inherit one of those boggy little estates in Ireland, so I suppose they'll go there once they're properly married. Naturally her parents have cut her off entirely. I wonder if they'll be at the ball the day after tomorrow."

"Who?" Cassie asked abstractedly, still lost in unhappy thoughts. "Miss Pearce and her new husband?"

"No, silly. Miss Pearce's parents. Well, we'll see. Come along now, the dressmaker is waiting in the morning room for our fittings. I do wish you weren't wearing mourning. However, there's no help for it."

"I shouldn't go to the ball. I can't dance until I'm out of mourning, and it's inappropriate for a companion to attend as a guest."

If she could stay home, she thought, she could search some of the rooms she hadn't been able to yet. The servants always took the evening the Lythams went out as a night off, leaving only a skeleton staff.

"Nonsense, my dear," Elaine said briskly. "I won't hear of you not attending. It'll do you good to have some entertainment."

Refusing to listen to more protests, Elaine swept Cassie down the hall to the morning room. Seated in one corner, a small, rabbity woman patiently hemmed seams. Elaine had decreed that Cassie was to attend Sir John and Lady Charlotte Dysart's costume ball as Mary Queen of Scots. A more comfortable costume was Elaine's choice: Queen Phillipa of Hainault, a woman of considerable girth.

Cassie changed into the dress behind a Chinese screen. With the stiff bodice hooked, she came around the screen and halted when Miss Woods darted forward with pins and scissors. Elaine nodded approval of the attractive picture Cassie made.

Black lawn rose to a high collar that filled in the low, square neckline of the heavily boned bodice which descended to a point at the waist. A full skirt spread normally about her. Only the tight sleeves felt odd. Heavily embroidered false sleeves glistening with jet fell open from the shoulders like a pair of wings past her waist and nearly to the floor. And the little seamstress had provided a small, winged cap, stiffened in a curve that pointed down over her forehead. The heart-shaped edge was also beaded with jet, and had a little veil covering the neck.

"We shall have to have Louis style your hair differently." Elaine frowned at the cap. "This will never go with your present style. It needs to be pulled straight back from the face."

A glimmer of laughter lightened Cassie's expression. "You mean my present lack of style. I wish I'd lived when curly hair was in fashion. Although anything this unruly never could have been."

"Well, you needn't worry with this. No one will see a single curl." Laughing, Elaine tossed the cap onto the rose daybed. "Now, while Woods pins your hem, I shall change into my costume. I'm so happy you're going to the ball. It'll be delightful to have you to chaperone."

Avoiding Cassie's protest, Elaine slipped behind the screen with her elaborate gold and green brocade costume trimmed with fur. "I spoke to Lady Dysart." Her words were punctuated with small grunts as she struggled with the fastenings of her dress. "They're delighted to have you coming. As much for your sake as for your poor father's. They were positively devastated when he died. If you hadn't come to me as companion, Lady Dysart would have asked you, so you needn't worry so much. You can help chaperone the young ladies appearing at their first costume ball. Dressing up sometimes goes to their heads even without masks. Not that you're old enough to make a proper chaperone." Elaine stepped back from behind the screen. "I warn you, my dear, I shall keep a stern eye on you, and shan't allow you to dance with Randal."

Pushing a vagrant tendril back behind her ear, Cassie apologized to the seamstress for jerking the hem. It bought the time she needed to find the proper offhand tone to divert Elaine.

"That gold and green brocade is lovely on you," she commented. "Randal's going to be there? I'd have thought the Great Exhibition would take too much of his time. It opens so soon."

"None of the Home Office misses a minute of the social whirl, Randal and my dear Lytham least of all." In a mirror placed perfectly to view Cassie's face, Elaine preened the ermine trim of the surcoat. "Lytham, you know, was very like Randal when we married. Not only in looks, but in the sweet way he behaves."

"Sweet?" Cassie's mind drifted back to the times when Randal had taken a devilish delight in teasing her. *Sweet* wasn't a word she'd use to describe Randal. Or Lytham.

"Oh, yes. Both Lytham and Randal are very sweet. At least—" Elaine fell silent, a frown darkening her eyes. Then she whispered so softly that Cassie wondered whether she'd heard it: "Except for the last year or so."

Randal was still frowning when he reached the library door. He'd wait for Lytham for a half hour, then go home. He wasn't concerned about the delay. He barely remembered the reason he'd come.

Absently, Randal entered the library. Why had that confounded woman grown so cold?

A kaleidoscope of memories filled his mind. Cassie warm and responsive in his arms. Cassie blushing faintly when he drew up a chair. Cassie laughing at his teasing. Then she'd turned distant, cold. What had he done?

Lost in thought, he walked slowly across the carpeted floor before he realized he wasn't alone. Randal cleared his throat. Lytham gave a violent start and looked up sharply while dropping several sheets of paper over a pair of wooden sticks on his desk. Matched spots of color blazed in his cheeks.

"Sorry to startle you. I didn't realize you were home yet. I was going to wait for you in here," Randal said easily, forcing his mind away from Cassie. "If you have the time, we've something to discuss."

"Time? Oh, yes, I've plenty of time." Lytham's finely modeled mouth lifted in a thin smile. He indicated one of the plain red leather chairs with mahogany arms and legs. "Pull up a chair."

Randal brought the chair up opposite the desk and sank into it. For several seconds, he sat staring sightlessly over his templed fingers. Lytham quietly added several more papers to the stack while Randal brooded. Finally, Lytham broke the silence.

"You had something to discuss with me?"

"What? Oh, yes. It's regarding one of the deliveries to the Crystal Palace that should have arrived a week ago. It hasn't come despite their promises."

"You've wired?" Lytham asked automatically. The mantel clock ticked steadily in the background.

"Several times in the last week. The problem is, I'm at a point where I can't let them set up any more displays in that section until this one arrives. It's too bulky."

Stroking his chin, Lytham nodded. "What's the missing display?"

"Some vast piece of machinery that's supposed to produce cold storage for food. It's called a refrigerator. It needs a space as large as your dining room to hold it, so you see my problem."

"Yes. But surely you could have asked young Harwell about possible reserves to fill the space?" Lytham shuffled several papers together with displeasure.

Randal nodded sheepishly. "He wasn't to be found."

"Well, I can't give you an answer this afternoon. It'll have to wait until tomorrow morning." Lytham tapped his fingers softly on his desk.

"I thought it would." Randal stiffened in his chair. "But I wanted to be certain you'd be there. You rarely are these days."

"Nonsense." Lytham picked up a dagger he used as a letter opener and smoothed the blade through his fingers. "Do you really believe the grand opening is so important?"

"Yes, and I've taken special pains to make sure it's spectacular." Randal looked past Lytham at the bookshelves. "The success or failure will be determined on the first day. The Royal Family will make the difference."

The mantelpiece clock chimed the half hour, and Lytham changed the subject. "Have you had tea yet?"

"Yes, with Elaine." Relaxing, Randal followed his lead. "Since you weren't home, I thought I'd thank her for last night's entertainment. The charades you chose were most ingenious."

Lytham flushed at the compliment, his eyes brightening until they were nearly silver with the barest hint of blue. "It was nothing. I thought everybody must be getting tired of the usual thing."

"A most refreshing change. And a most successful evening."

"Unfortunately, it wasn't completely so." Lytham contemplated the dagger in his hand. "I've had to speak to Cassie about the attentions she's received from some of the, uh, young men she's met at this house. Since she's under my protection, I can't allow her to do anything foolish."

"That must be quite a problem for you; she's both young and lovely."

Randal's answer was grave, but inside a bubble of relief floated. So that was why Cassie was upset? Lytham had spoken to her. He thought Randal's intentions dishonorable. Randal glanced at the clock ticking steadily on the mantel. Was there still time to see her again today? Surely Elaine's other visitors must have left by now, and Elaine wouldn't mind. She was his ally.

"A problem I don't intend to let get out of hand," Lytham said, unaware of Randal's elation.

"Don't blame you in the least. Some of these young blades are untrustworthy. What do you say to meeting tomorrow morning? Around eleven?" Randal rose with leisurely grace that masked his eagerness. "That'll give you plenty of time to look up possible replacements for that dilatory piece of machinery."

So his attentions to Cassie were so pronounced that even Lytham had noticed. It didn't matter. Lytham couldn't know his intentions. He wasn't certain of them himself. But he didn't want Cassie as reserved as she'd been this afternoon.

                    *      *      *

Cassie hurried down the stairs with Elaine's brush and hairpins. Nothing would do for Elaine but to try on the headdress that went with her costume. It was a stiff embroidered affair that rose steeply back in a curve with a crown atop it. Baroque pearls studded the headdress below the crown, and a tiny veil hung from the back. Cassie couldn't imagine it above Elaine's round face, just as her own heart-shaped headdress looked odd to her eyes.

"Cassie." Randal's soft call stopped her on the last step. "I thought you were a ghost."

"A ghost?" Bewilderment held her for an instant, then Cassie glanced down at her costume and smiled. "Lytham House wasn't built when this dress was the height of fashion."

"A ghost from a house which used to stand on this site." Randal looked theatrically around them. The light was dimming with the dying day, and the servants hadn't lit the candles placed ready in the sconces. "Aren't you afraid to walk these corridors alone?"

Cassie couldn't suppress her laughter. "Idiot. Of course not. Besides, I don't think a house ever stood here before. And if it did, why should a ghost from a previous house haunt this one?"

"'There are more things—'"

"'In heaven, Horatio.' I know the quote. But I don't think it applies." She paused. This wasn't holding him at arm's length. She tried to step around him. "Now, if you'll excuse me, I need to take Elaine these things."

Shifting so she couldn't get past, Randal extended his hand. Then dropped it. He had to go carefully, since Lytham had stuck his nose in where it wasn't wanted. "Why are you wearing that outfit?"

Cassie touched the fine black lawn gathered into

her throat. Her skin gleamed palely through it. "This is Elaine's selection for me to wear at the costume ball day after tomorrow."

"Lady Dysart's?" Randal's face brightened, and he took another step closer. Even with the advantage of the step she stood on, Cassie had to look up at him. "Will you be attending?"

Cassie nodded. He stood so close she could barely breathe. "The Dysarts were my father's friends. They've been kind enough to invite me."

"Will you save a dance for me?"

"I won't be dancing." She touched her black skirt with regret. "It wouldn't be proper."

"Then you'll sit out with me." Smiling, Randal captured the hand which had touched her skirt and stroked her palm with his thumb.

"If I have the time." His touch sent an odd combination of chills and heat radiating from her palm, just as it had last night. Before she caught herself, her eyes fastened on his lips. Was he going to kiss her again? "I'm supposed to chaperone, you know?"

"And who's going to chaperone you?"

"Elaine."

Smile widening, his brilliantly blue gaze caressed her barely parted lips. "Wonderful. I'll see you there."

He brought her palm up to his lips and pressed a kiss in it, then lifted his glittering gaze to hers. Triumph shot through him. Pleasure at his touch had turned her green-flecked hazel eyes golden, while something lurked in their depths. Did she hope he'd kiss her? Yes, she did.

He slowly leaned forward. Cassie froze, a delicate flush building. The innocent touch of her lips last night had stayed with him even when he managed to sleep. Now to taste her sweetness again even at the cost of another restless night.

His soft breath just brushed her lips when the sound of a door closing down the hall made them spring apart. Their eyes met for a fraction of a second.

Cassie whispered good-bye and watched Randal stride down the hall to the front door. She mustn't forget her intentions so thoroughly again. Yet despite her decision, keen disappointment swamped her. And keener annoyance at whoever had closed that door.

Neville tucked the plaid muffler more firmly into his overcoat and muttered a curse. As a private enquiry agent, he was accustomed to surveillance in all sorts of weather, but he'd never learned to like it. Once again the night had turned chilly, and low, thin clouds that promised rain scudded across the pale quarter moon. The lanterns marking the doorway of the Elephant and Cross where he was to meet Carstairs flickered in the wind. He wished Carstairs would hurry. Even though he was late, Neville knew he'd come. He was greedy.

A gust of wind whipped at Neville's shallow-crowned hat. He grabbed to prevent its flying down the dirty alley. In that moment a dark shape, plump and awkwardly furtive, darted across the street. Carstairs? Yes. There was no mistaking Carstairs' moon face in the dim lantern light.

Neville didn't cross the street immediately. Carstairs was to have come alone. When no one else appeared in the silent, wind-tossed street, Neville slipped down it and approached the inn from a different direction, watching for suspicious loiterers. He had no reason to expect trouble, but he never failed to take this precaution. Once it had saved his life.

Neville followed Carstairs into the warm, murky light of the pub and waited until he'd taken a seat, his back to the corner of the high plain settle. Carstairs' eyes darted about the room nervously before he relaxed infinitesimally. So Carstairs was frightened of being seen. That was the reason he'd chosen a rendezvous so far from the City where he lived and worked. Even more certain of his ground now, Neville stopped the single barmaid and ordered two pints of bitter for Carstairs' table. The entire room smelled of stale beer and sweat.

"Carstairs," Neville said. He slid into the cracked settle across from the McCrory and Chambers employee. He ignored Carstairs' start and the way his pinched, gray face paled. "I'm glad to see you arrived on time. And with no escort."

"You ch-checked?"

"Did you expect I wouldn't? Never mind. Here's some bitter. Drink up and we'll talk."

"Pretty cool, aren't you? But I warn you. I've got a hard head." Despite his bravado, Carstairs half-drained the tankard the barmaid set before him in one long swallow. He wiped his mouth with a dirty handkerchief and blinked at Neville. "So what do you want from me?"

"Something quite simple." Neville sipped from his tankard. Not the best he'd ever tasted, but he'd had worse.

"You'll p-pay me?"

"I'll pay you"—Neville took a five-pound note from his pocket, a tenth of Carstairs' inflated annual salary—"this in advance if you get me the information I want. And the same again when you deliver the goods."

Carstairs' eyes glittered at the sight. He licked suddenly dry lips and took another long swallow. Five pounds. More than a month's wages.

"What do I have to do?"

"Just find some documents in your files and bring them to me." Tobacco smoke mixed with smoke from the fire drifted across their table. It made Neville squint as he watched Carstairs.

Carstairs darted glances about the room. No one seemed interested in their low-voiced conversation. Men who gathered here knew better than to take too obvious an interest in other people's business.

"If it's an active file, you can't have it for long," he warned.

"It's not. That file's been inactive for some time. The name's Andrew Cardwell."

"The bloke who committed suicide?" Carstairs asked. Stories about it had made the rounds of the office.

Neville nodded. "You shouldn't have any trouble bringing me the file. No one else will want it."

A burst of laughter from the far end of the tavern startled Carstairs. Shoulders hunched, he licked his lips and darted a furtive look at Neville. "I suppose I c-could do it. For another few pounds." His eyes fastened greedily on the five-pound note lying beside Neville's hand.

"For the complete file?"

Neville smiled grimly. He was willing to pay a good deal more for it, but he didn't want more questions than necessary swimming about Carstairs' head. He was the sort of weasel who might try to make an extra pound or two by telling his superiors. Fortunately, a firm that sailed that close to the wind couldn't expect employee loyalty.

"It should be worth more than ten pounds, a

complete file should." Carstairs' gaze dropped again
to the five-pound note.

"We'll make it another ten pounds," Neville
agreed. "But the file must be complete."

"The complete file," Carstairs agreed. "Why do
you want it?"

"Why do you want the additional ten pounds?"
Neville asked softly, dangerously.

# Chapter IX

Cassie's first impression when she stepped out of the carriage behind Elaine and Lytham was of light. Light that dimmed the waxing moon and soft stars from the midnight-blue sky. Gas lamps drowned the front of Norwich House, the Dysart's home, with a clear-edged light that revealed every detail. Cassie followed the others as they joined the last few arrivals in climbing the the shallow steps leading up to the Palladian mansion.

Again, Elaine had been late. When she saw her husband's costume, Richard III, complete with hunchback beneath a red velvet mantle instead of the expected Edward III, it had taken the combined efforts of both Cassie and Lytham to soothe her tears. Finally, they had succeeded and gotten her into the carriage.

While Elaine chatted with their hostess, Cassie stood on the top step leading down to the ballroom. Couples swirled to the strains of a waltz beneath pink silk which turned the room into a tent. Her eyes moved restlessly over the dancers; then, against her wishes, she found Randal.

Resplendent in the costume of a Cavalier, Randal had his arm about a tall, plump woman wearing a yellow brocade gown from the court of Marie Antoinette. Cassie didn't recognize the woman, but Randal knew her. Quite well, if his easy conversation and laughter were anything to judge by.

"Ah, there you are, Cassie." Twitching her train around, Elaine stopped beside her. "You'll never guess what Lady Dysart has just told me." She drew Cassie on down the stairs to take them out of the traffic. "The Pearces haven't found the courage to attend, and"—she paused dramatically, excitement shining in her face—"Lady Albinia hasn't kept any of her social engagements in several days. What do you think of that?"

"Then Madeline won't be here?"

Elaine shook her head regretfully. Spotting one of her cronies, she waved and started toward one of the side rooms. "Lady Dysart suggests you join the young ladies who are sitting out over at that side since you aren't able to dance. But first, do you think you could find me a glass of lemonade? This heat is unbearable." She waved a feathered fan at her flushed, round face.

In green and gold brocade, her headdress rising nearly a foot above her, Elaine was impressive, far more impressive than most of the matrons attending the ball. They had chosen costumes better suited to their daughters. Elaine invariably showed excellent taste, as she had with Cassie's costume. Unfortunately, Elaine's own choice was too warm for the muggy night.

"Of course," Cassie said, smiling. "Where will you be sitting?"

"Me? Oh, I shan't be sitting along the wall, my

dear. I never do. I'll be playing cards. Lady Dysart is most sensible. She understands that many of us stouter ladies don't wish to make a figure of ourselves on the dance floor. I shall play whist while you— Oh, I'm sorry, I forgot. You can't. My dear Cassie. I hope you won't be too terribly bored." Glancing at the dancers, Elaine immediately spotted Randal. Her smile widened knowingly.

Cassie refused to follow Elaine's lead. "Don't worry, I won't. Let me get you established before I fetch a lemonade. Is it cool enough in the card room?"

With the heat from all the candles in the pink-silk-tented room and nearly four hundred people, Cassie felt comfortable. It was reminiscent of late spring evenings in Charleston. But most of the women and many of the men fanned themselves vigorously. Beads of sweat had formed on Elaine's forehead beneath her headdress.

"Yes, I'm sure it will be. That's one of the reasons I gave up dancing. Balls are always warm, costume balls especially."

She went lightly down the stairs and around the dancers into one of the rooms. Appreciably cooler, it was situated so matrons with chaperone duties could watch the dancers and enjoy themselves with whist at the same time. Cassie saw Elaine seated with friends, then hurried off to fetch the lemonade.

Skirting the dancers, Cassie caught another glimpse of Randal smiling down into the face of his partner. The music ended and couples streamed off the floor, laughing and chattering. Randal seemed to be enjoying his Marie Antoinette. Cassie repressed a pang of jealousy. If only Randal could dance with Mary Queen of Scots.

Sighing softly, she hurried up the steps to the re-freshment room. A throng of gentlemen intent on providing their partners with something cooling to drink arrived immediately after her. Slipping between them with the lemonade, Cassie went carefully down the stairs. At the bottom, a hand on her arm halted her.

"Randal! I mean, Lord Randal," Cassie said, conscious of people swirling past them. Some had heard her exclamation, and she didn't want to cause more gossip—enough had started after Elaine's evening of tableaux.

"Cassie! I mean, Miss Cardwell." Randal imitated her, amused. His tall frame clad in rich blue silk and lace with buckled shoes divided the stream of people heading up the stairs to the refreshment table. "Are you taking that to Elaine?" he asked, pointing to the lemonade.

"Yes, she's—"

"At the card table," he finished. "Let's get rid of that, then find a quiet corner where we can talk."

Seeing a break in the throng of people behind him, Cassie stepped around Randal, her hand cradling the glass protectively. "Aren't you dancing the next dance with—"

An Arab sheik, his robes flowing loosely about his short body, stopped her. "Miss Cardwell. Randal."

"Lord Playfair." What a relief. Playfair humored her in an avuncular way, but at least she knew how to deal with him. She still wasn't sure how to deal with Randal. "What an original costume," she continued.

Lord Playfair plucked at his fine woolen robe and let it fall back into place. "The concept of zero and the numerals we use are both Arabic inventions. Although I don't expect Rydal here to understand that."

"If I had the time, I'd resent that," Randal told

him, grinning. He stepped closer to Cassie. "However, I'm kidnapping Miss Cardwell, so if you'll excuse us?"

"Not so fast, young man," Playfair demanded. "Give that lemonade to young Rydal, Miss Cardwell. Prince Albert wants to meet you. Says he doesn't often get to chat with young ladies interested in mathematics. Normally your sex cares for nothing but the style of their hair. The number of flounces on their skirts is the closest they get to mathematics."

"I resent that on behalf of my sex," she told Playfair with mock sternness and turned to Randal. Cassie looked up appealingly into his face. "Would you take this to Elaine, my lord?" she asked softly. "She's in the card room over there." She nodded to the central door leading off the ballroom.

"I'd be delighted." Randal accepted his dismissal with grace. "Shall I see you later?"

"Oh, umh, I'm . . . not sure what Elaine wishes me to do. I'm supposed to help chaperone."

She glanced significantly at a group of young girls and their swains. They all looked as if they'd just been released from the schoolroom. While their flirtations hadn't exceeded the bounds of propriety, they threatened to. Three years earlier at her own debut, she had behaved just as skittishly.

"You aren't old enough to chaperone," Randal protested.

"The Prince is waiting," Playfair interrupted. "Come along, ancient Miss Cardwell, give the glass to Rydal. He'll take it to Elaine. Mustn't keep the Prince waiting."

He took the glass from her hand and thrust it into Randal's. Taking her arm, Playfair gently hustled her through the dancers returning to the floor as the orchestra tuned up for a waltz. Cassie cast a glance over her shoulder at Randal's rueful expression. Meeting the Prince was a singular honor. Why wasn't she more excited?

"You needn't worry, Miss Cardwell," Lord Playfair said. "Rydal will find you again. He's a very determined young man."

"And a very popular one, Lord Playfair. He'll be far too occupied to search for me."

A warm, fatherly smile softened his "Foolish girl."

Lord Playfair halted at the side of a plump, balding, blond gentleman in the costume of a courtier of Queen Elizabeth whose stiff ruff didn't suit his soft chin, although his carriage was erect. When he turned to greet them, her first impression was startling. She'd never seen a man who looked so tired.

"Your highness, may I present Miss Cassandra Cardwell, the young lady of whom I spoke," Lord Playfair said formally.

Cassie sank in a deep curtsy, murmuring, "Your highness."

Prince Albert nodded an acknowledgment and gestured at her black costume. "We're sorry to see you've suffered a recent bereavement, Miss Cardwell."

"Thank you, your highness. It's for my father and grandmother." His strong German accent surprised her.

"Please accept our condolences, but at least you have the consolation of your mathematical interests."

"Yes, your highness. Lord Playfair has been kind enough to tell me about the ciphers in the *Times*. I've enjoyed solving them."

"Your skills include cryptography?" the Prince asked, startled.

"Yes, your highness. My father taught me to

work simple ciphers as soon as I learned to read."
Humor lit her eyes. "It's amazing how fast I
learned, once he started leaving enciphered notes
telling me where my Christmas presents were hidden."

Only the beginning of a smile lit his stiff expression before a woman joined them. "A sad loss for
you," the Prince repeated with tepid warmth. "Ah,
you must allow me to present you to my wife, the
Queen."

A plump woman in the enormous wired lace ruff
worn by Queen Elizabeth in her portraits had hurried up to the Prince's side. The elongated line of
the bodice didn't suit her small stature. She looked
all bodice and no skirt. Why, the Queen was shorter
than she was, Cassie realized as she rose from another deep curtsy. She concealed her thoughts while
Prince Albert gave her name to the Queen.

"Your costume, Miss Cardwell," the Queen began abruptly. "It seems to be of the same century as
ours."

"Indeed, your majesty. Lady Elaine Lytham suggested I come as Mary Queen of Scots since that
lady wore mourning several times."

"Then you're in mourning also?"

"For my father and grandmother," Cassie answered patiently. Why was Queen Victoria's expression so stiff?

"You have our sympathy," the Queen said, her
voice even more devoid of expression. "As I recall,
our costume beheaded yours."

Dismissing Cassie, she turned to the Prince. The
Queen's tone softened miraculously when she spoke
to her husband. "Albert, one of the gentlemen involved with your Exhibition wishes to speak to
you."

Accepting her dismissal, Cassie curtsied deeply

again and turned to Lord Playfair. In a few steps they were lost in the throng. Unable to restrain her curiosity, a stunned Cassie looked at Lord Playfair.

He spoke before she could. "Our Queen does not care to have young, attractive ladies introduced to Prince Albert. Especially not when the young lady in question has something in common with the Prince that she can't share." He smiled at her surprise. "A love of mathematics. Where should I escort you? I should love to stay, but I'm engaged for this next dance."

Cassie looked quickly about her. Near the French doors leading out onto the terrace was relatively quiet. Yet it offered a fine vantage for watching the dancers. Watching for Randal, she admitted to herself. Even though she should think of other things.

"Over there looks comfortable, Lord Playfair. Thank you for your escort." His courtly courtesy called for equal formality. Was it his avuncular air that allowed him to tease her about Randal without offense? She didn't know; she was simply happy to know such a man. Her smile said as much when she accepted a small gilt and rose damask chair he held for her. It was comfortably near the open French doors.

"My pleasure, Miss Cardwell." His gaze ran over the crowd as he waited for her to settle comfortably. "I'll look for you at the next interval." He nodded toward a woman with tall green feathers sprouting out of her hair and a vaguely Scottish costume. "If you'll excuse me." He bowed and left to join his partner.

It took Cassie less than ten seconds to find Randal in the crowd of dancers again. Not that he was so much taller than the other men. The dancers swirled once again, and Cassie's gaze followed him into the middle of the floor.

He danced with a very young lady who looked as though she'd never been on the dance floor in her life. Cassie smiled. The girl's gypsy costume emphasized her youth and nervousness even though Randal smiled down at her. Displaying his partner's grace in the dance was a difficult task. The girl had the awkward grace of the very young, and she missed the beat of the music more often than not.

"Poor Cassie." She jerked around. Lytham stood above her. "I should have insisted you remain at home. It must be very dull for you, watching the other young people dancing."

"Good evening, Lord Lytham." Cassie hoped he hadn't noticed her start. "I'm enjoying watching," she assured him mechanically. Having no choice, she waved at the empty chair beside her. "Won't you have a seat?"

"Thank you. I thought you might feel thirsty with this heat, so I brought this." He extended a glass to her. "You do like lemonade?"

He absently pushed at the wadding beneath his mantle. Adding to his sweaty discomfort, his hunchback had slipped a bit.

"Yes, thank you, my lord." She accepted the glass and took a sip.

Beyond Lytham's shoulders, Cassie saw several dowagers with middle-aged gentlemen in attendance. They were exceedingly interested in Lytham's behavior. Gentlemen didn't fetch a drink for their wife's companion. But Lytham was intent on showing the world how considerate he was.

"When Elaine told me you were coming, I was quite against it," Lytham continued. In taking his seat, he had moved the chair closer to hers. Uncomfortably close.

"It's certainly . . . unusual for a companion to be included in invitations." Cassie took another sip of her lemonade and let her eyes drift back to the dancers. If she appeared uninterested, he might leave. "Even though the Dysarts were my father's friends."

"That's why I gave my consent. That and my certainty that your innate good taste would prevent you from doing anything improper. Your costume couldn't be more exquisitely chosen."

"Lady Elaine suggested that I come as Mary Queen of Scots." If he leaned any closer, he could drink her lemonade instead of his own.

"Your influence. Elaine, dearly as I love her, is something of a flutterbrain."

Not wishing to answer, she nodded toward the dancers. They had halted shortly after Lord Lytham arrived, and were now making up a new set. Waiting for the music to begin again were a particularly attractive pair Cassie had never seen before. The man was dressed as a Turkish pasha while his partner wore a simple Puritan costume that set off her fair, fragile beauty.

"What an unusual pair they are, my lord. Who are they?"

His glance flicked over them, uninterested. "Lord and Lady Mannering. They're still playing at turtledoves. You'd think they'd have gotten over that after five years of marriage and two children. The Queen set an unfortunate fashion."

"You disapprove of married love?" She should have kept her tone softer, less reproving.

"Certainly not, but there's no need to display it so ostentatiously. A good marriage should never be public." His gaze flicked sharply from the Mannerings, now dashing about the room to the strains of a polka, to Cassie's face. His gray-blue eyes disturbed her. "Don't you agree?"

"Quite possibly, my lord." She couldn't imagine a marriage that proper, that bloodless.

"After more than a dozen years of marriage, I can tell you that's the only correct manner for a couple to behave in, at least in Society. It's different in the lower classes."

He spoke slowly, quietly, as though arguing a point he'd been over many times. His gaze drifted unseeingly to the dancers again. He seemed to exist in a different world, far away from the ball. Flashes of something appeared in his face that made her uncomfortable. Why did he speak to her this way? Or was he talking to himself?

"I'm afraid I don't understand, my lord."

Cassie gazed directly at him. Why discuss such a subject? Had he been at the wine too much already this evening? Before they'd left for the ball, he had spent more time than usual over the port. But when they left, he was immaculate despite their exertions in soothing Elaine. Now the sprightly feather on Lytham's beret drooped toward his shoulder.

"What? Oh." Harsh color left his cheeks and the glitter died from his eyes. "I beg your pardon. The case of a friend of mine is weighing on me today. His daughter believed a man was serious when he wasn't. A simple flirtation. No harm done. Except, unfortunately, to the girl's heart. They fear she may go into a decline. I hate to hear of such a thing."

Relieved, Cassie encouraged him to tell her about it. The disjointed explanation made Cassie uneasy, but it was better than having his attention centered on her. His fulsome compliments when they were in public grated.

From his position in the midst of the dancers, Randal watched Cassie. Consideration for two girls he'd known since their school days kept him on the dance floor. Neither of the girls should have been forced into making her debut yet. Each was too shy and awkward. In a year or two, they'd be ready, able to enjoy the beaux who'd flock around them. But not yet.

He glanced down at his partner, a thin blond girl who blushed if he even looked at her. He'd never let his daughter make her debut when she was so unready. Although any girl taking after Cassie would— Randal cut himself off abruptly. Until he was certain, he mustn't create a family for himself.

Randal swung Miss Yalton around in a long curve, for a better view of Cassie. Yes, there was something wrong. Cassie kept looking away from Lytham. And why was he sitting so close to her?

As Randal watched, guiding Miss Yalton in a direction opposite to the other dancers, Cassie took another sip of lemonade. She turned her head toward Lytham and directed a question at him. Good. That had set him back a bit.

"I—is something wrong, Lord Randal?" Miss Yalton asked breathlessly, her cheeks fiery red. Long acquaintance with Randal gave her the courage to speak.

Randal, aware he'd been ignoring his partner quite abominably, smiled down at her. "Not in the least. . . . Tell me," he added, "are you enjoying your first costume ball?" Miss Yalton, at least, wasn't so tongue-tied as his last partner.

"Oh, yes. Mama said . . ."

Randal's attention drifted away from her artless prattle and back to Cassie. He was in time to see Lytham rising in response to someone's signal, while Cassie looked much happier once he was gone. Their eyes met and she looked away quickly, a slight smile on her face, to concentrate on the dancers and their colorful costumes. It must be lonely for her, knowing so few people. When this dance was finished, he'd sit with her for a few minutes. Before the next blasted dance with—Whom was he supposed to dance with next? He couldn't remember.

Cassie watched Lytham join a man she vaguely recognized from the tableaux. She hoped the conversation concerned something of importance to both men. Then Lytham wouldn't return quickly. If she did see him returning, she'd disappear through the crowd and find the ladies' retiring room.

Her eyes drifted automatically back to the dancers. In rhythm with the music, couples dipped and swayed. Their silks, brocades, and velvets caught the light of hundreds of candles. Cassie raised her fan and waved it slowly before her face. The room was becoming oppressively warm.

Then her fan paused in its regular beat before continuing more quickly. Randal again. He held a lovely young girl in his arms, blond and enchanting in her simple milkmaid's costume. She talked confidingly with him as he guided her steadily away from Cassie's chair. Cassie submerged a pang of jealousy.

"Miss Cardwell. I promised myself the privilege of speaking with you when I saw you were here this evening. May I join you?"

"Colonel Shelton, isn't it?"

Cassie smiled hesitantly at the small man in the army uniform of the previous century. With his distinguished features and gray hair, he was a hard man to forget. Yet Cassie couldn't have said where she'd met him. At one of Elaine's parties, but which one?

"Quite right, Miss Cardwell. Your memory is as perfect as the rest of you."

He took her recognition as permission to sit down. Pulling the chair around to block her view of Randal, he smiled confidingly at her. This close, Cassie could see tiny broken red veins threading his nose, and his faintly unfocused eyes. His breath reached her, too. He'd been drinking heavily, but controlled it well. She waited for him to begin the conversation, one she didn't wish to participate in.

"I hope you're enjoying your taste of Society," he finally said. "It must be difficult for a girl in your position and with no experience of Society's requirements."

"It would be more enjoyable if I could dance. I do so enjoy balls." Another one who assumed that because she'd grown up in America she must be a barbarian.

"You've been to balls before?" Colonel Shelton asked, surprised.

"Frequently in Charleston. When I joined my father in London, I was already in mourning for my grandmother."

Colonel Shelton blinked at her several times as he absorbed her calm demeanor. He seemed to believe she wouldn't be invited anywhere if it wasn't for Elaine.

"Your father?" he asked with a slight slur.

Cassie nodded aloofly. "Andrew Cardwell. He . . . died recently." Would she ever lose that break in her voice when she spoke of her father's death?

"So you went into Lytham's household, eh? Lytham always did know ripe pickings." His small tongue flicked out at one end of his drooping mustache.

"I wouldn't phrase it quite that way, sir." She didn't understand him, and she didn't want to. But even Lord Lytham was preferable to this man.

She let her gaze drift toward the dancers. It hadn't

worked with Lytham; perhaps it would now. If not, she could still retreat to the ladies' retiring room.

"Perhaps you'd care to consider an even better proposition?" He possessed himself of her hand and the fan in it.

"Colonel Shelton, unhand me." Flushing, Cassie pushed at his damp hand.

"You'd like living under my protection." He nodded wisely. "You needn't worry. If you accept my little proposition, you won't need to worry in the least bit," he repeated. His face was heavily flushed, and his breath came in little snorts. "When I mount a mistress, I do it handsomely."

All color drained from her face, leaving her eyes sparkling green pools of anger. "Colonel Shelton, you forget yourself. I have no idea what makes you think such a thing. If we were anyplace else, I'd slap your face!" She wrenched her hand free.

"Oh, I doubt it. Your position has been made plain by Lytham's attentions. He's a fool," Shelton sneered. "He even seems unaware of the gossip. Now, take my offer and you'll have much more fun. No running after my wife with glasses of lemonade. No sitting out every dance."

"Your assumptions are—are despicable, sir. Now, if you'll excuse me." He grasped her arm.

Cassie started to rise, spots of color burning in her cheeks. For such a small man, his hand was incredibly strong. He held her in place with no strain.

"You aren't going anywhere, Cassandra. Not till you agree to my little proposition. I'll be quite generous."

"I will not consider your filthy proposition. And if you don't let me go, I shall scream. Then how will you explain your behavior to Queen Victoria?"

Even the way he snatched his hand from her arm didn't satisfy the fury in her. She jumped to her feet. The jet trimming her false sleeves trembled with her rage. She intended to tell Colonel Shelton about both his manners and his morals when a hand on her arm stopped her. Swinging around to face her new tormentor, she sighed with relief. Randal.

His handsome face unaccustomedly stern, he looked from her to Colonel Shelton. "What did you say to upset Miss Cardwell, Shelton?" His voice was as icy as his eyes.

Colonel Shelton struggled to his feet. He stood squinting, his eyes not making it up to Randal's chin. "Nothing to do with you, Rydal. The young woman and I were talking."

"Sir, if you were not"—Randal's eyes, a wintry blue-gray, passed insultingly over the colonel and found him wanting—"beneath contempt, I should explain your conduct to you in terms even you can understand. If, however, you persist in your behavior, I shall be forced to give you instruction in how a gentleman acts toward a lady."

Paling until the veins on his nose stood out like red cobwebs, Shelton peered up at Randal's face, then turned to Cassie. "If I've said anything to offend, please be assured it was the wine." He bowed carefully and backed away.

"Come, Miss Cardwell." Icy fury still held Randal in its grip. His hold on her arm tightened until it hurt. "I shall restore you to Lady Lytham's care." Without another word, he led Cassie away.

Shock and anger kept Cassie upright. She felt soiled by Shelton's assumptions. How could he think such a thing? Had Randal heard him? She stole a glance at his face through her lashes. No, she didn't think so. If he had, he wouldn't be so calm. She looked around quickly. No one seemed interested in her . . . in them. The music and the hum of conversation had covered the incident. There would be no scandal. She felt faint with relief.

"It's all right, Cassie. There's no need to worry. Do you want me to escort you home?"

Randal's concerned gaze eased her turmoil as nothing else could have. She shook her head slowly. "I—I'm all right now. It's just—"

"There's no need to explain. The man's no gentleman. I can't imagine how he's tolerated in Society." Anger flared coldly in his eyes, graying them. Again, he reminded her of someone.

Cassie forced a trembling smile to her lips. "There are gentlemen and gentlemen," she said. "That's what my father told me. Fortunately, I haven't met any of that variety before."

"I'm glad of that. Now I'll take you to Elaine. Wait for me there, will you? I have to find"—he frowned as he fumbled in his pocket for the dance card—"Miss Loudon for this dance. It would be an insult if I failed to appear. But I'll join you for supper. We can talk about it then if you wish."

"Oh, Elaine? I . . . I couldn't face her. Not now."

Panic flooded her at the thought of facing Elaine in her flustered state. She needed time alone. Time to regain her composure.

Without another word to Randal, she tore free of his consoling grasp. Blindly, she walked through the dancers returning to the floor. Instinct brought her to the relative peace of a small, sparsely furnished room. Intent on not being discovered, Cassie curled up in a heavily draped window seat and drew the curtain closed.

The window looked out over the garden. Thin clouds playing tag with the waxing moon created ghostly shapes in the flowering shrubbery. A breeze danced through the bushes occasionally, making them bow to their neighbors even as the dancers inside did. Eerily, the bushes seemed to move in time to the muffled music.

Kneading a limp handkerchief, Cassie desperately tried to blank her mind. But she couldn't. How could Shelton assume she was— She broke off, then forced herself to finish it. Lytham's mistress? It made no sense. She considered Lytham. Lytham? How could anyone possibly assume she was his mistress? Just because he was given to fulsome compliments and patting her hand? Surely they knew of Lytham's need to project the best image?

Her thoughts squirreled around, producing no solution. There was none. She had to remain at Lytham House. At least until she proved Lytham had killed her father. Her instincts told her to run. She couldn't, though. No matter what Society thought her real position there was.

"My darling Cassie. He really upset you, didn't he?"

Gasping, Cassie jerked around. Randal. She blinked in the suddenly stronger light as he drew back the drape. He stood over her, his hand extended. The lace at his wrist fell softly over hers when she took it. Obeying the steady pull of his hand, she rose slowly to her feet.

With his free hand, Randal cupped her chin and asked, "Do you want to talk about it?"

Still bemused by his unexpected appearance, Cassie shook her head. If she told him, what would he do? Best to keep silent. Shelton's proposition was the product of a lecherous mind misinterpreting Lytham's public behavior. Nothing more. There was no need to involve Randal.

"All right. But if you'd care to at any time—?"

The opening chords of a waltz reached them from the ballroom. Randal stepped back and bowed, one hand clasping hers.

"May I have this dance, Miss Cardwell?"

Cassie glanced past his shoulder. The door was closed; no one would see her dance in her blacks. Randal's odd sense of humor helped drive out the unpleasant taste left by Shelton. With grave formality, she sank into a deep curtsy, her skirt spreading round her.

"I would be honored, my lord."

In the next instant, Randal was whirling her about the room in a series of graceful loops. The hem of her skirt frothed against the wall, the drapes, the one settee.

She'd dreamed of this moment since Elaine told her Randal would be at the ball. Her dreams were impossible, yet she'd dreamed.

Randal's handsome face hovered above hers, a half smile on his lips. His hand at her waist guided her firmly about the small room. His other hand clasped hers tightly. And the look in his eyes . . .

Each time they turned so that the moonlight fell on his face, his eyes grew warmer. As the strains of the waltz drew to a crescendo, he drew her closer until he held her almost fully in his arms. The blazing warmth of his gaze threatened to consume her.

The music ended in a triumphant crash. Afraid of revealing too much, Cassie dropped her eyes. With the final note, Randal drew them to a halt near the window seat. Her name escaped him on a soft breath, and he lowered his head.

Gentle passion enveloped her from the instant his lips found hers. First one hand, then the other crept from his shoulders to link about his neck. This had been in her dreams, too.

Cassie strained up against him, seeking something more, something she couldn't identify. His response was instantaneous. Randal swept her high off the

floor until she rested against his chest. His kiss taut-
ened, deepened.

Then a burst of noise from the ballroom reached
them.

Stiffening, Randal lifted his head and stared down
into her bemused eyes. "Cassie—" He broke off.
His eyes held a silver glitter.

"Yes?" Her voice was soft, slurred with desire.

Delicious tension ran through her. She'd known
from the night of the tableaux that Randal wouldn't
let himself be set aside until she'd found her father's
murderer. He'd just proved it again. Delicious danger waited for her in Randal's arms, danger she both
needed and feared.

Randal's lips curved in a wry half smile. "I can't
tell you. Not yet, anyway." He made the words
sound like a vow as he lowered her to her feet. Still
holding her hands, he stepped back from her. "I
think we'd best return to the ballroom before Elaine
looks for us."

Paling at the thought of Elaine's delight, Cassie
nodded vigorously. She cast a quick glance at the
door and started forward, drawing him with her.
Elaine could open it at any moment. His strong
grasp halted her.

"Not together. It wouldn't matter whether Elaine
found us here or not if we leave at the same time.
It's written on our faces. . . . Yes," he agreed when
Cassie drew her hands free to press them to her
checks, "mine too."

# Chapter X

"It's all going to work out perfectly," Elaine said.

The words dropped into the pool of quiet in the morning room. Cassie tensed and raised her head slowly from the pile of newspapers before her. There was no way to avoid what Elaine was going to say.

Still, it was worth a try. "You think Emory and Charlotte will be able to marry?"

The couple had been conducting their romance in a simple cipher over the past weeks, and Cassie had shown Elaine how to read their messages. Each day Elaine looked avidly for the newspaper until Minton had gotten into the habit of bringing it to them as soon as Lord Lytham finished. Her fascination with the romances gave Cassie plenty of opportunity to collect the ciphers her father may have meant. It had even given her the excuse to ask Minton for more back issues which he'd somehow found. Somewhere in them was what her father referred to. And she had guiltily made Elaine an accomplice.

Elaine frowned. "I'm not sure. There's a new pair using the same cipher. But they're talking some nonsense about an inheritance. I've no patience with them." She brightened, returning to her real purpose. "That wasn't what I meant."

"What, then?" Cassie kept her sigh to herself.

"I saw you go into that room last night."

"I wouldn't have thought you could see that end of the ballroom from the card room." Useless to deny she'd gone into one of the side rooms if Elaine had seen her. Wearing black made her unmistakable in most any crowd.

"Oh, Lady Dysart stopped to chat when I was on my way back from the ladies' retiring room. That dreadful headdress. I forgot to tell you on the way home, but Mrs. McIntyre told me that the headdress was quite the wrong century for my gown. I was never so embarrassed. Then it kept slipping the entire night, and it was far too heavy."

Cassie murmured something sympathetic. Perhaps the diversion would work. Once Elaine finished her complaints about her costume, there were always the amusing oddities they'd both seen at the ball. Such as the man who'd appeared in full plate armor. He'd clanked and squeaked the entire night.

". . . that's why I happened to see you. Lady Dysart and I stayed talking in the ballroom through the next dance. Then I saw Randal!" she finished triumphantly.

Here it came. "You saw Randal do what?"

Elaine put her newspaper to the side and leaned forward on the daybed where she had gone to rest after a late breakfast. "Well." She lowered her voice dramatically. "Randal was dancing with that nice Loudon girl. She's so attractive and an heiress too, but they've never been attracted to each other." She paused thoughtfully before continuing. "Now where was I?"

"Randal was dancing with Miss Loudon," Cassie said wearily. Might as well get it over now as later.

"That's right." Elaine beamed at her companion. "Well, ordinarily, Randal is the greatest of gentlemen and his manners are exquisite. He's always careful to stay with a young lady after the dance until it's time for him to find his next partner. But *not* this time," Elaine finished portentously. The clock struck in the hall, its mellow tones sounding through the closed morning-room door.

Were they talking about the same man? Randal's manners were faultless in many ways, but he'd never been a paragon with her. In spite of her wariness, Cassie's lips twitched.

"Would you like me to ring for tea?" Cassie asked. "I know it's early, but last night was tiring."

"It can wait until Minton brings it in." Too excited to stay still, Elaine wriggled a little farther down on the daybed. "Do you know what happened?"

Cassie shook her head. She could guess, but why spoil Elaine's fun?

"Randal simply dropped Miss Loudon off in the general area of her mother and practically ran through the dancers in the direction you'd gone. Now what do you think of that?"

Cassie frowned at the picture Elaine presented. Could Randal have so far forgotten himself as to run through nearly four hundred people to her side? Cassie considered it for a fleeting second and dismissed it. No. Elaine was exaggerating to make a good story.

"It sounds unlike Randal," Cassie answered casually.

Rising from the chair behind the desk, she went

to her needlepoint frame which stayed in the morning room except on Elaine's at-home days. Cassie threaded her needle with soft peach tapestry wool and began on one of the lady's gowns. The elaborate hunt scene with a castle in the background was going well.

"He didn't precisely run," Elaine admitted conscientiously. She clasped her hands before her. "Anyone who didn't know him as well as I do wouldn't have noticed at all."

"I didn't think he'd have forgotten himself so far as to run in a ballroom." The needle went in and out steadily while the canary chose that moment to serenade them.

"That's not the point. He did hurry after you." Elaine paused expectantly for Cassie's reaction.

There was nothing she could say. Nodding calmly, Cassie finished the small segment she'd been working on. She turned the frame over to allow her to attach the peach tapestry wool to the next part of the lady's skirt where the color appeared.

Realizing Elaine was still waiting, Cassie asked casually, "Anything else?"

Elaine's shoulders slumped for an instant. She'd expected a greater reaction, some consciousness, some change in complexion. Then she brightened. "Not for quite a while. In fact, not until after the next dance was over."

"You didn't go back to the card room?"

"Of course not. I was chaperoning you. . . ."

Flushing for the first time, Cassie nodded. Elaine should have been chaperoning a good deal more closely.

"Well, I was about to follow you when Randal came out. He was flushed as though he'd been dancing, and . . . I don't know quite how to describe it." Elaine considered the memory. "He looked concerned and triumphant and elated all at the same time."

Cassie didn't need to hear Elaine's description. She'd relived the memory of the elation, both his and hers. Hers had been mixed with confusion. How to deal with this unsettling new development?

She'd never expected to find love at Lytham House. With everything that had happened that year, she wasn't sure where she was or what she planned to do. She'd always been strong-willed and impetuous, but now her life threatened to get out of control. It was the element of passion, she decided, that was adding the confusion. And passion's name was Randal. She'd relived every instant in his arms during her dreams last night. By the time the maid had brought her morning tea, she'd given in completely. Neither Randal nor the thought of him could be pushed to the side any longer.

"Then you came out a few minutes later. And I knew what had happened." Elaine continued, eyes as expectant as a puppy at feeding time. Clearly she expected Cassie to say something, admit Randal had kissed her.

"And what was that?" Cassie asked. Deliberately she selected a deeper shade of peach tapestry wool and threaded it. She kept her head down.

"Randal kissed you."

"Yes. But I fear he's not serious."

"How can you say such a thing? Randal's a gentleman, and a gentleman doesn't kiss a lady without serious intentions."

"This wasn't that sort of kiss." Cassie shook her head, nearly overwhelmed by her impulsive lie.

These feelings were too new to be discussed by anyone, even Elaine. If there were to be discussions, they would be only with Randal alone. But the hurt she'd cause Elaine when the real reasons for coming to Lytham House were known tore at her tender conscience. And now she'd been untruthful to Elaine again, her one friend, by hiding her feelings about Randal.

"Of course it wasn't that sort of kiss." Elaine smiled indulgently.

"A man at the ball insulted me," Cassie countered. She stabbed at her needlepoint. "Randal saw the confrontation and rescued me, but he had the next dance with Miss Loudon. So he joined me as soon as he could. He'd always meant to sit out that dance with me. This time he let his kindness carry him away. It was meant as a comfort only." Cassie was glad her face was hidden.

"Nonsense. Randal intends to marry you. I can see it in his expression every time he looks at you, even if you can't. You're just not used to dealing with situations like this. But you needn't worry. Lytham and I will see that everything is done properly. You must promise me, though, that you'll visit me. I'll miss your company every day."

Sighing, Cassie got up and gave Elaine a warm hug. Then she let Elaine happily proceed to lovingly plan each detail of the wedding down to the date and the church. Only one thing stood in her way: Cassie's mourning. Because Elaine couldn't stand for Cassie and Randal to wait until the year was finished, her plans were restricted. She finally condescended to a small wedding and returned to her interrupted deciphering.

Once Elaine was happily reading Emory's and Charlotte's latest scheme, Cassie gazed unseeingly at the tapestry, her hands stilled. Elaine's plans sounded wonderful. She'd forgotten one thing, however: Randal hadn't offered yet. Tortured by the thought of him, Cassie wondered how, without compromising her search for the truth about her father's death and lost fortune, she could encourage him.

He was one more looming uncertainty added to her other problems. Another problem, at least, should be solved soon. The next afternoon, she was to meet Neville, according to a message from her solicitor. He had the keys. And some news. She concentrated on that, and not on Elaine's plans and Randal's magic.


The coffeehouse was nearly deserted this late in the evening. Only a few merchants occupied the box seats at their end. Most were more interested in the candle auction which was to take place at the far end of the long, high-ceilinged room. Already tradesmen had gathered down there waiting for the candle to be lit and the auction of the contents of a bankrupt snuff shop to begin.

His lordship nodded with satisfaction. During the time it took a candle to burn an inch, they would hold the auction. No one would pay attention to two men discussing business in this box. Just as he'd planned when he saw the auction advertisement.

He sipped his hot chocolate and let his hand tremble with a hint of tension as he replaced the cup. Convincing Barnthorpe he was worried his identity had been guessed would be easy. But it couldn't be too obvious. His lordship smiled coldly as Barnthorpe entered the coffeehouse.

"Barnthorpe," his lordship greeted the man coldly.

"My lord." Barnthorpe ducked his head in a nod as he took the settle opposite his lordship. "The last cipher was most interesting."

"Hush! Don't call it a cipher here." His lordship darted a glance around to underline nervousness.

"Do you see any difficulty in complying with the message?"

Barnthorpe began to smile. Signaling a waiter, he ordered hot chocolate for himself before answering. Once the waiter had left, he leaned forward to keep his voice low.

"Kidnapping is a major crime."

"You'll do it?" The question snapped out with more cold clarity than his lordship intended.

"Of course, my lord," Barnthorpe answered promptly. He swallowed hard. His lordship's icy stare unnerved him. "Well, my lord," Barnthorpe continued with a nervous laugh, "as I told you in my ci—message, certain of our friends are growing restless."

"Can't you put them off?"

The arrival of his hot chocolate delayed Barnthorpe's answer. "I tried, my lord. . . . I really did." Barnthorpe licked his lips. "But they wouldn't listen. They want to know when you'll meet them. Most of all, they want to know what you've hired them for." He started to lift his cup, and changed his mind when the chocolate slopped over into the saucer.

Barnthorpe was nervous and excited. Excellent. Now, how best to handle him? He had to be handled delicately, not hurried.

"You tried to reassure them?" his lordship asked quietly. It was too early to show more than a trace of nerves. Another few minutes of betraying concealed tension should do it.

"Naturally, my lord. But Alfie wants that money. And even more to make up for their losses while they're idle. They'll want even more when they learn it's a sn—kidnapping."

His lordship's brow rose in disbelief. "I didn't realize crime was so lucrative."

"According to Alfie it is. I had to promise him that money and a hint of your plans so they could prepare themselves." Barnthorpe tried to smile winningly in the face of his lordship's cold gaze. His sleeve skimmed the hot chocolate. It soaked into the pale gray fabric as an ugly brown blotch.

"They needn't worry."

"But they do, your lordship. They do. And I've got to promise more money to keep them quiet. Can I tell them it'll be over in May?"

Eyes flicking over the blotch on Barnthorpe's sleeve, his lordship nodded once. "It will be over by the first week of May."

"All right," Barnthorpe said. He nodded in relief. "Did you bring the money for them?"

His lordship handed him a package. Barnthorpe pulled it beneath the rim of the table. There he unwrapped one end and counted the bills. Thrusting them into his pocket, he smiled with more confidence.

"Two hundred pounds. That should keep them happy for a while. It's a pleasure doing business with the Marquess of Rydal. Or should I call you Lord Randal? I'm never quite sure of the correct social usage in these instances."

His lordship stiffened and cast a quick glance at the rest of the room. As expected, all the other occupants of the room were gathered at the far end bidding on the snuff shop's contents. The rumble of noise covered any sound they made down at this end, while all eyes were fastened on the auctioneer.

"'My lord' is sufficient. You needn't worry about committing a solecism." His lordship held himself still, watching Barnthorpe for any sign of uncertainty.

"When one is moving in the upper circles," Barn-thorpe said, his smile widening, "one wants to be sure."

"You desire to move in such circles?"

"Why yes, my lord. I hope my fortunes will permit it soon."

His lordship looked around nervously. "They will. I can also arrange to extend your acquaintance."

"It'll take a lot of money to do it right."

"I'm aware of that. Shall we discuss it after our joint venture? In late May, perhaps?"

His lordship watched Barnthorpe's face closely. Had he given in too quickly? No, he didn't think so. Barnthorpe was too eager, too ready to believe in blackmail. Everything was going according to plan. Careful handling was still necessary. Nothing else.

Cassie lifted her face to the sun, savoring the sensation. Another glorious day. The top of the Crystal Palace glittered above the treetops in the distance. A new wave of tulips provided splashes of color against the tender green of grasses and bushes. They promised the coming summer, just as Neville and her collection of ciphers promised a solution. He surely had good news for her along with the keys. And Randal . . . No, she interrupted herself, this afternoon she'd concentrate on her appointment with Neville.

Hurrying to keep it, she caught an interested look from a man strolling down one of the paths in Hyde Park. Lowering her head, Cassie focused on the path before her and sped to her meeting. She hoped Neville was already there. That man was following her, though. With relief, she saw Neville near the Serpentine and increased her pace.

"A problem, Miss Cardwell?" Neville asked as he joined her.

The man who'd followed her passed quickly on the other side when he saw Neville with her. Cassie contrived to catch a glimpse of his face, but didn't recognize him. Undoubtedly someone intent on accosting an unaccompanied female.

"Not any more." Cassie smiled sunnily at him. "Isn't it a lovely day?"

Neville's bland face broke into a smile to match her own. "Indeed it is, an unusually warm one for so early in the year. Would you care to stroll this way?" He indicated one of the quieter paths. "Or would you prefer tea?"

"I've had tea. Unless you'd care for some?"

"Thank you, no."

Offering her his arm, he led her down the path. He waited until they were unlikely to be observed and put his hand in his pocket. Pulling out a ring of keys, he cradled them in his palm. They looked like those she'd seen in Lord Lytham's night-table drawer. Cassie stared at them for a moment, then raised her head, beaming.

"They're identical," she exclaimed.

"They should be. When do you plan to try them?" Concern deepened the lines in his face.

"Not until Lord Lytham leaves for his office, of course." Cassie considered. "And Lady Elaine goes for one of her naps. There's not much chance she'd let me stay home while she shopped. Especially not now." Neville raised his brows questioningly. "She's decided to refurbish the entire house in Gothic style. Lytham's supposed to be out of the house all day tomorrow, though, and Lady Elaine will be attending the opera in the evening. She'll want a nap. So I only have to wait until tomorrow afternoon to try the keys." She grimaced, remembering her disappointments when she'd tried to make the impressions. "If nothing happens."

"An excellent plan." He watched her slip the keys into her reticule. "Shall we stroll on? We aren't alone anymore."

Cassie followed his gaze in surprise. While they talked, several people had taken this path which led off the main walk along the Serpentine. A pair of young girls peering past the edges of their bonnets giggled and whispered about a group of young men ahead of them. Cassie smiled. She doubted she had anything to fear from either group. But Neville was right. The less they were seen together, the better.

"Lord Lytham is involved with this Great Exhibition which is to open next month, isn't he?" Neville asked after they'd lengthened the distance between them and the other two groups.

"Yes. But I don't think there could be a connection between the Exhibition and Papa's murder, do you?" Had her father discussed it much in the weeks between her arrival from America and his death? She couldn't recall any special mention.

His lips pursed, Neville shook his head. "That's one of the first things I wondered about, since there's been so much controversy over both the Exhibition and the Crystal Palace. But I couldn't find anything. The closest I can come to a connection is the Marquess of Rydal."

"Randal? I mean, Lord Rydal?" Cassie stared at him dumbfounded. "What's he got to do with Papa's death?"

"Nothing that I can find. Other than being Lytham's colleague at the Home Office and one of the guarantors of the Exhibition. Those are the only reasons I know his name. Is he a . . . friend of yours?" Neville asked delicately. His smile was paternal.

"Yes," she admitted cautiously. Although *friend* wasn't the word she'd choose. How to describe her relationship with Randal? To most of Society, they were acquaintances. Only in Elaine's mind—and in her own—was there anything more.

Knowing her silence revealed more than she wished, Cassie hurried on. "You had some news for me?"

Neville patted the hand which rested on his arm. "You're in a difficult situation, but it may soon be over."

Cassie stopped, looking up at him alertly. He had good news for her. From the moment she received Mr. Marshall's note, she'd hoped. She'd imagined all sorts of impossibilities, everything from solid evidence implicating Lytham to a confession. She waited expectantly for him to tell her how foolish she was, but knew he wouldn't.

"One of the clerks at McCrory and Chambers is meeting me tomorrow with information. I'm hoping it'll provide some solid leads. But," he added, seeing the bright expectancy in her face, "don't expect too much. It's only the records of your father's accounts. I can't be sure what's there."

"But you think you'll find something?" Cassie asked. She wanted him to say yes, though she knew he couldn't.

"I hope so."

Satisfied, Cassie turned to go on and stopped. "The clerk—how did you get him to agree to bring you the file? A bribe?" He nodded. "Do you need any more money? You never told me how much the garnet pin brought, but I'm sure it can't have been enough to cover a bribe."

"It brought twelve pounds, and you're right, it wasn't enough. I'll need more money. You'll get a complete accounting when we're done."

"Here's a pearl necklace." She pulled a small chamois bag from the bottom of her reticule. "It should be worth more than the garnets."

"Thank you, Miss Cardwell. You're a most efficient businesswoman." His eyes twinkled. "Are you sure you wouldn't like to work as an enquiry agent once this is done?"

"Not unless you need a cipher broken. That's the only kind of detective work I'm interested in. Did I tell you? I think I have enough of that suspicious cipher to really begin working on it."

"You'll let me know as soon as you've broken it, won't you?" he asked. He surveyed the strollers who were beginning to fill the park. "I'll send you a message through Mr. Marshall if I learn anything tomorrow. I think it's best if we're not seen together anymore. I'll follow you at a distance until you get a cab."

Cassie thanked him and left. She walked slowly toward the nearest entrance to the park. Turning back once, she tried to spot Neville and couldn't. He had mingled with the crowd so thoroughly he was invisible.

Dismissing him from her mind, Cassie relaxed to enjoy the lovely spring day, the soft breeze on her cheek. There was a definite bounce in her step as she rejoined the main walk leading out to the street. With the soft afternoon breeze stroking her cheeks, she paid little attention to other strollers. Until one blocked her way.

"Sir," Cassie began frigidly, then: "Randal. What are you doing here?"

"I might ask the same of you." A disapproving frown drawing his brows together, he drew her arm through his. "I don't see a maid or a footman."

"Oh." Cassie cast a quick glance over her shoulder. Neville was still invisible. "I came to the park on an impulse when I finished an errand. It was such a lovely day."

She watched Randal carefully while she spoke. Had he seen her with Neville? She didn't think so. She wanted to confide in Randal, tell him her suspicions. But she couldn't, no matter how much she wanted to. For the first time, she realized how awkward her explanations would be without evidence. How could she tell Randal she'd been spying on the Lytham household, on Elaine's husband, his friend? She couldn't. Not yet.

"These American ways," Randal said, exasperated. He shook his head, trying to frown, but laughter danced in his eyes. "Maybe I should say these *colonial* ways. But you must be more careful. A lady of your quality doesn't go walking in Hyde Park without at least a maid to escort her."

"I didn't realize Englishmen were so dangerous." She lowered her lashes rather than meet his gaze. She knew one Englishman who was.

"Quite dangerous. And if you're not careful, I may prove it to you." His hand tightened on hers resting on his arm.

Cassie met his gaze with calm directness. "I think you already have."

"Nonsense." His warm expression belied the brusque word.

"What are you doing here at this time of day? You should be busy at the Home Office."

"I was busy at the Home Office until we ran into a problem at the Crystal Palace." He gestured toward the gigantic glass house with its light blue painted ribs soaring above the trees.

Seeing the laughter in his eyes, Cassie asked, "What problem?"

"There are three young elms complete with birds' nests in the middle of the transept, and we've been having a small problem with their, uh, droppings on the exhibits. The Queen, in her wisdom, realizing the gravity and magnitude of the crisis exceeded the capacity of the Home Office, insisted we consult the Duke of Wellington. I expected he'd loose a bunch of marksmen. An admirable suggestion, you realize, in the middle of a glass building in the heart of London." Even though he smiled, Randal tried to appear downhearted they hadn't tried it. "Instead he suggested we use sparrow hawks."

"And that's what you've been doing? Chasing sparrows?" A giggle escaped her that became a full-throated laugh when Randal joined her.

"That's exactly what I've been doing. I'm bird-catcher *extraordinaire* by appointment to the Queen. Have you ever heard a more ridiculous waste of time for a Marquess, a Duke, and a Queen?"

# Chapter XI

"If I might have your bonnet, miss?" Minton asked when he opened the door. "Lady Elaine wishes to see you in the morning room."

Something had upset Minton. Reluctant to lose the bubbling sense of laughter Randal left her with, Cassie handed Minton bonnet, gloves, and cloak, then went to the mirror to check her hair. Pushing and patting at the wayward curls, Cassie finally made a disgusted face and turned to the butler.

"Is anything wrong?"

"No, miss." A shadow of long-suffering patience crossed his face. "Her ladyship has found some new furniture."

Cassie stared at him, mouth open, and fought the urge to laugh. "More furniture?" she asked.

"Her ladyship's redecorating the west drawing room."

"She just decorated it last year."

Minton's gaze was focused over her head as he answered. "Her ladyship has found some quite, uh, elegant new pieces. They're to be delivered the day after tomorrow."

"What about the furniture that's already there?" Cassie hadn't much hope for the answer. It was just like Elaine to refurnish an overcrowded room with little notice to the staff.

"She hasn't decided, miss." Minton looked exasperated.

Sympathizing, Cassie shook her head. "Does Lord Lytham know yet?"

"No, miss. He'll be late again this evening."

A small jolt of elation shot through Cassie. Elaine would have an early night after the exertion of shopping. The servants would gather in their hall. With the house all but empty, she could open the strongbox. She caught herself. Not too enthusiastic, or Minton would wonder. Cassie lowered her eyes.

"Did his message say what time we can expect him home?" she asked, trying to sound barely interested.

"Quite late. Do you think you—" He broke off, appalled at what he'd almost asked.

"I'll speak to Lady Elaine, Minton. Don't worry. We'll straighten things out." A look of resignation crossed her face. "But we may need to have footmen standing by to transfer furniture."

Relieved at shifting the burden to another's shoulders, Minton nodded. "I'll arrange it." Somewhat embarrassed, Minton looked at his feet. "It would be of assistance if we knew what time the furniture will arrive."

"I'll find out."

"Thank you, miss." Minton bowed and hurried down the hall.

A bounce in her step, Cassie went to the morning room. Outside the door, she paused and took a deep breath. Smoothing her smile away, she entered and closed the door behind her.

"My dear Cassie," Elaine exclaimed, "I have the most exciting things to tell you."

Ensconced on the rose daybed, her forest-green dress peeping through the cobweb-fine wool lace shawl covering her shoulders, Elaine plucked at the brown lap robe she'd thrown over her feet and struggled to sit up. Contagious excitement burned in her eyes.

Smiling, Cassie went to her chair opposite Elaine. "Minton's already told me."

"How does he know?" Elaine frowned in disappointment. "Lady Hester only told me today, and in the strictest confidence. Surely Minton—"

"It's not about the furniture?" Cassie broke in.

"Oh, the furniture. I'll tell you about that later." Elaine was nearly bounding with excitement.

"What's so momentous?"

Cassie picked up a pattern card from the table and fanned herself languidly. There was no need for a fire, yet one burned steadily in the grate. Half a room away, fortunately. The heat made the canary chirp sleepily. It should have made Cassie drowsy after the freshness of Hyde Park. And Randal. But it didn't. Her goal was so close now.

"You'll never guess," Elaine began. She untangled her feet from the lap robe and planted them firmly on the floor. Leaning closer to Cassie, Elaine continued portentously, "It's about Madeline and Welton."

The pattern card paused for a moment before Cassie resumed fanning. "They've eloped?"

"I knew you'd never guess." Elaine lowered her voice dramatically. "Madeline's forced her parents to consent to their marriage."

"How?" Cassie stared at Elaine in astonishment.

"She spent an afternoon with Sinclair at an accommodation house. After that, her parents had to consent to the wedding. I believe it will take place next week, but Lady Hester said that was still uncertain."

"What's an accommodation house?" Cassie asked, puzzled.

"It's a place where ladies and . . . and other females can meet their gentlemen friends unchaperoned and in privacy." Elaine flushed painfully.

Absorbing the implications, Cassie remained thoughtfully silent. Madeline must have . . . have slept with Sinclair. Cassie wasn't sure what that meant, since her grandmother, who had raised her, had always been reluctant to explain. But she could guess. Especially since meeting Randal. It meant Madeline had to get married.

Randal's voice sounded in her mind. "The little vixen." Cassie's memory flitted back to earlier that same day. Miss Norworth's. Of course. She *had* seen Madeline enter Miss Norworth's. Randal *had* guessed when she told him about meeting Sinclair there. Cassie blinked as Elaine's prattle broke through her abstraction.

"Such a daring solution, don't you think?" Elaine's voice held nothing but admiration.

"Yes, quite daring."

The words felt dry in her throat. To actually do such a thing—Madeline must be very certain of Sinclair's love.

"It's not the solution for everyone." Elaine eyed her narrowly. "But for Madeline and Welton, it's perfect. They've loved each other for such a long time, and Welton's never looked at another woman since her debut last year."

Feeling her way warily, Cassie asked, "She's only

been out a year?" Elaine's calculating look worried
her. Was she planning something?

"Yes. Her ball must have been, oh, let me see, a
year ago this month. She's done well for herself
even though Randal was my first choice for her.
But in less than a week I knew they were too much
like brother and sister. Then, when I realized how
perfect Welton was, I decided he should become her
husband. And now it's all come true. Just as I
dreamed." Elaine sighed happily.

Pushing herself off the daybed, she went to her
favorite couch and rang the bell for Minton. "Join
me over here and we'll have our tea."

When the tea tray came, Cassie put dundee cake
and various other pastries and scones on Elaine's
plate. Eventually, when Elaine had only a single
scone and a slice of sponge cake left, she had completed her plans for next week's wedding and
paused for a sip of tea.

Putting her own plate aside, Cassie asked casually, "Where do you plan on putting all this new
furniture you bought?"

Elaine was quiet for a second, then, "Do you
think I could send some of it to the country?"

"Do you have room for it there?"

"No, not really." Elaine's fingers tightened on a
rum-soaked sponge cake. It cracked before reaching
her mouth. She dropped it back on the plate to pick
up the scone.

"You could sell some things," Cassie suggested.
"But perhaps Lord Lytham would prefer not to?"

Elaine bit into the cream-filled scone. "Dearest
Lytham? He won't care," she answered with a hint
of forlornness. "I'll try to discuss it with him before
the furniture arrives, but I'll be out tonight."
Clearly, neither questions nor sympathy were welcome.

Keeping her voice tightly controlled, Cassie said, "I hope you're going to a lovely party."

Sighing, Elaine shook her head. "A most tiresome party at Lady Carruthers to celebrate the birth of her grandson. Since Lytham will be at the Home Office this evening, it's something to do." She sent a troubled glance at Cassie sitting, still and attentive, in her chair. "But you'll be left alone."

"I'll have plenty to keep me entertained," Cassie assured her. She added almost as an afterthought, "It could make things difficult since you won't see Lord Lytham until tomorrow evening."

"What things?"

"The furniture will be delivered the day after tomorrow, won't it?" Cassie reminded her. "And we'll need at least a day to clear room for the new pieces. Perhaps the delivery should be delayed?"

"Perhaps you're right." Elaine looked downcast. "But where will I find the time to take care of it?"

Cassie offered to do it for her. She'd regret it. But it salved a conscience aching from the desire to hurry Elaine out the door as early as possible. Soon Cassie had a list of Elaine's purchases along with their approximate sizes. At least it was a reason for investigating the house. Especially those parts she hadn't found an excuse for searching. Even better, she'd have the library to herself tonight.

With Elaine finally gone, Cassie told Minton she'd find places to put the new furniture. Certain that she wasn't likely to be interrupted, Cassie began her inspection in one of the drawing rooms while the servants retreated below stairs for their evening's rest.

When she'd finished there, Cassie stepped into the hall and listened intently. Other than the steady tick of the clock, silence filled the house. List of furniture in hand, Cassie strode to the library. She had the keys, the privacy, and the excuse. Everything was going as planned.

Not all the library candles were lit; nor were the gas lamps. In the shadowed light, Cassie drew the steps to the shelves holding Balzac and Dumas. A single lit candle ready on the desk, she climbed the steps.

The shelf swung out effortlessly. In seconds, the strongbox joined the candle. Faint tremors in her fingers made it difficult to untie the handkerchief wrapped about the keys. But eventually Cassie had them out and ready.

The first key was too large, while the next was so small it fitted into the keyhole all the way up to the ring. Cassie's breath caught in anticipation when the third one clicked into the lock. But it refused to turn. Frowning, she took out the fourth key. She had a sinking certainty it wouldn't work, but she tried it anyway. The last one was so large it hid the keyhole instead of fitting into it.

Cassie stared at the key ring. Had she made a mistake? She tested the keys again, then again. None worked. Eyes desolate, she stared at the useless key ring. Useless? The keys fitted something in the house. The key to the strongbox had to be somewhere. She had an excuse to go practically everywhere in the house. Finding it should just take time.

Disappointment fading, she slowly rewound her handkerchief about the ring and returned it to her petticoat pocket. Cassie mechanically replaced the strongbox and the library steps.

Picking up the candlestick, she slowly rechecked the room. She'd searched here several times already. Lytham should hide his secret here somewhere. But where? She checked everything in the room. Even the small Chinese vases on the mantel. She then left the library, filled with determination.

She'd search what she could tonight. Then continue tomorrow, and for however long she could delay the furniture's arrival. Her energy failed by the time Elaine returned home, but there was still tomorrow.

The next morning, Elaine altered Cassie's plans. Randal had used his influence to get them a private viewing of the Crystal Palace. Elaine stressed the word *them,* though she clearly meant Cassie. Another strain of excitement underlay her announcement. Her dearest Lytham had volunteered to escort Elaine.

"When?" Cassie asked. She lowered a forkful of sausage onto her plate. Pleasurable anticipation coursed past disappointment.

"When? Oh . . . I know I have the invitation about somewhere." Elaine searched the litter of invitation cards and thank-you notes surrounding her plate.

"You've known about Randal's invitation for some time?" Cassie accused, suppressing amusement. Elaine must have arranged the invitation with Randal. After all, Lytham could have escorted them by himself if all Elaine wanted was to see the Crystal Palace.

"I kept forgetting to tell you." Elaine blinked innocently. "Here it is. At half past two this afternoon." Elaine paused, then held out another carrot. "Randal's found out about Babbage's calculating engine."

Cassie smiled absently, refusing to fall into Elaine's trap. "I look forward to hearing what he has to tell me."

Four hours remained to search the house—more,

depending on how long she postponed the delivery. And Randal to look forward to this afternoon. While she searched, she'd think of an excuse to leave Randal, Elaine, and Lytham in time to meet Neville. This morning's mail had asked for a meeting at his office that afternoon. Pushing her half-full breakfast plate back, Cassie rose.

"If we're going to Hyde Park, I'd better get to work. I'll also write postponing the furniture's arrival. If you'll excuse me," Cassie said, turning to the door. Elaine stopped her before she reached it.

"I've decided to postpone going to the opera. I'm so thrilled at Madeline and Welton's wedding that I've invited them to have dinner with us tonight. I've asked Randal to even up our numbers." Elaine's smile dared Cassie to accuse her of matchmaking.

Cassie returned the smile. She wasn't even exasperated. More complications, although Randal was a welcome one.

Randal watched them descend from the carriage. The sight of Cassie sent another jolt of fury through him. Beneath her short cloak, her full, flounced shot-silk skirt caught a burst of sun peering through the dark clouds. The weave of the fabric made the skirt shimmer with color as she moved. She looked so young, pure, and innocent. Thank God, Lytham would be late. Randal couldn't have controlled himself if they'd arrived together.

How could he have failed to notice? A parade of images flashed past Randal's eyes. Lytham patting Cassie's hand solicitously, attending to her at the ball, watching her closely whenever Randal was near. What had Lytham said to Elaine? That she was overworking Cassie. Elaine wasn't the only one. Lytham even had the gall to warn Randal off. As if honorable intentions were a threat. Well, they weren't honorable any longer. He had to think of the Rydal family honor. He wouldn't marry another man's mistress.

Yesterday evening, he'd gone into his club's smoking room to read the newspaper. Instead, he'd heard two members talking about Lytham. And Cassie. If it had been Shelton, he'd have ignored it after the Dysarts' ball. These two men gained nothing by spreading rumors that Cassie was Lytham's mistress. And their logic had been damning.

After they left, Randal had slowly pried himself out of the deep armchair. All the way home, images of Cassie in his arms, responding to his kisses, his caresses filled his mind. Responding with a passion no innocent young girl should display.

She hadn't protested against his liberties. Any decent girl would have. Well, his decision was made. The future Marchioness of Rydal would be pure and innocent, not just seem that way.

Yet he needed Cassie in his bed, a need that raged relentlessly. She must have agreed to be Lytham's mistress to replace the money her father lost. Then she'd return to Charleston with a tale of widowhood and buy herself a husband. Why hadn't she come to him? Randal snorted. The question was foolish. They hadn't known each other then. They did now.

The idea inflamed Randal. One path to assuage this fever in his blood was closed forever. But Cassie would find replacing her fortune far easier with him.

The soft blush on her cheeks must be very useful. And the soft black of her velvet bonnet accented it nicely. But he knew better than to believe it. She was a consummate actress, though his instincts refused to accept it. How could she treat Elaine that way? Randal's rage increased. It didn't matter. Cassic wouldn't be at Lytham House much longer. Before the exhibition opened, she'd be his mistress.

"Cassie," Randal greeted her, bowing fractionally over her hand. Her artistic little quiver as he took it was effective. "I'm delighted Elaine persuaded you to come." He bowed over Elaine's hand, squeezing it warmly. "Why don't we go in? There's a little chill in the air."

The day was like many other spring afternoons. Dark clouds gathered with the breeze, and it grew cooler instead of warmer. Cassie hadn't felt it until she met Randal's eyes. She lowered her gaze and sedately fell into step beside him. Had something gone wrong at the Home Office? Or with his Aunt Maude?

They entered the west end of the Crystal Palace. A warmth that reminded her of a Charleston spring enfolded them. Casting an assessing glance around the rim of her bonnet, Cassie knew that now wasn't the time to ask him. His handsome face was closed, forbidding. For the first time she realized how arrogant and remote his profile could be.

With a final glance at Randal, Cassie split up with Elaine at the statue of Richard the Lionhearted near the entrance. The display of pearls, gold, and snuffboxes, a bust of Prince Albert's greyhound, and vases carved from substances such as coal and zinc attracted Elaine. The coal vases caught the gray light. From one angle they gleamed brightly, while from another they seemed to absorb the light flowing through the glass panels of the Crystal Palace.

A small glass engine house drew Cassie. Randal followed her, while Elaine examined the snuffboxes a few yards away. The engine inside, he informed her in a neutral voice, powered this "machinery-in-motion" section of the Exhibition. The bright brass and steel engine worked energetically within its cage, the glass enclosure muffling its sound.

Cassie moved slowly about the engine house until Elaine called her away into the next completed display. The intervening area was to be the last filled. It was for nonperishable foods, but no one at the Home Office trusted the manufacturers' claims. They would be examined regularly for spoilage.

The next display held Cassie enthralled. The latest in transportation, from carriages to locomotives, filled the area. Some locomotives, the placards said, could reach speeds in excess of thirty miles per hour. They were certainly sleeker than any she'd seen. Before she finished her examination, Elaine grew tired of looking at carriages, whether elegant or utilitarian.

While she disapproved of Cassie's fascination with such masculine interests, she was tolerant up to a limit. And she'd reached it. Under her firm direction, they swept out of this first machinery exhibition area, drifted past several heavily ornate pieces of furniture, and eventually emerged into the central nave.

Beneath the soaring glass transept, workmen carefully constructed a complex crystal fountain to soar high over their heads. At Cassie's insistence, Randal told them about it. All but the last few sheets of glass were in place now. Glass columns led upward toward the arching ceiling high above their heads, ready to carry water soaring high only to fall back into the pond surrounding it. The Queen's dais was to be placed before the fountain, Randal said, and she would declare the Exhibition open here. It was beautiful.

A workman jockeyed another piece of glass into the exquisite fountain while she sought an excuse to be alone with Randal. Listening absently to Elaine's exclamations, Cassie didn't notice Lytham's entrance or Randal's reaction to it.

Lytham's proprietary glance at Cassie sent a flame of fury through Randal. Jaw tense, he stepped around Cassie to greet his rival. The way Lytham's gaze sought her was disgusting. It was time to separate them, begin his campaign.

"Why don't you take Elaine over to the textiles section?" Randal suggested once greetings were completed. "And that new Gothic bookcase the Austrians sent the Queen? I'll take Cassie over the rest of the machinery."

Elaine wouldn't let Lytham search for them. He could begin once they were away from the workmen. Best of all, Lytham found nothing amiss in his offer to escort Cassie. It must have been a relief, since he couldn't give his mistress the attention she deserved with his wife present.

In fact, Lytham was looking inordinately pleased with himself. He laughed. "I've had enough trouble with the machinery in this place. But you shouldn't have mentioned Gothic furniture in front of Elaine. Cassie's had to find a place to put the new lot coming tomorrow." He patted her on the shoulder, his hand lingering there.

She moved back, a fixed smile on her lips. She took another step back until Randal's hard-muscled frame stopped her. Tension radiated from him. Tension and anger. Did he guess how loathsome she found Lytham's attentions? The thought pleased her.

Lytham gave her a strange look, then escorted Elaine toward the textiles section where exquisite fabrics had already been arranged for display. He cast quick, furtive glances back at Cassie and Randal as he and Elaine walked away. A chill shiver ran through Cassie each time he looked at her. At last, the other couple disappeared in the maze of corridors leading through the incomplete displays. She was alone with Randal.

His forbidding presence burned Lytham from her mind. She turned to smile up into his impassive face, wanting to ask what had upset him, yet not daring to. Behind his head, a flash of light made the glass fountain glitter for an instant before darker clouds extinguished the fire. His frosty expression was as dampening as the clouds, and her smile began to fade. Then she realized why Randal looked the way he did. Lytham's touching her that way had upset him. The thought warmed her, making her face light up beneath her black velvet bonnet.

Confidingly tucking her arm into his, she asked eagerly, "Elaine said you'd found out about Babbage's calculating engine?"

That should give him something to think about beyond Lytham's nonsense. Cassie let him lead her to the next section of completed exhibits. The strong muscle of his arm hardened beneath her gloved hand.

"It's not completed yet," he answered. "And it won't be displayed." His mouth tightened. "That woman mathematician, Ada, Countess of Lovelace, hasn't managed yet to devise a means of feeding it information."

They walked slowly through the machines in silence until they were isolated from the workmen swarming through the building. Around them, exhibits blocked the public's view through the building's glass walls. Randal reached over, took her chin in his hand, and raised her face to his.

"Then there's this business about the family jewels."

The color drained from her face. He knew she

was an heiress! He must even know about Neville
and her spying on Lord Lytham. Jealousy hadn't
caused his remoteness. Disgust with her duplicity,
her behavior toward Elaine, her friend, had.

"There are extenuating circumstances," Cassie
managed in a low voice. Hopelessly certain he
wouldn't understand, she met his frigid eyes. "No
one would choose to do it without a good reason."

His mouth twisted. "Some things can't be excused. Ever."

She must have lost him, lost all chance of having
his love. Stubbornly, she tried to make him understand. If only his mind wasn't too closed against her
now.

"You shouldn't judge until you know all the
facts, my lord." At her words, his hand tightened
on her chin for an instant before he released it.

His deep voice answered slowly, "You can know
all the facts and still condemn the action. Like father, like daughter."

"What?" Her pale face filled with confusion. Her
father had been spying on Lord Lytham? There was
no reason for Randal to think that.

Looking down his high-bridged nose, Randal surveyed her coldly. "Lord Byron enjoyed creating
scandals. Ada, his daughter, is just like him. She's
been pawning the family jewels to fund her little
hobbies. And doing other things I won't discuss in
mixed company."

Cassie's pale complexion rapidly regained a
healthy color. "Ada?"

Sardonic amusement lit his eyes. "You do remember we were talking about the Countess of
Lovelace?" His eyes bored into her. "What did you
think we were discussing?"

Flush deepening, Cassie tried to drop her eyes. To
no avail. His strong hand tenderly held her chin

captive once again. She swallowed with difficulty and raised her hand to touch his cheek. "Try to understand—" She broke off, unsure how to tell him.

Somber, he sighed heavily. His eyes took on warmth. "I do understand," he said softly. "If you'd only waited—"

"Beggin' your pardon, your lordship."

Both jumped, and Randal's hand dropped away from her chin as they stepped away from each other. They'd been so intent on each other, they hadn't heard the workman approach. Wiping his hands on his smock, he stood before them, a smirk on his scraggly-bearded face. Sure he had their attention, he explained his mission while his eyes lingeringly explored Cassie's slender form.

"We've got a big problem with 'at there refrigerator." He pronounced the alien word with difficulty. "You'd best come quickly, my lord, or Lord Lytham's orders could slow things down." He turned to Cassie, licked his lips, and removed his cap. "Sorry to interrupt your pleasure, miss."

Her nostrils flared with anger and mortification. "Not at all. I'm sure you need all the assistance you can get." She turned to Randal. "You'd best take care of this problem, Lord Randal. I'll amuse myself looking at the equipment." She gestured toward the glazier's machine standing behind them.

Temper darkening his face, Randal informed the workman coldly, "Tell the foreman I'll be right there. I think he and I will have some things to discuss besides the refrigerator."

Insolence faded from the workman's face, and he quickly excused himself. Still frowning, Randal turned to Cassie. "I'll be right back to finish this. You're probably more knowledgeable about these machines than I am, anyway."

Watching Randal thread his way through the

maze of corridors formed by boxed and unboxed exhibits, Cassie felt torn between tears and anger. Damn that man! What did he understand, and why should she have waited? After several minutes' thought, she banished the problem from her mind. If he'd learned her reason for being at Lytham House, she'd have to find a way to enlist his help. Though certain facets of his behavior still bothered her, she soon lost herself in the wonder of the Crystal Palace exhibits.

Everywhere she turned, there were fascinations, and they led her from the areas where displays were set up to where exhibits were just out of their boxes. Finally she reached an area which was all unopened boxes; stacked crates cast dark shadows in the uneven light. She was lost.

What little light the low clouds emitted found its way between the crates in strange patterns. She was alone; not even the workmen had penetrated this far.

The blue girders, with their orange trim visible only inside the building, took on a nightmarish quality as she picked her way through the packing crates. Splinters of rough wood caught at the wide, shot-silk flounces of her skirt. In the dismal light, she turned to retrace her steps when she heard footsteps. Strange reflections, echoing from the stacked boxes and glass- and steel-beamed walls, made their direction uncertain. They sounded muted, as if their owner wanted to remain unobserved but was defeated by the way sound traveled in this strange building. Stalking some prey—the thought flashed into her mind and refused to be dismissed.

It had to be one of the workmen. Or Randal. But if it wasn't . . . Cassie shivered and listened intently for other, welcome sounds of the workmen coming to this end of the Crystal Palace. If they were near, they'd surely hear her if she screamed. Then she wondered why she felt she'd have to.

Even while she tried to convince herself she was being foolish, she slipped back between the crates. Her small size made it easy to push her way through openings no one else—her mind produced the image of Lytham—could enter. The footsteps sounded closer. Breathless, Cassie pushed between one last set of crates and huddled down into the dark shadows. She gathered her full skirts about her, hoping the bright colors would not catch the eyes of her pursuer.

Almost as if their owner had heard the rustle of her skirts in the silent building, the footsteps shifted direction. They sounded as if they were heading directly toward her. Once again, the sound shifted, reflections bringing the footsteps close one moment and far away the next. She peered around the protecting crate, hoping to see the stalker, identify him. Then she saw his shadow. He stood at the end of the corridor formed by this row of boxes.

Bareheaded and wearing a carrick, he was definitely a gentleman. And the profile was distinctive. But that high-bridged nose could belong to either Lytham or Randal. If it was Randal, she could come out of hiding and go to meet him, blushing for her foolishness. But Randal had no reason to prowl stealthily about. If it was Lytham . . . Cassie remembered clearly the cold anger in his eyes when he discovered her in his wife's dressing room. Since then, she'd wondered whether he suspected her. Now she wondered even more.

The shadow moved about, never coming close enough to identify. He walked strangely, as though to cushion each step, but his efforts were defeated by the grate of leather on stone. Each step made a

small sound reproduced several times by the echo.
He was clearly looking for something or someone.

Breathing as quietly as she could, she feared he'd
come close enough to hear her racing heart. She
shrank back as he approached her hiding place and
lowered her head so that the black velvet of the
bonnet cloaked the pale gleam of her face.

The footsteps stopped at the mouth of her hiding
place, but she dared not look up to identify him.
For unnervingly long seconds, he stood there. Then
went on. He hadn't seen her in the dark shadows
surrounding her. Relief flooded her. She had to fight
the urge to escape her hiding place and run back to
the safe center of the hall.

Gradually, the footsteps died. Still, Cassie waited.
No sound reached her beyond gusts of wind against
the panes of glass forming the walls of the Crystal
Palace. Then, holding her skirts close to her body,
she crept back into the aisle. Carefully, stealthily,
she retraced her path back to where Randal had left
her. Alert for every noise, she heard only sounds of
the wind against the glass.

"Where have you been?" Randal demanded as she
rounded a last row of crates. Then, seeing her pale,
tense face, "What's wrong?"

She never knew how it happened. In the next instant, she was warmly, lovingly cuddled in his
arms. He let her tears fall for several minutes until
she recovered a little of her composure.

"Are you all right?"

Tears glistening on her lashes, she nodded. "I was
lost," she explained simply. "Some noises frightened me." Even now in the haven of his arms, she
couldn't bring herself to tell him. The sardonic look
replaced the tenderness with which he had soothed
her.

"You're safe now. Trust me." His hands moved slowly, sensuously over her.

"Randal?" Cassie said, uncertain.

He ignored her uncertainty. With swift, experienced fingers, he flicked open the ribbons fastening her bonnet. A sound between a groan and a sigh escaped him. He took her mouth with a wild, sensuous freedom that drew an instant response from her. She wanted to resist, but couldn't.

After her fright, she needed him, needed all he meant to her. The sensation of his hands kneading the taut muscles of her back, his rich masculine scent enveloping her, became her world. Then his hands moved, pulling her fully against his body. Willingly, she arched up into his kiss, responding to his embrace.

Before, there'd been restraint in his touch, as though he feared frightening her. Now, he took her lips and explored her body with delicious freedom. His tongue plunged deep into her mouth and stroked hers knowingly. A heated explosion shook her, and she responded with wild abandon to Randal's probing tongue, imitating his actions innocently.

His caressing hands, the excitement of his passionate mouth, sent shivers of pleasure coursing through her. They gathered and built deep inside. She'd never felt anything like this before. Yet Cassie sensed something else, something of overwhelming importance lay ahead. Mindlessly, she sought that experience.

"Cassie, where are you?" Lytham's voice barely penetrated her mind.

Shuddering, Randal pushed her away, his eyes flaring brightly with shared passion. "Not here," he whispered, voice husky. "Lytham's coming. Later," he promised. He picked up her bonnet and gave it to her.

Uncertain, Cassie stepped back, wavering for an instant. "Later?" she asked, voice hushed. Somehow she got the bonnet on and the ribbons tied under her chin.

She'd taken another step, a step that took her into unexplored territory. From now on, Cassie knew, she would never again be able to flirt lightly with this man.

"Yes," Randal agreed harshly. "Later. I'll see you tonight."

Nodding distractedly, Cassie turned to greet Elaine and Lytham, who were dawdling past the stacked crates. Lytham was searching for Randal and Cassie, with Elaine slowing the search. Then Lytham spotted them in the shadows.

Elaine greeted them reluctantly. "Cassie, remember your appointment with Mr. Marshall. Do you wish the carriage? Lytham will find a cab for me."

And have the coachman tell Elaine she'd gone to Neville's office rather than Mr. Marshall's chambers? "No, thank you, Elaine. I'll find a cab. There are always plenty near Hyde Park at this hour," Cassie finished, waiting for Randal to protest her going alone.

But Randal said nothing this time.

Accepting Cassie's refusal easily, Elaine chattered about the exhibits she and Lytham had visited. Fortunately, the chatter covered Randal's silence.

His face was remote again. His withdrawal baffled Cassie. Perhaps he was suffering from the same unfulfilled ache that disturbed her.

"We saw the loveliest clocks. And the Gothic furniture. I wish I'd seen the Exhibition before buying my new things. I wonder . . ."

"We need to find a place for the things you've *already* bought," Cassie said quickly.

"She wouldn't listen to me, Cassie." Lytham smiled too warmly at her. "Would you like us to escort you until you find a cab?"

Refusing Lytham's offer, Cassie hurried to the nearest exit and out to the roads surrounding Hyde Park. There she found a cab and gave the driver Neville's address.

The first spits of rain carried on the gusty wind chilled her further as Cassie burrowed into the corner of the hansom cab. She needed to sort out the events in the Crystal Palace. Randal's aloofness when they first met. Lytham stalking her . . . it could only have been Randal or Lytham, and Randal wouldn't do such a thing. Then her reunion with Randal.

A flush mounted her cheeks at the memory of their reunion. Her headlong, passionate response wasn't proper. But she didn't think it had shocked him. Randal hadn't behaved properly, either. Deep warmth at the thought that she could inspire such impetuous, passionate behavior spread through her. Concern soon diffused the warmth. He hadn't protested her going to Mr. Marshall's office alone. He always had before.

Once inside Neville's office, her concern deepened at the look on his face. It was serious. She braced herself and took the Windsor chair he held for her.

"Late yesterday, I received the papers I told you about." He took a seat across the desk from her and touched a file on his desk.

"What's the matter?" Breath quickening, she felt her breasts press painfully against her stays.

"Look at these."

He pushed the file toward her, then leaned back in his chair, watching her closely. Contracts written in fine copperplate handwriting filled the file. Puzzled, Cassie read the unfamiliar contract terms slowly. "I don't understand. What makes these contracts important?"

"Look at the signatures," Neville directed.

She turned to the end of one of the contracts. There was Papa's familiar signature. Then her breath stopped. Randal George Augustus William Wakefield, Fourth Marquess of Rydal.

Blood draining from her face, Cassie whispered, "It can't be."

"I'm afraid it is, Miss Cardwell. He's signed every contract in this file."

It hurt to see the pain in her face, and he focused his attention on his clasped hands. Finally he asked, "What do you want me to do now?"

"I . . . I don't know." Shaking her head, Cassie recalled Randal's tenderness, then the sardonic harshness which confused her. She loved Randal. It was unthinkable that he was responsible for her father's death!

"I've spent this morning checking the terms of these contracts carefully. He's a clever devil. There's no proof he's broken the law here, so we can't go to Scotland Yard. We can ruin Rydal's reputation, but that's all. We need more evidence."

"Is it possible he isn't guilty?"

Frowning, Neville shrugged. "He's guilty of misleading your father," he said cautiously. "He may not be guilty of your father's death." He paused to let the words sink in. "And there's no proof here of anything illegal or fraudulent in his dealings with your father."

"May I take these?" Cassie pointed to the file. "I'd like to read them. Since I know both Rydal and"—she hesitated—"my father, maybe I can see something you'd miss."

"You aren't planning anything foolish?"

Face hardening with determination, Cassie rose impulsively. "No, my foolish days are over. I'll send you a message if I learn anything. Thank you, Mr. Neville." She turned to go, then remembered. "Was there any difficulty in disposing of the pearl necklace?"

"The necklace brought far more than expected, Miss Cardwell." Neville came around his desk to escort her downstairs. "A hundred and eight pounds. I'll give you a strict accounting of our expenditures when we finish, but you'll receive money back."

"Thank you, Mr. Neville." Cassie smiled distantly.

What did a pearl necklace matter? Nothing in comparison to Randal. Or her father. That she still loved Randal stung as bitterly as the tears that stained her cheeks.

# Chapter XII

"Cassie . . . it's time to withdraw."

Elaine's voice interrupted Cassie's thoughts. Realizing where she was, Cassie mumbled an apology and rose to follow Elaine and Madeline. The men would remain in the dining room with their port and cigars.

Her eyes met Randal's. The memory of passion they'd shared that afternoon shadowed his expression. Her traitorous body responded with a surge of warmth. How could she? He'd defrauded her father. Punishingly, she added the remainder of her suspicions. He had probably murdered her papa, then set out to seduce her. He'd nearly succeeded, too. His failure was her only bitter consolation. Why had he done it? Money? He had plenty.

Then she remembered the rumors. He was over-extended, and he'd retrieved his fortune with her father's. Then murdered him when Papa found out? But why the cold, calculating seduction? She flashed him another glance.

He had the gall to look . . . upset because she'd ignored him throughout dinner. Or was he upset? The few times she'd watched him, she'd seen fury and something else.

Randal still watched as she closed the door. In that instant, she knew. He intended to corner her when the men joined the ladies in the drawing room. The certainty hit her with a sickening jolt. She wasn't ready. The image of his face hard, handsome, implacable danced before her for a second.

Following Elaine and Madeline, Cassie searched for an excuse to leave for the rest of the evening. Elaine wouldn't help. She'd been disturbed at the lack of conversation between Randal and Cassie before dinner.

"Of course," Madeline said as they entered the drawing room, "we can't go on a proper honeymoon until October." Trying to include Cassie in the conversation, Madeline smiled at her. "It's the dreariest thing to have to share Welton with the Exhibition. At least this season promises to be especially glittering with all the foreign visitors. Don't you agree, Cassie?"

"It should be most interesting." Cassie smiled wanly. "I'm sorry, my head's been aching all through dinner."

"I knew something was wrong. Would you like a cup of tea?" Elaine offered.

"No, thank you. If I relax for a few minutes, perhaps it will go away." She didn't want to lie, but she had to leave before the men joined the ladies. "You were saying about the season, Madeline?"

"This one will be such a delight. Tell me, do they have a season in America?" Madeline asked with sympathetic interest. "In . . . Charleston, South Carolina." Waving her fan languidly, she asked,

"Do you miss your American beaux? Or are ours sufficient to make you forget them?"

"They're more than sufficient," Cassie admitted with a touch of grimness.

"Oh, I hope so. Welton is a particular friend of Randal's." Madeline looked at her archly. "I hope we shall be seeing a great deal of you after Welton and I are married."

"Certainly if you continue visiting Elaine," Cassie agreed tactfully. Eyes narrowed at the light glinting off the bright silver and brass candlesticks, she massaged one temple.

"Well"—Madeline's lashes brushed her cheeks, then flew up to include Elaine in her confidence— "Randal seems most . . . interested. And you appear to not be indifferent. It will be nice to have Randal happily settled."

"I'm sure it will." Cassie winced as though pain had stabbed through her head. It had. Pain that bore no relationship to a headache. "Elaine, please forgive me. My head's becoming much worse. If you'll excuse me, I'll lie down in another room."

"Do you need help?" Elaine asked, half-rising from her comfortable chair.

"No, thank you." Carefully Cassie smiled at them. "I'll try to return in time to bid good-bye to your guests, Elaine. If I'm not able to, Madeline, I wish you happiness in your forthcoming marriage."

Madeline and Elaine undoubtedly suspected a lovers' quarrel. But they'd protect her from any prying on the part of the men. It would give Cassie the time she needed, the freedom to decide.

In the morning room, Cassie huddled down into the safety of Elaine's favorite sofa. Knees beneath her chin, she stared into the glowing coals of the low-burning fire. A few candles were lit in the sconce at the far end of the room. Their shadowy light provided the perfect counterpoint to her thoughts.

Finally she could think. She'd fallen in love with a murderer. A murderer she had to bring to justice. Her father deserved nothing less.

And what of Elaine? Cassie couldn't stay at Lytham House. It wasn't just that Elaine would continue to matchmake. How could Cassie tell Elaine she was a spy, a traitor to her friendship? That Cassie had played on her sympathies to send Elaine's beloved husband to the gallows? Or that the man Elaine had chosen for her was a thief, a liar, a murderer?

Unconsciously, Cassie stroked the black watered-silk skirt covering her knees. Her hand encountered the odd stiff section beneath her skirt. The papers. The evidence that could destroy Randal socially. She fought the urge to destroy them.

Unable to help herself, she turned the skirt up, then the first petticoat. The small package lay pinned below it. With clumsy fingers, Cassie unpinned it and drew the papers out to examine them. In the brief hour between returning to Lytham House and having to prepare herself and Elaine for dinner, she'd scanned the papers. And she still couldn't bring herself to believe them. Especially Randal's signature at the end of each agreement.

She'd reached the last page when the door opened and closed. In a rush, she stuffed them behind her and swung around to face the intruder. The dim figure approaching her was masculine. Lytham.

As the figure approached the low light thrown by the dying fire, her heart sank. Randal. His handsome face was hard, intent.

"Lord Randal?" she acknowledged tautly after stretched seconds of meeting his hooded gaze.

"Miss Cardwell." He took another step. The fire

threw his face into high relief, the fitful firelight highlighting his furious countenance. "I was . . . disappointed not to see you in the drawing room. Elaine said you weren't feeling well. You do remember we have something to discuss."

The words were conventionally courteous; he was far more formal than he'd ever been before. She stood up to leave. "Please excuse me, I have a terrible headache."

"Nothing too serious, I hope." With the stock courtesy, he came another step closer to her.

"No." Cassie paused deliberately before looking at him with great directness. "I simply need some quiet to nurse it." Why did he watch her so closely? Her face must betray her, including her hagridden uncertainty.

Blue-gray eyes narrowing, then softening, Randal covered the remaining few feet separating them in two rapid steps. "Are you all right?" he asked, taking one of her hands firmly between his.

He sank onto the sofa, pulling her down beside him. Tugging at her hand, Cassie edged back. His warm touch reminded her of what she'd lost. She shrank from him. Behind her, the papers crackled loudly in the silence.

His hard hand fastened on her chin, bringing her face up to his. "I know what you've done. . . . What's wrong," he assured her. "I can make everything all right."

Cassie stared at him. She swallowed hard and pushed herself deeper into the sofa arm. But she couldn't free herself from his grip.

"I doubt you can help." Her voice sounded dry, thin in her own ears.

Expression warmer than it had been since he escorted her home from Hyde Park, he stroked the soft skin along her jaw. "Trust me."

Terror mixed with warmth throbbed through her. His eyes held her fascinated. She jerked against his hand, determined to fight.

His fingers gentle, Randal traced the fine line of her throat. "I've always admired your profile. You're quite beautiful, you know." His tone was meditative. "No one need ever know."

Confusion joined the excitement trickling through her veins. Each delicate touch was a subtle enticement.

His seeming reversion to the Randal she'd known before today made her fight all the harder. He wasn't that Randal. His caresses were impersonal, yet they made it impossible to concentrate. What if he reverted fully to the warm, loving man he'd been before? She'd succumb. The thought terrified her.

A curious half-smile on his lips, he bent to kiss her.

Cassie jerked free of him and fled around the sofa arm. Her fingers digging into the overstuffed upholstery, she glared down at him. He began to rise, giving the impression of calm certainty that he could possess her at will. Her anger flared. "Stay where you are," she ordered.

It was satisfying to see the look of amazement in his lordship's haughty face.

But it lasted only an instant. He came around the couch. "I can make you forget him." His voice was silken, intent.

Without thought, her small hand swung in a short arc to land with a stunning smack on his cheek.

"Why you—" A handprint flaming on his cheek, Randal reached for her shoulders to shake her, but Cassie eluded him. At the far end of the sofa, she stopped.

"I may not have proof you murdered my father,

but the evidence of your fraud is plain." His mouth set in shock and amazement, he advanced on her. Cassie swallowed hard and threatened, "One more step and I'll scream."

As though struck, Randal halted. He stared at her, then shook his head. "I've never even met your father."

"Oh, haven't you?" Cassie said scathingly. "Explain these." She swung around the couch and pulled the papers from behind the cushion. Clutching them, she was satisfied to see doubt creep into his eyes.

Quicker than she, Randal snatched the papers from her hand, leaving Cassie white with rage. Fool. To let him get so close. Now he had her only evidence. Pulse pounding in her throat, she watched him examine the papers one by one. He'd deny his signature. He'd deny he'd met her father.

"This isn't my signature. It's close, but not mine."

Nodding resignedly, Cassie sank back onto the couch. "I expected you to deny everything."

"Expected me—Why you little—" Randal grabbed her arm. "Look," he commanded. His grip hurt when he pulled her closer to the fire. The dimming, flickering fire was dangerously close. He could get rid of all her evidence in seconds. She lunged for the documents. His grip was too strong.

"What am I supposed to see?" Cassie demanded, panting. Randal held her with negligent ease. "A postscript stating these aren't real?"

He ignored her. But he didn't toss the papers into the fire. Instead, he pulled her to the sconce holding the lit candles. Picking up a candelabra from one of the tables, he lit each candle. Cassie pulled out of his grip again.

"I'm not going to run away."

Something akin to hope comforted her. He'd had the chance to destroy the papers in the fire, but he hadn't.

Randal thrust her down into the corner of the sofa and joined her. He unexpectedly thrust the candelabra into her hands. Clear, soft light fell on each page. He brought two of the signatures together. "Look at them," he commanded harshly.

"They're your signature. Both of them."

"Really? Why are they so remarkably similar?"

"Because they were written by the same hand." Cassie darted a glance at his angry profile and dropped her eyes back to the pages. She continued, her tone icy, "Yours."

"Look at your father's signatures." He pointed at them. "Is anything wrong with them?"

Slowly, Cassie shook her head. "No, they're Papa's signatures."

He shifted the pages. "Now look at both of them close together."

Bewildered, Cassie looked up at him after studying them for several seconds. "I don't see anything."

"Look at them again. Look at the slightly different shapes of the *w* and the way the *l*'s trail off. They're different each time your father signed his name. Now look at my name. Each one is exactly the same."

He was right. Hope flared in her, but she forced herself to doubt him. Randal knew how he affected her. He knew she wanted to believe him. And she couldn't yet. Her father's handwriting did have larger variations. But her father was older.

"Please return the papers to me." Cassie extended her hand, not really expecting him to. "I'll have my solicitor contact you and give you every opportunity to prove your innocence."

Randal folded them and put them in his breast pocket. "I'll take these to your solicitor tomorrow with evidence to prove I wasn't responsible for these signatures." His face grew even grimmer. "Then to Scotland Yard to find out who's been forging my name. Now let's return to the drawing room. I've been absent too long, and so have you."

Cassie stepped in front of him. "If you don't return those papers to me now, I'll be forced to tell Lord Lytham you stole them."

Randal looked down at her. "I stole them from you. You stole them from McCrory and Chambers. This should make an interesting conversation. Go ahead and tell him. It'll make a spectacular end to the evening." He took her arm. "Come along, my little thief."

Once in the drawing room, she joined Elaine without another word to Randal. Beyond a sympathetic glance from Madeline, no one commented on her return. Let them think what they would. It didn't matter. She had more than a dozen hours to get through before she knew whether Randal was guilty or innocent.

If he was guilty, she'd never see the evidence again and she'd be in great danger from him. If he was innocent . . . then Scotland Yard would pay attention to the Marquess of Rydal while they ignored her.

"Cassie." Elaine shook her arm. "Cassie, my dear," she said in a gentle voice when she had Cassie's attention. "You look tired and unwell. Why don't you retire?"

Grateful, Cassie went up the stairs to her room. Weariness creeping over her like a fog, she prepared for bed and blew out the candle. In the fitful light of the fire, she stared at the regimented trellises filled with deep pink and red cabbage roses that climbed the wallpaper. When she first slept in the room, they'd looked like a garden decorated for a summer wedding. Now they—

She slipped into sleep while trying to decide what they reminded her of. More than an hour passed. Time ticked steadily off the small clock on her mantel. Cassie turned restlessly in bed until she lay on her side, one arm beneath the pillow, the other atop it, a faint frown on her face.

In her restless sleep she dreamed. She stood, dressed only in her nightgown, in the gallery of the House of Lords watching Randal stand trial before his peers. He wore a gray frock coat and darker trousers while his peers filled the benches dressed in scarlet and ermine robes, coronets on their heads.

Witness after witness took the stand. Some pointed to Randal as a murderer. Others chose Lord Lytham. Each time an accusing finger was pointed at Lytham, Cassie cheered and clapped until a huge man dressed as a Beefeater dragged her down to the witness box.

There they demanded that she identify her father's killer. Randal's eyes caught and held hers, his glowing with blue fire that proved he was innocent. Silence filled the House while tears ran down her face.

She cried out, but the sound of men rebuilding the Houses of Parliament drowned her voice. In desperation, her gaze tore free of Randal's and found Lytham's. His held an icy layer of sardonic amusement in their gray depths. She desperately wanted for him to be guilty. Without intending to, Cassie pointed at Lytham.

But no one believed her. Another Beefeater marched over and placed a black hood over Randal's head. For one last time before the hood descended, their eyes met. In that instant, Cassie wept. Absolute certainty filled her. She'd love him till she died.

As they led him away to the hangman's cart, Cassie awoke and sat upright in bed, a gasped "No" echoing softly back from the cabbage rose–covered walls. The clock on the mantel said it wasn't yet one. She'd been asleep less than two hours, and already the bed was a tumbled wreck.

Stumbling to her feet, Cassie smoothed the sheets as best she could, then hunched beneath the covers, deeply chilled. She burrowed to get warm, her hands freezing when she pushed the curls which had escaped her braids off her face. Before sleep pulled her back into another dream, Cassie vowed no matter who had killed her father, she would testify against him at the trial.

But a trial was the farthest thing from her dream. Randal had proven himself innocent. And he had tenderly accepted her apology with a soft kiss. His eyes sparkling with warm humor as they used to, he chuckled when she blinked up at him. Then his fingers gently trailed down to the neck of her nightgown.

Her hand caught his, but he gently put it aside before he found the tiny buttons fastening the high neck. Flashes of fire spiraled out from each brush of his fingers against her sensitive skin.

Cassie moaned as he gently caressed her taut, full breasts. But he didn't stop. He lay beside her on the bed, tracing patterns along the nape of her neck. His breath on her cheek was as arousing as his touch.

Then he deserted her nape, and his teasing caresses drifted lower. Cassie arched against the dream hands. Randal knew every secret of her body, secrets she'd never dreamed she possessed. With a low moan, she stiffened when he swept over the curve of her buttocks and down the slender length of her legs.

She couldn't bear it any longer. Cassie reached to pull him down to her, opening her eyes. And screamed soundlessly. He wore a black hangman's hood, his eyes a brilliant blue flecked with silver through the slits in the black cloth.

The shock woke Cassie, a cold sweat filming her body. She lay shivering crosswise on the bed, the quilts and sheet trailing on the floor. Bewildered, Cassie sat up and groped for the edge of the sheet at her feet. It was so cold. But her robe was on the floor beneath the quilts.

Staggering to her feet, she steadied herself on the wooden footboard. The fire was almost dead, and the room bore the chill of an approaching English early spring dawn. It was past three in the morning.

Shivering, Cassie pulled on her robe and retreated to the fireplace a little more steadily. She needed to feed the fire. Jerkily, she knelt to stir it and add a shovelful of coals to the flames. They caught, and a breath of warmth stole out into the room.

Huddled before the fire, Cassie considered her tumbled bed. Did she dare to sleep any more? After two such dreams? She pulled the robe lapels closer about her throat and peered up at the clock. No, she hadn't been mistaken. The clock downstairs had chimed half-past three. She had to sleep.

Stiffly, she rose from her knees and went back to the bed to pull the top sheet and quilts back into place. Nothing but a complete stripping and re-placement of bedding would make it truly comfort-able. But at least she'd be warm.

Cassie reluctantly removed her robe and climbed into bed. Pulling the covers up to her neck, she tried to relax her tense body. Slowly, warmth seeped into her bones and she did relax, tiredness pulling her down. She slept peacefully, one braid flung over her shoulder, the other a curly mass which had been neatly controlled in its braid when she went to bed.

But peaceful sleep failed as dawn grayness began to creep through the curtains.

This time Randal stood, hooded again, in a cart taking him to the gallows. Cassie ran beside him, her bare feet and hands icy. She begged him to show proof that he was innocent, but he merely looked down at her through the hood and shook his head.

Cassie groped for something, anything, to stop him, stop the cart, but her hands closed on nothing. A few tears trickled down her cheeks, and she turned to burrow into her pillow. The soft lavender scent of the freshly washed pillowcase changed the dream again.

Randal was beside her with the proof and had come to take her away as his wife. Cassie couldn't accept. She still had to find her father's murderer. Trying to explain, Cassie caught his hands and held them. The more she explained, the more adamant he became. He would marry her immediately. As soon as the banns were called.

Then he drew her into his arms again to kiss her. Only, they weren't the tender kisses she expected. She tried to turn away from his searching, demanding mouth. But she couldn't. Nor did she understand the demands he made on her, though instinct urged her on. The ability to think faded beneath the insistence of his touch, and finally she could only respond.

Pressure built to the point of pain deep within her. His hands swept from her sensitive breasts, across the soft curve of her stomach, to the apex of her thighs. The pressure exploded when Randal touched the burning center. Writhing, she arched up against his hand. She was one burning ache, and she wanted, needed him. Cassie reached for him when an alien touch disrupted the dream.

"Good morning, miss." Carrie had already opened the drapes before she woke Cassie.

The bright morning light was at odd variance with the dreams that had tormented her all night. They'd been so real she had difficulty realizing this room with its bright-faced, inquisitive maid truly existed. Cassie rubbed her eyes and stretched. Her protesting muscles quickly convinced her that it was truly morning.

She blinked blearily up at the maid who brought her morning chocolate. Pushing the hair out of her face, Cassie sat up.

"You've had a restless night, miss. . . . Something wrong?" the maid, Carrie, asked. "Can I help?"

Speculation lit Carrie's face as she put the tray down on Cassie's lap. Plainly the servants had gossiped about what had happened the night before. Carrie wanted the prestige of her confidence, but she'd reveal everything as soon as she returned to the kitchen.

"Nothing's wrong. I wasn't feeling well last night. Today everything's all right." If only she were telling the truth.

# Chapter XIII

Cassie gratefully closed the door of the morning room behind her. The chef, Emil, was telling Elaine his woes in preparing for next week's dinner party. Cassie approved the menus, yet he needed to impress Elaine with the difficulties he faced. And Elaine enjoyed his wild gestures and Austrian floods of imprecation at the stupidity of English suppliers.

However delighted Cassie was to avoid both volatile personalities, she was reluctant to be alone with her thoughts. Randal had filled her dream-ridden night, leaving her empty and aching. Perhaps she could lose herself in the ciphers. Cassie drew them out of the desk drawer where they were hidden.

For the first time, it was possible to compare the messages without interruption. Only the canary chirped quietly in the background, a calming sound that helped her concentrate. The messages were polyalphabetic, definitely, but how long was the key word?

If only she had some evidence Papa had worked

on these ciphers. There should have been signs if he'd made an attempt to crack them. One of her tasks in the days following his death had been going through his papers. She'd seen everything. There were no notes of possible key words. No letter-frequency analysis. Nothing.

Yet, he'd warned her against breaking the ciphers, then been murdered. Cassie frowned at the sheets of paper spread across the desk. This polyalphabetic was the only one it could be, yet he'd warned her against solving it. She kept coming back to those facts. The other messages in the *Times* had been innocuous. Only this one remained.

Her frown deepened. Letter-frequency analysis would be worthless unless they'd begun their enciphering at the beginning of the key word each time. She had only a dozen messages now, which wasn't enough to test that theory. Turning back to the messages, she compared them line by line, looking for a weak spot.

There. In two messages, three letters repeated. It could be a coincidence. Or it could be a short word enciphered using the same part of the key word. The most common English three-letter word was *the*. If that was the three-letter word group, then a quick calculation should give her part of the key word. IED. What words ended in those letters? Frowning again, Cassie jotted down several possibilities. None worked.

Rising to hunt for a dictionary, Cassie froze at a tap on the door. It couldn't be Elaine or Lytham. They'd never knock. Still— Cassie considered the revealing litter of papers spread across the desk. No one could be allowed to see this. She scooped the work together and bundled it into a drawer.

A second, louder tap came. She called, "Come in."

"Thank you, miss." Minton stepped into the room and closed the door behind him. His perceptive, impassive gaze noted the shadows beneath her eyes, and his expression softened. "The Marquess of Rydal is here, miss. Are you at home?"

"He doesn't know I'm here?" Had Minton noticed the barest hint of a shudder? He must have. Her cheeks flamed, then grew pale.

"Of course not, miss. He said to tell you he has a message for you."

Cassie checked the clock. It was past noon. He must have been at the solicitor's office when it opened. He'd proven his innocence, she decided on a flare of rising hope. Otherwise why come in person?

"Lord Randal didn't say what sort of a message," Minton added regretfully.

"Show him in, Minton. The message must be important or he would have sent one of his servants with it." Minton said nothing.

After Minton left the room, she hurried over to her usual chair and waited for the door to open again. Her hands trembled until she pressed them firmly together in her lap. What would he have to say? Dreams that had been successfully banished while she worked on the ciphers engulfed her.

"The Marquess of Rydal," Minton announced at the door. Randal closed it after he stepped inside.

Hands clasped firmly in the folds of her skirt, Cassie rose from her chair. "Lord Randal."

"Miss Cardwell," Randal responded with equal gravity.

He strode through the forest of tables and chairs until he towered over her. He looked as tired as she felt. Fine lines radiated from the corners of his eyes, and his mouth was tight. His frock coat and trousers were the ones he'd worn in her first dream. But

the heavy envelope he held out to her had no place
in any dream. It was too real, too important.

"Your solicitor sent this. He'll send separate confirmation by post."

Cassie took it and waved at the sofa. "Won't you
have a seat?" she asked. Her name was scrawled
across the envelope in Mr. Marshall's script.

"I prefer to stand." He retreated a few steps.

Sinking back into her chair, Cassie broke the seal
and pulled out the contents. Mr. Marshall's strong,
angular script crossed the page.

Dear Miss Cardwell: Lord Randal
Wakefield, Marquess of Rydal, has shown me
evidence which makes it possible for me to
state unequivocally that it is not in the realm
of belief that he signed the agreements ob-
tained by you from the firm of McCrory and
Chambers. The dates and other evidence are
such that there can be no conceivable possibility of error. If you wish to discuss this in
detail, please visit my office at your earliest
convenience. I remain, Yours, etc., Edwin
Marshall.

After reading it twice, Cassie looked up. "I'm
sorry you were put to so much trouble, Lord Randal."

"Then you're convinced I neither defrauded nor
murdered your father?"

Stiffly, Cassie nodded. "I appear to have done
you a disservice. Please accept my apology. May I
have the papers you took? I shall need them."

"You're certain your father was defrauded?"

"More so than ever," Cassie answered firmly.
The shadows beneath her eyes stood out harshly.
"My papers."

"I'm taking them to Scotland Yard. I'll find out who forged my name."

"I wish you more success with them than I had," she said bitterly.

He closed the distance between them in a single long stride. "Should I use my influence to get Scotland Yard to reopen your father's case?"

"It wouldn't help."

A wave of depression swept over her. Cassie folded the letter and tucked it back into its envelope. She was back where she'd begun. Scotland Yard would only take an interest in the Marquess of Rydal's problems. She crumpled the letter with one hand. Slumped against the back of the chair, she shaded her eyes with the other.

"Try me." The offer escaped Randal.

Raising her head, Cassie looked at him. "You wouldn't understand."

Her hand dropped back in her lap and she braced herself to explain. But he gave her no chance.

"I wouldn't?" The faint tenderness in his expression dissolved. "Then perhaps I can understand this."

He lifted her into his arms. Expression twisting sardonically, he lowered his head. The grip keeping her pinned hard against his chest bordered on pain. Even in his anger, his touch held a tinge of gentleness.

"No, Randal, please."

He ignored her plea, inexorably stilling her struggles. The practiced movement of his hands across her back, dipping below her waist, sent strong tremors through her. Tremors that fed on the sensations her dreams had awakened.

The experienced, coaxing brush of his lips tormented her. She had to get away. Trying to dodge his caresses, she shoved against his chest. His muscles were like iron. No matter how hard she shoved, it had no effect. Her traitorous body softened in response to his practiced caresses.

His face was hard, keyed to his own desires. Yet he kindled hers. Her entire body was a sensitive mass of nerve endings eager for his touch. As though tuned to her, his touch became gentler, coaxing, undermining her will. Knowing this was her last chance to escape, she tried again to struggle free.

Then his hand found her breast. Gasping at the arcing shock of sensation tearing through her, Cassie raised her head. Whether to beg him to stop or to capture his mouth, she never knew. Randal pounced on the small surrender.

His mouth released a torrent of sensation. She arched against the coaxing pressure of his hand, his mouth. The need to surrender, to reach fulfillment shattered her control.

A low moan escaping her throat, Cassie blindly sought the crisp silk of his hair where it curved about his ears and touched his collar. She'd dreamed these sensations, yet she experienced them for the first time. They exploded, seared, until only the need for Randal existed.

Her fingers kneading his shoulders, Cassie felt a qualm when he lifted her in his arms and carried her to the sofa. The cool draft on her breasts disturbed her more. Somehow, he had unfastened the tiny buttons to her dress. Instinctively, she fumbled at them.

Randal's warm, strong grasp stopped her fingers. "I need you."

His rich voice was deep, warm, inviting, yet . . . Cassie lost the thought as he lowered his head again. Darkness shot with glowing jolts of pleasure descended over her. Slowly, delicately, Randal explored the curve of her shoulder beneath her opened dress.

The silken touch of his lips sent flutters of heat through her as though he brushed her skin with burning feathers. The heat traveled onward and down until it gathered deep inside to blossom into an unbearable ache. Unable to remain still, Cassie twisted beneath him.

He muttered something as he lifted his head when he reached the embroidered lace edge of her corset cover. With new freedom, her hands explored his strong shoulders, tugged inexpertly at his cravat, the buttons fastening his vest. A strange smile lifting his mouth, Randal flicked open the tiny hooks fastening the corset cover, first one, then three more in rapid succession. A low growl of satisfaction escaped him when he pushed it back.

There, edged with the lace of her chemise and the ribbons decorating her corset, her breasts waited, taut and silken for his hands. He buried his face in the soft hollow between them. Just as he had in her dreams, he was possessing her, carrying her to a realm she'd never explored before.

"Cassie!"

Elaine's shocked voice tore them apart. Passion fading, Randal rose slowly to his feet and turned to face Elaine. Finally free, Cassie felt bereft. Then shame washed over her.

Randal's cravat hung half undone; the first two buttons of his waistcoat were unfastened. How had that happened? Then she realized her own state. Flushing, she drew her dress back over her shoulder and fumbled at myriad hooks, ribbons, and buttons.

Elaine absorbed Cassie's actions in darting glances as she advanced into the room. Planting herself before Randal, Elaine surveyed him disapprovingly.

"Rydal, your behavior is reprehensible. Save it for the bedroom after you're married to Cassie."

From her seat on the sofa, Cassie darted a glance at Randal, her clumsy fingers stilling on her dress. "Elaine, it's my fault."

Ignoring Cassie, Elaine stared hard at Randal, but, expression insolent, he said nothing. He tied his crumpled cravat with practiced motions.

Flaring temper lit Elaine's face for an instant before she softened. "There isn't any alternative. You've not only compromised Cassie, but the scandal that would hit me—" She broke off, flushing.

Randal shook his head. "We can't have that, can we?"

Her mind functioning with uncomfortable clarity again, Cassie sprang off the sofa and glared at both of them, hands on her hips. She stated with as much emphasis as she could muster, "I won't be married to a man against his will."

"My poor dear Cassie," Elaine exclaimed. "You don't understand. If this should ever come out—"

"My reputation would be ruined?" Cassie demanded. She didn't care. Two days ago, she would have leaped at the chance to marry Randal. But not this way.

Elaine watched Randal's set face. "And Randal would be socially ruined, to say nothing of his career in the Home Office."

Randal nodded once, abruptly. "I thought so." He looked from Elaine to Cassie. An internal argument raged across his face. Then the ironic smile Cassie had seen before returned. "Very nicely done. It appears I have no choice. I'll go to Doctor's Commons for the license."

Cassie caught his arm. "We only have to keep quiet."

"These things never stay decently buried," Randal answered negligently, plucking her hand off his arm. He didn't bother to look at her.

"Cassie, you don't know what you're talking about. Someone, probably the servants, will talk. Minton showed Randal in here more than half an hour ago. That's too long for you to be together unchaperoned. The servants must be talking already."

"But they don't know that anything happened."

"I can't afford to have my career ruined. Not now." Face remote, Randal looked down at her. "And this will ruin it." His gaze drifted back to Elaine. "You'll have to beat some sense into her."

Beaming, now that Randal had accepted his responsibilities, Elaine nodded. "My wedding, dress is in the attic. We can have it altered this afternoon. Oh dear, this is my at-home day. To avoid gossip, we'll have to postpone the wedding until four-thirty. Can you be back with the license by then?"

"If Cassie will tell me what her birthdate is."

Expression mutinous, Cassie looked from one to the other. Both returned her gaze: Elaine sternly admonishing, Randal impassive. The clock in the hall gave a single bong, and the canary stirred to give a thin trill of song. One o'clock. They expected her to marry Randal in three and a half hours?

Shoulders slumping, Cassie's hands dropped listlessly to her sides. They were right. Randal would be totally ruined. Elaine would be abused for her companion's actions. And Cassie would lose all opportunity to find her father's murderer.

What should she do? Cassie knew she was weakening, and the satisfaction in Elaine's face said she knew it, too.

But why was Elaine so satisfied? Then Cassie remembered their conversation after Madeline had achieved the altar. Elaine thought Cassie had deliberately trapped Randal. He thought she and Elaine had plotted it between them. She was compromised. There was nothing she could do.

"My birthdate is March 15, 1830," she said in a low voice.

"The Ides of March." He didn't continue.

"Do you need to know anything else?" Cassie asked stonily.

"No. I'll be back in a few hours." He went to the door. "Oh, Elaine, should I arrange for the vicar? Or would you prefer to?"

"Our own vicar will be happy to officiate, I'm sure. And I'll send the announcement to the *Times*. Now, come along, Cassie"—she held out her hand commandingly—"we have a great deal to do before Randal returns."

As when her father died, Cassie had the sensation of walking into a nightmare. She caught a last glimpse of Randal's face. He didn't want to marry her. She would have sworn he did, only a few days ago. Why had he changed?

When he escorted her home from Hyde Park, his teasing, the glances they shared, everything about him had been tender, gentle. Then he'd changed. It hadn't been her accusation of complicity in her father's death. The change had come before that.

When they were at the Crystal Palace, his behavior had been unusual, not like the man he'd been the day before. Confusion filled her, and she was trapped in it.

"Cassie! Don't just stand there. We have so much to do."

Elaine's voice jolted her. Jerkily, Cassie went slowly into the hall, closing the door behind her. There was no avoiding it. She was to be fitted for her wedding dress.

"My dear," Elaine began when they were on the second flight of stairs. She panted lightly at their fast pace. "I couldn't be more delighted. It's been my dream for you to marry Randal. I didn't imagine it would be so soon, though. You must promise to visit me regularly. I shan't know what I'll do without you. Nor will the servants."

Cassie nearly missed a step. She would have to leave Lytham House. If Randal wasn't guilty, Lytham was the prime suspect.

"You will visit me?" Elaine repeated warmly.

"Yes, of course, I will."

Visiting Elaine was the only way. Yet it hurt to use her friend. Blast Randal. If he'd controlled himself, she wouldn't be forced to marry this way. Or if she'd controlled herself, she added honestly. She could have found some way to stop him.

"I'm so glad. Now hurry and tidy yourself while I have Simmons take my wedding dress out of storage and brush it down." Elaine put her arms around Cassie and gave her a big hug. Tears trickled down her plump cheeks. "I'm so happy for you."

Guiltily, Cassie slipped into her room and sank down on the dressing-table bench. How had it all happened? Her reflection in the mirror gave no answer. Then her appearance registered.

Most of the pins had fallen out of her hair. Only a few tenuously held the remains of a chignon. The rest of her hair curled and straggled wildly about her face. Randal must be responsible, although she didn't recall his touching her hair.

Then there was her dress. Half the small black lace collar stood up against her neck, while the rest of it was tucked inside. The front of her dress was misbuttoned, too. With a trembling hand, Cassie plucked at the collar, then her remaining hairpins.

Her mind blank, she brushed out her hair and

straightened her dress. When she finished, Cassie went down the hall to Elaine's room.

"See what Simmons found." Elaine held up a sheer lace veil that would sweep the floor when it crowned Cassie's head, and a circlet of silk orange blossoms. "I wore these at my wedding, as did my sister. We've both had such happy marriages that I wanted you to wear them too. You'll make such a lovely bride, my dear." A glitter of tears stood in Elaine's eyes.

Cassie blinked back her own. Elaine was doing her best to make it the wedding of her dreams. Touching the fragile lace of the veil gently, Cassie looked up at Elaine and smiled mistily.

"You will be my matron of honor?" she asked huskily.

"Of course, my dear. And dear Lytham shall give you away."

"You've told Lord Lytham?" Cassie asked sharply.

"I sent a message to the Home Office requesting that he be home by four since something of importance was happening. Now, let's try on the gown and see how it fits." She signaled Simmons, who had been standing patiently by. "The hem will have to be raised, but I think the rest will be perfect. You'd never believe it, but I was quite as slender as you when I was your age." She giggled sunnily.

Cassie unbuttoned her dress and stepped out of it with Simmons's help. In moments, she was hooked into Elaine's wedding dress. It was fashioned in the style of the mid-thirties. The neckline ran straight across from one shoulder tip to the other with large bows decorating them. The sleeves were puffed with another ribbon, then fell fully to slim cuffs. If the sleeves were odd, the waist was even stranger. It caught her on the rib cage only a few inches below the bust. Yet, the full flowing skirt that dragged the floor on all sides was charming. But best of all it wasn't black. It was a soft ivory silk.

She stood still while Elaine and Simmons darted around her exclaiming at the picture she made. An odd, floating sensation disassociated her from them. Cassie had last seen her mother alive in a dress very like this. And now she was to wear one for her wedding day.

While Cassie contemplated her reflection, Simmons settled on the floor with pins to mark the hem. Elaine was right: it was the only adjustment necessary. In less than half an hour, Simmons had pinned the hem, helped Cassie to change back into her clothes, and departed with the wedding gown to finish it.

"I'm delighted with your marriage," Elaine repeated once the door closed behind her maid. "It's the perfect solution for you."

Cassie's eyebrows rose in recognition of Elaine's one-track mind. Elaine was firmly convinced Cassie had planned today.

"Perhaps."

"Nonsense. This takes care of all your problems. Now you won't have anything to worry about."

Except tonight, Cassie whispered to herself, except tonight. What would happen when she left Lytham House this evening as the new Marchioness of Rydal? Randal wasn't the same romantic tease he'd been. Then she remembered her dreams. And the sensation Randal had drawn from her only an hour earlier. Yet he'd been so impersonal. A shiver went through her.

Elaine came sympathetically forward and pressed Cassie's hand. "Let's sit down over here. You must miss your mother at a time like this."

For a moment, Cassie didn't know what she was

talking about. When she realized, healthy color tinted her cheeks. "It's not necessary, Elaine."

"Oh, but it is, my dear. No one helped me, but I told my sister. She said it made her wedding night much easier."

"I really—"

"Now I won't hear another word. Just listen."

In brief, conflicting, confusing detail, Elaine told Cassie what to expect on her wedding night. Cassie felt more bewildered than ever when Elaine finished. If Cassie had been tense before, now she was afraid. Elaine cloaked everything in euphemisms, and her graphic description of the pain was at strange variance with the wonderful joy Elaine said to expect. Apprehension joined worry over Randal's inexplicable behavior.

As Cassie left Elaine's room, the clock in the hall downstairs chimed two. Two and a half more hours. There wasn't enough time left.

No matter. The wedding would go on whether she was willing or not, and no amount of dithering would change things. Cassie squared her shoulders. First she had to retrieve the cipher notes from the morning room before Lytham returned home. She dreaded Lytham's finding those ciphers.

With a quick look in both directions, Cassie hurried down both flights of stairs. The servants would either be occupied or resting or, most likely, discussing her rushed wedding. Cassie didn't want to meet any of them. Not yet. Not until the ordeal was over.

Luck was with her. On the ground floor, the hall and the morning room were empty. After gathering up her notes and the newspapers, she searched the desk thoroughly for anything else. Checking the hall to make sure it was empty, Cassie darted up the stairs with the bundle of papers.

The rest of the afternoon passed in a daze of packing and fittings. Simmons, her plain face dour, brought the wedding dress to check the hem before taking it away to press. Then she was back to help Cassie into it.

The trunks were packed, the ciphers tucked into the small bag that would go in the carriage with her, and she had changed into her wedding dress.

The chimes from her mantel clock echoed the single mellow bong of the clock downstairs. Time for her wedding. Cassie froze with her hand on the doorknob. She dreaded going down. But it was four-thirty.

# Chapter XIV

Randal wanted to reach out and comfort Cassie when she sank into her seat in the carriage. She looked so dazed. So innocent. His expression hardened. Too bad it wasn't real.

What was it Pearce said? "A neat parlay to have your wife hire your mistress as her companion. No cold trip at some ungodly hour when you're ready to climb back into your own bed."

They'd be whispering behind his back when the announcement appeared in the *Times*. The rumors would run that Lytham had foisted his discarded mistress onto him. And it was true. Although Lytham hadn't discarded her. His expression when he learned about the marriage had been sulphurous.

That was the one satisfaction in the entire mess. There weren't any others. When he'd first contemplated making Cassie his wife, he'd assumed she was as innocent as she looked, as inexperienced as she seemed. She must be a consummate actress.

Look at her now. Her still form gazing out the

window was the picture of purity. It was false, but a
perfect picture anyway. At least he couldn't blame
her for entrapping him. That was his own fault,
making love to her when Elaine could walk in on
them. He should have expected Elaine's reaction.

It was the easiest way of getting rid of her husband's mistress. Elaine would do anything to protect her dearest Lytham. And Randal had been
stupid enough to furnish the opportunity.

Eyes somber, he watched Cassie's small, cloak-
covered figure, her wedding gown hidden beneath
it. She'd been bewitchingly lovely, despite the old-
fashioned style. He'd have a wife, a political hostess,
to be proud of at his side. But first to put a stop to
the rumors about her. With Welton's help, that
would be easy. If only they weren't true.

Cassie started to turn her head. Randal jerked his
eyes to the window on his side. He couldn't speak
to her now, not and maintain the fiction of courtesy
between them.

Outside, a mist had begun to fall, coating the
cobblestones and brick buildings. The chill damp-
ness of another changeable spring evening forced its
way into the carriage. He neither saw nor felt it.
Pictures of the brief wedding and of the even briefer
toasts formed against the backdrop of buildings and
streets.

First there'd been the moment Cassie entered the
drawing room. He'd almost lost himself in the delight of her beauty. But the wreath of silk orange
blossoms in her hair reminded him of her duplicity.
His frown deepened at the memory. If he'd needed
any proof of her brazenness, her attire had provided
it. Orange blossoms were the symbol of chastity.

Then Lytham placed Cassie's hand in his. It felt
small, cold, in his grasp. Randal couldn't restrain a

warm, reassuring smile. With it came the satisfaction of seeing Cassie relax the smallest bit.

His fury returned when Lytham asked casually about Cassie's wedding and betrothal rings. How to explain that he'd found the time to go to his bank for the Rydal family rings despite the afternoon's rush. How to explain that even to himself.

After Lytham's curiosity about the rings, Randal hadn't been able to get out of the house fast enough. He hadn't permitted Cassie to change, but had hustled her into his carriage. Now she'd have to meet her new servants dressed like that. He stifled a flicker of sympathy. She'd used him. Let her pay for it.

But she didn't have to.

Once out of the carriage in the misting drizzle, Cassie had handled Pryor's presentation of her to the servants beautifully. She'd soon have his servants as much under her thumb as she'd had Elaine's, Randal decided cynically. Moving gracefully from one to another, she charmed each. Including his secretary, Glanville, and the girl Randal'd chosen as Cassie's maid.

"Have you ordered dinner to be served in our rooms, Pryor?" Randal interrupted harshly. The happy amity surrounding Cassie was irritating. Randal refused to look at his wife.

Pryor turned and bowed with majestic disapproval. "Yes, my lord. In one hour."

"Good." Randal looked at Cassie's new maid. "Fairleigh, take her ladyship up to her room, please. I shall see you at dinner, Cassie."

His precise bow and silent departure upset Cassie. But she wouldn't let the servants see her distress. Smile fixed, Cassie followed the maid up to her new room to change out of her wedding dress and into familiar mourning clothes.

Black was appropriate for her marriage. Randal had made his distaste clear. He'd barely spoken to her since Elaine toasted their health. Cassie hadn't minded during the carriage ride. But this abrupt rudeness in front of the servants!

Even if she'd been guilty of trapping him, she didn't deserve this. Except that wasn't his only reason. She'd accused him of defrauding and murdering her father. Cassie suppressed guilty sympathy for him. Perhaps, in his view, he did have sufficient cause for his behavior. A future filled with Randal's silent condemnation made her sigh as she dismissed Fairleigh.

Knowing her mood was simply a reflection of her nerves, Cassie looked about for something to keep her occupied. Her luggage was already unpacked, and not even the ciphers held the power to attract her this evening. She could explore the suite of rooms she was to share with Randal. Tension clutched her stomach at the thought. Would she ever be able to face Randal with anything approaching ease?

Abandoning her fruitless thoughts, she slowly examined her room, then went into the adjoining sitting room. Furnished in the light, airy style fashionable a generation ago, it was spaciously decorated in cream, gold, and pale blue luxury. Her room overlooked a small garden to the back. It was too dark to see now, but Fairleigh had assured her that Randal's mother had frequently taken her tea there when the family was in London.

A sitting room connected the bedrooms. Although smaller than either, it didn't have the appearance of an afterthought. Cassie could easily imagine working on her petit point here in the mornings. Or pouring Randal's tea. The image brought her up short, and she nervously banished Randal again.

In Randal's room, the furniture wasn't so light as in her own. Instead, it was elegant yet firmly masculine. Here the colors used in her room were deepened and reversed. A deep rich cream and gold accented deep blue hangings and wallpaper. Curious, Cassie moved about the room, examining velvet drapes, a satiny dressing table, the carved post of the bed. All were immaculately neat and clean after the cheerful jumble of Elaine's home.

But beneath the comparisons, other, more important thoughts ran. She stared at the bed. What would happen there in a few hours? Curiosity consumed her, yet she didn't want to know. She only hoped Randal had changed.

The sound of voices in the hall made her stiffen. Randal. She refused to be caught inspecting his rooms. Hurrying back to her own, Cassie found the cream-and-gold-figured damask drapes drawn against the murky evening. A small fire burned in the grate. Fairleigh had prepared the room for the evening. Cassie extended hands suddenly cold with nerves to the fire's heat and waited. The short burst of energy that had taken her on the tour was gone.

The wait wasn't long. The door swung open, and he stood in it. He'd removed his frock coat and replaced it with a brocade smoking jacket. Its velvet lapels and cuffs gleamed dully against the rich blue cloth. Leaning against the doorjamb, his eyes were dark, unreadable. The past hour hadn't changed him.

"You've resumed your blacks."

Cassie nodded. "It's customary when there's been a death in the family."

A flash of compassion lit his eyes. But he was distantly courteous. "Pryor's brought up our dinner. Won't you join me?"

"Certainly, my lord," Cassie answered, her voice colorless.

As she passed, his hand twitched. In silence, he accompanied her and held a chair at the small gateleg table Pryor had placed before the fire. On it, the first course waited in individually covered bowls. After seating her, Randal removed the cover from his thick mushroom soup.

"You'll find Jean-Paul the equal of Elaine's Emil," he said when she sat unmoving.

"What? Oh." Cassie returned to her surroundings and removed the lid covering her soup. If Randal could be coolly courteous, so could she. She took a spoonful and smiled. "Yes, he is."

She took another spoonful and let it settle warmly in her stomach. Here was why she felt so distant. She'd had neither lunch nor tea, and only a sip of champagne when Elaine prodded Lytham into proposing toasts to the bride and groom. She recalled the anger in Lytham's eyes as he pledged their happiness. He wouldn't be pleasant to Elaine tonight.

Her concentration was so great that she dropped her spoon when Randal's lightly tanned hand took the empty soup bowl away. So much for being coolly courteous. The butterflies of apprehension held at bay all afternoon returned in force, and she looked up at Randal with a fixed smile on her face.

"Sorry," he said perfunctorily. "I told Pryor we'd serve ourselves. He expected that"—Randal's gaze skimmed over her—"newlyweds would prefer to be alone."

She slid her chair back a fraction. "Would you like me to serve the next course?"

"That's not necessary." He took their empty bowls to a small sideboard along one wall to return with small servings of the fish course. "Jean-Paul feels newlyweds have small appetites, doesn't he? But we know better." There was an odd intimacy in his tone.

What did he mean? Something beyond the obvious. Her breath fluttered in her throat as she met his eyes. The innuendo was beginning to unnerve her. She raised her chin and answered him levelly.

"Not when one of the newlyweds has had nothing to eat since breakfast."

"Poor little Cassie."

"You've had just as trying a day," she said briefly, tasting the lobster in champagne sauce. She ignored the subtle mockery in his words.

Randal met her gaze over a pink-and-white morsel of lobster. "Trying? Success is never trying." Licking up a suspended drop of sauce before popping the lobster in his mouth, he contemplated her with half-closed eyes.

Her fork clattered onto the plate. "If you'll remember, my lord, I refused your offer of marriage. Nor did I attempt to ravish you."

"I beg your pardon." A self-mocking smile crossed his face as he changed the subject. "Do you often go to Miss Norworth's?"

Why such a question? To ease the tension? Not with that expression in his eyes. Her skin prickled as though she were chilled. Only, the room was almost too warm for this dress.

"I've been to Miss Norworth's only once," she said with an attempt at normalcy. "They had an utterly charming hat designed for half-mourning. I saw it that day I met Mr. Sinclair."

Then she remembered. Elaine had said Miss Norworth's was an accommodation house. Madeline had used it to force Lady Albinia into letting her marry Welton Sinclair. Why had Randal insulted her? She'd been forced into this marriage as much as he had.

"However charming the hats Miss Norworth's sells, I want you to patronize another milliner."

Furious, Cassie rose with her empty plate and extended a hand for his. "Certainly, my lord."

Silently, she went to the sideboard for the main course. The chef had chosen delicate lamb with the freshest of spring vegetables, all perfectly seasoned. Cassie carefully took the food from the silver serving dishes and arranged it on willow-green and gold china plates and took them back to the table. Though it was the best meal she'd had since arriving in England, neither heavy and rich as Emil's, nor bland as Papa's cook had prepared food, it tasted like sawdust.

Cassie responded formally to Randal's formal conversation. He described their itinerary for the year and when they would visit each of his homes. He apologized for not being able to take her on a wedding trip, but his duties at the Home Office prevented it. In the fall, once the Exhibition closed in October, he would take her to Rydal. In the meantime, she would have to amuse herself.

Listening numbly, Cassie began to dread what would come once they finished this meal. Soon those mysterious rites which would take place in that deep-blue-and-gold-hung bed would be mysterious no longer. But she didn't want to banish the mystery. She wanted to sleep in her own bed, not with the stranger Randal had become.

Plates which had held slices of a superb apple tart glistening with apricot glaze sat empty on the table. She didn't remember eating it. Randal rose to his feet and tossed down his napkin.

"Come along," he said brusquely.

Cassie rose slowly to her feet.

She couldn't look at his face. It was time; she placed her hand in his. It burned into her with a beckoning, frightening heat.

Cassie turned toward her room. "I'll ring for Fairleigh."

"You won't need Fairleigh tonight," he said, drawing her toward his room. "I'll help you."

He led her inexorably into his room. Her world shrank to that single burning contact between them. He stopped before the fire burning strongly in his room and inspected her pale face and slight form with detachment. "It isn't necessary, Cassie," he said, softly intent. "Remember, I know. I told you last night."

She stared up into his face. The pulse beat heavily in her throat, and she swallowed with difficulty. His gaze touched the pulse, then went back to her face.

Randal's mouth twisted wryly. "You do it so well."

He bent to take her mouth with harshly sensual freedom. His lips branded hers as frighteningly as the heated summons of his hand. Cupping the back of her neck, he forced her to meet his gaze. The hard glitter in his blue-gray eyes died. His hands grew gentler, and he leaned down to place a kiss in the soft cleft in her chin.

"It's all right." He sighed. "Come along."

Still bewildered at his abrupt change, Cassie obeyed the tug of his hand. In a large wing chair, he drew her down onto his lap and held her. The heat from his touch should have bothered her. But it didn't. She could almost believe herself back in the safe haven his arms had provided before. The safe haven that was truly Randal.

Then his fingers went to her throat to undo the tiny jet buttons marching from neck to hem of her dress. She tried to move away, but his hard grip at her waist wouldn't let her. His softly exasperated warning in her hair made her stop her struggle.

Something of her frozen incomprehension penetrated Randal's exasperation. His hand stilling on the fine buttons, he slipped his fingers beneath the springy curls of her loose chignon. Gently, he pried her face out of his shoulder and made her meet his gaze.

"I won't hurt you," he promised quietly.

Cassie blinked up at him. The warmth in his blue-gray eyes was the Randal who had kissed her during Elaine's charades. . . . Elaine had said the first time would hurt.

The frighteningly intense anger that had radiated from him at odd times during the day was gone. Instinctively she cuddled down into his lap and met his gaze. He said he wouldn't hurt her. She believed him.

"What do you want me to do?" she asked. He was her husband; she'd do her best to be his wife. Whatever that meant.

A low chuckle escaped him. "First, let me finish what I was doing."

With efficient fingers, he unfastened the long remaining line of buttons down the front of her skirt. Then lifted her to her feet and slipped her dress off her shoulders to let it fall on the floor.

"Don't bother," he commanded when she bent to pick it up. He ignored the faint color that deepened steadily in her cheeks.

Cassie straightened to stand before him, her dress a black pool at her feet. He reached for the tabs fastening her crin-stiffened petticoats at the waist. They too slipped to the floor, a white froth on the black pool. Cassie watched his handsome face. It was intent, but not frightening.

"Why you women wear such things," he murmured, shaking his head.

He flicked open the hooks of the corset cover. The gentle brush of his hands against her, the way his eyes touched Cassie, even through the remaining layers of fabric, sent delicate shivers racing through her. She shifted restlessly in the growing pool of clothing.

Even the inadvertent brush of his hands against her skin was a demanding summons. And the touch of his eyes— A shiver shook her. She started to reach for him, to tug at his tie, and thought better of it. Something—amusement?—lit his eyes.

"It's the fashion," she said huskily.

"What?" Randal barely heard her. Her small figure held all his attention. He drew her into his arms and covered her lips with his.

Heat flashed through her from a dozen different sources. His hands gently explored her. His lips tenderly possessed hers. The hard bands of muscle pressed into her breasts and stomach. When he held her back from him, disappointment welled and she tried to keep him with her. Then she realized he intended to finish what he'd begun.

A fine tremor shaking his hands, he reached for the row of hooks fastening her ribbon-trimmed corset. With the ease of an experienced lady's maid, he removed it and tossed it on the floor with an exciting hint of roughness. Without knowing how she knew, Cassie realized his control was deserting him. Next he turned to the buttons fastening her pantalets, and the garters holding up her lisle stockings.

In seconds, she stood before him, chilled and feverish at the same time. Wherever his gaze touched flamed, but the room which had seemed so warm before was filled with drafts now. Her toes dug into

the thick woolen carpet; it was all Cassie could
manage not to lift her hands to shield herself from
his gaze.

Mouth dry, Cassie tried to swallow. The instinctive motion broke some dam of emotion in Randal.
He pulled her into his arms and lowered his head.
The silken abrasion of his smoking jacket, the brush
of velvet and brocade against her soft flesh were incredibly arousing.

Cassie melted bonelessly into his strong grasp as
devastating kiss followed devastating kiss. This was
the Randal who'd kissed her on that makeshift stage
at Elaine's. After stretched moments that lasted forever, he raised her high against his chest to carry her
to the turned-down bed. She tugged the ascot tie
about his throat loose, then pushed at his smoking
jacket.

Randal's deep laugh as he lowered her onto the
sheet barely registered. Only the cool crispness
pressing into her bare back and Randal were real.
Swiftly unfastening shirt studs, he leaned down to
kiss her gently. Passion edged his touch, and a haze
of desire enfolded her.

Color flamed in her cheeks as Randal finished undressing. She couldn't tear her eyes away, even
though she thought she should. The enticing combination of satin-smooth skin and curling whorls of
hair over taut muscle held her prisoner. Swiftly the
muscular columns of his thighs with their thick
matting of tawny gold-flecked brown hair emerged
when he discarded the last of his clothes and turned
to face her fully.

Men were so different, Cassie thought, dazed.
Excitement glittered in his eyes, silver sparks dancing in the deep blue. He gently caressed her. His
fingers trailed over her small, rounded breasts, then
explored the fine dip of her waist and the rounded

flare of hips and stomach. Cassie moved sensuously, instinctively beneath his touch. Her fingers dug into the sheet beneath her and a soft sound rose deep in her throat.

Then he was lying full-length beside her, propped on one elbow, his free hand moving over the soft curve of her stomach toward her legs. This time she couldn't restrain her gasp. The beckoning heat concentrated beneath Randal's hand.

Her hands clutching his hair-roughened shoulders, Cassie raised her eyes to meet his. The shadows of the dimly lit room masked his face. But the turmoil that the furnace of his body created glowed in her eyes.

Then Randal bent over her. Trailing a string of kisses down her throat to the slope of her breast, he stroked and caressed, nibbled and tasted every inch of her body. Each touch, each kiss caused waves of fire until she was wrapped in flames that burned without harming. She writhed beneath him, unable to silence the desire he created.

She needed him. Clutching at his arms, his chest, his back, even his thighs, Cassie tried to bring him closer to her so that he could fill this relentlessly burning ache deep within her.

Uncontrollably aroused by her innocently passionate response, Randal positioned himself and thrust into her. Incredible pain burned through the desire consuming Cassie. Blinking back tears, Cassie forced herself to relax her sudden spasmodic grip on his shoulders. Passion no longer hazed her mind.

A beautiful smile swept across Randal's face. Controlling his taut body, he bent over her. His kisses were a gentle persuasion that slowly returned her to her dreams. She could feel him holding himself in check, taking the time to rekindle her desire. Trembling, Cassie clutched at his arms, his shoulders, stroking his hair, exploring his strong back with inexperienced hands.

"Gently, Cassie," he whispered warmly into the tumble of curls near her ear. "Relax and let it come."

Then he began moving gently within her. Uncertainly, then eagerly, she imitated him. Reality faded away as her world exploded.

Gradually it came back in focus and small things, small sensations returned. The distant tick of a clock. A draft teasing her side. And a beloved weight that rested lightly the length of her body. Randal. As he lifted his head from its resting place on her neck, Cassie opened her eyes. She needed to see him in this first moment, needed to see him when she told him she loved him.

"I'm sorry," he whispered against her ear. Slowly he lifted himself away and withdrew. "Go to sleep, Cassie."

She fought back tears. He held her, but he'd become distant. Unsure why he apologized, she craved reassurance. But pride kept her from asking. Closing her eyes, she willed herself to sleep. As she finally slipped into a light sleep, a few tears escaped and trickled down her cheeks.

Hours later, the flickering light of a candle fell across her face. Frowning, she turned, seeking the warmth that had lain beside her. Only, he was gone. Murmuring, Cassie stretched a hand to find him. The sheet had been warm, but now was cooling. A low chuckle brought her back toward the candle's bright light as she opened her unfocused eyes. Randal.

A magnificent ruby brocaded robe hung casually from his shoulders, shadow and light hinting at the tawny whorls of hair covering his body. Blinking back the sleep, she stared in fascination, then fiery color rose in her cheeks. Amusement crinkled the corners of his blue-gray eyes, and he set the candle down on the night table and settled on the bed beside her. Watching closely, he touched her shoulder, rising pale and satiny above the sheet and warm woolen blanket.

"How do you feel?" he asked softly when she neither tensed nor shied away.

The weight of his hand grew heavier, warmer, more comforting as it started moving over her. "Fine," she answered with equal softness.

It was as if she looked at him with new eyes. All the uncertainties of the evening were gone. She loved him deeply, but she couldn't tell him. Not when he'd been forced to marry her. Yet she needed to do or say something. Without intending to, she brought her hand from beneath the cover and traced the fine hair on the back of his wrist, her lips pouting with innocent invitation.

Delight darkening the blue of his eyes, he accepted the invitation. Leaning slowly forward, he sensuously explored the line of her jaw, dropped a kiss in the cleft of her chin, then flicked it with his tongue and found her responsive lips. He deepened their kiss into a sensual duel that seemed to go on forever.

As he lifted his head, Cassie met his gaze with shy willingness. Already a gentle warmth flushed her body from his touch. She reached up to loop her arms about his neck. And the blanket fell to her waist. Gasping, she flung herself against his chest and hid her face in his throat. Crisp masculine whorls of hair covering his chest brushed her breasts and sent a surge of passion through her.

"It's proper, little one. We are married."

His gentle, amused voice snapped her head back. "I had noticed, my lord," she said, trying to frown admonitorily. At his humorous expression, she giggled and burrowed into his neck again, while his hands swept beneath the tumbled, silken mass of hair to caress her back.

Tentatively, then with more certainty, she nibbled a trail of kisses along the line of his jaw. All the sensations she'd been too inexperienced to enjoy flooded over her now. She arched against him and nearly gasped at the soaring flame of pleasure. The taste of his skin beneath her lips. The enticing caress of his hands smoothing her back and the rounded curve of her buttocks. All kindled a fire deep within her that flared with each touch, each movement.

Randal gathered her fully into his arms, murmuring softly, passionately. She wound her arms about him as he laid her down in the middle of the bed. The lingering warmth where his body had lain enfolded her. He removed the remainder of the sheet and blanket covering her slender form and tossed his robe to the foot of the bed. It lay, a vivid, ruby splash of color against the mahogany, half on, half off.

Stretching out beside her, his eyes grew deeply blue and glittering with silvered flecks. With one gentle hand, he stroked from breast to hip. Cassie began to writhe uncontrollably with innocent sensuality. The need to touch him, to return this overwhelming pleasure, grew in her. Eyes heavy-lidded with desire, she stroked his cheek, the taut line of his neck, then his chest as he bent over her.

The curls of tawny brown hair tangling silkily beneath her fingers reflected gold in the candlelight. It massed around masculine nipples, then arrowed down to draw her on. Cassie traced its path, then gasped at where it led. He chuckled softly, the silver flecks dancing in his eyes. His firm lips closed over the crest of one rounded breast in a jolt of pleasure that was almost pain. Then her eyes closed convulsively.

Sensation soared through her until she trembled as ardently as he did. With abandon, Cassie surrendered to the exquisite pleasure of his touch.

Tenderly, he enjoyed the power of her total response and he explored the length of her pale, slender body from the perfect arch of her small feet to soft thighs, tiny waist, and the full globes of her breasts. His teeth and lips grazing her soft skin were flames licking over her body. She clutched at him, helplessly trying to bring him closer. Hovering above her, his eyes met her heavy-lidded gaze for long moments before he lowered himself fully onto her.

He moved gently within her, slowly building toward a crescendo. A haze of passion overwhelmed her. She responded eagerly to his touch, moved as one with him until they both reached a shattering climax at the same instant.

Minutes or hours later when awareness returned, Cassie snuggled close to her husband's side. He kissed her affectionately. Later, she could tell from his steady breathing, he slept. Before slipping off into sleep, though, he tucked the blankets warmly about her. How thoughtful, she thought drowsily, cuddlying closer into his shoulder. If only he loved her.

# Chapter  XV

A cold breeze fanned her bare shoulder. Mumbling a protest, Cassie snatched at the blankets and found nothing. A low masculine sound roused her from sleep, while a chill drift of silk touched her bare skin then withdrew to float over her again. Drowsily, Cassie batted at it. It drifted across her again, insistently. It wouldn't let her sink back into sleep.

Blinking, she pushed herself up on one elbow to search for her tormentor. A warm hand that wasn't her own tucked her tousled curls back behind her ears. Her eyes automatically followed to where a heavy ruby velvet cuff brushed the hand. Her gaze trailed up the sleeve to meet gleaming blue-gray eyes. Randal. Slow color climbed her cheeks.

"Good morning," he murmured and bent to brush kisses over each eyelid and her mouth. "I trust you had a good night's sleep."

Cassie nodded jerkily. "It was excellent," she answered, then realized what she'd said.

Well, it had been excellent. Especially the second time they made love. His tender attentions had banished her tears. For all her confused explanation, Elaine had been right. A loving husband was a delight. Randal's firm lips twitched.

"Thank you. I'd give an encore if it weren't for an appointment at the Home Office. So my sleepy wife has to get up. Pryor's bringing breakfast to the sitting room for us." He extended the confection of lace and silk he'd used to tickle her awake. "Put this on. As much as I enjoy you in that state, it might shock Pryor."

His warm, tenderly affectionate gaze drifted over the bare skin revealed by the turned-down blanket. Flush deepening, Cassie grabbed the mass of silk and lace from his hand. Holding it to her breasts, she waited for him to leave.

Randal met the appeal in her eyes with a smile. And waited.

Sitting up, Cassie winced at the soreness, but her eyes remained firmly on her husband. "Randal, please leave. Or at least turn around."

He bent down and planted a kiss on the tip of her nose. "Do you really want me to?"

Surprising herself, Cassie stretched up one arm to bring his head down to hers again and sketched a kiss along the corner of his mouth. He tried to draw her into his arms, but she held him sternly off.

"You have an appointment at the Home Office this morning, my lord," she reminded him.

"I could always cancel it."

"Umh, what a lovely idea."

She curled her knees beneath her and winced again. Randal's eyes narrowed with concern. He dropped another light kiss on her lips and straightened, going to the door leading into their sitting room.

"Unfortunately, it's with the Prime Minister. I can't cancel it." His gaze swept over her kneeling on the tumbled bed, the nightgown and peignoir barely concealing her lovely body. "Get up," he warned, his voice suddenly husky, "or the Prime Minister will have to wait."

The click of the door closing galvanized Cassie into motion. Hopping off the bed, she pulled the soft silk nightdress over her head, then pushed her arms through the sleeves of the peignoir. What she saw in the mirror made her grimace. Her hair hung in a tangled mass down her back.

Randal hadn't given her time to braid it. Was it going to be like this most mornings? Somehow, she suspected it would. If it was, she intended to have a brush in his room as well as in her own. This morning, she'd have to make do with finger-combing it and hope Randal wouldn't comment on the rather . . . wanton look it gave her. *Wanton* was the word she wanted. She'd never understood it before, but she did now.

Her image in the mirror was startling. More aware. Softer, yet more vibrant. Even though she'd worn silk nightgowns before, this one caressed her body. It was an odd, intriguing experience. And if she didn't hurry out to the sitting room, Cassie was certain she'd be in for another intriguing experience.

"I was about to come after you," Randal said softly. His ruby velvet robe crusted with gold embroidery accented the silver sparks of deviltry in his deeply blue eyes.

"Ah," Cassie shook her head, breathlessly playing up to him, "but the Prime Minister comes first." She paused. "Today of all days."

"For today," he agreed. "But I'll break away for a few weeks after the Exhibition. Is something wrong?" he asked abruptly. Cassie's expression had

altered subtly, her brows drawing together in a faint
frown, a shadow dimming her smile.

"Wrong? I—" Cassie halted. "I think we should
let the servants give us breakfast before I explain."

"The servants have already brought breakfast
up." He indicated a row of covered silver serving
dishes where their dinner had waited for them last
night.

Going to the sideboard, Cassie took a plate and
batted her lashes at him outrageously. "May I serve
you?"

When he refused, she filled her plate at random
from the dishes the cook had prepared. They ranged
from a revolting dish called *kedgeree* she'd first encountered on her arrival in England, to simpler
bacon, eggs, sausage and ham, and a rack of toast.
Pouring a cup of tea, she retreated to the table and
waited for Randal to join her. He wasn't going to
like this.

When he took the chair opposite her, Cassie
smiled tentatively at him. The smile died when his
expression didn't alter. This was going to be more
difficult than she thought.

"It's about Lord Lytham," she began with difficulty.

She stirred her scrambled eggs intently with her
fork. It would be easier without looking at him. As
quickly and briefly as she could, she told him her
purpose at Lytham House, what she believed, and
the sort of evidence she'd tried to find.

Finishing, she raised her eyes to Randal's face.
Whatever she'd expected, it wasn't this. He stared at
her, disbelieving. Then launched himself into a fit of
laughter. Her mouth tightened. What had she expected? No one but Mr. Marshall and Neville had
believed her before this. And they were paid to.

When he finally stopped, he looked at her, then

quietly rose and went around the table. Bending down, he kissed her. "It isn't what you're thinking, Cassie. Your husband is neither crazy, nor does he think it's funny." He paused reflectively. "I'm laughing at my own stupidity. No. I can't explain now." He returned as quietly to his seat, but his shoulders still shook a bit.

When he'd controlled his amusement, he asked, "You seriously believe Lytham killed your father?" At her nod, Randal frowned. "So, you think a guilty conscience prompted Lytham's offer to make you his wife's companion. Or that he wished to keep an eye on you after you complained to Scotland Yard that your father was murdered?"

"There's no other reason for him to offer me two hundred pounds a year to act as Elaine's companion. I was grossly overpaid."

Randal silently nodded. As she continued, he returned to his kedgeree, ham and toast.

"He always wants people to think he's the most generous man in London. But he could have hired me for half the salary and still have gotten the credit for his generosity. No." Cassie shook her head firmly. "There's only one reason to offer me so much money. I worried him. He wanted to keep an eye on my activities. And"—she paused significantly—"my accusations."

"Yesterday," Randal murmured, "I thought—"

He broke off, flushing. Startled, Cassie watched him intently. What was wrong? First the laughter and now this apology in his expression.

"Cassie, about last night," he began again.

It was her turn to flush painfully. "There's no need to explain. I understand how angry you must have been. To feel trapped into marriage with the daughter of a bankrupt suicide. But Papa didn't commit suicide, and I intend to prove it. And I'm an heiress."

"What?" Randal wiped his fingers mechanically on a napkin and dropped it on the floor rather than the table.

Smiling, Cassie nodded. "When Grandmother died just before Christmas, she left me fifty thousand pounds in jewels. Quite a respectable dowry, wouldn't you say?"

"Quite respectable." Randal stared at her. "Your father knew about this?"

"I told him when he met me at the docks. So you see why I had to spy on Lord Lytham," Cassie pressed on inexorably.

"Yes, I suppose . . ." His voice trailed off thoughtfully. "But that wasn't what I—"

"Papa knew we weren't bankrupt," Cassie interrupted rapidly. "He had no reason to end his life." Tears welled in her eyes. Whatever Randal wanted to explain could wait. She had to convince him to push Scotland Yard to investigate.

Randal shrugged. "Yes, I see your reasons. But why Lytham? It could have been someone else."

"Who else could it have been? Lytham sent Papa to McCrory and Chambers." Cassie pounced on the implication of Randal's slight frown. "You already know how trustworthy McCrory and Chambers' dealings are. They forged your name."

"Yes, I'm going to Scotland Yard today. Are you sure you want me to bring your suspicions to their attention?"

Some of the intensity drained from Cassie's face. "Will it do any good?"

"Perhaps. It's a bit difficult to believe. Think about it," he commanded, "without your natural involvement obscuring everything. Why should anyone want to murder your father? He'd only lived here for two years. He didn't have an enemy that you know of. So why kill him?"

"I don't know why," Cassie admitted quietly. "But," she warmed to her theme again, "I think he had proof that someone committed fraud. Why else would he warn me away from the *Times* ciphers. We'd solved ciphers like that since I learned to read. And why should he refer to himself as a bankrupt?"

Randal looked at her with his head cocked to one side. "You really have fifty thousand pounds?"

Cassie grinned at his bemusement and nodded. "I'm not a penniless bride." Her smile died slowly. "Randal." She hesitated. How to say it without hurting his pride? "The jewelry is available if you need it." His head came up with a snap. "It's just," she continued, "I've heard some rumors about—"

"My finances?" Randal finished for her with an ironic smile. "How could I believe that I could keep secrets from the most talented gossips in London?" He reached across the small table, lifted her hand to his lips, and gently kissed it. "Thank you, Cassie. But I'm not a pauper. My financial embarrassments stem from my guaranteeing the exhibition." At her quizzical look, he continued. "A number of wealthy citizens pledged to cover the losses if there were any. Unless it's a total catastrophe, my losses will be negligible."

Cassie hesitated, then asked, "And if there's another assassination attempt?"

"That would rank as total catastrophe," he admitted.

How could he be so calm about it? He smiled at her, then slowly lifted her hand again, this time to nibble at her fingertips. A curling warmth radiated from them to make her shiver. Cassie pulled her hand free as though she'd been burned. Men were unaccountable.

"It's unlikely there'll be another assassination attempt. Especially since we're well prepared. So the family seat won't go on the block." He looked at her for a second, and slowly smiled. "What else have you heard about my activities?"

Embarrassed, she dropped her gaze to her plate. "Nothing."

"Cassie, it's not polite to lie to your husband. You've heard Aunt Maude, if no one else, tell you about my reprehensible trips to Bluegate Fields. I've also frequented Seven Dials, an equally insalubrious locale." He relaxed and smiled at her. "You'd best know the whole horrible truth. I've set up several boarding schools for poor children recently." He paused, growing serious. "As a result of working with Prince Albert on housing for the poor, I received a prepublication copy of a study called *London Labour and the London Poor*. I had to do something." Randal took a sip of coffee. "Unlike our 'Great Philanthropists,' I disapprove of publicity for good works."

A warm, affectionate smile lit Cassie's face. "You've misled me horribly. There's nothing a wife likes better than correcting her husband's faults. I had real hope that this 'Bluegate Fields' would give me a chance to redeem you." She mopped at her eye with a damask napkin. "All my hopes are undone."

Randal lifted her hand again and sensuously nibbled her fingers. "I'm amenable to acquiring some real corkers for you to correct."

She tried to hide the effects of his touch. "You have enough to be a challenge even now. I'll start with that abominable sense of humor. It's going to get you into trouble someday."

The French mantel clock sent silvery chimes into the silence between them. "Starting right now if I don't leave for my appointment now." He rose and stood towering over her, a thoughtful frown turning his face serious. "Let me take care of your worries over your father."

The gay world of bantering with her husband collapsed around her and Cassie shrugged. "Somewhere in Lytham House there's proof my father was murdered. I know it."

"You can visit Elaine," Randal commanded. "But don't try to be a spy. It may not be safe. I'll visit this private enquiry agent you've hired and talk to your solicitor. You crack that cipher. I'll have Glanville get you the newspapers. But nothing more."

"But—"

"No," he ordered with quiet authority. "If you're right, it's too dangerous. If you're wrong, you could cause a scandal by accusing the wrong man."

"You will help?"

"I'll help. I don't know whether your father was murdered. But I'm willing to find out. All right?"

Cassie nodded. "I'll be very careful. But I intend to visit Elaine today."

"That's all right. Just don't search the house anymore."

"I've searched every corner of the place, and I haven't found the key to the strongbox. That's where the evidence is. But I don't know where the key is."

"Don't try to find it," he ordered again. "Now I have to dress. Once I finish with the Prime Minister, it's Scotland Yard, then your private enquiry agent. I'll be home for tea."

Randal unexpectedly leaned over and took her

mouth with devastating passion. Helpless, Cassie
linked her arms about his neck. In seconds, her
weight rested against him, her toes barely touching
the floor. With increasing confidence, she explored
with fingers and lips the finely carved curves of his
ear, the odd way his left brow grew into a peak, the
curl of fine, soft hair peeking from beneath the neck
of his dressing gown.

As she touched his throat, Randal set her back on
her feet and looked down at her, breathing deeply.
"The Prime Minister is going to have an awfully
long wait."

With innocent coquetry, Cassie's lashes dropped,
then swept up to half veil her eyes. "You have to
go?" Where had the question come from? Color
stained her cheeks, but she was glad she'd asked.

"Unfortunately, yes, wench. Now behave yourself." He set her on her feet and patted her rump as
he gave her a gentle push toward her bedroom.

The silk of her nightgown clinging to her skin,
Cassie pointed out with assumed outrage, "I was
behaving myself."

"All right. Now be good or at least quit tempting
me."

Giggling, Cassie disappeared into her bedroom.
She would love to prolong the moment and see
where it ended. But Randal took his responsibilities
at the Home Office seriously.

After all, he'd married her rather than face the
possible ruin of his career.

The memory struck so coldly that Cassie nearly
missed a step on her way to ring the bell to call
Fairleigh. Ridiculous. Saving his career wasn't the
only reason Randal had married her. It couldn't be.
He loved her as much as she loved him. She pushed
the doubt firmly to the back of her mind.

But all through her bath and choosing a walking

dress for a visit to Elaine that afternoon, Cassie was plagued by her doubts about Randal. They were still with her when she rang the doorbell to Lytham House.

"Good afternoon, Minton. Is Lady Elaine at home?" she asked, tugging off her gloves.

"No, miss . . . milady. She's helping with Miss Edgar's wedding." Minton managed to look crestfallen, yet hopeful. "Unfortunately, Lady Elaine lost the list of where to place the new furniture. If you could remember what was on it." Minton held the door open wider to admit her. "I know I shouldn't ask."

Already undoing the ribbons fastening her bonnet, Cassie handed it to him. "Nonsense, Minton, I'd be delighted." How odd to hear Minton call her "milady." It brought home the change in her position as nothing else had. Or could.

"Thank you, miss. And, may I say, milady, that the staff joins me in wishing you every happiness."

"Thank you, Minton. That's very kind of you. Please convey my thanks to everyone." Cassie smiled up at him. "Now, I'll try to re-create that list. If I might use the morning room?"

"Certainly, milady."

Less than half an hour later, Cassie came out of the morning room with a list of where the new furniture was to go. It would be simpler to take the list to him in the pantry than to wait while a footman went to fetch Minton to the morning room.

"Cassie!" Lytham's surprised exclamation brought Cassie swinging around from the dining room door. "I thought— Does Elaine know you're here?"

"I don't believe she does, Lord Lytham," Cassie replied formally. A hint of tension underlay the words. After his strange behavior yesterday, uneasiness filled her. "She's at the Edgars. I'm redoing the list of where to place the furniture that arrives today. Elaine misplaced it." She was explaining too much, but he made her nervous.

A flash of warmth lit Lytham's gray-blue eyes at Elaine's latest misadventure. It died quickly. Opening the door into the library, he gestured for her to join him.

"It's kind of you to trouble yourself," he said mechanically. "Won't you come in? I have something I need to discuss with you."

Hesitantly, Cassie went down the hall to join him. "Yes, Lord Lytham?" she asked. Close up, Lytham looked decidedly strange. His jaw was clenched, and his eyes, when they inspected her, flamed coldly.

She stepped past him into the library and went to the chairs she and Randal had occupied the first day they met. But cool quietness made the library feel entirely different. No comfortable crackle from a fire burning on the hearth sounded today, although the mantel clock ticking steadily in the silence tried to fill the room.

"Elaine shouldn't have talked you into marrying Rydal," Lytham began. "What will people say?" He paced restlessly up and down the length of the rug before the fireplace while Cassie silently watched.

Lytham was only concerned about his reputation. That wasn't too bad. She smiled placatingly, but he didn't stop pacing until she spoke.

"The wedding was private because of my recent bereavement." She touched her black skirt. "Randal put our wedding forward to help remove Lady Albinia's objections to Madeline's marriage. It would be just like him to try to help a friend."

Lytham stopped before the chair opposite Cassie and dropped into it when she finished her explanation. "It might work." His unfocused eyes sharpened when she moved her hand and the Rydal betrothal ring flashed blue fire. "It's lovely, isn't it?"

"This?" Cassie lifted her hand and looked clearly at the Rydal betrothal ring for the first time. It was a marquise-cut sapphire surrounded by diamonds in a fragile setting. She'd never seen a lovelier one. "Yes."

Lytham shrugged irritably. "The Marchioness of Rydal always wears the ring." He shifted in the chair, crossing and recrossing his legs. "Elaine and I have never been blessed with children," he continued after a moment's silence. "Rydal might have an heir before I do."

"Oh, well—"

Cassie broke off, uncertain how to answer. In all the turmoil of yesterday and the confusion of waking up in a strange bed with a husband, she hadn't thought of that. What if she was already pregnant? From Elaine's incoherent explanation, Cassie gathered that she might well be. A young Randal. She smiled tenderly. The smile faded when she met Lytham's gaze. Why was he looking at her like that? His expression made her want to escape.

The crackle of the list as her fingers tightened gave her an excuse. "If you'll excuse me, Lord Lytham, I must take this list to Minton. The new furniture is due anytime."

"How do you come to have the list?" Lytham asked, frowning.

Hadn't he been listening? His strangely unfocused eyes made her wish Randal were with her. "Elaine mislaid the list," she repeated, "and Minton asked me to rewrite it."

"The Marchioness of Rydal is above that. I'll speak to Minton."

"I didn't do it as the Marchioness of Rydal," Cassie said quietly as she rose to her feet. "I did it as Elaine's friend."

After a moment, Lytham stood also. Still frowning, this time at the empty fireplace, he asked, "Are you and Rydal planning to attend the opening of the Exhibition?" A smile crept over his face. "It'll be a day of surprises." A long pause followed. "They installed the refrigerator yesterday."

"The refrigerator?"

Lytham explained briefly. "That won't be the only thing worth seeing at the exhibition. There's the Queen and Prince Albert. The Prince of Wales will be there, too."

"Randal hasn't told me his plans." Cassie edged quietly toward the library door, more uncomfortable than ever.

"I'll urge Rydal. It should be a most interesting spectacle." Lytham's smile turned inward, as though he saw an image available only to him.

Murmuring agreement, Cassie took one careful step, then another toward the door. Lytham didn't see her. His gaze had returned to the empty hearth. Grateful his attention had wandered, her hand was on the doorknob before he spoke again.

"You must make the effort to attend the opening. It promises to be one of the most memorable events of our age. The Great Exhibition!"

Her hand still on the knob, Cassie met Lytham's eyes. Strange gray flames flared in them as he looked at her. She swallowed before she replied.

"I'll tell Randal," she promised, then fled the library.


The slut hadn't even bothered to open the curtains. Barnthorpe strode fuming into his small room high above the city street. He tossed the newspaper on the rickety desk in the middle of the room, sending the cipher engine onto the floor. The smaller stick lodged in a crack.

Grunting, Barnthorpe fumbled with his penknife for several minutes before he pried it out. And nearly stabbed himself as he grabbed the end he'd brought above floor level. He swore viciously and struggled to his feet again. Soon he wouldn't have to live like this.

His mind drifted to the lodgings he'd soon have. First, there'd be three rooms. A guest room in elegant mahogany with a fine carpet on the floor and damask drapes at the windows. A sitting room with gleaming woodwork, comfortable, fashionable chairs, and a sofa before a fine marble fireplace. Then his room. Wardrobes filled with the finest clothes. A bed with hangings for each season. A dressing table holding his brushes and a gilt-framed mirror that showed his well-tied cravat. But most of all, a couple to take care of him. The wife to cook proper meals and keep woodwork gleaming and linens fresh, the husband to handle all the other details of a well-run household.

And Rydal would pay for it.

Shaking himself out of the pleasant dream, Barnthorpe turned to the agony column and copied the latest message out onto a sheet of paper. With the message laboriously deciphered, he leaned back to read it. Then read it again. Rydal must be mad.

Barnthorpe pushed the message aside and rapidly enciphered a reply. This had to go in the next edition of the *Times*. When he finished, he left it at the newspaper. Barnthorpe broke into a cold sweat. There wasn't enough money in the world.

Cassie raised her face for Randal's kiss after he closed the library door on the amused servants. After nearly a week, she was accustomed to Randal's displays of affection. If only he'd *say* how he felt.

Something beyond physical passion. There was more than enough evidence of that. But it wasn't enough. She needed more.

Randal raised his head from his gentle exploration of her mouth. "What is it, little one? Something bothering you?"

Cassie forced a smile as she traced the curving arch of his upper lip with her finger. "Just the usual." Did he love her? Not just want her. She hungered for him to love her with the same intensity she loved him.

"Elaine wasn't home?"

Gently he bit her finger, sending a shiver through her. Nodding, Cassie stretched up to kiss his nose. "She's always at Madeline's planning every detail of the wedding. Fortunately, it'll be over in a few more days. Then I can get Elaine's attention."

"She enjoys these weddings as much as though they were for her daughters," Randal said, amused. "By now, Madeline's sorry she's got a helper. It's too bad Elaine doesn't have any children. Then she wouldn't spend all her time matchmaking."

Cassie looked away. Did their precipitous wedding still rankle? The dowry should have helped. But there was still something, something that kept him from saying he loved her.

Randal swept her off the floor in a gargantuan hug and carried her over to her desk. Plopping her into the chair, he dropped another light kiss on her waiting lips. The thin silk of her simple, low-cut evening dress floated about her, then settled.

"You've gone away from me again. Does it worry you so much?"

Cassie blinked up at him. "A little," she admitted, then pulled his head down for another kiss before he could ask any more difficult questions.

"Umnh. You taste like the first strawberries in June," he whispered, shaping her breast with one hand. "I have work to do. Now behave yourself and stop tempting me."

"Me? Tempt you?" Cassie smiled with a sensuality she'd discovered less than a week ago. "I didn't know I could."

"Oh?" The mischievous look was back in his eyes and he raised her lightly to her feet.

"Randal, you have work to do." She pushed against his hard-muscled chest without effect.

Taking a small step forward, he trapped her between his body and the desk. He traced the line of gauzy black silk across the tops of her breasts with one lazy finger. Laughter lit his face as she shivered responsively.

"Now behave yourself." She tried to keep her voice serious, but the words giggled out. Playfully pushing him harder, she tried to free herself.

With a languid sensuality, he lowered his lips to her throat and nibbled his way up to her earlobe. Her hands kneaded his strong shoulders, while her traitorous body responded seriously to his amorous play. Shots of pleasure filled her when his hands found her breasts. Slowly he brushed seductively against her. A low moan escaped her, and her hips began a slow, sinuous dance of their own.

This was rapidly getting out of hand. "Randal, what if Pryor should walk in now?"

"Let him get his own woman," Randal's muffled voice growled back.

He swept her into his arms and carried her to the couch. His mouth closed on hers, and, to his joy, her lips parted willingly, eagerly, to give him entrance. Frantically, with slipping control, he freed

her swollen breasts from beneath her gown and caressed them, then started to explore the rest of her
ready body.

A knock on the door forced them to part. Breath
still coming in tattered gasps, Cassie covered herself
and smoothed her hair while Randal checked himself in the mirror. Finally he called in an almost normal voice, "Come in."

The door opened very slowly, and Pryor entered
in his stateliest manner. "When will you desire your
evening tea, milord?" Only a slight upturn of the
mouth gave indication of his amusement.

"I'm afraid we'll have to do without tonight,
Pryor," Randal replied seriously. "As her ladyship
has been reminding me, we have a lot of work to
do."

Cassie was glad the butler had carefully averted
his gaze from her after one glance. The look on her
face, if not the condition of her hair, would surely
cause amusement among the upper servants tonight.

"Very good, milord. I'll see that you and her
ladyship are not disturbed further." In spite of his
best efforts, his mouth cracked into a small smile as
he closed the door behind him.

Cassie rose from the couch quickly and headed
for her desk, carefully skirting her husband out of
arm's reach. Laughter lifting the corners of his
mouth, he followed.

"Randal, did you notice how Pryor waited until
you gave the order to enter?" She held her breath
and watched him closely. If he started teasing her
sexually again, she'd respond whether she wanted to
or not. And she found herself wanting to often these
days. Without intending to, she drifted back to his
side.

"The servants are all laughing," Randal said. "If
we move dinner much earlier, we won't have to get

up from the lunch table. Or would you have all our meals served in bed?" He observed her blush with satisfaction. "It's getting harder to make you do that these days," he said, tracing the curve of her cheek. "Now let me get my work done. Then I'll get you off your feet."

Pressing a kiss into his palm, Cassie regretfully settled back in her chair and shooed him to his own. "You seem to have a great deal of work these days," she said at random, watching him settle at his desk. He'd placed her desk so they could see each other.

"Lytham's work in addition to my own," Randal explained, his mood turning serious. "He doesn't appear at the Home Office more than once a week, and his assistant's useless."

Cassie frowned, remembering Lytham's queer comments the day after her wedding. "Has Scotland Yard reported on the forgeries?"

"There isn't enough evidence to make them investigate Lytham," Randal repeated mildly. Lytham might not be a murderer, but his erratic behavior was making Randal more and more suspicious.

"Are they any nearer to discovering McCrory and Chambers' principal?"

"Not yet." Frowning, Randal focused on the low-burning fire in the grate across the room, its heat welcome on a cool spring evening. "They're afraid of scaring him off. I can't make them move any faster."

Cassie looked down at the latest copy of the *Times.* "When I break this cipher, they'll listen," she stated firmly.

For about an hour they worked in silence, both conscious of the other's presence. Each time she looked up, he seemed to be watching her. She wasn't sure how much he accomplished, but work on the ciphers went nowhere until she examined the latest one.

The first and fourth words were the same. Both were three letters. It just had to be the word *the*. With a little calculation, Cassie came up with a new key word. Not a word containing the letters IED, but a three-letter word: *die*. It couldn't be that simple. Unbelieving, she tried deciphering the rest of the message. Except for one typographical error, the words fell into place.

"Randal," she called faintly, her voice trembling, "Randal, come here." The candles on the desk flickered with her breath.

Instantly he swung around her desk and draped his arm about her shoulders. "What is it?" he asked, concerned.

She handed him the clear copy of the message.

Frowning, he looked up when he reached the end. "You're certain this is right?"

Cassie nodded in stunned silence. It had to be a grisly joke. But Randal was taking it seriously.

"I'll go to Scotland Yard tonight."

"Are they insane?" She swallowed against rising nausea.

"They must be." He extended his hand. "Give me the newspaper." Rapidly checking against the paper, Randal nodded, then looked at her. Cassie's pinched, worried face made him pause briefly. With a strained smile, he squeezed her hand reassuringly and asked, "What's the key word?"

*"Die."* She handed him the newspaper, frightened. "Do they really mean to kidnap the Prince of Wales at the Great Exhibition?"

# Chapter XVI

"'is lordship's fit fer Bedlam." Alfie's mug sloshed over when he slammed it down on the table. He licked the ale from his fingers.

Barnthorpe darted a glance at the next table to be sure no one was listening, then nodded. "I told him that in a cipher. I told him we didn't want any part of it."

"Yer bleedin' well better believe it." Alfie took a long swallow of ale and wiped his mouth on his sleeve. "There ain't enough money in the 'ole bleedin' world fer that job." He gave a covert inspection of the raucous crowd. "Too bad we didn't get more money, though. The boys woulda felt better about it, bein' laid off all this time."

"I gave you the money. I haven't got any more."

Barnthorpe pulled a scented silk handkerchief from his pocket to dab at his sweating temples. Alfie and his crew mustn't learn about the hundred or so pounds left. He needed that money. He'd worked harder for it, taken more risks than they had.

"Some money would come in 'andy w'en I splits up the gang," Alfie said, watching Barnthorpe closely.

Barnthorpe smiled winningly. "If I had any, I'd share it with you. But his lordship won't even pay my expenses unless I agree."

Had Alfie swallowed it? He was greedy, cunning, and unprincipled. He'd also save his own hide first. Therefore, Barnthorpe had to emphasize the danger.

Barnthorpe leaned closer and lowered his voice. "I'm destroying all evidence linking me with this." He looked around with exaggerated caution. "If the Yard gets wind of this, it's the drop. I don't intend to give my business to the hangman." Taking a drink of his ale in deliberate, distasteful imitation of Alfie, Barnthorpe wiped his mouth on his hand. "You'd better clear out. Destroy any evidence. Any evidence at all."

Had it worked? Barnthorpe hoped so. As fast as he patted his temples dry, more sweat beaded there. Alfie would assume he was terrified of the Yard. The Yard was only a distant possibility now. Barnthorpe had to frighten Alfie into cutting all connections between them.

The crash of a bench hitting the wall made Barnthorpe jump. A pair of drunks swung wildly at each other. The barman collared them and hustled them outside into the cool evening air. Barnthorpe watched their exit nervously. Alfie didn't lift his head from contemplation of his half-empty mug.

"Anything written," Barnthorpe emphasized, licking his dry lips. "There can't be anything to connect us. We must break the link."

"Wot do yer take me for? First thing a man

learns," Alfie told him, "not t' write anything down."

Swallowing, Barnthorpe nodded and leaned forward. He didn't notice the sticky puddle that soaked into the fine gray broadcloth of his sleeve. He lowered his voice confidentially. "I've destroyed everything connecting me to his lordship and to you. This will be the last time we meet." Barnthorpe didn't say "Thank God," but he felt it. "If you've told anyone anything— Well, I leave it to you."

A frown marred her normally placid expression as Elaine approached the library. He'd been acting odd. Gone every night. Irritable and sullen when he was home.

"My dear, I hope you're not busy tonight." Elaine slipped into the library and closed the door behind her. This was the first time she'd been there since Lytham decreed no one was to enter the room without him. "But I must speak to you, and I haven't had the chance."

Lytham folded the newspaper spread open on his desk with careful precision and placed it in a drawer. He didn't recognize her for an instant. Then, smiling thinly, he rose and gestured at the chairs before the fireplace.

"I'm never too busy for you, Elaine."

Her shawl slipped from her shoulders when she took the chair he offered. She waited expectantly for him to take the one opposite. He didn't. Instead, he looked at it with undisguised distaste. With quick nervous steps, he paced, sending darting glances at the chair.

"I don't like that chair," he said abruptly. "It reminds me of the wedding. She sat there. That wedding never should have taken place."

Elaine brightened. "I'll find you another chair. I

won't be able to look until after Madeline's wedding, but would next week do?"

"Next week is fine." He shrugged. "There's no hurry." He settled in the despised chair as though her suggestion had pleased him; his long legs stretched across the hearth. "Now what can I do for you? I'm busy."

"It's about Cassie's replacement," Elaine began.

"You never had a companion before Cassie," Lytham protested, his attention fully caught.

"I don't know how I existed without one. Only look how she arranged the new furniture. And took care of its delivery even after she married," Elaine added as if it clinched the matter. She took a breath and sailed on in a different direction. "Oh, I put my new bookcase in the morning room. It's perfect for keeping all the little notes and things I need."

"You shouldn't ask the Marchioness of Rydal to arrange your furniture for you." He shrugged her attempt at self-justification away irritably before she spoke. "Do we need another young woman to keep you company?"

Elaine's smile saddened. "The household is in turmoil without someone. I know she won't be as sweet as Cassie. Nobody could be. She made such a difference."

His eyes a cold gray, Lytham looked beyond her chair, focusing on an unseen image. His mouth stretched tightly.

"So," Elaine continued eagerly. As she gestured, her shawl slipped onto the chair. "I need someone like her. Minton and Emil are both distracted. Could your man of business find someone?"

"He'll advertise for a likely candidate," Lytham agreed absently. "Anything to help the house run smoothly." His attention snapped back to her. "Now, I must ask you to excuse me. A most important matter." Eyes unfocused, he touched the arm of his chair. "A most important matter," he repeated.

"Dearest husband. It's nearly bedtime, and we've spent so little time together. Can't it wait until tomorrow?"

"No." Lytham's gaze went to the portrait of the previous Lord Lytham that hung above the mantelpiece. "No, it can't wait."

The door closed behind Randal, and Cassie turned to deciphering the other messages from the *Times*. Even with the key, it took long minutes that stretched into hours. All were disturbing, but none so disturbing as the one Randal had taken to Scotland Yard.

Her tension grew as she read each one. Her fingers tightened on the pen, and a drop of ink splattered on the last message.

"Milady, the last mail delivery for the day has arrived." Glanville brought it to her at the desk. "Is there anything I can do?" He smoothed the letter where his grasp had crinkled it. "I'd be delighted to stay up if I can be of service."

Cassie smiled tiredly. "No, thank you, Glanville. You'd best retire for the night." As he went back to the door, she stopped him. "Did Lord Randal's message reach the Prime Minister?"

"Yes, milady." He hesitated. "Pryor's locking up now. Are you sure there's nothing further?"

"No," Cassie repeated. "Thank you. I'll wait up for his lordship. Pryor's had some coal brought in, and I've got my needlework, but thank you anyway."

She wished she had another cipher to break, anything to keep her mind occupied. But she didn't. And Glanville's company wasn't soothing. All she needed was Randal beside her, able to answer all her questions.

Realizing he was still standing by the door, she nodded dismissal to the little man. He meant to be kind, but she couldn't tolerate more of his company. His solicitude made her worry, and worrying was foolish. Randal was safe. The Prince of Wales wouldn't be kidnapped. Still—

The sound of paper crumpling when her fingers tightened reminded her of the letter. The postmark was Ireland. Who could be writing her from Ireland? Breaking the seal, she unfolded the stiff sheets of parchment white paper. Aunt Maude! Of course, she was in Ireland for the birth of a grandchild. Cassie scanned the blistering letter, her mouth quirking.

Turning back to the beginning, Cassie began reading. Shortly she was laughing. Frances, whom Randal termed a corker, had lived up to her reputation for being scatterbrained. Apparently, according to Aunt Maude, counting higher than the fingers of one hand was beyond Frances.

"My daughter-in-law presented us with a son," Aunt Maude continued. "Quite properly. Unfortunately, the girl seems unaware of the normal period required for the production of a child. When she told Arthur to expect the baby in early May, she neglected February. Consequently, she was brought to bed the day after I arrived, a full two weeks ahead of the announced time, and nearly nine and a half months from initiation.

"The boy is a healthy baby weighing nearly eight pounds. There's no calling this one premature. Arthur married Frances on the first of September. I have informed Arthur of my disapproval. He assured me that his next child would take the usual nine months. With Frances, one can't be sure."

Chuckling, Cassie turned to the next page, which contained a lengthy description of the heir whose courtesy title was Viscount Clonroche. Recalling Randal's affectionate teasing of his aunt, Cassie knew he'd enjoy this letter. Especially Aunt Maude's pithy comments about Frances' inability to nurse her infant son. Then she reached the last page. Randal couldn't be allowed to read this part.

"I have received word that you and my abominable nephew married a few days after my departure for Enniscorthy. I am delighted to welcome you into the family. My disappointment lies in not seeing that rapscallion led to the altar. Although I saw his interest the day you visited, I assumed the wedding would be sometime this fall. However, I look forward to greeting you as my niece and hope to find you emulating Frances. Not, I hasten to add, in her inability to count, but in the celerity with which she ensured the succession. I worried that the line might become extinct with Randal unmarried. It is a great relief to me, and would be to his mother were she alive."

Plainly Aunt Maude wondered, as must all of Society, why the marriage had been so precipitate. Recalling their one meeting, Cassie had no doubt the old lady would have the full story inside ten minutes of her return.

Cassie shrugged. Aunt Maude's intelligence service would rout out the reason if she failed. But she'd failed to discover the real reason for Randal's visits to Bluegate Fields. Should Cassie tell her not to worry? No. It was Randal's secret. Not hers.

Glancing at the clock, Cassie pulled her needlepoint frame to a comfortable chair before the fire. Nearly eleven. Randal would be home soon. Setting a candelabram on a nearby table, she surveyed the canvas for an interesting spot to resume.

With meticulous care, Cassie chose the color needed to complete a huntsman's tabard. Soon this needlepoint canvas would be finished and ready to stretch for Elaine. What should she do next?

A smile touched her lips. Looking over the canvas for another place requiring this particular intense shade of blue, Cassie decided on a tapestry of Randal's principal seat. With an artist's drawing, she could have it ready for either his birthday or Christmas. It depended on whether they could visit the estate before the Exhibition closed.

The horror of the kidnapping plans receded behind daydreams of their future. Cassie added colors to the canvas. The ticking of the case clock on the mantel provided a soothing counterpoint to the fire's crackle. Midnight's chime startled her. She focused sleepily on the clock face.

Midnight, and Randal wasn't home yet. Shivering, Cassie stretched, and tucked her shawl closely about her shoulders. The fire had died down. Yawning, she rose to add more coal to it. Randal would need a warm room after the night's chill. She cuddled back down in the massive armchair, her eyes slowly closing.

A teasing trail of kisses along her cheek and down the side of her neck woke Cassie. Smiling, she stretched an arm up to loop about his neck. Randal allowed her to draw his head down, and she caught his lips in a welcoming kiss.

"Hello, sleepyhead. You shouldn't have waited up," Randal whispered when their lips parted. His strong arms moved gracefully about her body. He picked her up and sat down with her on his lap. His cheek was cool beneath her searching fingers.

"Oh, I'm so cramped." She straightened her legs. Then she remembered. "What happened at Scotland Yard? Did they believe you?"

His smile tired, Randal nodded and rubbed the high bridge of his nose. "Remember, one of my responsibilities at the Home Office is coordinating security for the Exhibition. The Yard knows me very well."

The tension drained out of Cassie. "I was so worried," she whispered. "Is the Royal Family going to appear at the opening?"

"I don't know. The Prime Minister's going to tell the Queen tomorrow . . . I should say"—he glanced at the clock—"today. Don't worry. Scotland Yard's put every available man on it."

"You think they'll catch them?"

He stroked the gentle curve of her cheek. "I think they will." He wished he were as certain as he sounded.

Straightening, he stretched. "Now." He stood her on her feet. "Let's go to bed. I have to meet the Prime Minister at two to learn the Queen's decision. And be at the Home Office early to solve the other problems that have sprung up overnight."

Out of the safe haven of his lap, Cassie felt wobbly. Her legs were still numb, but Randal steadied her.

She laughed up at him. "I'm not sure I can walk yet. I must have slept on my legs wrong."

In answer, Randal swung her up in his arms. "Put your arms round my neck," he commanded. "With all those clothes, you're no light weight."

Giggling, Cassie followed instructions and stole a kiss.

"And make yourself useful. Open the door."

"Slave driver. What would you do without me?" Cassie stretched down for the doorknob.

Randal waited for her to close the door behind them before he raised his brows. "You'd be amazed at the number of things I can do." He dropped a kiss on her nose. "For one thing, you won't need to ring for Fairleigh."

Cassie blinked up at him innocently. "I'd hate to get the poor girl out of a warm bed." Cassie shivered in the cool air of the hall. "For that matter, I wish I were in a warm bed."

"I'm working on that."

A sensual smile tugging at his firm mouth, Randal shifted her higher against his chest and set off. He strode down the hall and up the stairs to their rooms. Hands sliding caressingly over her body, he carried her into the dusky warmth of his room.

"One last chance to ring for Fairleigh," he offered softly.

Her lashes swept down, then up, as she smiled with slumberous invitation. Trailing teasing kisses up his throat to his inviting lips, she smiled up at him. "Should I trust you?"

"No." He took her lips with sensual abandon. Then slowly lowered her to her feet. "Now turn around." He patted her rump. "Why do women insist on such finicking little buttons?"

Her reply was low, husky. "It makes unwrapping the package more fun."

A slow smile lit his face. He worked at the offending buttons. A cool draft crept down her back, marking his success. Shivering, she looked over her shoulder at him, pouting lips softly inviting a kiss. Randal took advantage of the opportunity, but his hands never left their task.

He slid her dress off her shoulders and past her waist. It caught on the billow of her petticoats before it reached the floor. The pale skin of her shoulders glowed above her chemise in the soft light of the dying fire and pair of candles. Arms sliding around her, he kissed his way down her straight back. Eyes heavy with desire, Cassie turned in Randal's arms and reached for his tie.

"It's the same every night," she murmured. "You never do these things right."

"Don't I?" His left eyebrow with its endearing peak rose quizzically as he pulled free the tapes fastening her petticoats. Suddenly, she was standing in her pantalets, corset, and chemise, a froth of black-edged white petticoat about her feet. "I'll have to practice more."

"You're getting enough practice now."

Tilting his head back, he looked down at her, eyes sleepy. "Do you want me to restrain myself?"

"No." She buried her face in his chest. The smooth broadcloth of his coat felt cool beneath her heated cheek.

"Randal," she murmured, her voice husky, hesitant, deeper, "I've been wondering," she began slowly. "Am I— Is it all right for me to . . . to feel, be so wanton?"

"Wanton?" Surprised laughter echoed in his voice. He bent to kiss the tip of her nose. "Where'd you learn the meaning of that word?"

"You taught me." Cassie smiled with increasing confidence.

His smile widened. "As long as it's with me, I love you being wanton. I wouldn't have you any other way."

An incoherent murmur escaped her, and she drew his head down. Her lips on his, she tugged at his tie and worked at the buttons fastening his waistcoat. She needed to touch him, not his clothes.

He unhooked her corset, his fingers stroking her sensitive skin after each hook. Already her breath came in long sighs. His agile fingers stroked the globes of her breasts, the trembling curve of her stomach, as he freed her from the confines of clothing. The tremor in her fingers increased until she couldn't undo a button. Would she ever be able to control herself long enough to undress him? She doubted it. And she didn't care.

Brushing her hands away with a smile filled with promise, Randal lifted her from the last of her clothes and carried her to his bed. Lovingly, he laid her down on the turned-back sheet. The soft linen, cool on her heated skin, made her shiver. Pouting seductively, Cassie linked her arms behind his neck.

Randal allowed only a single kiss before he pinned her arms against the pillow. "No, my dearest," he whispered at her protest, his voice heavy with desire, "I have to finish undressing."

Her eyes half closed, Cassie sketched a kiss. Each time she lay like this, tinglingly aware, she wondered at the strong, perfect power of his body. No softness marred the rippling muscles beneath his skin. Tawny brown hair covered his chest, arms, legs. She shivered at the memory of his hair-covered skin touching hers.

His heat branded her when he slid into bed beside her. Then in an amused growl, he ordered, "Move over, wench."

Her hand sketched down his ribs to stroke his hip. A ripple of response tightened the muscles under her hand satisfyingly. "If you like, I'll go to my own room." The throb of desire underlying her voice belied the offer.

Catching her hand, he brought it up to his chest. "No, thanks. Your bed's too small."

"I didn't invite you to join me."

Her lips pouted invitingly up at him in the dim light. Knowing it would arouse him more, Cassie plucked at the soft hairs surrounding the flat, masculine nipples. Heavy, throbbing tension deep within her needed to drive him wild slowly.

"It doesn't matter." He accepted the invitation of her pouting lips. Raising his head a fraction, he studied her face. "Courtesy demands you stay here."

"Which etiquette book is that in?"

"Mine."

The sudden harshness in his tone signaled the end of his patience. He captured her mouth and settled full-length against her. He was a fiery blanket burning into her. With a sensuous shiver, she encircled his strong back with her arms and arched up to meet his passion. Yet he didn't enter her.

Each time was new, different, yet the same. The same delicious, fluttering uncertainty, the need to tempt him, the need to return the pleasure he gave her. Each time she learned something new that pleased him. And tonight she needed release of the tension that had gripped her all evening.

Hands sweeping down his back to the hard muscles of his thighs, Cassie wriggled against him, knowing the brush of her soft, supple breasts against his chest aroused him as much as it did her. Only, Randal was in a different mood.

Instead of urging her on in a game of advance and retreat, he pinned her arms above her head and ravished her mouth, one strong hand resting on her belly. When he lifted his head, Cassie recognized a need in his silver-flecked blue eyes she'd never seen before. She tried to free herself to soothe and comfort him. Only, he refused to let her go.

"Randal?" she whispered.

A beautiful, reassuring smile swept over his face. While he trailed gentle touches over every inch of her skin, his lips and hands inflamed every place they stroked until she writhed beneath him, wild to return his caresses. Yet, he wouldn't let her.

"Please, Randal," she begged.

Immediately, he stretched the full length of her body. His hard strength a commanding force waiting, he dropped a tender kiss on her lips and whispered her name. In the next instant, he entered her and set a demanding rhythm she followed helplessly.

His compelling rhythm brought them to the edge of ecstasy. And then over the edge.

Long minutes later, Cassie returned to awareness. Randal lay, a beloved weight above her, his face buried in her throat. In the final frenzy, he had released her hands, and now she reached gently to encircle his weary body. Never before had it been like this.

Triumphantly, she knew she'd given him something he needed. Cassie smiled tenderly. Even more than her physical satisfaction, that thought pleased her. Perhaps she meant more to him than he admitted even to himself. Her lips curving sweetly, she slipped into sleep, clinging to him.

# Chapter XVII

Expression gentle, Randal watched Cassie sleeping soundly while he finished dressing. Sometime during the night, he'd awakened chilled, and found he lay more on than off her. Gently he'd eased himself off, despite her sleepy protest. Pulling up the thick covers, he'd slipped back into sleep with Cassie held tightly to his side.

If he hadn't had Cassie last night— A shiver went through him. All the dark urgency which had ridden him returned. The danger to the Prince of Wales, the helplessness of Scotland Yard, the danger to the Rydal fortune if the Great Exhibition failed had sent him home frustrated and worried.

Then he'd found Cassie sleeping, waiting for him like a child. No, not a child. He remembered the abandon with which she responded to his touch. And she was his alone. Never mind the dying gossip.

With Welton's help, he'd stopped that. Everyone believed Shelton had started it in a rage because she'd rejected him. His lascivious attempts to seduce attractive women made it easy for Society to accept that explanation.

Randal tucked the blankets about Cassie's bare shoulder and brushed a kiss over her cheek. She was small, fragile, yet so strong. When this business with the Prince of Wales was done, he would find her father's murderer. All his doubts were gone with this latest evidence.

Finally he had a motive. Her father must have learned about the planned abduction. She thought Lord Lytham was guilty. Randal doubted his involvement. There was no reason.

Lytham's going to the Cardwell home the night of the death was Cassie's evidence. Along with the offer of an exorbitant salary for a companion. And his recommendation of McCrory and Chambers. Maybe that explained Lytham's employment offer. Feelings of guilt that his recommendation had made Cardwell come to grief had prompted it.

Randal intended to meet her enquiry agent after his meeting with the Prime Minister was over. But first to visit Scotland Yard. Lord Russell would want to know what the Yard planned.

The clock chimed softly. He had to hurry if he was to reach Scotland Yard before meeting the Prime Minister. Once he learned the Queen's decision, he'd have plenty to do to ensure the Prince of Wales's safety. Only then would he be free to turn his attention to the other business.

During his first meeting with Neville, Randal had suggested several avenues for investigation. The enquiry agent might have news by now. And Randal had more questions to ask now that he'd had time to think about the case. He hoped to return home with something positive to tell Cassie.

Smiling though his eyes remained grave, Randal

bent to kiss her throat. She smiled and snuggled deeper into the warm bed as though in the midst of a pleasant dream. His tired eyes lit with pleasure. He tucked a note beneath the cover by her hand. She'd find his promise to be home for tea, if possible, when she woke.

Checking the set of his cravat and gray frock coat in the mirror, he let himself out into the hall. He hurried down the stairs and met Pryor, who knew something of the disturbance last night and hoped for an explanation. Perhaps later, but not until the Yard had safeguarded the Prince of Wales. The slightest rumor would send the kidnappers to ground.

"No breakfast this morning, milord?" Pryor asked, eyeing the carrick Randal carried.

"No time," Randal answered briefly. "Call a cab for me, please."

"Certainly, milord. Mr. Glanville desires to see your lordship. In the library, milord."

In the library, Randal met Glanville's questioning gaze. The secretary had been studying a stack of monthly reports from the Rydal estates. "There's no news yet."

The secretary sighed. "I'm sorry to have disturbed you. It's just that I'm anxious."

"Don't worry about it." Randal nodded at the reports stacked on his desk. "More problems there?"

"No, milord. It's good news. The early crops are huge, and Stevenson thinks he can find a buyer for the unentailed properties. One willing to pay enough to cover the guarantees for the Great Exhibition. That is, of course, if it's needed."

Shrugging into his carrick, Randal's lips twisted wryly. "I'm glad. There hasn't been much good news recently."

Glanville smiled colorlessly. "As you say, milord."

With a nodded good-bye, Randal returned to the front hall. Brilliant sunshine poured through the fanlight, and a gentle breeze carrying the scent of spring flowers came through the open door. A hansom cab, the horse's coat shiny with the care lavished on it, stood waiting for him in the street.

Randal hurried into the cab, telling the driver to take him to Scotland Yard. Soon he'd know what the Yard planned to do, and what the Queen had decided. She might keep the young Prince safely at home. But he doubted it. The Queen refused to be cowed by assassination attempts. She considered it her duty to set an example for her subjects. Her eldest son wouldn't be allowed to do any less, even though he wasn't yet ten. That left Randal and Scotland Yard with the task of finding the kidnappers. Or stopping them.

Stirring her tea rapidly, Elaine sat upright on the couch. Cassie had never seen her like this before. Dressed in a dark brown summer dress of the previous year, Elaine had led Cassie to the morning room.

Even the sun streaming through the windows couldn't brighten that dress. It left Elaine's complexion muddy, and underlined the dark circles beneath her eyes. Something had upset her badly. But the barrage of words kept Cassie from leading her to talk about what was disturbing her. Was it Lytham? Perhaps. Whatever it was, it wasn't Madeline's wedding.

"It's going to be a small wedding," Elaine concluded, "with just a few attendants." She took a tiny mouthful of dundee cake. "You'll receive a letter from Madeline asking you to be bridesmaid. Randal will be best man, while I shall be matron of honor."

Cassie stirred her tea and took a sip. This was the opportunity to lead the conversation to Elaine's husband. She might learn something, and help Elaine at the same time. That possibility was a consolation.

"Will Lord Lytham be able to attend?"

"Lytham?" Elaine blinked and put down the full plate she'd held on her lap for more than half an hour. "I'm not sure. It's so close to the opening, I'm surprised Randal and Welton are able to take the time. They hold such responsible positions."

"Madeline and Welton aren't leaving on a wedding trip after the ceremony, are they? Randal and I won't go on our honeymoon until after the Exhibition closes in October."

"Oh, my dear Cassie. That is much too long to have to wait for a wedding trip. Can't Randal get away sooner?"

Shaking her head, Cassie poured herself another cup of tea and held up the pot to Elaine questioningly. When they settled in the morning room, Cassie had poured Elaine's cup and prepared her plate as she had the past few weeks. Elaine had been content to let her. But Elaine had eaten little. Despite half an hour of chatter, the scone was untouched while the cake had only three tiny bites out of it.

"Randal says we can't. I'm content to remain in London until I'm out of mourning. I'll feel more like traveling with a new wardrobe. I'll be able to shop for it in September." Cassie waited for Elaine to brighten at the mention of her other favorite pastime. But she didn't.

"You'll need a complete new wardrobe. All your things from last year will be behind the fashion,"

Elaine agreed absently, accepting the fresh cup of tea. As before, she stirred rapidly without taking a sip. Then she took a large gulp of the hot liquid and gasped.

Elaine's problem must be Lytham. Cassie brought him into the conversation again even though she felt guilty. "Will you and Lord Lytham be able to go to the country when the season's over?"

"This summer?" Elaine's fair brows drew together in a troubled frown. "I'm afraid not. We usually visit Wandsley Hall. We spent our honeymoon there, it's so lovely."

"It's selfish, but I'm glad you'll be here for the summer. I know so few people."

Elaine smiled and started to relax. Instead of sitting bolt upright on the couch, she rested against the back for a moment, pleasure lightening her round face. Then some memory destroyed her enjoyment. Elaine straightened again, only the remnants of anticipation left in her face.

"You haven't been introduced," Elaine said distractedly. "After the Exhibition is over, I shall sponsor you at one of the Queen's drawing rooms for your formal presentation as the Marchioness of Rydal. . . . Oh," she added, remembering, "it can't be until next year when you're not in mourning. The Queen wouldn't approve."

"I'll be delighted to have you stand sponsor for me. Will you be able to take an active part in the season?"

Elaine's half-full cup joined her full plate on the table. "We always have in the past. But this year . . . this year has been so difficult. I'm hoping in May we'll accept more invitations."

Elaine wasn't ready to talk. All conversational gambits led back to the Exhibition. Most of London talked of little else. But Cassie wondered what was really bothering her friend.

Putting aside speculation, Cassie turned her attention back to Elaine. She had reverted to Madeline's wedding, some animation returning. But the food on her plate remained untouched, and she occasionally shivered as though chilled, despite the warm spring afternoon.

After the fourth time it happened, Cassie asked, "Could I get you a shawl, Elaine?"

"Shawl?" She looked vaguely about the morning room. But the maid whose task it was to clear the room had done her job. Nothing was draped over the furniture. "There doesn't seem to be one here," she said vaguely, "but there's a shawl in the library."

Elaine only realized she'd answered when Cassie began to rise. "My dear," she exclaimed, "I didn't mean for you to go after it. You're the Marchioness of Rydal now. Lytham wouldn't approve."

"I'm your friend," Cassie said gently, unmoved by Lytham's concept of propriety for a marchioness.

"I'll send one of the maids." Elaine's brows drew together in perplexity. "Except, Lytham won't allow them in the library unless he's there. Something to do with his papers. I'll have to send one of the maids upstairs for another shawl."

"I'll fetch it from the library. I'm not one of the maids, so you haven't broken his prohibition. I won't touch his papers."

"I would appreciate it." Rubbing her arms as though chilled, Elaine smiled up at Cassie. Her eyes were tired, sad.

"The *Times* couldn't give Scotland Yard information on who'd placed the ciphers in the personals, but they'll save all future correspondence they receive. Beyond that, the Yard's checking their informants for anything they may know. I don't have much hope they'll find anything. And there're less than two weeks left before the Great Exhibition opens."

Brushing his tawny brown hair from his forehead, Randal shrugged tiredly at the question in the Prime Minister's dark eyes. It had been a long day with little time for rest or refreshment. Long since, he'd regretted refusing Pryor's offer of breakfast. There'd been no time for lunch, and he wouldn't arrive home in time for tea. Cassie would be anxious for news, but he couldn't spare the time.

"About as I'd expected. There's been too little time since the discovery," Lord Russell said, tiredly closing his eyes with a sigh. "I waited on the Queen this morning."

From Lord Russell's face, Randal knew the answer. "She won't agree to postpone the opening or keep the Prince of Wales and the Princess Royal at home?"

The Queen would descend from her carriage with Prince Albert and their two eldest children, Bertie, the Prince of Wales, and his elder sister, Vicky, the Princess Royal. As always, the Queen's nickname for her eldest son irritated Randal. What if he styled himself "King Bertie"?

"Precisely. 'It ill becomes a member of the Royal Family to acknowledge such threats,'" Lord Russell quoted, imitating the Queen. His fine dark hair drooped over his forehead, making him look more melancholy.

"Then the children will be on the dais when she opens the Exhibition," Randal finished for him, rubbing his aching eyes. Even with Cassie beside him, the fate of the children had haunted his dreams.

"One thing, Rydal," Lord Russell said slowly. He folded his hands on the desk before him. "I know your wife is an expert at breaking these ciphers, but— Is it possible she's made a mistake?"

"I wish she had, but the chaps at the Yard agree with her. If you'd like, you can see their copy of the deciphered message. After I gave them the key, they arrived at the same thing without benefit of seeing Lady Rydal's. They even found the same typographical error. There's no chance of a mistake."

Randal handed the Prime Minister the two copies of the message, one in Cassie's handwriting, the other in the unknown Yard expert's. He knew them by heart:

THE GOLD IS THERE IF YOU HAVE THE COURAGE. THE VICTIM IS THE PRINCE OF WALES. KIDNAPPING TO TAKE PLACE AT THE OPENING OF THE GREAT EXHIBITION.

Once the Prime Minister had compared both, he sighed and put them down. "And the only thing we've accomplished so far is the Queen's promise she'll hold Bertie by the hand while they're at the Crystal Palace."

"Hold Bertie by the hand?" Randal repeated in weary disbelief. "That should scare the kidnappers off."

Lord Russell nodded. "And Prince Albert will hold the Princess Royal by the hand."

"I suppose the kidnappers are interested in either child." Randal hesitated, then continued. "If the Yard hasn't found these people within a couple of days of the opening, I'd like to take some direct action."

Lord Russell looked at him hard. "What can you do that Scotland Yard can't?"

"I'd like to place an ad in the *Times* using their cipher. Something to this effect: 'All is discovered. Flee for your lives.' It's a slim chance, but it's something."

Astounded, Lord Russell emitted a low chuckle. "I'll agree. Even if they still try the kidnapping, it's always nice to confuse your enemies."

"Thank you, sir. I'll start working on one patterned on their old ciphers for the style of phrasing." A cloud descended over Randal's face again. "Why kidnap the Prince of Wales in the first place, though?"

"For ransom? Or some other purpose? After those attacks on the Queen last year, we have to look at all the possibilities. The Irishman who fired at her loaded his pistol with blanks, but other Irish radicals may have gotten an idea."

"You mean ransom the Prince of Wales or the Princess Royal in return for Home Rule?" Randal asked, his brows rising. The answer showed in Lord Russell's expression. He shook his head. "I doubt it. Although, how do they intend to collect a ransom?" Rubbing an aching temple absently, he frowned.

"What else bothers you, Rydal?"

"The key word," Randal answered slowly. He shifted in his chair and met the Prime Minister's gaze. "It's *die*. Scotland Yard feels the key word for a cipher usually has some meaning. What if a madman's behind the plot? What if he doesn't intend the Prince of Wales to survive?"

"Kill him in the Crystal Palace? That's not likely."

Randal shook his head thoughtfully. "No, or there'd be no sense in a kidnapping. So it has to be ransom. What kind of ransom, though? I still can't shake the feeling that the key word has some significance."

Cassie felt the eyes of the previous Lord Lytham watching her from his portrait over the mantel. With care, she moved about the room, checking places she'd checked time and again. Minutes were ticking off the clock, and she'd found nothing. Just more dust than usual. Lytham must be serious about not letting the maids come in unless he was there. From the look of it, no maid had been in the room since her wedding.

Why had Lytham suddenly forbidden the maids to come in here? While none of the servants was good at his job, none was a thief. Nor did they pry into things like his papers. Most could barely read, and thought it a waste of time. So what had caused Lytham to make such a radical change in household procedure? It was all of a piece with his odd behavior the day after her wedding.

Dismissing the problem as insoluble, Cassie opened a desk drawer for one last search. In the back, thrust carelessly behind a number of envelopes and the letters which came in them, lay a long metal box. It hadn't been in the drawer before. This was her third search of the desk in the past month.

Her hand trembling faintly with excitement, Cassie drew the box out of the drawer. The lock looked as though the smallest key on the ring she'd had made up would fit perfectly. Quickly she took the set out of her petticoat pocket. Thank the Lord she'd brought it with her each time she visited Lytham House despite Randal's prohibition. The guilt over disobeying her husband was minor in comparison to the excitement.

Holding her breath, she inserted the key into the lock. It fit perfectly and turned with oiled precision.

Making as little sound as possible, she opened the lid. And stared at the contents.

Two carved wooden sticks on a padded bed met her gaze. A cipher engine! The quarter chimes reminded her to return with the shawl. Noting their order in the box, Cassie picked up the varnished alphabet sticks and put them aside. Was anything hidden in the padded sides, bottom, or lid? Listening for a betraying crackle of paper, she searched the box with sensitive fingers. Nothing.

So the cipher engine was the reason for this box. There was nothing additional to be learned from the varnished wood of the cipher engine. The longer stick held two consecutive alphabets, lines incised between each letter for separation. The shorter stick was a duplicate with only one alphabet. Reluctantly, Cassie put them back in the box, closed it, and returned it to the drawer where she'd found it.

It wasn't illegal to possess two wooden sticks. Cassie might be certain they'd been used for the ciphers her father warned her against. But Randal was right. There was no motive for Lytham to cheat and kill her father.

Sighing, she turned to the litter of papers covering Lytham's desk. Someone must have interrupted him while he was working. Never before had the desktop been messy. A fine coat of dust covered the bare wood. She'd have to be careful not to leave finger marks. They'd reveal her presence in the library as nothing else would. Lifting pages delicately, so that Lytham wouldn't be able to tell they'd been disturbed, Cassie read them one by one.

As expected, they held no interest. But the blotting paper did.

She stared at it for what seemed like frozen hours. Then raised her head to stare sightlessly at the filmily curtained window that allowed rich golden sunlight to pour into the room. Dust motes, bright flecks in the motionless air, floated in the sunbeams.

She'd stared at those words long enough last night. She didn't need a cipher engine to help her read them, even printed backwards as they were on the blotter. It was the cipher she'd tried to break for so long. The cipher with *die* for a key word.

Fear clenching her stomach muscles, Cassie carefully replaced the papers as they had been before. Then she went to the shawl and picked it up. The shawl pressed to her stomach, she checked one last time that the desk didn't appear disturbed. It didn't. Good.

Her pulse beating rapidly, Cassie hurried down the corridor to the morning room. Elaine mustn't know anything was wrong. Taking several deep breaths to calm her nerves, Cassie opened the door and smiled at Elaine. One question kept pounding through her mind.

Why had Lytham done it? Why?

# *Chapter XVIII*

"Good afternoon, milord," Minton said. "You're home early. Lady Elaine will be delighted."

"What? Oh." Lytham handed the butler his black overcoat and shallow hat. His eyes drifted to the library door and stayed there. "Don't tell Lady Elaine I'm home. I'm not sure how long I'll be able to stay."

"Very good, milord."

Lytham nodded distantly and brushed past Minton. Replacing that fool Barnthorpe and his gang of thugs had to be his first priority. Forget Rydal's possible heir. That could be handled later. If she proved to be pregnant.

All morning Cassie had occupied his mind. Damn her soul. And damn her father's. At least Lytham had the comfort of knowing her papa was burning in hell.

How Cardwell had discovered his plans, Lytham still didn't know. But he'd taken care of him. Everyone assumed Cardwell committed suicide to avoid the disgrace of bankruptcy. Everyone except his meddlesome daughter. Only she hadn't believed her father had hanged himself. If it hadn't been for her— But she was so lovely. Why hadn't she accepted the story?

And now Rydal was involved. Scotland Yard's call at his office questioning him again about Cardwell's actions the night of his death made his own plans more difficult. If they'd hoped to trick him, they'd failed. He'd repeated his story exactly. And they'd left believing him. But he'd have to be careful.

Lytham shrugged. It wasn't important. He'd handle Cassie if she became a threat. A smile flitted across his thin face. He'd enjoy that. But she wasn't likely to become one, except as Rydal's wife. The potential mother of his heir.

A confused look on his face, Lytham scanned his desk. Ah, yes. That was why he was here. Barnthorpe's latest message. The confused look dissolved into a sneer. The fool could still be bought. Enough money would persuade him to find a less cowardly bunch of thugs to do the deed.

And they wouldn't know whom they were kidnapping until the morning of the grand opening. Lytham decided to tell them personally. That would impress his face in their minds. They'd make good witnesses. The last group had too much time to think about it. That was the only problem. This time, all would go well.

A high chuckle filled the quiet library. What a perfect opening for the Great Exhibition. He could see it now. The Queen shrieking her head off. Scotland Yard running in circles trying to find the Prince of Wales. The Exhibition ruined. The Rydal fortune being used to pay the creditors. And then his final triumph.

First, to dangle more money before Barnthorpe's nose. A thousand pounds should work. It was a sum large enough to entice a man like that. Besides, it was Cardwell's money, not his own.

Lips stretched in a thin, mirthless smile, Lytham removed the strongbox from behind the hidden panel. He'd get the cipher engine out before he composed a message bringing Barnthorpe back in line. Then his concentration wouldn't be broken.

With the strongbox on the desk, he took the key from his wallet and opened it. Then stared into the strongbox. Other than a few pound notes, it was empty. Where was the metal box containing the cipher engine?

He searched with his fingers to check what his eyes might have missed. But there was nothing beyond bare, cool metal walls. Lytham tossed the money back and closed it with a thud.

A frown knitted his fair brows. Not only was the cipher engine missing, but also the letters that set up the account he'd used for bribing Barnthorpe and his crew. For the past few days, he'd been increasingly careless. That was why he'd stopped everyone from going into the library.

Worried, he sat down in the tall chair behind the desk and stared at it sightlessly. Lytham opened the desk drawers roughly and sighed. There were the letters and the narrow metal box. Collapsing back in his chair, he rubbed the high bridge of his nose exhaustedly. Now he remembered. He'd been very upset at Barnthorpe's traitorous note. Then, in his hurry for his meeting with the Prime Minister, he hadn't time to get the strongbox.

He'd thrust the cipher engine box in the drawer along with the account information. He'd been certain they'd be safe in his desk drawer. Now he wasn't quite so certain. He reached for the box and paused.

Hadn't the account letters been on top of the box? They looked different somehow. If only he could remember. He visualized the drawer. It was no help. He shuffled the letters to one side. The box seemed all right. He hesitantly picked it up. It was unlocked. He'd locked it before he left. He was certain of that.

He was still standing beside the bell pull when Minton entered. Lytham's face blazed with an agony of fury. Some intruder had dared to violate his privacy.

"Who's been in here?" Lytham demanded before Minton could speak.

"In the library, milord?" Without changing expression, Minton looked offended. "Your lordship gave orders that no one was to enter without your being present. Neither I nor the staff would disobey a direct order, milord."

The fury in his face died slowly, and Lytham sagged. Sighing inwardly, he nodded. "I'm sure you wouldn't, Minton. Where's Lady Elaine? She may have come in for her shawl."

His eyes drifted toward the chair. He'd deliberately avoided looking at it since entering the library. The last time he'd seen Cassie, she'd used that chair. Her image was there haunting him every time he looked in that direction. No matter how hard he tried to push her away, she was there, taunting him. Now the chair drew his eyes inevitably, inexorably.

Elaine's gray and rose shawl was gone.

"What, Minton?"

Minton remained expressionless. "Lady Elaine is in the morning room, milord, taking tea. Will that be all?"

"Yes, thank you, Minton."

The door closed behind the butler, but Lytham didn't hear it. His gaze was back at the empty chair that wasn't empty. Cassie's bright golden hair, her green-flecked hazel eyes, the pure beauty of her face, and small, slender, luscious body—he could see her clearly, mocking him by her very existence. Yet, the smooth leather chair sat somnolent in a beam of dust-laden sunshine empty of Cassie, empty of the shawl. Yes, the shawl.

He let himself quietly into the morning room. Elaine sat staring at the fire, an elaborate tea tray beside her untouched. Poor old girl. He'd make it up to her once this was over. She'd enjoy a visit to the seaside. Clearing his throat, he threaded through the forest of tables, chairs, and sofas to her side and brushed a kiss on her cheek.

"Lytham!" Elaine's face brightened magically. A sparkle came into her large china-blue eyes. "How lovely. I was wishing you could come home and keep me company."

"I was able to get away from the office for a little while," Lytham lied easily. "The advertisement for your companion will be in the newspaper tomorrow. My man expects a deluge of applicants. Once they're screened, you'll have several to choose from."

He mustn't question her too quickly. There was no sense in arousing Elaine's suspicions. Accepting a cup of tea and a scone, he took the chair across from her.

"Dearest husband"—Elaine's smile was joyous—"how like you to think of me in the midst of your busy schedule. I don't know how you found the time. The Home Office works you too hard. If Lord Russell keeps this up, I'm going to speak to him. You've lost weight and you're not getting enough sleep. There are terrible circles under your eyes." Elaine paused, and deliberately, coquettishly tilted her head. "Must you go back to the office this evening?"

A flash of affection lit his gray-blue eyes, then slowly died. "Don't make a fuss, Elaine."

"Well, you have to eat more than that poor lonely scone," she commanded.

Reaching for his plate, she added a raspberry tart and a slice of plain sponge. He didn't care for her favorite, dundee cake. He accepted the plate with a smile, and she added some cake to her own plate. For the first time today, she felt hungry.

"Thank you, my dear." Lytham took a small bite from the scone. Clotted cream oozed into his mouth, and he took several quick swallows of tea to wash it down. With difficulty, he repressed a shudder.

"Have you been alone all day?" he asked when his mouth tasted clean again.

"Oh, no. Cassie came for a visit just after luncheon. She's a dear. Did I tell you that she's to be bridesmaid at Madeline's wedding?"

"No. I hope you two had a delightful cose." His eyes swept down to the gray and rose shawl that lay on the sofa beside Elaine.

"Oh, we just talked of this and that. Nothing important. I'm going to help her with her new wardrobe when she goes into half-mourning in September. She and Randal will go on their wedding trip after the Exhibition closes in October. So she'll have a new wardrobe for the trip. Then I get to help her buy a normal wardrobe early next year just before the Season starts. It'll be such fun."

Behind him, the canary sent a rapturous song into the still room. Frowning, Lytham stiffened. His cup rattled against the saucer before he caught himself.

Meeting Elaine's concerned gaze, he managed a smile that reassured her.

"We may be able to leave London earlier than October."

Color rushed into her pale cheeks. "Oh, when, Lytham? I so want to visit Wandsley Hall again."

"I'm not sure yet." His gaze dropped to the shawl. "I see your shawl was taken from the library. I hope one of the maids didn't get it for you. I should hate to think one of them had disobeyed me."

The gentle admonishment in his voice killed Elaine's excited flush. She stroked the shawl beside her and numbly shook her head.

"Cassie got it for me. She didn't disturb anything, and she isn't a servant. I thought you wouldn't mind." She looked anxious.

"Not in the least, my dear."

Mentally blocking Elaine's rush of chatter, Lytham took a contemplative sip of tea. So Cassie had been in the library. She'd searched his desk. And had a set of keys to his cipher engine box. He'd been right. She was spying on him.

Her father had described with parental pride her skill with ciphers. So she should recognize a cipher engine. Something had to be done before she talked to anyone. Like Randal. That couldn't be allowed. That couldn't be allowed at all.

Cassie looked up from her desk as the butler entered the library with afternoon tea. "Is there any message from Lord Randal?"

"Yes, milady." Pryor put the tea tray on a table near her chair and handed her a note. "Will that be all?"

"Yes, thank you, Pryor." Cassie looked at the

teacup and array of cakes and scones the cook had sent. The solitary teacup meant Randal would be late. "Please tell Jean-Paul that tea looks delicious."

"Very good, milady." Pryor bowed and withdrew.

She was right. The note said Randal had been delayed and wouldn't be home until time to dress for dinner. He'd be home for dinner. But he wouldn't get to eat it. He'd leave for Scotland Yard as soon as she told him about the cipher engine and the cipher on Lytham's blotter.

Cassie rose stiffly from behind the desk. Shaking out the creases from her silk skirts, she went and settled in the armchair. Awash after her visit with Elaine, she still sipped her tea while staring at the list she'd made up.

Any way she looked at her discoveries, they were bound to hurt someone, Elaine most of all. But now she had a motive. Maybe her father had learned about the plot to kidnap the Prince of Wales. But still no one would believe her. There was still nothing connecting Lytham to Papa's murder. Scotland Yard would agree about Lytham's complicity in the kidnapping plot, but not that he'd murdered Papa. Somewhere there had to be evidence Papa knew Lytham was planning the kidnapping.

She put the list aside and finished the cinnamon muffin. After Randal returned home, she'd tell him about Lytham and the cipher. She wanted to put it off until she found evidence linking Lytham to her father's murder. But she couldn't. Even if she told Randal now, she knew what would happen. First, he'd be exultant that the Prince of Wales was out of danger. Then he'd realize the consequences and be upset. For Elaine's sake. And because she'd searched Lytham's desk again.

"Well, I didn't *exactly* promise not to." The words sounded hollow, just an excuse. Randal was right. If Lytham had come home while she was investigating his desk— In retrospect, Cassie shivered at the thought.

A brisk tap on the door broke into her melancholy thoughts. Pryor entered with a note centered on a small silver tray. Even from a distance, the paper looked yellowed and roughly handled.

"This arrived for you, milady." Nose wrinkled, he held the disreputable-looking note at a distance as though it might contaminate him. "A young person delivered it. I was reluctant to accept this but decided it might have some bearing on last night, milady."

The servants had speculated endlessly since Cassie had cracked the cipher last night. Now each word from Pryor was a broad hint asking confirmation. Cassie smiled and gingerly took the grimy message. It would be foolish to discuss the plot with the servants. There was too much chance of rumors reaching the kidnappers before the Prince of Wales was safe.

"Possibly, Pryor. Thank you," Cassie said mildly. The cleft in her chin deepened with amusement. Pryor was trying so hard to find out what had happened, yet wouldn't demean himself by asking. She nodded dismissal.

After the door closed behind him, Cassie waited an extra minute, oddly reluctant to read the note. She considered waiting until Randal came home, then shook her head.

Smudged and tattered, it was difficult to read. Uneducated handwriting trailed so haphazardly across the page, Cassie had to squint. After reading it, she wished she'd obeyed her cowardly impulse to wait until Randal came home. Hands shaking to

match the turmoil in her stomach, she read it again
with slow deliberation to make sure she hadn't mis-
understood.

> If you want to know who murdered your
> father, come alone to Argyle Street, number
> 17, immediately. I want two hundred pounds
> or the equivalent in jewelry. Bring this note to
> prove your identity. If you don't arrive alone
> within the hour, your hope of finding your fa-
> ther's murderer is gone forever.

Her eyes rose to Randal's empty desk. If he were
here, she could count on his aid. But he wasn't, and
she had to act immediately. Should she obey the
note and go to 17 Argyle Street? Cassie frowned at
the paper. Now that the initial shock was over, she
realized it had the feeling of a trap. Despite the uneducated handwriting, the note came from the pen
of someone who was literate. The choice of words,
correct spelling, and proper punctuation belied the
rough paper and coarse handwriting.

There was a chance that someone from McCrory
and Chambers was responsible. She could understand the request for cash. But why suggest jewelry
as an alternative? The Rydal betrothal ring flashed in
the evening light. Of course. It didn't refer to her
inheritance. The Rydal jewels were justly famous.
Everyone would know she had access to them.

She pondered the note again. If she waited for
Randal, she'd be late and lose her only chance of
identifying Papa's murderer. And she couldn't do
that. She didn't dare tell the servants. They'd be
useless and prevent her from going. Randal would
dismiss any who didn't stop her. If they knew. So
she wouldn't tell them.

But to go alone to Argyle Street would place her

at their mercy. They could kill her or hold her for ransom after they'd gotten the money.

She was going. Papa deserved it. So did Randal. Her mind made up, she felt better. She'd go, but take safeguards. And informing Randal was the first one. She could almost hear him now: Stay home and let him handle it.

But she couldn't. She only had an hour. To wait was to lose her chance to remove the stigma of suicide from the Cardwell name. No, she'd go. But first the precautions.

Going to the desk, Cassie made a copy of the note. She'd follow the letter of the instruction, not the spirit. Then Randal would know where she was.

She glanced up at the clock. Randal was due home in three-quarters of an hour. Cassie hurried to write another note explaining her actions. He deserved that. By the time she finished writing and changed clothes, he'd only be fifteen minutes behind her. Randal would follow even if she asked him not to. And she wasn't that foolish. Hurriedly, she finished and folded the pages together.

Original note in hand, Cassie went into the hall where the butler lurked. "Pryor," she said pleasantly, "I must go out immediately. It's important. I've written an explanation for Lord Randal and left it on his desk. He must get it as soon as he arrives home."

"Of course, milady. . . . But"—he hesitated— "should you go alone?" The question overstepped the bounds of propriety, but the cheeky scamp who'd brought the message worried him.

"I'm just going to seventeen Argyle Street," Cassie answered. There, one more defense. "Please find a cab while I change."

Cassie hurried up the stairs and tore out of her dress. Randal was right. They did have too many

buttons. Choosing an older, warm woolen dress
she'd worn on the voyage to London, she pulled it
on. Her hair was escaping its pins, but she didn't
have time to fix it. She had to be gone before Randal got home. Tucking her wayward hair beneath
the cloak hood, she hurried down the stairs, heart
beating in her throat.

More weary than any time since his father died,
Randal left the cab. Dusk was closing in. A snatched
tea with Neville had done little to placate the growl-
ing in his stomach. He was hungry and needed to
tell Cassie what he'd learned. Most of all, he needed
Cassie.

The butler stood in the open door with a worried
expression. He'd never seen Pryor this upset. Randal felt too weary to listen to some domestic crisis
that had disturbed his phlegmatic butler. Let him
talk to Cassie or the housekeeper. But Pryor
blocked his way.

"Yes, Pryor?" Randal asked, removing his hat
and carrick. Pryor didn't take them.

"It's Lady Cassandra, milord."

"What's the matter?" Tension pushed his weariness away.

"Something's happened, my lord. She left in a
hurry. There's a message for you on your desk. You
were to read it as soon as you got home. The address was seventeen Argyle Street."

The address meant nothing. She must be playing
spy again. He couldn't allow her to pursue some
wild start alone. Chill certainty of danger licked
along his nerves. She must have discovered her father's murderer. It didn't seem likely, but nothing
had since he'd married her.

Fighting to keep himself in tight control, Randal
asked, "How long ago did she leave?"

"Some time ago, milord. Do you wish a cab?" He hovered near the door. "Or would you prefer your carriage?"

"A cab will be faster, Pryor, but I need to read that note before I leave."

Hurrying to the library, he tossed hat and carrick on a chair. Several pages covered with Cassie's handwriting lay on the desk. Scanning the note, a curse escaped Randal. Cassie had been right. If Lytham was involved in the plot to kidnap the Prince of Wales, he probably had murdered her father. Then Randal read the copy of the note that directed her to Argyle Street. It had to be a trap. It must be more important to her than he'd realized to prove her father's death wasn't suicide.

She must have left some clue behind. Lytham must know what she'd found and chosen her father's murder as bait because he knew she'd take it.

Lytham must be mad. Pushing tawny hair back from his temples, Randal swore again softly. He should have recognized it before. It explained Lytham's erratic behavior. His absences from the office. His anger over their wedding. The wild mood swings.

Randal took out paper to write a message to Scotland Yard. Just say he'd received word that the kidnapping attempt's organizer was at number 17 Argyle Street. Send men immediately to arrest him. But he'd better warn them to be careful. The kidnapper had a hostage. Cassie was in Lytham's hands by now. He hadn't a chance to escape, but could harm Cassie, perhaps even kill her.

At the thought, Randal closed his eyes. An image of Cassie danced before him. As Lytham's prisoner. As a madman's prisoner.

★   ★   ★

Fading light straggled through the new leaves on the trees. Argyle Street was old, decrepit, though the houses were large and lined the street solidly. The cab pulled up before number 17, and the driver descended to hand her down. Eyes on the house with its peeling paint and sad shutters, Cassie extended a pound note to the driver. She didn't even feel him take it from her. The dilapidated, sinister-looking house held all her attention. It had an uncared-for look that set it off from the others on the street.

"It's too much, miss," the driver protested. "I got no change fer a quid."

Cassie moved around him absently, her gaze fixed on the house. "Consider it a tip for bringing me here so quickly."

"Thank you, miss. Should I wait fer you?" The driver touched his hat respectfully.

She turned and smiled at him. "No, thank you. My husband will be here shortly."

Cassie started slowly up the steps, oblivious of the cab moving down the street. There was no light in the windows. The other houses showed candles flickering or gas lamps lit, but this one was dark. Only reflections of the lingering sunlight glinted off the panes.

At the top of the steps, she rang the doorbell. From inside came the echo of the bell's clang, but no footsteps hurrying to answer the door. Cassie rang again. Again the echoing clang, then silence.

Going back down the steps, Cassie surveyed the house. Still no signs of life. She looked down the street. The cab had already turned the corner.

This quiet side street was empty. No other cab would come down it, not even an old-fashioned hackney. And it was two or three blocks to a street where she could find a cab. Walking unescorted that distance—unescorted in this type of neighborhood—frightened her more than entering the house.

Shivering, Cassie tried the doorbell one final time. Again the bell sounded and died to eerie stillness. Cassie glanced at the other houses. Should she ring one of those doorbells and ask for help? No. Randal was following her. He'd expect to find her here.

The door was unlocked. Carefully, she stepped inside and closed it behind her. A musty, unused scent hit her nostrils. This house had been empty for a long time. But dark shapes of furniture were visible in the thin light.

Hesitantly she moved into the downstairs reception rooms. A hodgepodge of furniture styles filled them. No holland covers draped them to protect the upholstery from dirt. Since they weren't dingy with accumulated grime, they must have been moved into the rooms recently.

Slowly, then with more confidence, Cassie went from room to room. In each one she found the same scene, a jumble of furniture thrown into the room with abandon. A dining room table was flanked by a wing chair, a long couch beyond it. Side chairs from the dining set stood forlornly beside a sofa.

There was no rhyme or reason to the furnishings. It was as if someone hoped to give the house an air of being occupied. He hadn't succeeded.

Each room gave the impression of forlorn abandonment. Not even candles which stood ready provided a sense of occupancy. The dying daylight made the old house even eerier. Cassie lit a candle with relief.

Candle in one hand, skirt gathered in the other, she climbed to the next floor. The silence was unsettling. Not even a clock ticked. As if the house had been made deliberately dead. The solid walls and floors absorbed the sound of her footsteps. She wouldn't hear anyone behind her.

The thought nearly sent her running down the stairs to safety. But Randal would be here in a few minutes. Unless he was late. She didn't know how long she'd been here. It seemed forever. She'd crept through so many halls and endless rooms with their crazy-quilt arrangement of furniture.

A shiver went through her, making the flame's shadows waver on the mottled walls. The house seemed empty. She'd finish the search, then wait for Randal at the front door. Someone had played a monstrous joke on her. After Randal lectured her, they'd return home to one of Jean-Paul's dinners.

With the candle's light to help her miss the helter-skelter furniture, Cassie searched each room on this floor. Then she climbed to the next. The rooms were the same. No one had occupied them for a long time.

Finishing the last room, she paused. There were no more to search. She'd looked into each, even the linen cupboard. There really was no one in the house, she realized, a tide of relief washing over her. Now to go down and wait for Randal.

Then she spotted a final set of narrow stairs. They led up to the attics. The servants rooms weren't up there. Cassie had found cubbyholes at the back of the house on this floor for maids and footmen. Quietly, she looked up the dark and narrow staircase.

The candle's flickers on the walls revealed a strange lack of marks. As though no one had ever used these stairs. At the top, a heavy wooden door barred her progress. Hand on the doorknob, Cassie hesitated. Then turned it. She had to step off the small landing and down two steps to open the door. Cautiously, she climbed back up the two steps. The room was fairly dark despite a small window opposite the door. Ready to flee, she thrust the candle inside the room.

Her stomach unknotted. It was empty except for a cot set forlornly in the middle of the room. Smiling for the first time since entering the house, Cassie stepped inside to finish a cursory inspection, then head downstairs.

Reaching the center of the room, she heard the door swing partly closed behind her. Heart in her throat, she swung about, her skirts swirling about her legs. He was standing there.

"Randal," she exclaimed, starting forward. "Do you know what a start you gave me?"

She'd almost reached him before she realized.

It was Lytham.

# Chapter XIX

"Lord Lytham. You startled me. Didn't you hear the doorbell?"

The breath caught painfully in her throat. Swallowing, Cassie watched him tautly. His face was an unreadable mask, an angel's face, inhuman in the light from her candle. His presence here would convince Scotland Yard. If she lived to tell them.

A thin, mirthless smile distorted his features. He must think she'd been foolish enough to follow his instructions. Let him. Randal would be here long before anything could happen.

Lytham's thin smile stretched further, then became gentle, almost peaceful. "This room is soundproof," he explained courteously. "I wanted you to come up here."

The room stretched low, cavernous, empty in the wavering light of the candle. In the deep silence, Lytham took a leisurely step toward her. The candle flame reflected as twin points of fire in his eyes.

"Why?" Fighting the need to back away, she held

herself still and assumed a polite, puzzled look. She couldn't get around him. Randal would get here soon. She clutched at that reassurance.

"You won't disturb the neighbors up here."

The words dropped into stillness broken only by her breathing and the restless brush of his shoes on the wooden floor. Constantly in motion, he was jerky, awkward, his face cadaverous. He'd changed in the past week. But he seemed unaware. Unaware of the change, of his movements, almost unaware of her. His eyes bored through her more than saw her.

Into the frozen silence, he suggested, "Why don't you rest?" and motioned to the bed standing solitary in the middle of the room.

Cassie glanced at it and barely repressed a shudder. "I'm fine here, thank you."

"Are you sure? It might tire you to stand while I explain why I had to bring you here."

Lytham was insane. Insane enough to plan the Prince of Wales's kidnapping. Insane enough to murder her father. Insane enough to murder her and even Randal when he arrived. Beneath her cloak, she hugged herself tightly. He wouldn't harm Randal; she wouldn't let him.

Keeping her voice calm, she said, "I'd rather stand. But you look so tired. Why don't you sit down? Please, don't stand on ceremony with me."

He probably wouldn't take the suggestion. But if he did, she'd bolt through the door and lock it. A creak from below startled her. She strained to catch any sound that drifted through the half-open door. But it didn't recur. Just the creaks of an old house settling after a day of sun.

"And while I'm over there, you'll run out the door." Lytham smiled. "No, thank you. I shouldn't try it," he continued pleasantly. "I'll take great pleasure in restraining you." The look in his eyes belied the pleasantness of his voice.

"Run?" Cassie protested ingenuously. "You were going to explain why you brought me here." To survive, she had to keep Lytham talking. When he stopped— She fought to keep from looking at the bed.

Lytham rocked slowly, steadily, from heel to toe. His finely modeled mouth moved into a warmer smile as though he contemplated something he didn't want to share with her.

"My reasons will interest you as the Marchioness of Rydal." He stopped rocking. "Or I should say as the wife of a usurper." He spat out the last phrase with venom.

"I don't understand." She was bewildered yet interested. And she needed the time.

"You thought you married so well with your little plan. You even tricked my poor Elaine into helping you." A hoarse chuckle echoed in the low-pitched room. He slowly started rocking again. "Rydal is already married. So you can't be the Marchioness of Rydal."

"Randal is married to me!" she protested.

Her vehemence upset Lytham. Poised on his toes, a bewildered look came over his face. Then he settled back on his heels, and a peculiarly sweet expression transfigured him. He shook his head. And laughed.

How long had it been since she left home? Randal might even now be entering this house. She hadn't found a way yet to warn him. And she had to. Her attention snapped back to Lytham as his laughter broke off.

"Randal's an imposter," he said sharply. His hand cut through the air in a vicious movement. "*I* am the Marquess of Rydal."

"Your father was Lord Lytham," Cassie protested, wide-eyed. "I've seen his portrait in the library. You look like him. You're as blond as he was."

Frowning, Lytham snapped, "I take after my mother. She was blond"—he hesitated—"and very beautiful."

"I don't—"

"The Baron Lytham was a dupe for the second Marquess of Rydal, my real grandfather," Lytham sneered. "Baron Lytham married my mother. But she was already carrying me. Yes," he confirmed, seeing the dawning comprehension in her eyes, "I am Randal's elder brother."

"Your mother was Randal's father's mis—" Cassie broke off, afraid of the reaction.

"Mistress?" Lytham finished for her. "My father swore he'd marry her when he came of age. But my grandfather stopped the banns because she wasn't an adequate match. So he bribed the poverty-stricken Lord Lytham to marry her after his son, my real father, got her with child."

Lytham was lost in his own little world. But every tiny motion she made, every flicker of the candle flame riveted his attention. Finally risking a look at the single small window in this attic, Cassie realized it was nearly dark.

"Didn't your real father protest?" she asked with quiet, soothing interest.

"No. He found it expedient to marry elsewhere." Lytham giggled, and a sweet smile reappeared to curve his perfect lips. "But Randal was their only child. The female who usurped my mother's place was too weak to perform her duties." Lytham began silently pacing up and down over the uneven floorboards.

Cassie watched him for silent minutes. He

seemed unaware of her until she took a tentative step toward the door. He cut his path short and turned back through her escape route. Cruel pleasure flared in his eyes, but he turned again to pace away, then returned. Finally, he stopped before her, giving her another disarming smile.

"There hasn't been more than one male in the Rydal family for generations. It's a judgment against them for letting my younger brother take my rightful place." The strange smile lifting his lips, he gazed into the distance with unfocused eyes. Then he looked at her. "That's why I had to kill your father."

Pain glazing her eyes for an instant, Cassie stared at Lytham. "You killed my father," she said huskily when she could finally speak, "because Randal had no heirs?"

"He discovered my plans," Lytham answered quietly.

Forcing her voice to stay level and steady, Cassie asked, "What did he discover?"

"That I was responsible for taking his fortune. I planned to blame it on Randal. Society would shun him. His career would be ruined. Then I'd arrange Randal's death to look like a suicide caused by his disgrace. I'd even written a new will leaving everything to his old friend, me." Lytham spoke with calm, simple pride in his own ingenuity.

"Then somehow your father found out I'd swindled him." Confusion crossed Lytham's face. "I don't know how he found out. I was so careful." A beatific smile replaced the confusion. "He pledged he wouldn't tell anyone about it if I returned the money. He swore he hadn't told anyone. That wasn't very smart."

"But you don't need the money. You're rich."

She shouldn't have spoken. Lytham's eyes focused on her again.

"The purpose was to disgrace Randal. Besides, the money my grandfather paid to Baron Lytham wasn't enough. Not for disinheriting me. Not for putting my younger brother in my rightful place. The Rydals had to pay. And not just with money. When I removed your father, I hoped to blame it on Randal. But the need to dispatch your father quickly made that impractical. Even my original plan was too dangerous now."

Shaking his head, Lytham spread his hands, palm upward. "If your father found out about me, someone else might. I liked your father. I had no choice but to kill him. You can see that."

He was asking for understanding and approval. Swallowing quietly, Cassie agreed. "It was wrong of him."

"Everyone but you believed he'd taken his own life. After you'd gone to Scotland Yard, I knew you were too dangerous not to keep an eye on. And when I caught you searching my bedroom, I was sure. I was never foolish enough to believe your righteous indignation. I tried to catch you at the Crystal Palace but couldn't find you."

An angelic smile lit his face. "Are you certain you wouldn't like to sit down? It's not good for a young lady to stand so long." He slowly looked toward the half-open door. "You shouldn't have come here without a maid. It's not proper."

His lecturing tone gave her hope. "My maid's downstairs. I'll go get her." She started openly for the door.

Lytham cut her off. "I'm not stupid, you know. You came here alone." His expression glazed but intent, he took another step toward her.

"What did you do when your original plan was ruined? I don't think I would have had the courage to go on." She dipped her head and fluttered her lashes. He couldn't see the intense calculation in her eyes. For a moment, her feminine flirtatiousness had no effect. Then, slowly, overweening pride replaced his fierceness.

"I realized I could not only destroy the imposter, but make the name Rydal a curse. They stole my birthright. I'd destroy the family name. I'd take Randal's pride and joy and use it to destroy him." Lytham licked his lips. His eyes remained glazed, but his voice took on a silken purr each time he used the word *destroy*.

"At the grand opening, I'll kidnap the Prince of Wales. I'm surprised that wasn't my plan in the first place. It's so perfect. The Great Exhibition ruined. The Rydal fortune forfeited to the creditors. Randal dead." Lytham's eyes were fully, blindly open. "I'll even take the credit for rescuing the Prince of Wales. My reward is my rightful elevation to marquess, perhaps even duke. The House of Lords tries Randal and sentences him to death. While I receive a huge grant from a grateful nation."

"That's clever." She forced herself to praise him. Randal should have been here by now. "But why have him tried before the House of Lords?"

"How else could I kill him without staining my hands with my brother's blood?" he asked in surprise. Lytham grew calmer. "It was so easy. All I had to do was darken my hair a bit and wear some makeup. Everyone will swear I was Randal. Especially that fool Barnthorpe." Lytham smiled vindictively. "He expected a life of genteel blackmail after he identified Randal."

"You still intend to kidnap the boy?" If only she'd

brought a weapon. In this bare room, there was nothing but the candle.

"Naturally." Lytham looked at her in surprise. "Randal must hang." Another wave of confusion contorted his face. "You're so very beautiful. I'm glad you're my marchioness. I'll make you very happy."

Taking a slow step, he reached toward her. The sudden, sensual intent in his expression galvanized Cassie. She threw the lit candle at his face and broke for the door.

He grabbed her cloak and it came away in his hand, tangling about his feet. She ran for the staircase. The scuffling sound of Lytham fighting off the cloak made Cassie run faster. She made it through the door and far enough down the stairs to close it.

She turned, but there was Lytham, his face contorted. Cassie tried to slam the door. He was too close, and his strength overpowered hers. Stumbling, she ran on down the stairs, clutching the bannister for a guide in the darkness.

Then he caught her skirt. Lunging forward, she tried to escape. A few inches of her skirt tore free, then it held. He swung her about and forced her against the wall. She struck blindly in the dark, intent on doing as much damage as possible. A ringing slap stopped her for the moment, and Lytham pulled her hard against his body, telling her with graphic detail what he intended to do.

Insolently, he explored her, his hands massaging her breasts, ripping at the small collar of her dress where it fastened at her throat. Nausea surged through her. His mouth covered hers in an excruciating kiss, and she clawed at his eyes.

He struck her again and forced her up the stairs. He was incredibly strong. She couldn't fight free.

He thrust her toward the bed in the center of the room so hard she fell. Regaining her feet, she faced him warily. Lytham breathed deeply, passionately as he stalked forward. Defenseless, she faced him.

"Where's the cab?" Randal demanded.

"I've been searching, milord. But there are none to be had. Is Lady Cassandra in danger?" asked Pryor, his expression troubled.

Nodding, Randal extended a note. "Have a footman take this to Inspector MacPherson at Scotland Yard. Tell him to meet me at this address as quickly as he can."

"Very good, milord." Even with his mistress in danger, a lifetime of habit held. "Would you care for your carriage?"

Randal shook his head, turning toward the library. "It'll take too long. I'll get a cab in Belgrave Square."

He could take some servants, but they were more likely to get hurt or hinder than help. He'd trust Scotland Yard. And himself.

In seconds, Randal was inspecting the loaded double-barreled percussion pistol kept for protection against burglars. He thrust it into his waistband and left the house.

Where were all the cabs? In the dimming light, there wasn't a single hansom in sight. He raced on down the street. And nearly knocked over an elderly lady. Steadying her with his strong hands, he gasped an apology and ran on. His breath tore at his throat and his chest ached when he finally reached Belgrave Square. He stopped, gulping in great drafts of air, and looked wildly about.

The peaceful square was devoid of cabs. Where to find one? Restlessly he scanned the street. Not even a private carriage he could commandeer. Then he saw it. Up ahead, a hansom cab rounded the corner from Upper Belgrave Street and halted to let down its passenger.

Almost before the traveler had paid his fare, Randal hailed the driver. "A ten-pound note," he panted, each word an effort, "if you get me to seventeen Argyle Street in ten minutes. It's urgent. A life is at stake!"

The driver scanned the quiet traffic. "For ten pound, I can make it in eight minutes, guv. Jest 'op in." He whipped his horse into motion before Randal had the door closed.

The minutes stretched to eternity, with nothing but his imagination for company. And his imagination produced vivid images. Randal ground his teeth. How could she be so foolish? Visions of her dead, violated body floated before his eyes. No, she couldn't be. She had to be all right.

Couldn't the cabbie get his horse to move any faster? He knew he was being unreasonable. The man was doing his best. Still, Randal barely stopped from shouting for him to hurry each time the cabbie checked the horse for some delay in traffic. The driver almost hit an elderly gentleman stepping incautiously from the curb.

Then the cabbie turned into a quieter street off the main thoroughfare. Argyle Street? Randal looked quickly around, but could see no street sign. The cabbie sprang his horse once they turned the corner. Randal sat tautly still against the jolts of the poorly maintained street.

But he paid little attention. Instead, his mind returned to Cassie. He understood her reasons. If she'd only waited for him. Lytham's arrest for the plotted kidnapping wasn't enough. She needed proof Lytham'd murdered her father. So she'd gone to find that proof. Lytham must have guessed she'd found the cipher engine. And planned to kill her. Lytham must intend to kill him as well. Randal touched the pistol thrust into his waistband. Lytham had a surprise waiting.

"Pick up the candle," Lytham ordered. When she didn't move: "If I have to pick it up . . ." The threat emphasized their isolation, her vulnerability.

Tearing her eyes away from the bleeding scratches on his face, Cassie looked down at the candlestick. Amazingly, it was still lit. It lay midway between them. To get it, she'd have to approach him. Her gaze flicked back up at a sound, and she began to move. His face told her she had no choice. She took a step toward him and it.

Then another step closer. Crouching as far away as she could, she stretched for it. The flame burned her fingers, and she barely restrained a gasp. Daring to take her eyes off him, she located the candle holder, then snapped her watchful gaze back. He hadn't moved, though he watched her intensely. His anger faded as she obeyed him. She slowly retrieved the candle, fearful that any rapid motion might set him off again. Warily, Cassie rose and took slow, cautious steps back.

"That's better." Lytham's voice was silken in praise. "You should always obey me. It's your duty as my wife."

"Why do we stay here? Wouldn't we be more comfortable if we went home?"

Keep him talking. Randal should be here soon. Except, he wouldn't know to come up here. Lytham had closed the door. It didn't matter; Randal would check the entire house. Then her face went pale. If Randal walked in here unprepared— But he'd know from her note. He'd figure it out. But, if he didn't, Lytham might kill him. She'd have to keep Lytham talking. And find a way to escape.

"The Prince of Wales will stay in this room. At the Great Exhibition, our dear, foolish Queen will display her little dears to the public. Once my men"—a frown clouded his eyes for a moment— "kidnap him, the Exhibition will be ruined and so will my younger brother."

"How will that ruin Randal?" Cassie asked softly. She'd listen to it all again to keep him talking.

"I told you." He threw a surprised glance at her. "The estate agent met me as Randal. So did the dealer who provided the furniture downstairs. Even my little brother helped pile up evidence against himself." Lytham shook his head, revulsion curling his mouth. "How could Randal bring himself to frequent Bluegate Fields? Undoubtedly his mother's blood coming out. It doesn't matter. I appreciate the help."

A dry, rasping chuckle rattled in his throat. "His excursions to Bluegate Fields made me search there for the tools to carry out my plans. Unfortunately, they were weak, not up to my strength. But I shall find strong, unafraid men. Men who are brave enough to grasp their destiny. And your father's money will make it possible."

The candle flame trembled with Cassie's trembling hand. She steadied it so the weird shadows no longer danced on the cavernous walls. The casual way Lytham referred to her father's death, to the kidnapping, to Randal sent shivers of fear through her.

"Randal didn't—" she whispered involuntarily, shaking her head. Lytham only saw the motion.

"Didn't you know, child?" Lytham said in surprise. "All society knows about it. Not only his visits to Bluegate Fields, but he's let his financial

problems become public knowledge. The fool."
Pulling at his lower lip, Lytham frowned. "He
should have known he couldn't keep it secret. He's
blackened the Rydal name! My name."

"Has Randal been seen in Bluegate Fields that
often?" Cassie asked.

The question triggered an unexpected fury. Berat-
ing Randal for his behavior, for his abuse of the
name, Lytham strode up and down the room
pounding his fist against the wall. Each thud made
Cassie wince. She had to find some way of soothing
him before he turned his fury against her. Before
Randal arrived.

"But wasn't that useful for you?" she suggested
in a pause in Lytham's fury. "If Randal hadn't gone
to Bluegate Fields, it would have been much harder
for you. You'd have had to impersonate Randal
there. That would have been very difficult." Cassie
simpered coquettishly. "But I'm sure you would
have done it as well as you've done everything
else."

Pleased, Lytham stopped his frantic pacing and
pounding. "That was kind of my little brother,
wasn't it?" Glee lit his face, and he hooked his
thumbs into his waistcoat pockets as he resumed
rocking. "I shall have to thank him for his consideration before I kill him," Lytham continued casually.
"He can't escape me, of course. He's no match for
the real Marquess of Rydal."

Even to please him, she couldn't admit the possibility that Lytham would succeed in killing Randal. "What happened to the men you hired from
Bluegate Fields?" Cassie asked quietly. "You said
they'd failed you?"

She kept her voice quiet, steady, soothing, her
questions prompting him to keep talking. But any

question could also trigger his rage. Or his lust. The memory of Lytham fondling her made her sick.

Lytham nodded thoughtfully. "It's just as well the men I originally hired were too cowardly for the job. They couldn't identify my little brother. But the fool who hired them for me can." He laughed harshly. "And he will. He's identified me as Randal. Then when I meet the new gang the morning of the kidnapping, I'll impress Randal's face on their memories. Nothing could be better. That was the problem with the first group. I shouldn't have hired them so early."

"The kidnapping's still planned for the first of May?" The soft prompting focused his attention on her again. Her heart's thudding threatened to shake her to pieces.

"Yes. Only two weeks away. I won't have any trouble hiring new tools before then. They won't have to wait long, so their nerve won't fail." He shrugged irritably and resumed pacing. "I should be working on the cipher now. I'd be doing it if you hadn't interfered."

Bewildered, Cassie shook her head. "How did I—"

"You searched my desk and found the cipher engine." Lytham halted, menacingly close.

"I never went near your desk."

His face showed he didn't believe her. Elaine must have told him she'd been in the library. But how could he know she'd been near the desk? She'd returned the cipher engine box to the correct spot. And replaced the letters. Had she relocked the box? It didn't matter. He'd spotted something wrong, and she had to convince him she hadn't done it.

"What's a cipher engine?" Cassie tried to look innocently curious.

"Hmph," he snorted. "Your father told me all about your knowledge of ciphers. How could any father be proud of so unfeminine an interest? And Elaine has told me all about you and the *Times* ciphers. How you've helped her read the love notes. Elaine never keeps anything from me." Pride lit his face.

"Just simple substitution ciphers," Cassie protested, her heart sinking. "Nothing so complex it would require a— What did you call it? A cipher engine?"

"It's no good." Lytham looked annoyed. "I don't understand how you broke that cipher. Not without the key word." He hesitated. "If you could do it, maybe your father could too. Those messages to McCrory and Chambers were in the same cipher." His gaze pinned her. "You and your father have inconvenienced me greatly."

Hands dropping from his waistcoat, Lytham started forward before she could protest again. She backed away, the candle trembling faintly in her grasp.

He took two more steps, expecting her to run. She didn't, and his gray-blue eyes began to glitter with approval. Another step closer. Almost within range. Another step. She thrust the lit candle at his face.

Giggles echoed in the room as Lytham batted the candle away and caught her wrist in a punishing grasp. "Very good, that's to be expected from a woman worthy of me." Inexorably, he drew her toward him. She didn't struggle. There'd be no more than one opportunity. She'd go for his eyes. Watching him closely, she waited for it.

Then Lytham patted her cheek gently. He was so close, his breath touched her face. But incredibly, he looked courteous and normal, even regretful. She'd

seen the identical expression on Randal's face when
he had to leave her to go to the office. The chilling
echo of Randal's expression in Lytham's face frightened her more than anything else had.

"I'm sorry, my dear. I shall have to postpone our
love for a bit. I'm sure you'll forgive me."

Blinking, Cassie tried to speak and couldn't.

"I've just had the most marvelous idea." Lytham
smiled beatifically at her. "You probably left a note
to my little brother. I'll go prepare for him."

Fear enabled her to speak. "What are you going
to do?"

"I shall write another cipher. One that will appear
to come from Randal." Lytham stroked her cheek
gently. "When my dear younger brother charges to
the rescue, I shall kill him and leave the cipher engine on his body." Laughing softly, he enveloped
her in a hug, then held her away from him, hands
on her shoulders. "No more need to deal with fools
like Barnthorpe. No need to depend on weak reeds
like those I found in Bluegate Fields."

"But how can you plant this cipher engine if it's
still at Lytham House?" Cassie asked, desperately
trying to keep him up here with her. She preferred
even that to the possibility of Randal's death.

"The cipher engine's downstairs. I brought it to
work on a message for Barnthorpe while I waited
for you. It took you too long to get here. My wife
must obey me instantly."

"I'll do better in the future," Cassie promised.
His fingers dug deeply into her shoulders. She'd
have bruises tomorrow. If she was still alive.

"Of course you will." His eyes snapped back to
her tense face. "You needn't worry, my dear, I'll
make you happy before you die. . . . You must
die," he added conversationally. "I'm sorry, but
Randal can't have an heir to carry on the Rydal
name. Besides," he added prosaically, "you know
too much."

# *Chapter  XX*

Randal swore silently and looked at his watch. He'd been in the cab only minutes. It seemed hours. Ahead, a group of revelers heading to a costume party blocked the street. With a lurch, the cab swerved onto the sidewalk and past the outraged party goers. One, dressed as a monk, chased them shouting, then was lost in the distance.

Randal thrust the watch into his pocket and checked his pistol again. If Lytham harmed Cassie in any way— He broke off the thought sharply. She hadn't been there long enough to be hurt. Or had she? Pryor hadn't been sure how long ago Cassie'd left. If Lytham harmed her, he wouldn't live to stand trial.

The driver barely slowed at a hackney's tangle with a dowager's landau, and his wheels sideswiped the hackney. Oblivious to the hackney driver's curses, the cabbie cracked his whip above the horse's ears. London traffic, even at this hour, was no place to spring a horse. Yet, for ten pounds the driver was doing it. He knew a swell toff like Randal would pay for any damages. Dusky twilight from nearing nightfall made it even more difficult to avoid hazards.

His jaw clenched to stop from shouting at the driver for even more speed, Randal leaned forward and searched for a street sign. Within a minute of Belgrave Square, the driver took him into unfamiliar streets. This area contained neither the elegant homes surrounding addresses like Grosvenor and Belgrave squares, nor the squalor of Bluegate Fields. Well-to-do merchants and civil servants lived in the large, neat, well-cared-for houses lining these streets.

But with each second, the neighborhoods grew worse. There were few fashionable carriages and more hackneys now. The cabbie barely missed a lumbering wagon as Randal spotted a street sign. To no avail. A flowering tree partly blocked his view, and concealed some letters. Then it was gone, and they were past the corner, the driver urging his horse on with reckless speed.

Street after street came and went before the driver again slowed his horse. He turned into a narrower road. Argyle Street? Daylight had faded so far that Randal couldn't read the street sign. And the lamplighter hadn't lit the gas lamps yet in this down-at-heels neighborhood.

Randal checked his watch. It was now too dark to read it, but they must be almost there. He took a ten-pound note from his wallet to save time. Another ten-pound note along with a fiver remained.

A change in the cab's motion made him look out at the street. Was the driver slowing to a stop? No, not yet. But they should be there soon. They had to be there soon.

*    *    *

A tear dripped from her jaw and hit Cassie's hand in the silent room. Angrily, she wiped the moisture from her cheeks. This wasn't the time for tears. Lytham was planning to kill her husband. She had to stop him. If she was killed trying to escape to warn Randal, well, that was better than waiting for Lytham to return.

Holding the candle high, she inspected the room. If Lytham had chosen this room to hold the Prince of Wales prisoner, there'd be no easy avenue of escape. The room was soundproof, so it would waste precious time trying to attract attention by screaming.

Two blank walls greeted her inspection. They were low where the roof met them with no openings in either. Of the remaining two walls, one held a door and the other a window. The thunk of the lock turning when Lytham left still echoed in her ears. Perhaps she could fit through the window.

The last light filtering through it outlined rooftops stretching into the distance. The candle flame wavered with her movements. It was a forlorn hope, but better than going down the stairs past a murdering madman. Yes, she'd fit through it without her petticoats. But she couldn't open it.

Nails fastened the window casement to the frame. It would take a crowbar, and it wasn't worth trying. A small, almost invisible metal mesh in the glass stopped her from breaking it. Worse, the window looked out over a sheer drop into the alley. And the next house had no window, only a steep roof opposite her aerie. No wonder Lytham had chosen this room to imprison the young Prince.

The door was her only avenue of escape. She had to open it and stealthily creep past Lytham. If he caught her, Randal was dead. She'd be dead, too, after Lytham enjoyed his personal revenge.

Skirting the cot, she went to the door and tried the handle. She'd heard correctly. It was locked. And the hinges were on the outside. That left the door panels. They were solid, thick. Even with part of the cot's frame, she couldn't break through in time. A chill that had nothing to do with the room's coolness prickled her skin.

The candle would burn out soon. The thought of waiting in the dark for an insane murderer bent on rape sent shivers down her spine. But if she had to, she was going to be armed. Glancing back at the cot, Cassie smiled grimly. Part of its frame could serve her as a weapon.

Then she remembered. The sound of the tumblers had echoed harshly over her soft sobs in the quiet room. And she'd heard his footsteps fade down the stairs. But she hadn't heard the scrape of metal as Lytham pulled the key from the lock.

It was a slim chance.

Cassie knelt on the bare floorboards before the lock. A splinter bit into a knuckle as she reached for the candle. She ignored it.

Holding the candle just below the doorknob, she tried to look through the keyhole. It was too dark now in the hallway to see. And there was no telltale reflection from a key. Cassie took a hatpin from her frivolous hat of jet and velvet.

Leaning against the door, she probed carefully with the hatpin. The keyhole was blocked by the key. Her sigh echoed in the silence. Now, to push it free, then bring it into the room.

There was about an inch between the bottom of the door and the floor. She tested the opening with her hand palm up. Small as she was, it wouldn't quite go under. She forced herself to breathe slowly and think. What could she use?

The note Lytham had told her to bring.

Cassie took the tattered, grubby paper from her

pocket, carefully smoothed and unfolded it. Looking at it, she wondered if it was large enough. It had to be. Positioning the paper directly beneath the lock, Cassie pushed it delicately under the door.

It caught on a crack in the floor. She tried again, and it caught again. Sliding it to the side, she tried once more. At last her fragile hope slipped out of sight beneath the door.

Carefully, she positioned it and cast a tense glance back at the candle. Hitting the floor twice had damaged it. The wax melted lopsidedly and ran down a crack chipped in it. There were only a few minutes left before it guttered. If she failed to get the key, she'd need a minute or two of light to break the cot into a weapon.

Then would come the long, dark wait for Lytham. The thought of waiting for him froze her with fear, but she shook it off. Her only real defense against rape and murder, her only real chance of saving Randal's life, lay in escape.

Ignoring the fast-burning candle, she worked to free the key. The hatpin slipped sideways, jamming her hand on the doorknob; she drew the hatpin back and tried again. The key *had* given a bit. Gently, now. If she pushed too hard, it might fly down the stairs. Bit by bit she worked at it until, with a final scrape, the key fell out. She heard it hit the floor and bounce. Then silence.

She pulled slowly, and one corner of the tattered paper tore away in her fingers. Taking a deep breath, she gripped it and began again. With exquisite care, Cassie worked at it, afraid the paper would tear, afraid it would catch on a splinter in the uneven floorboards and the key would fall off, unreachably distant. Time stretched intolerably. But gradually the paper with its precious cargo appeared under the door. The key sat squarely on Lytham's note.

Eyes closing with a moment's grateful prayer, Cassie sat back on her heels. She'd done it. Now to make it down four flights of stairs and escape without Lytham's discovering her. It sounded impossible.

Scooping up the key, she rose stiffly. With the hood of her cloak over her head, she'd be practically invisible in the darkened rooms. She pulled her hatpin from the lock. It was a laughable weapon, but Lytham would feel it if he caught her. Even this small defense boosted her spirits.

The candle flickering behind her, she felt her way onto the steps and closed the door. Only a sliver of light crept under it. Soon, even that would be gone.

Everything had to appear normal when Lytham came up for her. The longer he suspected nothing, the longer she had to escape. When she ran her hands over the door, everything seemed normal. Except there was no key in the lock. She debated leaving it behind, but nothing would induce her to give him the opportunity to lock her in that room again.

Cassie listened intently before starting down the staircase. Darkness surrounded her. Darkness and tiny noises. They weren't footsteps. They were faint brushings and scratchings in the distance. Mice. In this old house, there must be mice. Unless there were rats. She shuddered at the thought.

Hand gripping the bannister, Cassie slowly felt her way downstairs step by step. Each creaked with agonizing loudness. Her skirts brushing against wall and bannister rustled noisily in the quiet, and she feared the sound must be audible all over the house. She paused every few steps to listen. The house was silent except for the creaks, mice—all the little inexplicable night noises that assaulted her now she was free of the deadening stillness of that locked room.

Finally she neared the end of the imprisoning tunnel of darkness that was the staircase. Pausing again, now able to see faintly, Cassie could hear more sounds. A carriage rattled and clopped down the street. Randal? Cassie barely subdued the urge to rush down the stairs and warn her husband. With a sigh of relief, she realized the carriage had passed the house and was continuing down the street.

In the distance, a dog barked. Then she thought she heard a door close. Breathless, Cassie strained to hear the sound of footsteps on the stairs. There was only silence. In the faint light, she fought her fears. Lytham wouldn't be coming up here yet. He couldn't have had time to finish his cipher. Still, Cassie hurried down the last steps ready to flee into the nearest room.

On the landing she paused, her heart pounding. The bare windows off the hall provided some little light. Enough to see the next flight of stairs. Enough to find a refuge. She'd see Lytham by his candle. But in the dim light, he wouldn't see her. Hurrying, yet fighting to remain quiet, she found each floor easier than the last.

Until she reached the ground floor.

Bright light spilled from a room opening onto the hall. Lytham. Freezing, Cassie estimated her chances. Could she slip past on the far side of the hall? To even reach the back entrance, she had to pass his open door.

She took a step, then froze. Lytham walked between the lantern and the door. His long, threatening shadow fell across the hall, then wavered back and forth as though pacing.

Cassie watched the doorway anxiously, ready to hide in the nearest darkened room. She willed Lytham to go back to his cipher. From the corner of her eye, she saw the sun had already set. Only dim twilight remained.

The shadow paused as though struck by an idea. It swung about and faded from the bare floor that separated the hall carpet from the drawing room. Cassie took two tentative steps toward the front door, her eyes on Lytham's room. He must be seated now.

Cassie moved quietly. Fortunately, no furniture lined the hall. Just dust and the dismal scent of mildew. She hugged the far side of the hall without touching the wall. The sound of her dress brushing it would be disastrous.

A sound behind her made her turn around quickly, but she could see nothing in the dark hallway. Except the light streaming from Lytham's room.

At last she reached the front door, its key gleaming. She tried the doorknob, but it was locked. Swallowing quietly, she turned the key. The bolt slammed back with a loud, dull thunk that shattered the stillness.

Then with incredible swiftness Lytham was on her. He must have followed her into the hall. His breath hot and moist on her cheek, he overpowered her and dragged her toward his room. It was useless, but still she screamed for help. Infuriated, Lytham hit her until she quieted. His fingers dug bruisingly into her arms. She aimed a kick at his kneecap, but the stiff folds of her petticoat softened the blow too much to do any damage.

"Behave yourself." Lytham threw her into the lighted room.

He stood menacingly between her and the open door. Rubbing her bruised arms, she stared proudly back. "I'm Randal's wife."

"My brother?" Confusion struggled for a moment before the angelic smile lit his face again.

"No. You're the Marchioness of Rydal. You're my wife."

There was no chance of getting past him. She hid the sharp hatpin. It was a feeble weapon, but she could use it to get around him and out the unlocked door. Once she was in the street, her screams would be heard.

He stepped toward her.

His voice became gentle, loving. "I've made you wait too long." Lytham gestured toward the couch. "Prepare yourself."

"No."

"I'd enjoy punishing you for disobedience, my dear." Expression darkening, he cracked an order out. "Prepare yourself."

She stayed where she was.

He started toward her. "Take off your clothes and be dutiful."

Cassie shook her head and shifted onto the balls of her feet, hatpin ready. She had to wait for the right moment.

"Obey me!"

Face contorted with rage, Lytham charged. With a great openhanded blow, he stunned her and sent her reeling toward the couch. Ripping her cloak off, he threw it toward the door. Then he caught her arm and pulled her toward him, imprisoning her struggling form. He savagely ripped from her lips a kiss that left her feeling unclean.

As Lytham released her and ripped at her clothes, a low, wordless moan escaped his lips.

"No." She gasped and thrust the hatpin at his face.

At last the driver slowed. They turned onto one last dark street, the horse down to a fast walk now. The cabbie peered at the numbers and pulled up before a house with a single lit window.

"This the one yer wants, guv?" the driver asked, swinging down from his perch.

"If this is seventeen Argyle Street," Randal answered.

Randal swung out of the cab and climbed onto the sidewalk, inspecting the driver for the first time. He was an older man, near retirement. Useless in a fight. Worse than useless. But useful for getting help. Randal looked consideringly, eyes narrowed and bleak, at the house they stood before. Help might be necessary.

The driver coughed apologetically and held out his hand. "Yer promised me ten pound."

Randal pulled the ten-pound note from his pocket and handed it to him. "There's another five pounds waiting if you find a bobby quickly and bring him here. Ten pounds if it's within five minutes."

The driver cast an uneasy glance at the silent house, then looked back at Randal. "Wot's wrong?"

"A man's holding my wife in there for ransom." Randal gestured toward the house. "I've sent a message to Scotland Yard, but they may not get here in time."

Scrambling back onto his perch, the driver took up the reins. His whip cracked, and he sent his sweating horse running down the street. Was he going for help? Or just getting away from danger. Randal didn't have time to worry.

Running up the front steps, he tested the door. Unlocked. The door swung open silently at his touch. He entered, leaving the door open for Scotland Yard. The air inside struck cold, close, unused.

Scuffles and thumps echoed in the silent house coming from the lit room down the hall. He ran toward it, a screamed "no" lending speed to his feet.

At the doorway, Randal yanked the pistol free of

his waistband and took aim, then hesitated. On the floor, Cassie struggled with Lytham. Her bright, golden brown hair spilled over the dirty floor, while a streak of blood stiffened Lytham's. The torn skirt of her black wool dress was pinned under his knee. She hit him hard, and he pulled back to strike her.

In two quick strides, Randal reached the struggling pair. With savage pleasure, Randal swung the pistol butt against Lytham's skull. It hit with a satisfying thud, and Lytham slumped to the floor. Randal grabbed his unconscious foe and threw him to the side, then knelt and gathered his trembling wife into his arms.

"Are you all right?" Randal asked. Her frightened face stared up at him blankly for a moment before she recognized him. Relief filled her face, and she threw her arms around him.

Tenderly, Randal picked her up and laid her on the couch. Shuddering, she held him as he stroked her tangled hair away from her face. Finally, when her trembling eased, Randal sat back.

"Are you all right?" he repeated.

"Y-yes," she whispered. Her small, slender fingers held him as she shivered again. "I am now that you're here."

Randal knelt before her, his hand moving comfortingly over her shoulder.

For the first time, she looked toward Lytham's slumped figure. "Is he—?"

"Dead?" Randal shook his head; a bright lock of tawny hair fell forward against his forehead. "No, just unconscious. I won't let him harm you. And Scotland Yard will be here soon."

"Before they get here," she began breathlessly. She raised wide eyes to her husband's face. She had to tell him about Lytham. That he was Randal's brother. Shivering, she rubbed her shoulders and

winced. Marks left by Lytham's hands were already
darkening on her pale skin.

"You're cold," Randal interrupted. "I'll get your
cloak."

He hugged her, then went to it. She needed the
warmth. And she'd be more comfortable covered
when Scotland Yard arrived. Then he'd take her
home. Away from the horror of this house.

Ignoring Lytham's crumpled body, Randal went
for the cloak near the door. At Cassie's startled
shriek, he swung around. Knife in hand, Lytham
launched himself at Randal, but Cassie intercepted
him. She clawed at his face, his arm. With a vicious
swipe of his free hand, Lytham slammed her to the
floor. Dazed by the blow, Cassie grabbed his leg
and held on grimly.

Enraged, Lytham raised his knife, the blade glittering. From half the long room away, Randal's
pistol cracked twice. Lytham staggered back and
fell, dead before he hit the floor.

Silent tears streaming from her eyes, Cassie rose
to stand trembling. Until strong arms closed about
her.

Randal kissed her tenderly. "I'll take you to another room," he said as her eyes strayed to the
bloody, inert heap that had been Lytham. "After
Scotland Yard arrives, I'll take you home."

"Randal, I need to talk to you," she said breathlessly.

"It can wait, my darling. Let me get your cloak."
He looked down at her dust- and blood-streaked
corset. "You'll feel more comfortable."

Cassie let him put the cloak about her shoulders
before she pulled him back to the sofa. She kept her
eyes carefully averted from Lytham.

"I want you to rest," Randal said, settling her
back against the sofa arm.

"Randal, sit down." She pressed her fingers to her temples. "There's something I must tell you before they arrive."

Stroking her bright, tumbled hair soothingly, Randal reassured her, "You won't have to talk to them if you don't want to."

Catching his hands, she drew him down beside her with surprising strength. "I know why Lytham was going to kidnap the Prince of Wales."

She had his attention, and quickly explained what Lytham had said. His discovery that he was Randal's half-brother. Lytham's feeling that he should be the Marquess of Rydal and the way it had grown until he was convinced he actually was Rydal. His plan to discredit Randal through her father's dealings with McCrory and Chambers. His murder of her father because he got in the way. And finally, his intention to implicate Randal in the Prince of Wales's kidnapping.

Several times, a protest formed in Randal's eyes. But he controlled it. Then, when she finished: "I heard that my father's first love was a local girl." He nodded thoughtfully, a faint frown drawing his tawny brows together. "But my grandfather wouldn't permit the banns because there was insanity in the family."

Face shadowed, he looked at his half-brother's body. "I'm sorry it happened." Hands flexing, he shook his head. "What an inadequate, useless thing to say. But I am sorry."

Cassie reassured him gently, stroking his cheek tenderly and pushing the lock of tawny brown hair back from his brow. "What about Elaine? She'll be devastated if this comes out."

Randal's gaze came back to her. "We'll have to protect her."

"But how?"

"I'll tell the Yard about the plot to kidnap the Prince of Wales. I can get them to keep it quiet. If we publicize this, someone else may decide to carry out Lytham's plans for his own purposes. To the rest of the world, he met his death at the hands of a madman. It won't be that far from the truth."

"What do we tell Elaine?"

"That he died protecting you from a madman." The thought gave him a little comfort. "You'll have to tell her. I'll be busy with the Yard, and she should find out from a friend." He looked at her. "You'd best go home and change before you see Elaine. Seeing your torn clothes would be an additional shock for her. I'll contact Welton to send Madeline to relieve you." Randal listened intently. "Here's Scotland Yard. At least, I hope it's MacPherson and not the bobby I sent the cabdriver for." He rose to his feet and went to the door.

Hours later, Cassie still heard Randal's explanation ringing in her ears. Inspector MacPherson hadn't liked it, but he'd accepted it. Randal's quiet, steely insistence that Prince Albert and Queen Victoria wouldn't care to have the story publicized helped.

Her papa would remain a suicide to the rest of the world, but she didn't think he'd mind. He wouldn't have wanted Elaine to be even more distressed. She'd taken the news of her husband's death badly, but Cassie's repeated reassurance that he died protecting her from a madman seemed to help.

Still, the hours listening to Elaine cataloguing Lytham's virtues had worn on her until Cassie felt as bruised and drained mentally as she did physically. Eventually, she'd gotten Elaine into bed. She was quiet now under the doctor's sedatives. After Madeline arrived it was obvious that, though she accepted the story, she didn't fully believe it. Cassie offered to stay and help, but Madeline finally sent her home to rest.

Now only Randal remained.

After arriving home, she quickly shed the dress she'd changed into before going to Lytham House and got into a warm nightgown and robe. Taking the pins from her tightly bound hair, she sat brushing it at the dressing table, trying to quiet the nervous shivers that still shook her. The door connecting her room to the sitting room opened, and Randal stood there in a magnificent dressing gown.

"Are you all right?" he asked abruptly. The expression in his eyes was uncertain, concerned.

Cassie rose, smiling tremulously, and ran across the room and burrowed into his arms. Finally she felt warm and safe. Her instinctive action reassured her husband. He relaxed as her arms closed about his waist.

Tipping her head back to meet his gaze, she reached up to stroke his worried face. "I'm fine. Don't worry."

"I can't help it." He caught her hands and pressed them against his chest. "If he'd hurt you—"

"But he didn't," Cassie reminded him gently.

"Is Elaine all right?"

Nodding, Cassie reassured him. Then she gathered herself together. "There's something I need to tell you," she began, eyes fixed on his chin.

"I'll still love you," he said, "even if I do want to beat you for going there alone."

Her gaze flew up to meet Randal's troubled, loving eyes. "You love me?" she whispered. Happiness flared in her eyes, erasing her exhaustion. "Idiot," she said lovingly. "Nothing happened."

"Than what do you have to tell me?"

"Only that I love you. I thought—" She shook her head wonderingly. The bright hair spilled over her breasts and rippled down to her waist with the movement.

Randal stroked the long slender column of her neck before he brought her close. The familiar teasing gleamed in his silvered blue eyes. She shivered with the delicious promise there.

"You thought I was only interested in carrying you off to bed?"

Cassie nodded solemnly.

"You're right. And we haven't christened yours yet." His lips hovering above hers, he continued softly, "I think I'll show you how much I love you."

Cassie reached up to pull his head down. From the moment his lips touched hers again, passion flared as never before. Stroking his cheek, she gloried in the smooth/rough texture of his skin beneath her fingers.

She smiled dreamily up when he finally raised his head. The ascot at his throat now was out of the way; Cassie's fingers snuggled confidingly against the comforting warmth of his skin. Their robes lay pooled, brilliant red and pale blue, on the floor. Tenderness lit his face: a greater tenderness than she'd seen before.

Randal bent to drop another kiss on her parted lips before his strong fingers found the row of buttons marching down the front of her warm gown. Smiling, he deliberately brushed her flesh with a thousand minute caresses as he progressed down the row.

"Too many buttons?" Cassie asked huskily.

"Umnh," Randal murmured, concentrating fiercely on freeing her from the enveloping folds.

Cassie plucked the silk ascot from about his neck,

then she touched him with a new freedom. He
loved her. That alone drowned the memories of the
day. Until Randal saw the bruises marring the fine
pale skin of her breasts and arms once he pushed the
unfastened gown from her shoulders. His hardening
face warned her what he was thinking.

"It's over with and he'll never hurt us again.
Now"—she took his hand and led him toward her
bed—"let's christen this bed." Cassie sent a fleeting,
seductive smile at him over her shoulder.

Sweeping her high against his chest, Randal took
the final stride. There, he laid her gently down and
bent over her, the solid muscularity of his form
blocking the light from candles burning on the
dressing table.

Silently, Randal knelt beside her and brushed tender kisses over each bruise. A wave of love overwhelmed her. With urgent hands, she tugged at his
shoulders, pulling him alongside her on the bed. In
moments, he was as aroused as she, but not out of
control. Tentatively, as though afraid of frightening
her, he lifted himself over her soft, pliant body and
poised above her, waiting.

Cassie, eyes wide with passion in the candlelight,
wondered why he waited. Then she saw his uncertainty. With a low, sensual murmur, her fingers
closed on the taut muscles of his buttocks and urged
him toward her. In the next instant, they were together, lost in their mutual love.

The candles were burning low on the dressing
table when Cassie moved in his arms. Instantly,
Randal was alert. "Are you all right?" he asked.

"All right?" A contented smile lit Cassie's face.
She burrowed closer into his arms and drifted into
sleep.

# Note to Readers

Prince Albert's Great Exhibition was bitterly opposed by Parliament and the public on economic grounds, because they feared the Crystal Palace would collapse and also believed that it would draw foreigners and criminals to London. In addition, all previous national exhibitions had been financial disasters despite their vastly smaller scale, while an international exhibition had never even been attempted. Consequently, Parliament refused to fund the Great International Exhibition of Arts and Industry, forcing Prince Albert to ask wealthy, public-spirited men to guarantee its success with their own fortunes.

Some of the fears had a foundation. Not only had all previous exhibitions failed economically, but the architect of the Crystal Palace, Joseph Paxton, was not even an architect. He was gardener to the Duke of Devonshire where he had charge of a giant Amazonian lily whose leaves were so strong they were able to support his daughter's weight. Using the

pattern of the ribbing on the lily's leaves, he designed the Crystal Palace. Virtually no orthodox architect believed the concept sound.

The furor over a building for the Great Exhibition in Hyde Park seemed ready to continue forever
when Paxton published his design in _Punch_ maga-
zine. The public fell in love with the brilliant and
unique design and forced the building selection
committee's hand. Reluctantly, they accepted the
gardener's design. In late 1850, building began, and
it was completed in March of 1851. The Crystal Palace required a third of Britain's glass production for
an entire year and covered nineteen acres of Hyde
Park. Enclosed within the soaring roof line one hundred eight feet above the ground were the three elm
trees with their infamous sparrows. Queen Victoria
did, indeed, call in the Duke of Wellington to solve
the problem of bird droppings. His keen tactical
mind suggested sparrow hawks. More than six mil-
lion visitors to the Crystal Palace were thus able to
view exhibits free of unsightly leavings from the
sparrows.

Despite the fears of all the nay-sayers, the Great
Exhibition was a fantastic financial and cultural success. The net profits were used to purchase land in
Kensington adjacent to Hyde Park. On this land
were built the Victoria and Albert Museum; the Science, Geological, and Natural History Museums;
the Imperial College of Science and Technology; the
Royal Colleges of Art, Music, and Organists; the
Royal Meteorological and Entomological Societies;
and the Royal Albert Hall, among others. Not all of
these buildings were funded solely by the Great Exhibition, but the Exhibition provided seed money
and purchased the seventy acres these buildings
stand upon.

In 1852, the Crystal Palace was dismantled and

taken to Sydenham, where it was used for various exhibitions until destroyed when some exhibits caught fire in 1936. But it never succumbed to wind or hailstones or the vibration of millions of feet walking through as its detractors feared.

Some other fears of the Exhibition's detractors had better cause. Following the birth of Prince Arthur in 1850, Queen Victoria was attacked twice: once by an Irishman brandishing a gun, the second time by a man who attacked her with his cane. Consequently, attempts to safeguard the Queen from this kind of incident during the grand opening were strenuous. And a complete failure. The division of responsibility between the military outside the Exhibition, and Scotland Yard inside the Crystal Palace, made the grand opening a weak point in security.

According to Lord Playfair's diary, as the Queen declared the Exhibition open, a Chinaman in rich silk robes flew from the crowd and prostrated himself before her. Assuming he was a representative of the Emperor of China, officials placed him between the Archbishop of Canterbury and the Duke of Wellington in the procession the Queen led around the Crystal Palace. The next day, Playfair says, they learned the Chinaman was the captain of a Chinese junk docked in the Thames boat basin. For a shilling, his junk could be hired for a trip on the Thames.

Ada, Countess of Lovelace is credited as the first computer programmer. Although Babbage's calculating (or differencing) engine was not displayed at the Great Exhibition (in fact it was never completed), Ada devised a method for feeding the machine information. In her honor, the United States

Department of Defense has named its new high-order programming language ADA.

A fine mathematician, she had one failing: a love of gambling. Her compulsion led her to pawn the family jewels, creating as much of a scandal as her father, Lord Byron. Like him, she died at the age of thirty-six. Cancer caused her death in 1852, while her father was shot during the successful Greek War for Independence in 1824.

One final point concerns the action of the doctor and coroner in a suicide of the sort described. It was common through the later Victorian period in England for a suicide to be listed as death by natural causes or by visitation of God when a death certificate was issued at all. Physicians were not legally required to give death certificates until 1874, while coroners were not paid for an inquest unless justices deemed that it had been duly held. The justices invariably took a strict interpretation of "duly held." Consequently, murders where there was no outward evidence of violence were dismissed as either suicide or due to natural causes. This changed in 1860 when the County Coroners Act put coroners on salary and made them largely independent of the justices.

# *Sweeping Tales of Destiny and Desire*

**BEYOND ALL FRONTIERS by Emma Drummond**
Charlotte Scott, imprisoned in a loveless marriage, is captivated by a man whose taunts she cannot refuse. Set against the grand panorama of Imperial India, this is a provocative love story with all the splendor and passion of *The Far Pavilions*.
_____ 90077-5   $3.95 U.S.

**FORGET THE GLORY by Emma Drummond**
From the exotic splendor of India to the bloody battlefields of the Crimean War, Mary follows the man society forbids her to love. "Rich in historical and emotional details."          —*Publishers Weekly*
_____ 90678-1   $3.95 U.S.

**AT THE GOING DOWN OF THE SUN by Elizabeth Darrell**
Three spirited, passionate brothers and the women who loved them are caught in the heartbreak and glory of World War I. "Gripping ...irresistible."          —*Booklist*
_____ 90044-9        $4.95 U.S.

**KIMBERLEY by Colin Burke**
A sweeping saga of love, war, and empire in the glorious diamond capital of the world. "Evocative...an absorbing and lively read."
—*Kirkus*
_____ 90501-7   $4.50 U.S.        _____ 90526-2   $5.50 Can.